The Moving Water

BOOK TWO OF THE
RIHANNAR CHRONICLES

THE MOVING WATER

SYLVIA KELSO

FIVE STAR
An imprint of Thomson Gale, a part of The Thomson Corporation

Detroit • New York • San Francisco • New Haven, Conn. • Waterville, Maine • London

Sequel to Everran's Bane.

Set in 11 pt. Plantin.

LIBRARY OF CONGRESS CATALOGING-IN-PUBLICATION DATA

Kelso, Sylvia.
The moving water / Sylvia Kelso. — 1st ed.
p. cm. — (Rihannar chronicles ; bk. 2)
Sequel to: Everran's bane.
ISBN-13: 978-1-59414-606-0 (alk. paper)
ISBN-10: 1-59414-606-3 (alk. paper)
1. Large type books. I. Title.
PR9619.4.K456M68 2007
823'.92—dc22 2006038257

First Edition. First Printing: April 2007.

Published in 2007 in conjunction with Tekno Books and Ed Gorman.

Printed in the United States of America on permanent paper
10 9 8 7 6 5 4 3 2 1

For my parents
Here and *in absentia*

With thanks to Lillian Stewart Carl for more than ordinary editing.

The title of this book comes from Robert Payne's translation of a famous Li Po poem, variously titled "Conversation among the Mountains," "Green Mountain," "Question and Answer," etc. The translation first appeared in Payne's anthology of Chinese poetry, *The White Pony*, in 1947, and the third line reads, "The peach blossom follows the moving water": an allusion to TaoYaun Ming's even more famous prose tale of the peach blossom fountain whose waters led wanderers out of their world and time. I have been unable to get permission from Mr. Payne's estate to quote the entire poem.

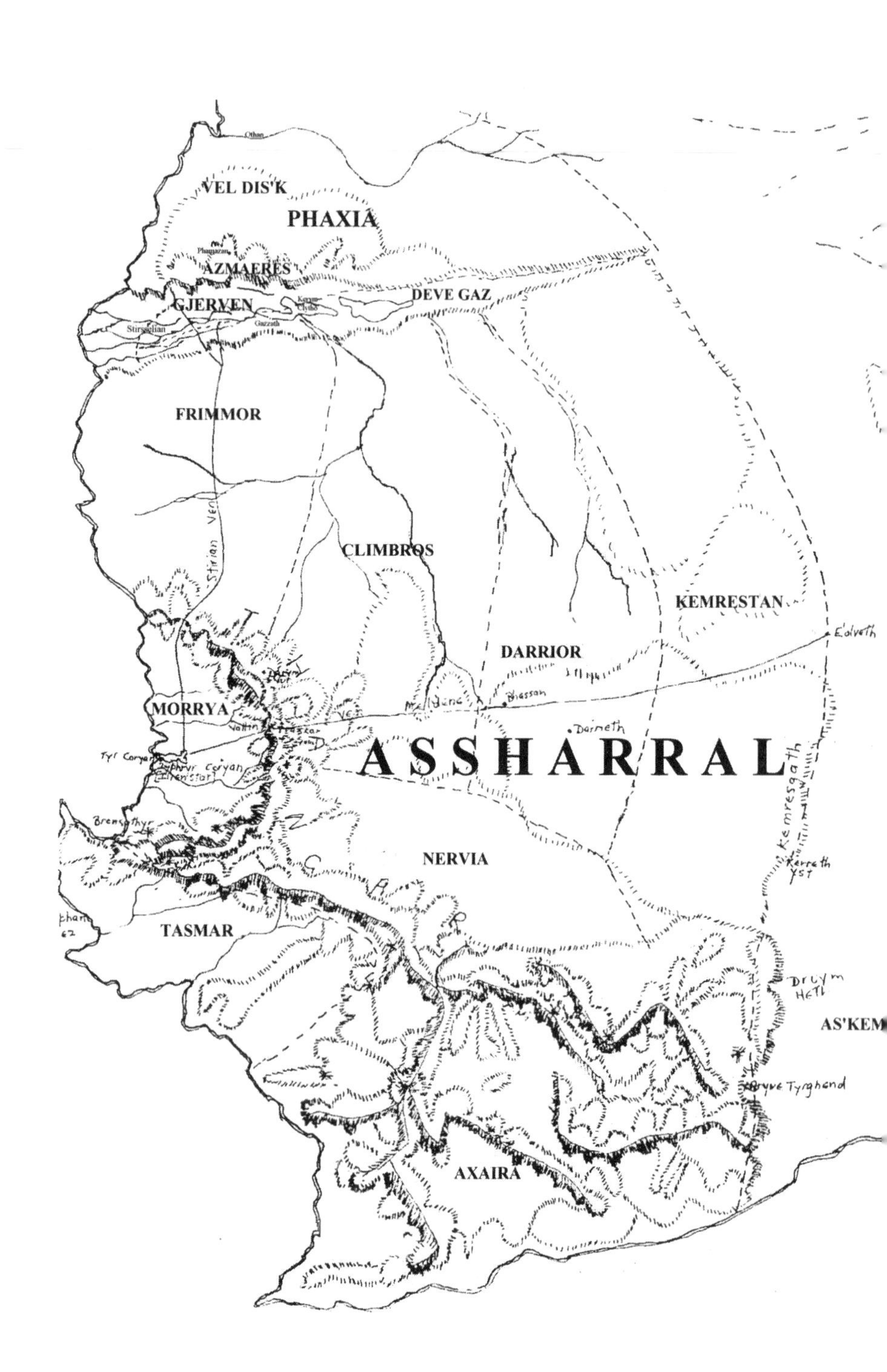
Othan
VEL DIS'K
PHAXIA
AZMAERES
GJERVEN
Gazzath
DEVE GAZ
FRIMMOR
Strian Ven
CLIMBROS
KEMRESTAN
DARRIOR
Darneth
MORRYA
ASSHARRAL
Kemresgaath
NERVIA
TASMAR
AS'KEM
AXAIRA

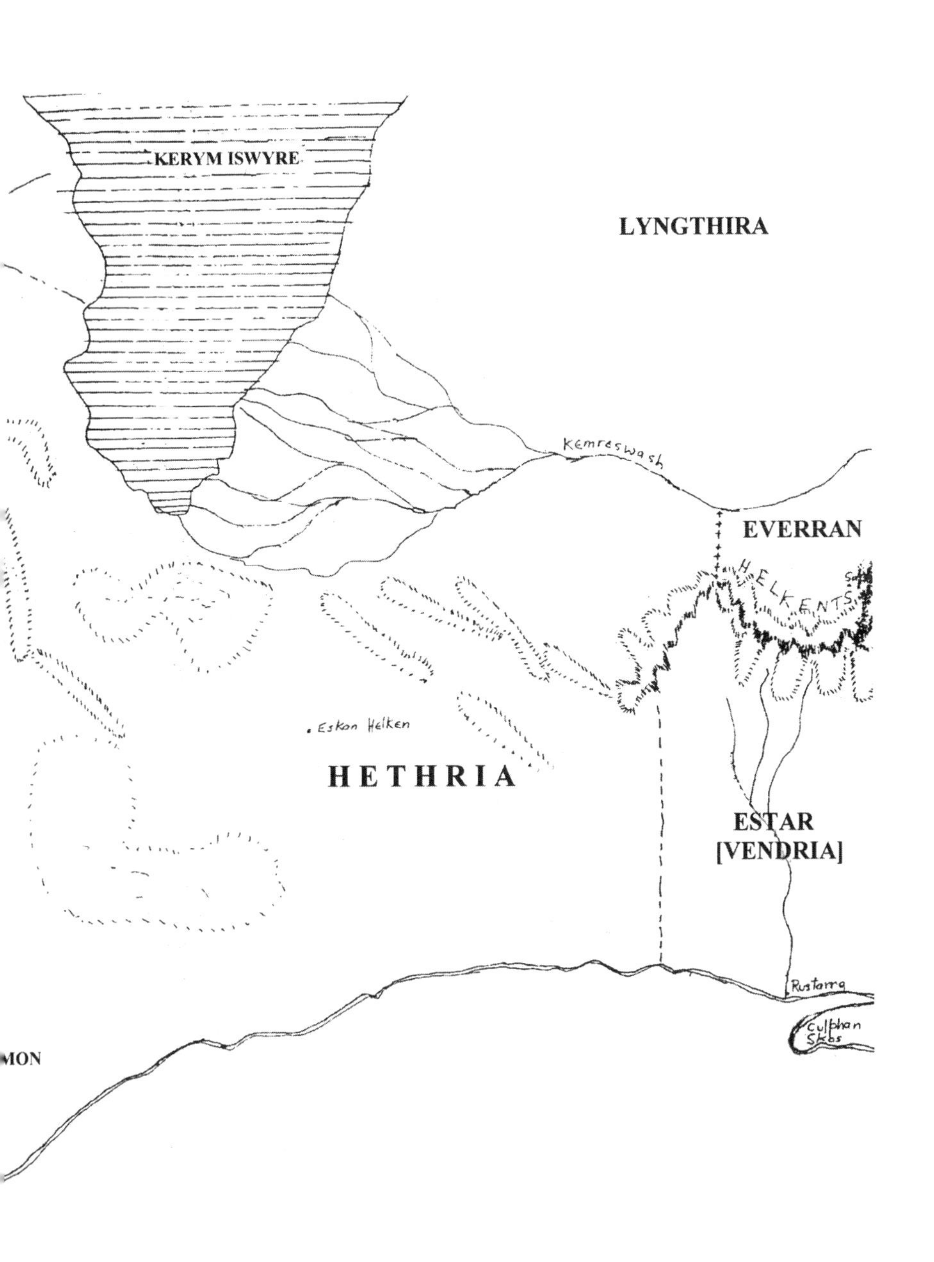
KERYM ISWYRE
LYNGTHIRA
Kemreswash
EVERRAN
HELKENTS
Eskon Helken
HETHRIA
ESTAR
[VENDRIA]
Rustarra
Culphan
Skos

CHAPTER I

It is a long road to Eskan Helken here in the wastes of Hethria, and longer still when you do not know you are traveling it. As I did not. The day my journey began, I had never heard of Eskan Helken, and only vaguely of Hethria. All I knew was that, after morning inspection, the Lady Moriana wanted words with me.

Hardly momentous? But no one who served the Lady Moriana answered such a summons without a degree of sweat in the palms and tallying of his own and others' recent sins. Certainly not the Captain of her Guard. Certainly not the newly promoted Captain of her Guard.

That was in my second's manner when I said, "Hear defaulters for me, Evis. I'm going up there," and he nodded without meeting my eye. It spoke from the rigid stance of the two sentries I had just posted, as I clanked between them up Ker Morrya's green marble entry steps. From the schooled face of the steward with moontrees on the back and breast of his black silk surcoat, when I said, "The Lady asked for me," and he replied, "This way, sir." It persisted in the fit of my helmet, which was too tight, in the slip of my boots, which were too loose. In the chill of the first long colonnade whose tiles were scalloped moss-green, jade-green, by each archful of morning sun, in the piercing sweetness of a black-beaked eygnor's song, and the suddenly lovely curve of each water-fern's drooping frond. Such things grow precious when you may be seeing them for the very last time.

Ker Morrya is a huge pile of a place. The Lady would add or subtract from it as fancy took her, so some part was always rebuilding, another being torn down, and the intact pieces fitted with no rhyme or reason clear to a soldier's mind. From the first colonnade we entered a circular gallery with pillars leafed in gold, branching capitals entwined above elegant white marble bas-reliefs: the Lady in profile to the left, to the right. Contemplating a mirror, a serpent, a pomegranate. On the crimson carpet beneath stood a Gjerven swamp-tribe's gargoyle, six feet of garishly painted red-and-blue wood.

Left turning, we emerged in a garden of pools and pergolas, geometric as a phalanx between hedges ruler-clipped. It was scented by herbs, pungent, unruly, sweetly dangerous. Under the central pergola little black Morryan bees had built a head-sized clot of a nest. Beyond rose a mezzanine hall, a wreathing maze inlaid on its russet-and-mahogany parquet work. From its central pit grew the ferny leaves and gold and scarlet florets of a dwarf delryr tree. A langu, one of the great northern pythons, slept like a round bale of tapestry against the trunk.

Two steps led out and down to a tapestry loggia, its solid wall masked by a myriad tiny bejeweled figures, dancing, reclining, beneath trees in smoky-lavender flower. A staircase turned in and up to a complete guest suite, white plaster walls inset with delicate powder-blue medallions under molded cornices: the Lady burning incense, playing with a dove, tying her girdle, discarding a shoe. The bedroom's rear wall was torn out, the table of gold and crystal tiring ware and the four-poster's dove-blue silk hangings open to the bricks and ladders strewn outside.

We crossed the trampled mud, wiped our feet on a Tasmarn silk rug's gray-and-crimson damascene, some southern weaver's masterpiece, dodged the spikes of a helymfet that had gone to sleep on its meal of ants, and entered a vestibule composed in green: malachite floor, jade-inset ceiling, green marble fretwork walls that latticed Ker Morrya's living drapery. Beyond rose a flight of open, rough-hewn steps.

The steward stopped, lowering his voice. "The Lady is . . . by the fountain, sir."

He vanished. I looked at the stairs and found my mouth was dry. The Lady received as she built, in kitchen, boudoir, hall or buttery. But it was rarely anyone met her by the fountain, and more rarely that those who went to such an interview came back.

It was chilly in the vestibule. The mountain beyond was already breathing back the sun. I could see facets of black, glassy rock, pockets of moss and fern and palm, glitters of silver water amid the green and black. A vague roar rose from the streets of Zyphryr Coryan, sprawled busy and populous far below. Clearly, through and over it, I heard water, a crystal, fluent tinkle, swift, unfaltering, bubbling out into air and the mountain's emptiness.

The sun met me halfway up. I could not help a glance back, and then a halt, for the view would distract you from the Lady Moriana herself. I was on the very shoulder of the Morhyrne, the huge lopsided triangle of mountain visible a day's sail east of Zyphryr Coryan and three days' march to the west. Its bare black cone loomed over me. At my feet a vista of the city's crowded roofs fell in red and white and fallow-gold patchwork to the lands of Assharral, spreading south and west and north to the horizon. On the other side, the city's huge, peacock-blue-and-green-tinted harbor coiled away to the breadth of the eastern sea.

I lingered a moment. The air was brisk. The green things near me were tingling with it. It did not seem a fitting day to die.

The stairway ended at a living arch, the blended foliage of two tall trees that drooped sweet-scented speckled brown-and-gold sprays of flower. I knew they were the legendary rivannons, which few Assharrans have ever seen.

Beyond them a semi-circular terrace had been scooped in the mountainside, its diameter the cone's black native rock, its arc a low parapet of lustrous dark-red porphyry. Inside was a tangle of fragrant shrubs and flowering trees. At its center the sun played black and silver on the fountain of Los Morryan, an endless dance of scintillant bubbles and sweet-tongued sound whose spray showered down over the glittering black rim, fanning moss over pavement where ancient symbols had been blurred by feet and time.

The bower was dappled by shade and water, fragrant, remote as paradise. It was also empty. Of the Lady Moriana I could see no sign.

It would be correct to say I was at a loss. You would not summon the Lady like a serving maid. Nor would you charge bull fashion into the bower of Los Morryan. Nor, as I very much wished, could you summarily retreat.

I tucked my helmet under an arm. The crisp air breathed on my skull. Then, beyond the fountain, I saw a shoe.

A frivolous, high-heeled golden sandal, encasing a high-arched, blue-veined foot. Its owner sat under the broad silver spearhead leaves and golden fluff-lance flowers of the perridel tree beyond the spring. Now I looked, I could distinguish, through the falling water, a hem of white flowing silk.

I advanced, silently cursing my unsilent boots. The Lady Moriana leant sidelong in the onyx seat, elbow on the parapet, fingers adroop. On the curve of her wrist, motionless as the Lady, rested a great gold-and-purple butterfly.

At first sight of the Lady Moriana you would think, A girl. A girl in girlhood's crowning flower. The simple white dress, the ebony hair fallen from a center part to a loose coil in the nape of the neck, the pensive downbent profile, slightly parted, unpainted lips, smooth round chin, swannish concave stem of throat, high rounded brow. It would all seem a sculptor's idealized innocence.

Then you would see the bracelet of nut-sized thillians coruscating on the slender wrist, the huge eclipsed-moon gold signet on the right thumb, the quiet, cruel arch of bridge and nostril from the lids drooped over the slumbrous coal-black eyes, and you would know without instruction that she is neither innocent nor a girl, and that a goaded coffin-snake is less dangerous.

Neither lady nor butterfly paid the slightest heed to me. I stood at uneasy ease, feeling my breath stop. I also knew I had begun to sweat. Fine symptoms for a man who looked unmoved on a Phaxian battle-front.

The fountain tinkled, the shadows stirred. At last, the Lady drew a breath.

"Fly, then," she murmured. Los Morryan's music had broken into syllables. "Fly."

The butterfly opened its wings, beat them once, an imperial trumpet blast, and looped away. The Lady gazed after it, chin on the back of her hand.

"Tell me, Alkir"—that muted music was half somnolent—"was I a butterfly dreaming it was Moriana, or Moriana dreaming she was a butterfly?"

Never was I so thankful for formality. It let me respond with correct and perfect blankness, "Ma'am."

Her lips curved. The pull of a tightened bow. Her eyelids rose. Black depths I saw, powdered with golden galaxies, and looked carefully an inch above. Her brows were black and fine, her forehead had a glow of youth, just tinted by the sun. Every time I saw the Lady Moriana I had to remind myself that she was ten, twenty times my age.

She turned full face, the edge of my vision caught her eyes' waking, and I am not ashamed to admit my backbone chilled.

"Never mind, Captain." Now the music too was lazily mocking me. "You were not meant to understand. It was for something else that I wanted you."

I came to attention, thinking, You can at least die soldierly. But she reached into a corner of the seat, and the sun blew up in dazzling, transparent fire.

The dazzle passed. A sheet of colorless light flared in her cupped hands. A dewdrop big as a fist, it looked, but retaining its orb shape, its thillian-gem brilliance, in her grasp.

"Ker Morrya's spyglass," she said.

I could not help the questioning note as I repeated, "Ma'am?"

"Even the Lady Moriana"—the music kept its drowsy threat—"sometimes needs to help her eyes."

Finally, I nerved myself. "And, ma'am. . . . What do you see?"

Her gaze moved past me, out over Zyphryr Coryan, over Assharral, into blue's infinity. Her voice was flute song, just audible.

"Something is coming. Coming here."

I was relieved to unearth tangibles, and tangibles within my sphere. "An enemy, ma'am?"

Her lips curved. To this day I cannot decide if that smile held hate or love, hope or dread, eagerness or enmity.

"All things in the Dream," replied that low, absent melody, "seem as you see them. Rose, thorn. Treasure, serpent. One, the other. Both."

I hoped she was not listening to my thought. Respectfully, I did not say, Are you babbling? but, "If the Lady has need of me. . . ."

"Oh, yes." She was still gazing westward. Her words fell cool and crystal clear. "You are going to meet it, Alkir. Bring it to me."

I tried not to swallow. "Yes, ma'am. Er. . . ."

She turned her head. Her mouth spoke what I knew her eyes would hold. Knowing, languid mockery.

"Hethria," she said. "You've never heard of it."

"Er—yes, ma'am." You dare, sometimes, to contradict even the Lady Moriana. But very, very respectfully. "It's a desert. Beyond Kemrestan. I served garrison duty out there once."

"How very"—silken menace—"convenient."

Looking over her head at the glittering black rock of the Morhyrne's shell, I felt the toes curl in my boots.

"It is coming," she sank back, letting the dew-globe slide down into her lap, "from Hethria. To . . . let me see . . . Etalveth. You know the town . . . no doubt."

"Ma'am." My mouth was dry.

"A fleapit," added that drowsy lilt. "Full of bored dogs, lazy soldiers. And Sathellin."

The picture assembled in my mind, white dust between white mud flat-roofed shanties, searing sun, sanctuaries of shade jammed with donkeys, dicing soldiers, beggars, peddlers, and the black-turbaned, blue-gowned figures of the Sathellin, the desert sailors whose caravans wind in from oceans only they can chart, laden with the craziest blend of rubbish and treasure-trove. Ochre-daubed amulets, tall pointed jars of wine from an unknown vineyard, maerian gems and goat-skin sandals, dried serpent skins and the priceless tapestries hung in her own loggia. . . .

The image faded. Los Morryan twinkled, the perridel's golden bloom and silver leaf were dancing, while the Lady looked past me with that odd smile in her coal-black eyes.

"You will go to Etalveth, Alkir. Take . . . two pentarchies of the Guard. And collect this gift."

"Ma'am." I saluted. My heart bounced ridiculously halfway up my throat. After my forebodings, this lunatic order was a gallows reprieve. And then the omission occurred to me.

The Lady smiled. Now the laughter was cruel, alert, and aimed at me alone.

"Yes. How very remiss of us. You are looking for a man, Alkir. A man with a scarred face." She drew her fingers down the flawless porcelain of her right cheek. "With a crippled arm." She moved her right arm on the parapet. "And. . . . Oh, yes. He has green eyes."

Los Morryan did fulfill part of its reputation. It seemed a mere minute or two we spoke there, in the first quarter of a fine Dry-season day. Yet I descended into late afternoon, to find the Guard in turmoil, Evis unsure if he was a second or a new-made commander, and Callissa occupying my work-room amid a swarm of upset children and a flood of half-stemmed tears.

"Yes," I told Evis, untangling a wife from my breast-plate and a son from each leg. "But not for long. Yes, dear, I'm alive. No, son, nobody's eaten me. I just have to go away for a while."

Callissa substituted frightened query for frightened relief. We grew up on two of Frimmor's little neighboring farms. She was never fully reconciled to my quitting it for the army, even after I married her and necessity rather than ambition kept me aiming for captaincy of the Guard. Without influence, it takes a good deal more than simple addition would predict to feed four mouths. She had never said a word against soldiering, the Lady, Zyphryr Coryan. Only I knew that if I ever asked, "Do you miss Frimmor?" we would be striking camp in a week.

"Nothing to worry about," I told her, smiling to calm those clear brown eyes. She has clear skin too, and a cloud of fine brown hair, and fine bones that looked elfin before Zem and Zam arrived. "I'll tell you at home. Just let me grind Evis' nose a little flatter first."

Before we talked I also had to bed down the twins, supply a

condensed saga of the latest Phaxian war, and warn them that my trip was "in security." I doubted the Lady's whim was for open talk, and that was enough to lock their mouths. Then I disarmed and bathed and Callissa silently kept an eye on the maid serving roast beef and vegetables. Servants were still not customary to her.

She did not exclaim on the Lady's vagaries, speculate on the stranger's aims or provenance. There was no "Etalveth's such a long way" or "When will you be back?" or "Why must it be you?" or even "Is it safe?" There never had been, even when I marched to Phaxia. Only at the end, not raising her eyes, she said quietly, "I suppose it had to come sometime."

"What on earth do you mean?" In peace or war, our kind mislike cold prophecies. "This is just an errand. Inside Assharral. I'll be back before the boys need more new shoes."

She turned the silver on her plate. A Captain of the Guard needs silver tableware, naturally, and naturally it bore the moon-tree crest. So did most things in our large old house above the main barrack square. Cups, hangings, chairs, fan-light, the round moon with its crowning tree looked back at you everywhere.

"Oh, you'll be back." With anyone else, I would have called that note defeat. "Only . . . things won't be the same."

"Tell me," I said, taking her hand, with gentleness.

"Nothing." She turned her hand to clasp mine briefly before removing hers. "Just stupidity."

If it is shorter than the way to Eskan Helken, the road to Etalveth is journey enough. Four of Assharral's ten provinces it crosses, from the coastal farms of Morrya to Thangar's ranges with their timber forests and tingling air, then the long grain lands of Climbros, and Darrior's mines and cattle-camps; before the ever-more-arid shepherd lands of Kemrestan change from half-desert to wilderness, and a fringe of garrison towns marks the edge of no-man's-land, the prelude to Hethria.

We were a fortnight on the way, despite post-horses and the silver moontree on our black surcoats that gave us precedence over everything but chance. A fortnight is ample time to think. Yet I had reached no conclusions when I informed Etalveth's flustered garrison commander that I was on "an informal inspection of the western defenses," and he quartered us in his half-empty fort.

The western garrisons are little more than the Lady's whim, or the army's nursery. When Assharral looks for trouble, it is northward, from Phaxia. My ten guardsmen livened the brothels and enriched the gambling sharps, I spent half my days in military trivia and the rest at the caravanserai, the huge colonnaded courtyard with its crumbling brick walls and monstrous old keerphar trees and babble of a dozen different dialects, where the Sathellin camp in Etalveth, when they come at all.

Only in the last two generations have they come. No one then knew why. There were many rumors, all baseless. Wild stories of a realm beyond Hethria, a cluster of realms called the Confederacy, wilder stories of a witch dwelling in Hethria, who dammed a great river to make the desert flower and bade the Sathellin carry wares from one to the other end of the world. There were curious tales of wizards, and another sea. Everyone knows there is only Gevber, which borders Assharral and Phaxia, and keeps the islanders of Eakring Ithyrx trading instead of invading us. I heard a good many yarns in that week I haunted the caravanserai, from grooms, sweepers, peddlers, merchants. All Assharrans. No caravan was in.

I wrote to Callissa and sent the boys toy Hethrian spears, blunted to prevent massacre. I extricated two guardsmen from the civil jail and a third from an imputed paternity suit. The caravan master took to nodding, then to offering mint-tea. He had once visited Zyphryr Coryan and felt himself the Lady's intimate.

On the eighth morning my humoring of his humors paid off. A sweeper met us setting out to inspect a nearby signal tower and said, touching his brow, that the master thought I might be interested. Some Sathellin were due.

"Nomads," I told the blank-faced fort commandant. "Homeless. Masterless. Have you never thought, what a perfect communication line for a spy?"

His jaw dropped. He never paused to wonder what you would spy on in Kemrestan, or what value it would be at such a transit's end. We rode out past Etalveth's wattled sand-levees, to where the works of man sink into insignificance, and confronted the pebbly curve of sky that is the threshold of Hethria.

The caravan was approaching from slightly north of west. At first it was only a snailing dust smear, like an infantry column in extended march. Then it became a slowly swelling red cloud. Then blurs patched the fog. Then heads stuck out at long intervals, black-turbaned heads. Then the bobbing ears of horses, donkeys, mules appeared, interminable squadrons roped in sixes and sevens to each other's pack-saddles, with a Sathel riding at each troop's head. They ride side-saddle, controlling their mounts with a stick tapped on quarters or neck. "Barbarians," said the commandant, comfortably superior. "Never heard of a bit."

Most rode donkeys, but here and there was a horse of another breed to the heavy, shaggy clumpers laden with water-skins, fodder and firewood, along with human goods and provender. And these horses, in the days before Zem and Zam made horses a forbidden luxury, I would not have disdained myself. Most were black: fine-boned, blaze-faced, with a proud bearing and a look of tempered stamina. But at the very rear of the caravan another kind caught my eye.

It was more like a war-horse, tall, well-boned, though so finely proportioned it did not seem heavy, with splendid shoulders and rein and a fine if placid carriage of the head. It was gray. A silver dapple-gray, like a piece of moonlight come to life.

The rider, swathed to the eyes in blue robe and black turban, resembled all three accompanying Sathellin, except that he had no stick to control his beast. I watched him as they rode by. Then, thinking it would make a pretext for scout-work, I said, “I wonder if there’s a price on that horse.”

The commandant laughed. “With Sathellin,” he said, “there’s a price on a sister’s virginity. Just so long as it’s high.”

I went down to the caravanserai at dusk. A pretty time, in any camp. The fires gild the dust, there is a comfortable smell of cooking and off-saddled beasts, the babble of a long day relived in talk, a romance in the mundanities of picketing. The caravan-master was delighted to sip mint-tea and school me in the scandalous habits of Sathellin, while through his door arch I watched horses, donkeys, mules being watered, and the blue-robed figures that passed with their swift, gliding walk. But nobody brought a gray horse to drink.

Presently I disengaged to take a stroll. Some Sathellin were already haggling. In this or that room tallow lamps caught a vehement mouth, a waving finger, an eager, skeptical, impassive, wary curve of cheek, the gleam of metal or sheen of fabric, the glitter of other, more precious stuff. One buyer was sampling wine. It ran redder than heart’s blood in the glow of the lamp. But nowhere, loose or picketed, could I catch a glimpse of a gray horse.

Having patrolled the entire court, I was forced to clumsier tactics. As the next Sathel passed I halted him and said, “When your caravan came in, there was someone riding a gray horse.

Do you know where he is?"

Though he was a mere blur in the dusk, I sensed a withdrawal, a stiffening. "Why was you wanting to know?"

"I rather," I said, "liked the look of the horse. I should like to see it again."

"Ah," he said at last. He stopped another passerby. I caught only a quick run of words, ending in one intelligible phrase. "Thorgan Fenglos." The Moon-faced King.

Sometimes there is vantage in surprise. "Thorgan Fenglos," I repeated. "Is that the man? Or the horse?"

One Sathel twitched. The other let out a snort. Both seemed to withdraw. Then the second said under his breath, "Ah, well." He jerked a thumb. "Down the end there. Last keerphar."

I had walked past. Walking back, I found a door had been masked by the tree's wide, gnarled trunk. I ducked under the prop that upheld one huge low limb, stumbled on a hump of root, and looked up into a rectangle of deeper darkness from which came a faint silver gleam, and the sound of someone humming, as you do at a pleasant task.

It was a man's voice, clear, low, with a lurking gaiety. Under it ran a brisk rhythmic brushing noise. As I came up the humming broke off. The voice said, "Stand over, then." Hooves clopped on stone, and a faint tingle coursed my neck. Whatever the context, it is impossible to mistake the tone of a military command.

I hesitated in the keerphar shadow, oddly ill-at-ease, wishing for light. The humming ceased. The voice said with that good-humored authority, "If you don't fancy Assharran water, madam, that's all I can do for you." A shape came swiftly from the doorway, straightening and checking so we stood face to face.

He was tall, taller than I, and even in Assharral I am no dwarf. I could see only the shape of robe and turban, but two things struck me at once. His right shoulder was somehow mis-held, and he showed no surprise.

"Yes?" he said. The lurking gaiety persisted. "Were you looking for me?"

"If you own a gray horse," I answered, "yes."

"Fengsaeva?" A low chuckle. "Oh, she owns me."

My wits must have been quickened by something in the air: the Sathel strangeness, the freakish search. Or some infection from him. I am not usually witty. Nor, usually, am I recklessly cordial. "Then perhaps," I said, "she would permit you to eat with me?"

The amusement had deepened. "Why not eat here? Then you can inspect us both at once."

I should have been startled. Later, I was, and not merely by the idea of dining with a horse. At the time I replied as if it were commonplace, "A pleasure. But I fear I'm not an owl."

With another half-chuckle he turned on his heel. "Move up, madam." His shape vanished. There was a flash, a flare, I was still wondering how he could be so quick with flint and tinder when the door filled with lamplight, and he called, "Come in."

The mare's quarters nearly filled the door. His voice said, "She won't kick."

Nettled, I stepped by. A tiny traveling kettle sat on a clay brazier. Saddlecloth and saddlebags had been tossed out on the floor, a vague heap of belongings lay beyond. As any soldier would, I looked for his weapons. And could not find a knife, let alone a sword.

"I don't carry one." He was stooped over a saddlebag, the amusement open now. He tweaked out a cup. Left-handed, I noted as my wits rallied. The mare blew gently on my elbow, distracting, reviving me.

"A self-invited guest," I said, "should add something to the board. And at his host's behest."

"Very good." He turned around. I had the most curious idea it was not the offer he meant. "Then in honor of Assharral, we might pass up mint-tea for once. You'll favor me, Captain, if you relieve that old rogue Langis of a measure of wine." The laughter flickered. "Tell him Thorgan Fenglos asked for it."

I retreated, in ostensible good order. The wine-seller, in a way that had my complete sympathy, gave me the measure without a word, a demand for payment, a glance at my face. At the time it seemed quite reasonable.

"This," said my host, "should come after eating. Let's begin."

I forget what we ate, though I have the clearest vision of the mud-walled room, the mingled smell of horse and burning tallow and traveler's distance from his gear, the mare's big black liquid eyes and shimmering face poised over us, the lamplight that made everything mysterious, indistinct. We ate in silence. Then he filled the cups, left-handed, as he had done everything else, poured a drop on the floor, drank, and let out a long breath.

"From Stiriand," he said. "Gesarre valley, I should think."

"You know where this wine is made?" I could not help myself.

He nodded. For once the underlying laughter was quite gone. "Yes," he said softly. "I know."

I was still deploying words when he supplanted them.

"It comes from Everran. A kingdom west of Hethria. The mare's not for sale, she belongs to a friend. But then, you didn't really want to buy her, did you? And I'm Thorgan Fenglos because of this."

He had loosed a fold of turban to eat. Now he pulled it all off in a tangle and lifted his face to the lamp, revealing the huge scar that darkened his right cheek. It also, for the first time, showed me his eyes. They were narrow, almond-shaped, alive as sun on running water. Deep, vivid green.

"How did I get it?" He raised his brows at my dumbstruck face. "The same way I got that." He slapped his right arm, still swathed in the robe, and the swing told me it was limp. Paralyzed. "Hotheadedness." His eye-corners crinkled. "Military hotheadedness. But then, you knew I was a soldier when you heard me speak."

Whatever my face said made him grin. "A friend of mine once did the same to me. 'Too full of How and Why to choose a First. I'll tell then, and save all our tongues.' So now you've found what you were looking for, why were you looking for it?"

I must have swallowed nothing at least five times. He had turned to the mare. When I did not answer, he went on easily, "The only reason I came to Assharral is . . . to see the sea."

"The. . . ." I croaked.

"The sea. They always said there was another east of Hethria. I didn't want to spoil it by looking. I wanted to see with eyes."

Some basic inconsistency in this eluded me. I still felt as if the entire Morhyrne had hit me in the wind.

He went on, not quite gravely, "You'll grow used to it. Getting answers before you speak, I mean. And now, why were you looking for me?"

Finally I managed to assemble something resembling wits. "I have"—orders was too tactless—"an invitation from the Lady Moriana. She wishes you to . . . visit her."

Those eyes danced, making me perfectly sure he knew just how I had paraphrased.

"I shall be delighted," he said gravely, "to visit the Lady Moriana. Whoever she is. So long as she lives near the sea."

With that same alarming clairvoyance he forestalled awkwardness by saying, "You can leave me here overnight. I won't decamp. But I hope you don't need to travel post-haste, because I can't leave the mare. She's unbroken, you see." I did not see at all, and could find no way of saying so. "So we'll meet," he finished crisply, "at the town gate tomorrow morning." And finding I had answered, "Sir," without the slightest hesitation, I knew that if he had been a soldier, it was in the highest rank.

I was glad we did not travel post, because in those weeks' escort duty I rediscovered Assharral. The Kemrestani herds of long-tailed sheep and flamboyant black and white goats, I learnt through his eyes the splendor of their vivid splashes on the dun and tawny wilderness. The Darrian watermen drawing with a yoke of tall red bow-horned oxen backing to and from the well, I had never noticed their ingenuity. Nor had I appreciated the iron-miners who pump water by some kind of screw and use their spill to reshape the countryside. The Climbrian dancers, fifteen-year-old living candelabra in cloth of gold, ruby and emerald tinsel, with headdresses high as themselves, I had never plumbed the beauty in their swaying mime of Assharral's legends, Langu the snake that ate the Ocean, Fengela the Moon-mother who stopped a flood in the River of Heaven with a net of her branching hair. The make of a Climbrian stump-jumping plough, the ram-headed Kemrestani cups, the style of a Thangar axeman's cut, the blue-spotted Darrian cattle-dogs, he showed me it all. At first I was uneasy. But I soon understood, with the perception beyond reason, that this was not the scrutiny of a spy. It was more like that insatiable innocent curiosity of a boy on holiday.

Finally he caught my sidelong look as he watched a pair of herd-boys wrestle a fractious calf, and grinned. "I've been so long in Hethria. Everything's new."

I revolved openings on that topic. Then, as by Los Morryan, an image formed in my mind. A wide, barren, hard, hot, red and golden country, beautiful in its savage way, scattered with staging point farms and nomad savages. And thrusting from its heart a cluster of rock domes, bubbles of rusty vermilion against a harsh blue sky.

"Eskan Helken. Someone else does live there, but she's not a witch. Aedr is the proper name. Just as it is for me."

I concentrated hurriedly between my horse's ears.

"Yes, we did dam a river and run the water south into Hethria. It was a femaere's own job." In old Assharran it means an evil spirit. Catching my look, he grinned. "First to get her interested, then to build the thing. I was never my own engineer before. It's a cursed sight easier to say, 'Build me such-and-such,' than to go out and do it yourself. That's what kept me so long in Hethria. But it was worth it. If only to open the road for the 'Sathellin.' "

My mouth opened too. Two generations they've been coming. . . . It danced in my head. Yet the lamp had revealed a man of seeming early middle age, forty, no more, deep-lined face, gray in coal-black hair.

"Don't worry." I could hear the smile. "Aedryx live longer than ordinary people, that's all."

I should have followed that up. A mysterious, powerful—wizard—led like a pony into the heart of Assharral? It would sound Alarm to the merest ranker, let be Captain of the Guard. But I never even paused to wonder why, instead, I thought about the Sathellin.

"No, they don't come to spy," he said. "Or to drain gold from Assharral. They do take some things. Seeds, new animals. Your silk. But that's not why the road was built."

This time, I had to ask. "For what, then?"

He was gazing ahead, though not at the wide lands of Kemrestan. "Roads," he said softly, "are for carrying ideas."

What sort of ideas? I wondered warily.

"Oh," he said, "nothing dangerous."

This has to stop, I thought furiously. *I can't call my thoughts my own!*

"Forgive me," he said. "It's so simple, and saves so much time. And living with—Fengthira—I've grown used to it. It's just Scarthe, you know, reading your verbal thoughts. But if it worries you," contritely, "I won't do it again."

After two or three swallows I managed to ask, "Scarthe?"

"One of the Mind-Acts. Ruanbrarx. The aedric arts."

He watched a red kite plane across the road. You are, I told myself, Captain of the Lady's Guard. You should be equal to this.

"We call them rienglis," I said. "Morglis is the other sort, with sharper wings."

Not at all startled, he glanced round, giving me a rare look full in his eyes, which were bright with interest, and oddly pleased. And seemed again to have a life of their own, a motion as if the very irises were awake.

"Morglis? That's Black-nose, to me. A southern cape." Then he nodded at my sword-belt. "Do your smiths use tempered or laminated steel?" And next moment we were deep in military technicalities.

More than technicalities. Presently I found myself saying, "Of course, the Guard's mostly a parade unit. But you have to pass up the real stuff, when you're a married man—"

I broke off, more shaken than by anything he had done. Even to myself I had never admitted how I saw the Guard, or what had put me there. But he only nodded, with sympathy, understanding, and a strange touch of envy in his voice as he said, "Everything has its price."

That made me wariest of all the surprises he handed me, and those began with our first bivouac. It was a post-house, whence the usual swarm of ostlers rushed at sight of the livery, to be taken aback on finding a desert Sathel in our midst. And more than taken aback when he said as he slid to earth, "Thanks, I'll see to the mare myself."

I opened my mouth. Shut it. Bade my senior file-leader,

"Carry on, Zyr," and followed the mare and her rider and the inn's protesting rank and file stableward.

"Water," he told them. "A loose box. Hay. Handful of oats. That's all." He bedded her down. Then he beckoned the head groom and said sternly, "For your own sakes, see nobody fools with her."

The mare was gazing placidly over the stall door, looking sweet-tempered as an apple and mild as any clumper that ever hauled a cart. His eyes flickered at me. "You're as bad as the rest. I'll give you all a demonstration. You, Captain. Walk up to her."

At ten paces her ears went back. At five, she showed the whites of her eyes and jerked her head. Not fear, but the challenge of the man-eater, proclaiming readiness to savage you.

"Whoa," I said, trying to sound soothing. "What's the matter? You know me."

She bared her teeth. I took another pace. She did not snort or squeal or rear, she hit the door with her full weight and a wicked scything snatch of the jaw that plucked my surcoat sleeve before I shot out of range.

"You see?" her rider asked the thunderstruck yard. "So don't go meddling."

"Wreve-lan'x," he said as we walked off. "Beast mastery. Another art. She's never been broken in the proper sense. But it's hard to make people believe she's only safe when I'm around."

"Safe!" I exclaimed, and he chuckled. "At least that hatchet-faced red lad of yours won't go trying to play horse-tamer behind my back."

My guardsmen were too well trained to think much, but that episode began to change their view of him from lofty disdain to rank distrust. Isolation is part of command. We were not battle-knit, even old enough rankmates to overstep rank, so I could neither share their speculations nor air my own; and I was naggingly aware my thoughts might be shared elsewhere, unbeknownst. But you need not know men to gauge their mood.

Theirs grew bad enough to distract me from the riddle in our midst, and was not bettered by the evening in Darrior when his saddlebag fell open halfway across the yard. He said, "Oh, drat!" and kept walking, while cups, spare girth, bootlaces, kettle and knife and salt-box whirled up in his wake and popped back into the bag like autumn leaves on a backward wind.

"My apologies," he said, when we sat, as usual, over supper in one of the inn's better rooms. "I've really upset them now."

I felt it the most masterly understatement I had been privileged to hear. I did not say so. With surprise, I found I had accepted speech was unnecessary.

He nodded, at the agreement or the realization or both. "I forget you're not used to aedryx. And I've used Axynbrarve so much it's easier than hands. Especially," a somewhat rueful look, "for me."

I looked at his arm, and asked instead, "Axynbrarve?"

"Another art." His eyes shot a green flash. The beer jar slid to my elbow, and he chuckled at my recoil. "Easy, after you've spent whole days knocking over trees. Oh, yes. You can do almost anything with it, if you're strong enough. And I usually am."

With his turban down in coils about his neck and the scar hidden by warm human laughter in those extraordinary eyes, he looked like a disheveled, impudent boy, and I succumbed to the spell behind the powers.

"Trees and beer jars," I said. "Just make an exception for me."

"Sir." He parodied a salute, and for the first time we shared a laugh.

But when we rode into Bhassan he did not laugh at all.

It was a normal high day. The magistrates had already sacrificed in the temple, which was palatial for a province, granite portico, high-relief frieze, gilt columns, solid gold image inside. A pleasant smell of burnt meat and incense wafted over the colorful crowd, there was a medley of sacrifice vendors in the forecourt, a babble of greeting and chaffering and noise from the doves and cocks and lambs on sale, and for once he questioned me outright. "What's all this?" he said.

"High day." I was surprised. "They're offering sacrifice."

"Sacrifice?" For once the tables were turned. I had startled him.

"Animals. Or incense, if you're rich enough. In thanks, or a petition." It was on the tip of my tongue to add, How on earth do you worship in Hethria? His eyes silenced me.

"You mean . . . you kill things? For the Four?"

"The Four?" Surprise was back with me. "We worship the Lady. I don't understand what you mean."

"The Lady? What Lady?"

"The Lady Moriana," I said patiently. "What other could there be?"

He turned full round. Though he rarely met your glance, from him it did not seem shiftiness. But now his eyes were wide open, and I pulled mine away, for those irises were no longer green but pure black, and his horror was solid as a blow.

"You worship your ruler? She lets you treat her like a—a—Sky-lord? Another human being?"

More insulted than shocked I said indignantly, "She is our Lady. And you may be long-lived, but she is immortal. Why should we not worship her?"

He let out his breath. Very low, utterly appalled, he said, "Imsar . . . Math."

"Do you"—I was still in arms—"behave differently?"

He tore his eyes from the beasts.

"Sacrifice? To the . . . the Four ?" He sought for words. "We fly kites for Air. Light fires for Fire. Plant trees for Earth. Give wine and flowers to Water." His eyes returned to the animals, as to some indelible obscenity. "But those are Sky-lords. Not a—a—"

"No wonder," I snapped, "you made a desert of Hethria."

Shock nearly made him laugh. "Oh, I'm the Four's only follower in Hethria. Fengthira just believes in Math. The Good. I can't explain, it's too complicated. But she doesn't give it anything at all."

He jerked his eyes free and clicked to the mare. We had changed horses and were a mile outside Bhassan before he spoke again.

"Your Lady. You call her undying?"

Still stiff, I retorted, "I am the tenth Captain of her Guard. And she is still a girl."

He caught his breath. Shot a glance at my surcoat. "Moon-tree," he muttered. For a second his eyes went vacant. Then he said bleakly, "I see."

"See what?" I snapped.

"This—immortality. Does it touch others too?"

I recalled my predecessor's fifty-year reign, my minute-long day beside Los Morryan. "You might share some of it, if you were close to her often enough."

"I see," he repeated, with another sort of glance, and I said furiously, "I don't want to live forever. I have a family to feed!"

"Of course," he agreed mildly. Provoked, I charged on.

"She's a good ruler! Assharral is safe, wealthy, orderly, strong. What more could you ask?"

"And nobody," he retorted softly, "sings."

"Nonsense!" I was thoroughly enraged now. "I'm not afraid

of her! Nobody is!"

He gave me one brief inexpressive look and words died on my lips.

"Very well," I said, half a mile later. "So people . . . disappear. They are rebels. Troublemakers." He did not reply. "It's a small price to pay!" He still did not answer. "What ruler is different?" I found myself near shouting, and hastily dropped my voice. "What if she does have moods? Play cat-and-mouse? Get rid of—of—bad elements? If you think that's cruel, you should go to Phaxia!"

He glanced round then. His eyes were still and sad and gave an odd impression of grief not only suffered but relived.

"You needn't defend her, Captain." He sounded almost tired. "I understand. I probably understand far better than you."

Chapter II

He did not mention it again. Only he looked away from the next Assharran fendel whose pure gold and beautifully minted moontree had formerly delighted him, and some of his pleasure in the land itself was marred. Between what he did and what he made me do and his effect on the men, it is small wonder I grew distracted, and was careless with the weather, as no commander ought to be.

It was the second day in Thangar that I bypassed an over-early halt, then compounded the error by misreading a Thangrian storm. We were in the high cold broken country that lifts sharply to the range crest, and we had watched the storm march from left to right across our front, veiling the black crags and thick emerald rucks of forest about Vallin Taskar, the Horned Gate. Having picked those irregular swaybacked jambs from the skyline I judged we would evade the storm, but I reckoned without the lie of the land. West of Vallin Taskar the waters run back to Kerym Scaur's fathomless blue pit, and they run with the pace of a bolting horse. The storm was still on our flank when we found a ravine that held a tangle of rent timber, undermined piers, and a brown torrent coming down like a Phaxian cavalry charge, more than wither deep. Worse still, a glance told me the storm had veered. It was going to clinch its attack with a frontal assault.

Too risky to advance, pointless to retreat. The men were muttering. "Kestis'd never've done it. . . . Should've known. . . .

What'd you expect?" I bit my lip. The worst of a parade unit is that you have no chance to blood yourself in with them, and precedent dies very, very hard.

The storm trumpeted in the crags. The one fault worse than negligence is vanity, and I was guilty of that too. At the last change, perhaps in some unadmitted rivalry with the gray mare's rider, I had let them saddle us with four or five green colts. My own flattened his ears and spun tail to the wind, another began to plunge. The light became the gloom of a storm's skirmish line, the narrow gorge resounded to its advance, the beetling cliff vanished in a boil of white. Furiously I yelled at the guards, "Shut up and hang on to your horse!"

Our sole mercy was that no one drowned. It was a ferocious storm, bad lightning that struck with shattering, numbing cracks, earsplitting thunder, water coming off the ravine-side knee deep, vision lost in a white murk lit by fitful whiter flashes that showed me horses standing on their heads in rain fit to wash away your skin. When it passed I was wet under my very helmet crown. To make it worse, we were nearly in the dark. The stream was impassable. A bitter wind had got up. We were stuck on the mountain, tentless, rationless, shivering drowned rats.

The sole choice was to make the best of it. "You and you," I said, still too angry to give them names, "go and scout. Cover. Dry wood." It was asking the impossible, and I did not care. "The rest of you get the horses back in the lee of the hill."

By then we were all shivering, horse and man, the gray mare and her rider by far the worst. Probably, I thought, they never had storms in Hethria. In the uproar I had had no time for more than a glimpse of the mare braced head down and quarters humped into the rain with a crouched shape on her back, and halfway through, an odd sense that the colt was easier to handle, which I somehow connected with him. But it was time to pay attention now.

I got off my played-out beast and sloshed over, trying not to sound as mortified as I felt. "I beg your pardon, sir. I've not found you much of a camp."

He straightened. Slowly. With surprise I saw his left wrist was shaking under the sodden robe, then identified the note of exhaustion in his voice. But he said quite calmly, "Never mind, Alkir. I've guessed worse." I might have known he would divine it all. "Owf!" he shook himself. "I haven't seen a storm like that since Hethria. And it's warmer there."

A wet bivouac is everyday to Phaxian veterans, but now I had horrid visions of reporting to the Lady that I had let her gift die of lung-fever from a night of Thangrian cold. "We'll start a fire," I said hastily, and he nodded as he slid to earth. "Good." He glanced at the mare. "If this one takes a chill I'll have explaining of my own to do."

The scouts had naturally found neither fuel nor shelter, and were sullenly ready for rebuke. I set them all to collect wet timber, and someone reluctantly ceded tinder and flint, but it was beyond a spark. The heap of sodden boughs sat dourly in our midst, and I could hear the internal grumblings.

The ringleader muttered, "Oughta ride back to Mallerstang." The stars shone coldly crystal, the ravine rumbled to the flood. A wet branch emptied down my neck. With cold fury I said, "A night out won't kill you. Get the horses head to tail and make them lie. We'll shelter behind them."

But a post-horse is not a warhorse. Never a one could we get down. We were still wrestling them when a crisp voice demanded, "What in the Four's name are you doing with that fire?"

"I'm sorry, sir." I could not help my stiffness. "It's a little difficult."

There was a growl around me, just under the level of punishable insolence. Someone said, louder, “No flint. ’N the wood’s all wet.” Unspoken behind it hung, And what’ll you do about that?

I heard him give a quick sigh. “Stand away,” he ordered. In a much kinder tone, “Turn around, girl. Stand away, I said!”

They obeyed that peremptory ring. He drew a breath that seemed endless. Then there was a vivid green flash, a crack, and the entire wood-heap burst into steaming, bubbling, green and blue-shot flame.

“Make two or three more off it and we’ll get between,” he said into the hush. “The way Hethox nomads do. Much warmer. Well, man, what are you waiting for?”

They fairly fled. Daring neither comment nor query, I busied myself with my horse, watching from an eye-corner as he used his turban to rough the mare’s wet hide. When four fires were alight we crowded men and beasts between them, and in time grew warmer. But not more comfortable.

“Look,” he said, kicking a stick into the fire where he and the mare stood all alone. “That was an art. A, a mind-act. Wreviane. Fire-mastery. You can learn it. I did. If you have the aptitude, it’s no more mysterious than—than water-seeking. Don’t you have diviners over here?”

Nobody replied, but I saw one or two make the horn sign with their offside hands.

“It isn’t witchcraft.” He was pleading, I had the sense, with far more than ten sulky frightened men, pleading a case he had lost before. “I am flesh and blood, just like you. I don’t eat babies, or call up demons. It’s just a skill. Would you rather have done without the fire?”

When there was still no reply he turned away, clicking to the mare. She folded herself down in the mud, he scrambled in among her legs with a fine disregard for hooves, curled against her belly, and in ten breaths was asleep. Which, I reflected, as I sent off the first wood-party, had done his case no good at all.

In morning watch I snatched a doze against a leaky tree, and woke to full dawn: a limpid, piercing day, the sky freshly blue, the wet forest silver and emerald, birds rejoicing everywhere. I, on the contrary, was wet, cold, stiff, hungry and sour. Eyeing the muddy square with its charcoal-heap outposts, the limp horses, the limper men, my charge still blissfully slumbering, I wished heartily that I had never set eyes on him. Then two guards bracketed me, and I knew real trouble had arrived.

"Ranks' prerogative," the first said curtly, with no attempt to salute. It is a euphemism. It means, accept our ultimatum or face a mutiny.

What, I thought, have I done to merit this? With a bitter pang I saw my dismounted troopers battling through the Stirsselian swamps, rotten with fever, riddled with ulcers, rife with dysentery, fighting, dying, abusing me at every turn and deserting me at none. And these fat flawns curled up after a single open bivouac.

The spokesman was still talking. ". . . nothing personal. But either we get rid of this—warlock—or else."

"Else what?" My hand itched for a sword hilt.

"Or else," he repeated, and evaded my eye.

"You fat louse." I kept my voice down, for effect, and not to wake a man who would never have encountered mutiny. "You parade-ground parrot. You creeping belly-ache. Your orders are escort duty to Zyphryr Coryan. There's no 'or else' for you."

He had gone purple. Hopefully, I watched his sword-hand. But he was a guard.

"You're not fit," I said, "to wash a surcoat, let be dirty one. A soldier wouldn't wipe his boots on you." Still he did not bite.

"Get away from me before you end where you belong. In the mud."

More purple than ever, he persevered manfully, "Is that your last word?"

"No," I snapped. "This is my last word." I wrenched at my sword, he sprang away, and a yell of, " *'Ware backs!*" nearly burst my ears.

I spun as any fighter would and my feet shot from under me as the second man's point speared between my right arm and ribs, I rolled and kicked with the spokesman charging my other flank and my frantic whip-lash just cleared his thrust, they closed in, I heard shouts and running feet and prepared to end under the pack of them—then the one who had struck from ambush dropped his sword, clapped both hands to his eyes, and folded gently down beside me in the mud.

I sat up. Retrieved my sword. Got to my feet. Nine whey-faced muddy black posts confronted me, slack-jawed, paralyzed. My charge emerged from behind them in an equally bedraggled blue robe. I took one glance and jerked my head away. He had no face. His eyes obliterated it, a glare of blinding, white-shot green.

"Sorry," he said curtly, "to interfere."

When none of us managed a word he came over to the man in the mud. Bent to feel a wrist. Straightened up.

The changed expression told me before he spoke. "I'm truly sorry." The voice had altered too. "He's dead, Alkir."

"Sorry?" I was still airborne with rage. "For what?" I rounded on the rest. "Anyone else want to exercise 'ranks' prerogative'?"

No one did. Sheathing the sword, I turned to my rescuer. And stopped.

After a moment I said, "Mutiny. Trying to kill an officer. The kindest he could hope for was to lose his head." He did not look round. "One more barrack-rat. The Lady won't worry.

She's more likely to string me up for negligence."

He sat on his heels over the corpse. I found I had put a hand on his shoulder as with one of my own subordinates. I said, "There was nothing else you could have done."

He might not have heard. He was staring, mute, deaf, as if nothing but the body existed. As if he had never seen a man die before.

I took the hand away. My skin crept. I heard myself say, too quietly, "Could you?"

There was a pause so deep I heard a foot squelch in the mud, drops spatter from the trees. Then, all of a piece, as a sliding boulder moves, he turned and looked at me.

I had taken a step back. But it was not me he saw. Those eyes looked past me, laughter all blown out. Dark and deep as a sunless forest pool. And blind, as if they had been stunned.

Then they shortened focus. That time, all of us stepped back.

"Could I not?" He barely whispered, but it cut like a whip. "Not knock the sword out of his hand? Stun him? Throw him a sarissa-length away? Stop him in his tracks . . . But no. I had to use A'sparre." Suddenly he buried his face in his hand. " 'A brick-maker stitching silk.' . . . Oh, Four. Any brick-maker could have bettered that."

With a degree of wounded dignity I said, "You did save my life. Or perhaps you'd rather have saved his?"

He just shook his head to and fro. Then, muffled in his arm, he said, "Fengthira was right."

"About what?"

He ignored that. But something in the bow of his shoulders made me burst out, "Don't tell me you're scared of your poxy witch!"

In another moment he looked up. His eyes were still stunned, but the shock was changing. Now he looked nearer to despair. And oddly forlorn, as if I had deserted him.

"You don't understand," he said. And it was not blame, but grief.

I stared. He looked back to the corpse.

"That . . . he . . . was unique." He said it very softly. The grief remained, as if he were speaking some great hero's eulogy.

"There never was, there never will be another of him. It took all time, and everything that ever was, to put him here. And I destroyed him. Blew him out, Phut! Not because I had to." His head went back in his arm. "From sheer . . . blind . . . criminal . . . incompetence."

I could not fathom the technical terms, I was uncomfortable at the depth of his remorse, baffled by this extravagant metaphysical breast-beating over a scurvy back-stabber who had got his deserts, and it gave me an odd sense of falling short, of lacking some value I could not even define. That, like all awareness of deficiency, made me angrier.

"He's still dead," I said brutally. "And that's all there is to it."

There was a long pause. Then he took his hand down and stood up, and when I saw his face I knew there would never be words I would wish so bitterly to have left unsaid.

"Yes," he said.

I beat a thankful retreat to the practical. The other curs were well to heel. They saddled up with speed, and I had just ordered, "Dakis, Krem, tie that crowbait on with his stirrup leathers," when a voice behind me said, "Alkir, wait."

He seemed to have recovered a little or, at least, to have begun to think. "This was my fault," he said. "All of it." An echo of that grief ran across his face and I wanted to look away. But he went on at once, "There'd have been no trouble if you weren't escorting me."

That I could not agree made me no more amiable.

"So . . . he could have drowned yesterday. We could bury

him here. And"—he swept a glance round the ten of us—"finish it."

Was I to clap or swear? Conspiring with your men to falsify a death and conceal an aborted mutiny, entrusting your career to a pack of toy-shop heroes' malice or drunkenness—if they did not read his mercy as weakness and kill us both. Nothing is so rancorous as pardoned crime. Before taking the chance he did I would have struck the mare. But perhaps such gambles, or an insight that makes a surety of them, are the mark of high command.

Before anyone produced a word or, I daresay, a thought, he said in open relief, "Thank the Four." Then he looked surprised and, almost under his breath, amended it to an equally fervent, if more cryptic "Imsar Math."

"In the name of Math," *what?* I wondered irritably, as with no sound but blundering horses we rode into the ravine; through the girth-deep, neglected ford. Back to the road. Silence held as we dipped and climbed amid a forest wet and glittering as new-polished shields. A Thangrian timber jinker passed, fourteen horses, a giant of a log, skill and power joined. An orchid collector, a pack of rainbow exotica on his back, his tree-boy running ahead. I was still unsure of the guards, he noticed none of it. No one would ask about those moments over the corpse. But finally my confusion marshaled on a single idea.

"I don't see why it was . . . incompetent."

The forest shook to the roar of a falling giant. I heard the clap of another axe beyond. Still staring between the mare's ears he said, "It's not a snub. Will you give me time to think?"

We had reached an inn, breakfasted, and set out again before he said a word. Then, as our horses breasted the first rise, slowly, all but fumblingly, he began to speak.

"You think what I did was justified. Self-defense. For act or worth, he—Gevos—deserved no better." I nodded. "But everyone's stupid when they're afraid. Nor was that all his fault. So much for him."

My neck told me the curs had grown six inches extra ear.

"And for me?" A wry smile. "It was about as fair as a mouse against a tiger-cat. I needn't have killed him. Why I should not is the heart of it."

He was still staring ahead, almost back in that morning's somberness.

"Fengthira told me, when I left. Warned me. 'Tha'st been safe, in Hethria. T'will not be so easy, among the temptations of men.' "

I did not have to find a prompt. His mouth tightened and he said too quietly, " 'I'm usually strong enough.' I actually said that. I'd forgotten—after trees, and rocks, I'd forgotten how fragile it is—flesh and blood." He looked up into the dew-starred forest canopy and added, yet more quietly, "And I'd forgotten Math."

I let the silence ask, Math?

"I follow the Four, I said to you. I thought Math was—an idea. A theory. Fengthira's business . . . something I just had to hear about. I know now, it's not."

I just managed not to blurt, "Eh?"

"It isn't a theory." Now I could hardly hear him at all. "For an aedr. . . . It's inside you, part of you. When you damage that, or break it. . . ." He made a little sound that was poles from a laugh. "Then you find what it means, to say, This'll hurt me more than it hurts you."

I must have twitched or somehow else betrayed myself. His eyes came right round and he said it for me. "I'm sorry. You don't understand. You don't know anything about Math."

I tried to make it sound neither pressing nor accusing. "No."

He frowned. "I don't think I can explain this very well,

because it's Math, to begin with. And I'm new to it. And I was never very good with words. But I think . . . 'Math' is twofold. The—vision. And the rule. For the vision, Math means, Reality. That-which-is. For the rule . . . Fengthira says, the simplest is, Respect that-which-is. Trees, beasts, men. Because every single one is the sum of Math, and you can alter or destroy them, but to make them is beyond us all. It takes the whole world and all of time, it was never done before, and will never be done again."

It was almost, I remembered, what he had said over the dead man.

"And the more power you have over that-which-is, the more reluctant you should be to exercise it. A little fire won't temper a sword-blade, but nor will it turn a master-sculptor's marble into lime." I nodded. "I am an aedr. I can damage that-which-is more than—just about any living thing. I can misuse power. The way I did this morning. What's worse, I could come to enjoy misusing it." He looked down at his crippled hand. "When I learnt the arts, Fengthira gave me a lesson on that I'll never forget. But the temptation lasts. Power can rot you. It can make you"—his voice grew careful—"destroy yourself."

"Go on," I said.

He shot me a glance, and looked away. Perhaps, I thought, he changed what he would have said.

"Um . . . so, the greater the power, the greater the obligation to respect Math. Be good, so to speak, to keep goodness good." I wondered what the ears would make of that. "So when I kill a man by incompetence, I'm not only a bungler at my trade. I am a destroyer of Math. And because my power's the greater—so much the worse is my default."

"You mean," I was floundering, "if I step on a grasshopper, deliberately, it's still better than if you do—what you did—by mistake?"

He answered bleakly, "Yes."

I stared. I had never dreamt of such a power, nor one which could so implacably condemn itself under a statute only its own consent could enforce.

"We are all responsible for Math"—he stared ahead of him—"according to our power. I'm an aedr. I used to think I had problems when I was just a king."

His vague and enigmatic Math went straight out of my head. But the somber set of the mouth, the eyes still dark as malachite, warned all too clearly, Don't ask. Not now.

His mood had not lightened by our midday halt, though he was hardly quieter than the guards. Girthing up again, I wondered what might distract him, when he had ridden unseeing in the trenchant upland air under the mightiest trees in Thangar, past traffic that a day ago would have rotated off his head. Then a bend showed me the closest skyline. I eased my horse back a little behind the mare, and waited on events.

The hoof-noise told me the rest had closed up on us both. The mare flicked her ears, but he paid no heed. Then the light changed, and as you would expect his head came up.

He shot upright on the mare. His mouth fell wide. Then he cried, "Alkir, you louse!" and fairly flew from the mare's back to the highway edge.

If it is a whim of the Lady or her engineer I cannot say, but whoever built it had a craft to match the sheer audacity of the design. The Horned Gate lies on the very range brink, at the end of a long rising ridge that sweeps round from south to east; but at the bend-head the road diverges to spring clean across that bight of valley almost as deep as the range, rising on the gentlest of gradients to Vallin Taskar's port, upheld by pylons that elongate in center valley until the trees are green cauliflowers beneath each dizzily perpendicular stone jet, and the crowning span bears you across the sky like a spider on a giant's thread. While under the parapet the range falls in tiny, defeated folds to eighty miles of Morryan coastland and the knuckle of the Morhyrne and the tenuous, unending, aquamarine circumference of the sea.

There is no warning. Just a last jink of the tree-shuttered road and the bridge fires you out into immensity. Glancing round at nine grins wider than my own, I thought what joy there is in seeing others' joy take them by surprise.

"You femaere," he said when I dismounted and walked over. "You never said a word."

"You did say," I pointed out, "that you wanted to see it with your eyes."

"So I did." He was still devouring it, too rapt to comment again, even in superlatives.

When he finally moved and sighed, I said, "We call the ocean Gevber. The Eastern Sea. The land is Morrya province. That little hill's the Morhyrne. Zyphryr Coryan's on its seaward side. And above Zyphryr Coryan is where the Lady lives."

"Oh, yes." At that moment she could not have mattered less. But at last he turned away, to scan the bridge again, and then remark, "Must be some good in Assharral, when they build something like this just to show off something like that."

When I said, "Thank you," he looked delightfully abashed. Then he said indignantly, "Sneak that under my shield, you can expect a kick in the teeth." And I swung back astride laughing, so relieved to have him himself again, I dismissed questions of kingship along with his baffling Math.

The byplay had touched the guards too, though it was hardly perceptible. Just a minute sense of atmosphere grown indefinably easier, as we passed Vallin Taskar and the road began its zigzag down a vertical cliff into the forest depths.

Lisdrinos' trees are mammoth, its undergrowth impassable.

Bird and beast flourish in that wet green labyrinth, but you catch only rare glimpses, like the spell-cast vistas from a road shoulder: half a waterfall in the fern, a segment of Morrya past a vine-hung cliff. If you are lucky, the frigid quiet may yield one syllable of a ferrathil's slow, chiming call. It was in there, soon after we left next morning, that one of the horses chose to cast a shoe.

"Take him back, Wenver," I told his rider, "with my nastiest compliments, and get another one." I felt the cold war had eased to such small levities. "The rest fall out, but sit on the road, unless you want to banquet the whole family Leech." I had been through such forests before. Then, thinking there could not be too much danger, I lay down with my head on the curb and my feet in the sun, and promptly fell fast asleep.

<Alkir,> said my charge, <wake up.>

I came upright inside out clawing my sword as I spun to meet a mass assassination attempt. He was nowhere in sight. Eight amazed faces stared uphill at me. "What—where—" I had just begun to yell when he broke in, sounding oddly flat.

<Fifty paces uphill. An earthfall across the right ditch, a big brown tree-fall five paces beyond. You'll see us there.>

Then how in the Lady's name, I almost shouted as I ran, could you talk to me down here?

<Quieter,> he commanded. I tiptoed. Shadow and creeper resolved into a crouching blue back and a guard's wide black rump. <Don't talk,> he countermanded himself. <Just do a stalk up here. And then think what you see.>

As if after a Phaxian sentry I slithered up to the father of logs that was their ambuscade, with sour thoughts of leeches nestled to its spongy bark, inched my head up to gauge his line of sight. And forgot everything else.

Ten paces away a tiny glade of bracken ferns was caught in a shaft of blue-white sun, dazzling as liquid thillian in the greenish gloom. The light framed a tall earth mound. I had vaguely heard a racket suggesting a whole barrack-room of birds. Now, as sight slowly became perception, I knew there would be only one.

At first it looked like a filmy white helmet crest shaken out just above the ground. Then the two long bronze and gold-spatched outer feathers came into focus, framing the white plumes in their open-heart curve, two finer ones rising to repeat the heart above. A black flash of foot beneath the silver arch. A shine of bright black eye. And it had assembled, facing me, tail arched forward high over its head as it performed the mating dance. A heart-tail bird, a clythkemmon, or as some say, a terrepher, a silver dancer, or a tingan as others call it, a many-tongue, because it can mimic any sound on earth.

The silver fan quivered. Slid gracefully to the left. On the final hop I had a glimpse of wings. It sidled back. The calls had passed from a ferrathil's chime to a gerperra's whipcrack cry to the salvoes of a gweldryx flock. Now, quite distinctly, came the clop of hooves and the very timbre of my commands. Hearing my charge's breath of a laugh I nearly thumped his shoulder, for they are the shyest of all birds.

But it was all right. The sun flamed on the trembling silver curtain, the gold and bronze feather bars glowed, distinct as beads, the dance went on. Advance, halt, retreat. The hen must be somewhere close, I thought.

A crying child, a windlass's squeak. A rovperra's splutter of raucous man-like laughter and the fan swept shut. A dull brown bird with an ungainly tail edged coyly up to a stump, saying, "Choo . . . choo." Another patch of dowdy brown fluttered down to it, and then the forest had drunk them both.

After a long time the three of us sighed in near-perfect unison, and sat back. I glanced at my charge. He was on my right, still staring into the gloom, turban fallen round his neck, which let me study his undamaged profile: as I took in the long jaw, springing nose, black-lashed green almond of eye, sweet-tempered mouth that belied the bone structure of command, it struck me that women must once have found him a more than handsome man.

Silently, as behoves beauty unindebted to men, we filed back to the road. As we started down, he said, "I'm glad you called me, Sivar. The captain says it was a clythkemmon. Or a tingan. Or a terrepher. By any name, it makes Assharral a lucky place."

More thought-reading, I deduced resignedly. And then, galvanized: How did he do that? How did he get any of them to speak to him, let be follow him up there alone?

<He thought the noises were 'odd.' Wanted to raise the alarm. And,> blandly, <the only other officer was asleep.>

I did not pull a face at him. I knew Sivar had picked up "the captain *says*," too.

That first implicit praise had made him preen as well as mumble. Now his eye-whites were showing. I waited for him to run. A word, a bare glance from the menace would have been enough. But my charge ignored him, making steadily on downhill.

Another three strides, crunching on the road's damp stone. The others were watching, not yet in earshot. I caught Sivar's indrawn breath. Then the half-cleared throat, and, with more than natural awkwardness, the word.

"Sir . . . ?"

My charge made an encouraging noise.

"Sir . . . but . . . Fylg . . . ah, the captain—never said anything."

Does he know, I thought, that this is an overture from the shyest of all birds? Does he guess how much rides on this?

But of course he had.

"Not aloud," he answered matter-of-factly, not looking round.

"But we couldn't talk up there. So I had to read his thoughts. It's just another art."

At Sivar's, "Oh," my heart sank.

Then other concerns yielded to my own query. "Apart from picking my mind, just how did you get me up there?"

"Oh, dear." He stopped, and scrubbed at his hair. Sivar, I noted hopefully, had stopped too, showing more inquisitiveness than fear.

"You see," he smiled disarmingly, "about the first art we learn is Mindspeech. Lathare. And I couldn't shout for you." The smile broadened. "Though if I'd yelled as loud aloud as I did in Lathare I'd have brought the whole of Assharral. You have a great talent for sleep."

As Sivar gleefully joined the laugh curiosity bested my own wariness. "Can anybody hear—and talk—like that?"

Sivar broke in with a jealousy quick as his about-turn to interest, "C'n I, sir? Or is it just officers?"

"You have to be taught," he answered thoughtfully, "to speak. But many people can hear. It's like an ear for music. Doesn't seem to matter who you are."

"Ah," said Sivar, and he returned, <You see?> and laughed so infectiously Sivar forgot his fright.

I had already thought of something else. "How did you know I could?"

His eye glinted. "You jumped round quick enough the other day when I told you to ' 'ware backs'."

Sivar's thought had followed mine. A question, a puzzle, a struggle for courage fermented in his heavy face.

"Sir," he was still painfully timid. "Gevos. Just what—did you do?"

My charge's face shadowed all over again. He answered quietly. "The Arts use several of what we call direct Commands. The main one is Chake." He pronounced it "Sha-kay." "If you're strong enough, you can stand someone on his head with that. But the only real difference is the scale of power. Knock somebody over, knock them out, blind them, kill them. That's A'sparre. I meant to knock him out. But I hit too hard."

For a moment he could have been back kneeling over the corpse. I could find nothing useful to say. But Sivar was also hunting consolation, and, I should think, a quite unwonted tact. What he achieved was an outright herald's staff.

"Well, sir, everybody's gotta make mistakes. My old man used to say you gotta be toes-up before you don't." He withdrew hastily on camp. "Sir, permission to check me horse. . . ."

Watching him scuttle away, my charge said slowly, "You know, I think that's the kindest thing anyone ever said to me."

I found myself gagged by my own base, ridiculous jealousy. He went on, thinking aloud.

"Fengthira was right. 'Th'art never Round but Through.' I thought he'd never get it out. I wanted to jump in and answer before he said it, like I can with you." My gag dissolved. "But if I had . . . it would have tipped the scales, sure enough." He looked absurdly pleased with himself. "I think I'm getting the hang of Math."

Whatever Sivar told the rest worked faster than any herald's staff. By nightfall they were all trying to ride in earshot. Next day in the inn-yard both Zyr and Ost, the second file-leader, dared an outright glance at him and a mumbled, "Morning, sir." At the midday halt Sivar hovered, then sidled up to hazard, "Where did you come from, sir? Before Assharral?" In a couple more days the lot were all but climbing in bed with him.

With the wall down they wanted to know how he had learnt and how it felt, to have their thoughts read and be taught to "speak," with explanations of the rest and demonstrations thrown in. They never tired of dropping things and saying plaintively, "Sir, do you think . . ." or piling wood for noonday mint-tea and asking, "Sir, would you start . . ." or pleading, "Sir, couldn't you just tell this horse. . . ." I had to forbid boasting at post-houses and restrain collectors of everything from bulls to butterflies and curtail a flood of talk on all the minutiae of Assharral.

Against imposition he was his own defense. He would bear with them as long as he chose. Then he would smile, raise his brows and say pleasantly but firmly, "Well, now," and they would subside, mild as milk. At times I wondered if I was leading an escort or a harvest festival.

We reached Zyphryr Coryan in late afternoon, riding from farmland into the virgin forest belt that girdles the city like an outer wall, the road swinging in a wide curve about the Morhyrne's base, with glimpses of black rock cone through the silver-green, sparse, long-fingered foliage and close-packed slender white trunks of Morrya's helliens. The boughs were clamorous with birds. Big gray coastal lydwyr hopped leisurely from our path, making him exclaim. "We only have lydyrs in Hethria." He glanced at me and half-smiled. "Little hoppers. Nothing like that."

Then we rounded the long curve onto the cliff above Rastyr, and all Tyr Coryan opened at our feet, a shining labyrinth of apple-green and azure wound among silver-gray wooded spits, edged with bayside villages' dabs of white and ochre above the trelliswork of naked masts. Up from the quays on the left flank rose the spur that backbones Zyphryr Coryan, a stepped chine of white, brown, rose, gold, granite gray and steely blue, the green of street and park trees laced along its side, the city wall showing in discreet black patches at its base. And above, where the Morhyrne's shoulders rear into the rock cone, lay the sinuous varicolored necklace of Ker Morrya, lapped in its gardens' green.

We had all reined in, watching his face. He gazed a long time, occasionally sniffing the tang of city and salt, at first with frank pleasure in his look. "Smells like Hazghend," he remarked. "A country I know." Gradually the pleasure became interest, then assessment. Then his eyes lifted a little, and grew quite blank.

At last Sivar broke out, "Not a bad little village, is she, sir?" As a local, he did have the right of disparagement.

"It's a fine city," he agreed. Sivar looked pleased. He could not have caught the hint of trouble in the voice.

By the time we hurdled over the harbor hills it was sunset, and traffic had dwindled to a few tardy pedestrians, the lull before wagons began to pour in from the farms and up from the harbor for the markets' opening at dawn. He dutifully admired the tall double city gate between its bastions, and ran a soldier's eye over the city guard in their green surcoats, which Sivar and company viewed with disdain. He studied the big squares lined with courtiers' and nobles' mansions, the sight-seers' rally points of temple, tower, public garden and colonnade, the government buildings, the observatory, the beetling outer wall of the treasury. When we reached the military quarter the light was nearly gone, and a fresh problem confronted me.

We left our horses at the post-house. I said, "Dismiss." He said, "Wasn't such a bad road, was it?" And before that smile could elicit drinking invitations I said firmly, "Sir, I doubt the Lady will expect you at this hour." There were tales of how she spent her nights, tales which had perturbed Callissa when I was promoted, despite all assurances that I was hardly pretty enough to make a favorite. "Would you care to lodge the night with me?"

The guards clattered away with a volley of parting remembrances. He nodded. "Yes, Captain," he said. "I'd be pleased."

Chapter III

As we mounted the two steps to the gate amid its yellow-flowered emvath brambles, and the house lights shone through a tangle of ornamental shrubs and helliens, he said, "I like these door-gardens." Crunching up the path, I whistled the Stand-to as usual. And as usual there was uproar behind the moontree fanlight, squeals of delight and cries of reproof, the pounding of small boots and lighter, larger feet, then the door flew back and two small thunderbolts hurtled across the porch with Callissa exclaiming in the rear.

"If only I'd known you were coming, there's no dinner—no, of course it doesn't matter, just so you're back—you little wretches, let me to your father—thank goodness. . . ." She submerged, to resume beyond our greeting kiss. "Rema can find something, she—what did you do with the—never mind, you'll tell me after—oh!"

I had moved. The hall light, occupying my shadow, revealed the tall shadow at my back.

"My wife Callissa," I said. "One of these is Zam, the other is Zem. Callissa, this is—" I broke off, discomfited yet again.

"My name is Beryx." With a tinge of amusement he brought me smoothly off the reef. "I come from Hethria."

Callissa's usual guest front, already shaken, fell into abject rout. "I must see Rema," she gabbled. "Alkir, you'll look after—see to—excuse me—I mean, please come in. . . ." And she fled.

The twins were not disturbed. They escorted us from hall to

guest reception room to our living place, oversaw the deposit of saddlebags, the doffing of helmet and turban, the disposal of chairs, with silent unwinking scrutiny. I was on tenterhooks over their reaction to his scar, not to mention the rest, but there was no hope of banishing them. Not that night.

Seeming unconcerned, my guest scanned the big room under the hanging lamp, the floor strewn with boys' debris and Tasmarn rugs, the medley of old and new furniture, Callissa's sewing spread over a table and three chairs, my account-desk neck deep opposite. "So this is a house," he said. "I never had one myself."

"A palace," he expanded as my jaw dropped. "But you inherit that. Then I shared with Fengthira." For a moment it could have been envy. "Not like this."

I sought for cover. "Will you drink something before we eat? Not Everran wine, but they make a barley-spirit in Morrya. . . ." Retiring on the tall dresser that housed our alcohol I was just in time to hear a small, clear, uncompromising voice enquire, "What happened to your face?"

I spun round. Zem, I think, was planted before his chair, Zam usefully posted on the right flank. Aghast, I wondered if it would be worse to call them off or let them go. But my guest had already responded, perfectly assured.

"It got burnt."

I cringed. Sure enough, the interrogation began.

"How did it get burnt?"

He scrubbed at his hair. "You see, there was a dragon. They spit fire, you know? I came too close, and it spat on me."

"A dragon?" The flank force discarded tactics, the frontal assault goggled as wildly as its sire. "A real dragon? With wings and claws and everything?"

"And everything," he agreed. At which the flank guard elbowed past the van, scaled his closer knee and ensconced itself as with me, perched on the chair-arm with both feet on his thigh, to announce in a fair copy of my defaulters' voice, "You'd best tell us all about it. From the start."

Over their heads his eyes met mine, green chips of mirth. "We should," he suggested blandly, "ask permission first."

I levered my mouth shut. "Not at all—please don't—only if they don't bother you—"

His laughter brightened. "Don't you," he suggested demurely, "want to hear it too?"

"Femaere," I said, and brought over the drinks.

He sipped, choked, and still half-smiling, began. "Once upon a time"—they wriggled ecstatically—"there was a kingdom called Everran, and I was its king. One day a dragon came. Its name was Hawge, and it had every intention of eating everything in Everran that was eatable." They nodded. It was orthodox dragonry. "But I had no wish to see my kingdom eaten, so I declared war. No, I didn't send a herald. The dragon would have eaten him too. I mustered troops—three hundred troops. Not cavalry, horses don't like dragons." A shadow crossed his face. "They wore leather because the dragon fire would have made steel armor too hot, and," with a chuckle, "they didn't much care for it. We marched off on the dragon's trail, burnt houses and eaten cattle and—other things—" That memory held no mirth at all. "We found it near two farms it had just burnt, and we attacked. Yes, with a battle-order. Hollow square of spearmen, archers inside. To shoot at its eyes." More knowledgeable nods. "Hawge woke and saw us, and up it flew.

First it tried to break the spears, but they were too sharp for its liking, so it spat fire instead. The troops were very good. They stood fast, just as your father's would." He was smiling, but I could see the memory's grief. "Four times it spat fire, and they never broke." The twins were enraptured, lurid visions weaving in their eyes. "Then one archer put an arrow in a wing and brought it down, so we charged. The trouble was, the worst thing about a dragon isn't the fire, it's the tail. When we came in range it knocked the whole front rank over. Then it spat fire and bit and clawed the rest of us, and in the end we had to give up."

Zem and Zam did not. "But what happened to your face?"

"I," he said lightly, "was more stupid than any commander ought to be. I took a spear and blindfolded my horse and charged it myself. No." He grinned wryly at their idolatrous looks. "I didn't kill it. The horse and I came off worst."

He touched his cheek. "As you see."

His eyes lifted to mine. "Military," he murmured, "hotheadedness."

They drew breath to burst. I was beyond speech, for I could put fact between the carefully edited lines. Phalanxmen, the troops must have been. Against a dragon. I knew in theory what one was like. My hair rose at thought of what had to be no bare defeat but a massacre. Hotheadedness? Sheer berserk. . . .

"Lunacy," he supplied. "Homicidal nerve," I corrected. He shook his head. "Desperation," I amended. "That," he answered dryly, "came later." And before the twins could rend him for details he was moving their feet in readiness to rise.

"I'm sorry to be so long," Callissa was in the doorway. "Rema's just—"

She saw the twins. A hand flew to her mouth. "Zem, Zam," she snapped, "come out of that. Come out!"

They gaped, amazed as I. He said swiftly, "They're all right, ma'am. I won't hurt them," and she grew positively wild-eyed. The whole by-play still had me mystified when the twins took advantage of the gap.

"Mi, mi, he's fought a dragon, we can't go yet, he hasn't told us the rest, we haven't talked to Da, it's not time, we always have supper with Da first night home—"

Two small square faces reddened, four gray eyes glistened ominously. "Halt!" I said in a hurry. "You eat with us, but you're quiet. Quiet or the cells. Right?"

They were quiet. At least, until our guest hesitated at the lamb cutlets Rema had "found," and Callissa intervened, too kindly for kindness. "I'm so sorry, I didn't think. Would you like them cut?"

I wished wives were subject to army discipline. He gave her a steady, unresentful look. "I can manage, thank you, ma'am. If you don't mind Sathel manners, that is."

The boys' eyes were already circular. When he took up a cutlet left-handed, discipline broke. "What happened to your arm?" the nearer one burst out. "Was that the dragon too?"

"Yes, Zem," he replied without the slightest hesitation, and I heard Callissa gasp. She too had been sure it was Zam. "It threw the horse and me up in the air with its tail. I smashed the nerve in that arm when I came down."

"It's a wonder," I exclaimed, impulsive as my son, "you're alive at all!"

"No wonder," he answered mildly. "Just a very good friend to pick me up."

"My husband," Callissa observed, "has been wounded too. Was it five times, dear? Or six?"

What, I signaled, is the matter with you? She ignored me. He said, "The war with Phaxia?" She agreed, in detail. Full detail. Two-year campaign, begun as a troop-leader, promoted to squadron-leader, then wing-leader, three pitched battles, a turn with the swamp guerillas, victory pulled from the fire when an ambush commander fell, two mural crowns in the forts beyond Stirsselian, a corps commander at the peace. He heard her out. Then he said modestly, "I can hardly compete with a hero like that."

"Da says," Zam announced before I could retaliate, "that

there are no heroes. Just dead clowns and lucky ones."

"Da," replied my guest with feeling, "is right. When you get your first command, Zam, remember it."

Their eyes met across the table, in equality, harmony, perfect understanding. Then Zam said, so quietly I knew he meant it, "Yes, sir. I will."

"You've had your supper." Apparently unable to tolerate even this minor apostasy, Callissa used the tone that meant no appeals. "Now you'll come to bed."

Meekly they left their chairs, came for my goodnight hug, went out, hanging back from her hands for a last look. He watched the door close. He did not have to tell me he would have given his magic, probably his former kingdom, for just one son of his own.

Before I could hide my pity he had turned and was smiling, so quickly I wondered if I had imagined the rest. "Well, Fylghjos?" A brow cocked. "That's what the escort call you, you know. Granite-eyes." Mischievously he let me consider its present delicious inappropriateness, until Callissa returned, and he was all formality again.

"You got on so well with them," she said as we all sat down. "Quite surprising, really."

I tried not to gasp. Inept in noble company she might be, insecure enough to boast about her husband, but this was clean out of character.

He replied with perfect courtesy, covering the lapse, negating the spite.

"I'm sure anyone who took the trouble would get on with them, ma'am. Their manners are a credit to you."

"Oh, that's Alkir. I just bandage the knees and patch the pants." She donned her social voice. "Are you married, my lord?"

His face shut like a door. He said, "Once."

I tried to kick her under the table, and missed. Brightly, she charged on. "Then you've no children of your own?"

If you are unlucky, you may see such a face in battle, as your spear strikes home. He said in a low voice, "No."

"Oh, such a pity. I'm sure you'd be good with them. . . ."

How, I thought in furious unbelief, can she have missed it, can she go on trampling over what even I can tell was not just a pity but stark tragedy? Wildly I sought words, something to drop, to overset. But my brain was numb, the table cleared. Callissa was prattling still. "Children make your life I always feel, they're troublesome at times, but all the same. . . ."

In a moment she would be pitying his wife. He took a breath I heard. Then, looking full at her, he said, "She has—had—children afterwards. Not . . . mine."

I could no longer offer so much as the paltry aid of keeping rank, pretending to see nothing wrong. Kicking the chair back, I said, "Let me show you your room.

"You can see clear to the harbor." I shoved the window wide in some fuzzy idea of comfort, amends, knowing his silence for the voice of the unsealed wound.

He came to lean on the sill. I blurted, "She's never like that. I don't know what's got into her."

"Mothers." The sadness held no grudge. "She doesn't know what I am. She doesn't have to. She just feels I'm dangerous to them."

What could make amends for that? And the full sense of that last cruel confession, its sequel in questions no man could possibly ask, was still racketing round my head. She had children later. . . . There is no more terrible way to be maimed. In my extremity I actually hoped that he would read my thoughts and extract the speech I could not muster, for the solace nothing could give.

"Just sterile. Not impotent." He not only read my thoughts,

with paralyzing candor he answered the question I could not ask. "Don't upset yourself, Fylghjos. After all"—the tiny quiver of amusement was the bravest thing I ever heard—"it could have been worse."

With shame I admit myself unable to match it. I said goodnight and fled.

Next day I sent breakfast to his room to ensure the twins would be off to school and Callissa to the markets before he emerged. Despite her tearful protests that "I never meant to upset him. How was I to know? I don't know why I said it, he just—made me," I was convinced he would go on striking truth from her as he did from me, and I had been scarified enough. So it was well into second watch before we set out for Ker Morrya.

He scanned our route with his usual bright-eyed interest, quite unconcerned by his own effect on passersby. I asked if he wanted to inspect the mare, stabled at the post-house with orders to "Wait here for me. And behave yourself." He merely narrowed his eyes, shook his head, replied, "She's all right," and resumed his study of carriages, sightseers, officials, workers, people of every trade and province surging by, while I thought yet again that his eyes had a freakish life of their own.

With the sunny street making his pupils pinpoints, his irises had the constant swirl and variegation of light in flowing water, mint, bayleaf, laurel, sea and moss and royal jade-green, changes swift and bewitching as his moods. . . . I lost sight of the city. I even forgot to ask how he knew about the mare. But then he nodded at some Gjerven tribesmen with wooden spears, bones in their noses and towering feather helmets, saying, "Imagine charging in one of those—and the chinband breaks." So we were laughing as we reached Ker Morrya's gate.

No steward was there. Passing the sentries I felt a sudden need for support, and nodded to the guard officer, saying, "I'll take the four on stand-by." Their boots made a solid, reassuring clump behind us on the marble steps.

The court was in the central gallery. Its hexagon is big as any temple, one side giving on the forecourt, the rear wall a backdrop for the Lady's white-gold throne inlaid with onyx moontrees, under the canopy which is the boast of Assharral: a single mighty rock crystal cut and polished to transparency, shimmering above the dais like a curve of visible air, a foil for the flamboyant walls and floor and roof.

The walls are of alabaster so thin the sun shines through them, turning the stone-grain to huge whorls of sunset rose and tangerine and gold, the floor is black marble spanned by a moontree of silver: flowing boughs, voluptuous orb. The ceiling is yellow amber imlann wood, coffered in geometric mazes whose woven triangles prison the eye, an ebony star at each one's point.

I had never felt at ease there. Today I found myself reflecting that a tenth of this ostentation would have fed my troops properly in Phaxia. Among it, perfectly at home, chattered and postured the rainbow of silk, satin, jewels and outrageous fashions that composed the court.

Nor did I ever like the court. They are nobles, I am a farmer's son, yes. I am a soldier, they were play-people, yes. But to me there was something immoral in the sight of Assharral's wealthiest, wittiest, best-bred and most beautiful frittering their days away in empty ritual and squabbles over trivia, while a few governors, a horde of scribes and a couple of generals turned the Lady's chariot wheels.

I watched the latest favorite, a willowy gallant in royal purple with sleeves that brushed the floor, thillians in his shoe-heels, scented to smother you at a spearlength, orange and scarlet-dyed hair in two horns above his temples, fooling with a gold stave of office he could barely lift while he changed frivolities with two ladies whose costumes are beyond my description. I saw other heads turn, the arch of painted brows, could imagine the catch-word repartee at our expense.

Then it struck me like a thunderclap that I did not merely dislike them, was not merely afraid my charge would disapprove of something Assharran, but was feeling actively defensive. Of him.

"It's been nothing but surprises," I grumbled under my breath, "since I ran into you."

"Surprises can be healthy," he replied blandly. He scanned the gallery. "Handsome." His eye gave me his opinion of the fops. "None of the Council here yet, I see."

"Council?" I was off-balanced again. "What council? We're not at war."

"Advisers." He grew surprised too. "Doesn't she have advisers? Nobles—elders—province delegates—people's representatives?"

"No." I felt shame, as over Gevos' corpse, for some elusive defect that had never seemed so before. "The Lady . . . sees what's happening. Everybody just . . . does as she says."

I sensed he was as deeply shocked as at Bhassan, but less surprised. "Ah," he said. Then a steward reached us, murmuring, "The Lady is by the fountain, sir."

The guest suite had become a picture gallery, dove-gray walls and cream ceilings with primitive daubs from Axaira glaring out at us. At the last stair's foot he broke stride, sniffing. "Rivannons! I've not seen them since. . . ." The chance-met joy faded. "Up there?" he said, non-committal, and we began to climb.

Los Morryan's clear music filled that balcony of light and air. The escort clumped sheep-like at the stair head. From the nearer side of the fountain, disposed sidelong on the onyx seat in a flame-scarlet silken dress with huge frothing skirts, the Lady Moriana said in her soft, inherently mocking voice, "What have you brought me, Alkir?"

I think I stepped aside. Or something moved me. My eyes vouched that neither of them stirred. My inner senses claimed everything was moving, up in a tightening spiral as if the Morhyrne itself were coiling to explode. The sun was too bright, its rays shivered, overcharged. The Lady Moriana's eyes had grown enormous, black lakes shot with motes of brilliant gold that flew with dizzying velocity, a comet shower in space. Flashing through them ran a quicksilver sparkle of green, hot white green, dragonflies that taunt as they elude your clutch, and unlike the meteors they had their life and origin in unquenchable merriment.

I blinked. A man and a girl confronted each other, one seated, one standing, one the epitome of luxurious, lethal sovereignty, the other a landless vagabond whose mind was dominion enough. But something was still happening. I had a sense of thrust and riposte too swift for thought to pace, of duelists engaged with weapons so subtle my very mind found them invisible.

Then it was over. He put up his hand, shaking back his turban. That faint smile said he had not come off worst.

He said, "He brought you this."

No one has ever seen the Lady Moriana in a rage. And lived to tell of it, that is. I could only deduce from the arch of her fingers, the tiny hint of color in her cheek. But her voice was an indubitable purr.

"You are somewhat prodigal with my guards, Alkir."

He put up his brows. "Unworthy." The hidden laughter had slid into his voice.

Infinitesimally, her eyes widened. His mouth corners pucked. He said, "You brought the audience."

One nail drew a tiny click from the parapet. He nodded. The swarms of golden meteors stilled.

"You disapprove," she said.

"It is very beautiful."

"And rotten to the core."

"Only in the head."

"But then, you were only a king."

"I knew my place."

"Not well enough, it seems."

"Seeming's in how you see."

Her head tilted just a fraction. Her eyes held a fleeting, triumphant smile, a chess player noting a future vantage point. "As in . . . A'sparre, perhaps."

"We all make our own mistakes."

"I do agree." She drew it out. Taunt. Riposte. Threat. "Welcome to Assharral."

"How kind of you. It's pleasant to be among kin."

"You astonish me."

"You astonish *me*. Moontree. Obviously a descendant of Lossian and Fengela. You don't know the Moontree's roots?"

"All commoners are fanatic about history."

"Ah, my blood goes back to the Flametree itself. Lossian's own line. A little later, of course, than yours."

"And, of course, so worthily."

His eyes danced. "I never heard Lossian went in for marrying."

"So little point. For those who can get children, that is."

I caught my breath. But he had his shield today. "Or those who can but won't."

"Some of us," she stretched, a lazy cat, "have no need."

"Fountains do run dry . . . eventually."

Again that tiny, triumphant glitter. "And now you are here, what will you ask of me?"

He let his eye travel down her body's length. The glitter brightened. "I am, unhappily . . . fastidious."

"And that place is occupied."

"Temporarily."

"In his case, at least."

"In every case, I find. But perhaps it's different, in Hethria?"

He gave a sudden spurt of laughter. "Very different!"

"Then I should warn you. Assharrans respect their beasts."

I think I gasped. He merely grinned. "Pouring the lees already?"

"Dressing to fit my company."

"Dear, dear! Madam, you seem to have wounded you."

"I can forgive myself."

"That must be easy, for a—divinity."

"Divinely so. One sees everything."

"I daresay," he murmured, "that you do." There was a tiny stress on the "you."

"You wonder that I expected you?"

"One hardly expects an enchantress to boast of prentice arts."

I had a fleeting impression that he had caught her out, forcing a deflection of the attack. "How is Fengthira nowadays?"

"Happy. A rare thing, I find."

"I daresay it's easy to be happy with a—horse."

"Easier than with men, it would seem."

"One does grow bored with them."

"I daresay a—divinity—does."

"Ah, then you'll be lucky, won't you?"

"So I think. And Fengthira too."

Her eyelids drooped. "Her age is showing, I expect."

"Some of us do it gradually," he sounded equable. "Some wait a long time, then do it all at once."

Her lips curved up. I wanted to shout, as to a careless swordsman, Watch out, it's coming now!

"Some of us never do it."

"Some have imagined so."

The thillians in her bracelet spurted blue-white fire. She had shifted, reaching for something in the seat corner. Her hands rose. The great dew-globe glistened between them, shimmering against scarlet silk, shattering the sun, its own depths unmoved, profound and colorless.

"And some of us"—the ambush was sprung, the triumph blatant—"need not imagine it at all."

His eyes had shot wide. He went stiff all over, his face blank. Not control, but shock.

She caressed the globe, looking under her lashes, savoring the foretaste of victory.

"You know what it is."

He sounded breathless. "I know."

"You thought it was the fountain, didn't you?"

"I didn't use Pharaone." Though he spoke sharply, the word war was forgotten. "It would have made no difference. That"—he gestured with his eyes—"wears a Ruanbraxe. No aedr would realise till he saw."

Again I had the sense of incomprehension matching mine, bypassed as irrelevant. "And you know what can be done with it."

His face changed again.

"You," he said flatly, "do not."

Her fingers stilled.

"Immortality?" He was not teasing, nor on the offensive. His face was stern, grim. "Tyranny? Godhead? You have no idea. It shows in every move you've made."

"Of course you know so much better."

"Enough to know what I wouldn't do."

"Castrated," she said sweetly, "by morality."

The shaft bounced straight off. "You do know what it is. And you abuse it. Play with it! Using that for Pharaone, imsar Math! Practicing Wreve-lethar to keep yourself young! Who was your teacher, in the Four's name! Or were you blinded in the nursery?"

In anyone else that tiny shift of brow might have signaled a frown. Then it was gone.

"Oh?" she was purring. "So what should I do?"

"Something about Assharral?"

Her voice was flat. "It's mine."

"Mine!" He tossed his hand up. "There speaks a true Morheage. Just leave it mine, and who cares what else happens to it? Mine! You don't know the meaning of the word!" He had quite forgotten he was in combat, and I knew she had not. "Rule it! Exploit it, tyrannize it, terrorize it, batten on it, play your piddling tricks—rule? It's pure shameless incompetence!"

She had not been drawn. She watched him, contained, poised, and again I wanted to cry, Look out!

Then she smiled. "Here, then," she said. And held out the globe to him.

His hand jerked away as from a snake. He very nearly recoiled.

"Don't you want it?" she purred.

His face moved. Not in shock or wrath or any other emotion he had shown. This time it was vulnerable. Naked, as in physical desire.

He swallowed. Then he said harshly, "No."

"But I'm incompetent." She knew she had the whip hand, and was showing it. "You could do so much better than I."

He took a quick hard breath and licked his lips. I did not understand the fence. I simply knew he had lost his guard, and was being pressed beyond hope of recovery.

"No," he said fiercely. "I don't want it."

She merely looked at him. We both knew it was a lie.

"You're not . . . competent?"

The light writhed in his eyes, the pupils flared, they were

turning black. His hand lifted, and was wrenched violently back to his side.

"Just think," she murmured, "what you could do for Assharral. From the court to the painted savages. No more terror. No more tyranny." He choked as if hands had him by the throat. "And not only Assharral. Hethria. Everran. The Confederacy. You know what this is. You know you needn't stop at that. You could change the entire . . . world."

He shut his eyes. That one small act was a bitterly contested, cruelly expensive victory.

"That is not Math." His voice shook. He was not stating a belief but reciting a prayer. "Math isn't doing. It's doing only what you must."

"But surely you know it must be done? You were—are—a ruler too."

"No." Sweat ran down his jaw. The scar glared purple. He clenched his fist.

"No." It came on a longdrawn, struggling breath. "I . . . will. . . ." His voice cracked, I barely heard the clinching whisper. ". . . not."

She had missed the pivot point. She still sounded soft. Concerned. Pitiless.

"You'll turn your back? On all that? Even on Assharral? Is it Math to see something so evil and to . . . walk away?"

He opened his eyes. The irises were bleached, the sockets looked bruised, evidence of a fight that had taken every atom of strength. But the exhaustion was at peace.

"Moriana," he said. "Give it up. Please."

Her eyes went blade sharp. "To you?"

"Not to me. Not to anyone. I know you don't understand Math, but even an imbecile knows Ammath when it touches him. And this is Ammath. You're not a Sky-lord, however much incense they burn for you. Do you taste all those butchered sheep? Four, of course you don't. You've perverted something like—that—" He gestured at it, not looking. "And for what? What pleasure is there in playing morsyr to ten lives' favorites?" I knew he meant the black spider who eats her mates. "Working some bastard form of Fengthir on poor clowns like those?" He jerked his head at the guards. "Terrorizing decent soldiers, emasculating your nobles, toying with an empire? Believe me"—the plea deepened—"it might do for a while. It won't fill an 'eternal' life."

She bent her head away, a swan's pure curve. A little, willful smile played on her lips.

"But," she cooed, "it amuses me."

"Amuse—!" He caught his breath and wiped sweat off with a jerk. "Moriana, there are other, more amusing things for an aedr to do. Four, you've never been prenticed! When I talked about Pharaone you didn't know what I meant." It was pity, rigorously concealed. "You rot away by your little fountain, abusing something that—well, never mind that—and you think there's the rest of time to do it in. When it may already be too late."

She leant back, feigning consideration. Her voice half-teased, half-protested, a flirting woman's denial that she is ready to yield. But I knew this No was real.

"If I left this . . . I'd turn into a hag."

"For Math's love! You'll come down a girl, you just won't stay that way. Women! It's your head that matters, not your face!"

"Oh." Blandly demure. "But . . . what would I do—out there?"

"You could begin," he answered grimly, "with amends to Assharral."

Her eyelids lifted. She gave him a long, silent stare.

"So," he said after a moment. "That may be true. It wouldn't matter. Not if—"

"Not matter?" Her fingers arched on the globe. "I'm to leave my palace, renounce an empire, give up 'eternal' life. And then, when my 'loving subjects' hound me into exile, probably hunting my blood, when I'm out in the road, growing old, 'ignorant,' ugly, not to mention penniless—then just what becomes of me?"

The grimness shattered, burst by spring-light that was all too familiar, all too inevitable. I never had time to bellow, No! Not here! Not now!

"Welllll," it came in a drawl. He cocked his head, appraising her like a tavern wench. "Even then . . . I'd probably marry you."

Her eyes spat. Her cheeks flamed. In a flash she was not merely aged but hideous.

"You ape! You oaf! You limping hobbledehoy! You—" Her eyes slashed past him. "You gaping ninnies, take him! Truss him up! Cripple him!"

He spun on the advancing guards, I felt some blind compulsion seize me and found I was advancing too, sword out lest he resisted, mind aware of what he was and that I was a friend to him, limb and muscle refusing to hear and will accepting it.

He whirled back to me. I saw his eyes flare, green-white, blinding, and knew he would use A'sparre, in a moment I should be dead as Gevos. I had no way of preventing it, and no fear. Whatever impelled me did not care.

His back arched, his breath drew in. Then, like a bough breaking, the intent snapped.

As my sword-point touched his ribs he said, "I won't fight, Alkir."

I could not feel relief, let alone thankfulness. Something was appeased, I knew that. I also knew where we were to go. Down into the city, to the Treasury, whose vaults had once been the imperial prison for rebels of common blood. There were still chains riveted into those clammily weeping walls, their key in the Vault-keeper's custody. I would lock them on, and restore the key to its rightful guardian.

The guards about-turned and fell in on either side. Without protest he swung and started to walk.

Chapter IV

I had climbed back to Los Morryan, handed the key to the Lady, and re-crossed the square outside Ker Morrya's gate, when I regained my will.

Waking up? No, for I had never slept. Escaping a glass cell? No, for glass you can smash for yourself. Growing up in a single breath? But a baby lacks a man's coherent memory. I could remember everything. But now it all had meaning. And I was free to make a response.

The passersby must have thought me a lunatic, running full-pelt in the street. The Treasury scribes certainly did, for I barged straight back to the Vault-keeper's room and on down the long flight of steps into those dim tunnels, past the torch we had left in a bracket, snatching it as I tore into the dank crypt where that other will had directed me, yelling, "What happened? For the love of anything you like, what happened up there?"

He stood as we had left him, back to the square rough wall blocks whose faces ran sopping red in the torch-glow, red as the pools on the uneven floor. I had done my duty well. A long fetter ran to each manacle, another to the leg-iron on each ankle. He could hardly have lain down, had there been inducement. But whatever we did, he had recovered his own guard. His eyes caught the light, narrow, sparkling green.

"To me?" he said. "Or to you?"

"To, to—" I found then what it means to grow incoherent with rage.

"You were given a Command. Not pure Chake, a blend of some sort. There's something odd about all you Assharrans, it must come from—up there. You're all permanently half under Letharthir—half mesmerized."

"Mesmerized!"

"Bewitched, then." His brows came down. "Did you never think, on the way here, to ask what you were doing? To say to yourself, Here's a very strange fellow, peculiar powers, quite unknown quantity, could be highly dangerous—so I'll just conduct him straight to my ruler's doorstep and see what he'll do?"

"I, I—"

I stopped as it hit me, winding as a door in the face. All that way, clean across Assharral. The Captain of the Lady's Guard. With a wizard under my shield-arm, worrying about spies and the doings of the Sathellin.

"Then, when you do get a Command, you go clean under." The eyes twinkled. "Like sleepwalkers, you were."

"And you, you cackling idiot!" It is wonderful what liberties affection permits. "You let her get away with it!"

The laughter snuffed. "To stop her," he said flatly, "I would have had to kill you all."

I gasped. He nodded. "Or challenge her, and try to break the Command. There wasn't time."

Water plopped. I heard the scurry of a rat. Then my own voice, sounding shrunken, small.

"Could you have—done it?"

"You mean, was I able? Oh, yes. Was I willing? Never. No."

I stared. He sounded quiet, stern, pure adamant.

"I will never," he said, "save myself by killing innocent men."

The torch guttered between us in the sodden air. He had had the power to win. He had chosen defeat, shameful bondage, rather than abuse that power. For the sake of his enemy's tools.

And whether she understood his power or not, whether or not she had gambled on his integrity, the Lady had been ready to see us slain. For malice, revenge. Victory.

I should have agreed. Every soldier knows his life may be the price of winning, and counts winning the end that justifies all means. And unquestioning obedience, unswerving fidelity, are the corners of a soldier's earth. But mine was no longer firm.

"She," I said, "just wanted to win."

He nodded, silent. Even now, he would not stoop to calumny.

"However she did it. . . ." Slowly, a conviction formed and firmed to intent in my mind. "I'm going back to get that key."

"Alkir!" His voice spun me round and his eyes were white-hot crystal. "You'll do nothing of the sort!"

"But—but—you said yourself, it's against Math! It must be stopped! You can't sit here and refuse to—"

"I refuse," he said between his teeth, "to get you killed."

"Killed!"

"Wake up, man. Stop thinking you're a big brave sword-swinging soldier and she's just a slip of a girl. If she let you up there, you couldn't do a thing. She could walk you straight over that parapet. And she would.

"Don't drop the torch," he went on after a moment, rather hastily, but I knew the smile had revived. "I'm not that fond of the dark."

I groaned. He, I could hear, smiled. "When Fengthira taught me Lathare I spent two days tied on a rope-end. This is just damnably wet. And uncomfortable."

"And," I said bleakly, "there's no way out."

He was testing the manacles. "I don't . . . think . . . Axynbrarve is up to these. If it were, I'd have to cut down a wall of sleepwalkers upstairs. And probably the whole guard outside." He gave me a cryptic look. "Including you.

"And don't get sacrificial," he anticipated me. "I loathe sacrifice."

"Then what in the name of your Math," I bellowed, "is this?"

"Oh, this is tactics," he answered cheerfully.

Looking round, I saw a fetter-ring, and stuck up the torch. "I don't even know the ensigns, and I'm in the middle of a war. Do you think you could explain, at least? To begin with, what *was* that—thing?"

"Not a thing." For the first time he showed reverence. "*That* was Los Velandryxe Thira. The Well"—reverence deepened—"of Wisdom's Light."

"But what *is* it?"

A fetter cramped the familiar scrub at his hair. "Nobody really knows. Fengthira tells a very old story that it's a drop of water from Los Therystar—do you know the Ystanyrx, the Great Tales? No. Anyway, there's one about the Xaira, the separation of aedryx and men. The Mothers of men and aedryx were sitting by Los Therystar, the Well of the Purple Flowers, when Arva Aedryx saw in its water the first vision in Yxphare. Foresight, you'd say. The Mother of Men laughed and Arva Aedryx struck her blind. So ever since, aedryx and men have been"—an old wound spoke in his voice—"different."

He looked at my face, and shrugged. "Math knows where Los Therystar was, if it was at all. The Tales are truth, not history. And nobody knows the origin of Los Velandryxe, because at some stage some enterprising soul put a Ruanbraxe, a mind-shield, on it. You can't see it with the Sights, not with Pharaone or Phathire, and Fengthira says Yxphare's the same. One reason why that Sight's so dangerous."

"Sights?"

"Pharaone is farsight. How I checked the mare this morning. Phathire is vision of the past. Yxphare, future-sight, is a gift, it can't be taught. Because of the mind-shield, I didn't know what

Moriana had. I thought she was just Ammath. Evil. An aedr gone rotten. For her line, it would be in character."

"Never mind her line. What about this—this—heirloom?"

"Um. . . . The lower arts, like the Sights, and the Commands, even A'sparre, deal with minds. The higher ones are different. Wreve-lan'x, Axynbrarve, then the harder ones, Wreviane, Wrevurx, that's weather-work—"

"You can control the *weather?*"

"Oh, yes." He was quite matter-of-fact. "I could have turned that storm in Thangar. But Wrevurx is the first art where Velandryxe really matters. Wisdom. Justice, judgment, and Math."

My head swam. "I thought Math was respect for that-which-is?"

"Part of it, yes. The rule part. Just as a storm's part of that-which-is. Before you meddle with it, you have to judge if your reason's pressing enough. To push a storm about may drown someone here, or ruin someone there, who needed rain for his crops. It may spoil remoter things." His look was unfathomable. "So you must use judgment as well as power. And guide the judgment by Math."

"Respect for that-which-is." I clung to that talisman. "But where does this Well come in?"

"At the very top. The supreme art is Wreve-lethar. The old aedryx never told prentices about that at all. You had to be a master to know and a Velandyr so much as to think of trying it. And of the handful who tried, only one, so far as I know, managed to succeed."

"But what did he actually do?"

He grew very quiet. "Wreve-lethar means, to control the dream. And what aedryx call the Dream is—what you call the Universe."

My head spun right round. I grabbed for solid stone. When the Lady said, "You could change the entire world," I had thought she meant something ordinary like conquering it.

"You need wisdom," he was saying, "and more skill than I'll ever have, and the sort of strength I only dream about. Most aedryx said it was for the Pharaon, the creators, and forgot it. A few tried, and lost their minds. But one succeeded. And he changed the Dream. He brought Math into the world."

"Who . . . was he?"

"Th'Iahn." He spoke the name with care, respect, but not reverence. "The first Heagian. Founder of the Flametree, from which both my and Moriana's lines were a branch. . . ." His eyes came to sudden life. "But I'll show you. Look here."

His eyes seemed to swallow me into gulfs of black. Then a tiny world rushed toward me, I was in it. Part of it.

He was on his feet looking straight at me across a work-table cluttered with mementoes, gems, bird-skulls, artifacts. His coppery hair flung back from his temples as with the wind of flight, his eyes bore down on me like runaway green fires, leaping from that volcanic face. "You'll want and wish as you like," he hissed, "but I say you *will!*"

I literally tumbled backward from that impact. Beryx looked down on me sprawling amid the puddles with a somewhat wry grin.

"One of his happier moments. Makes you wonder how he could sire Math?"

I reformed my wits. "So he used Wreve-lethar and—and changed the world by dreaming Math?" He nodded, I scrambled up. "At least my outposts are set. But how does this Well come in?"

"Wreve-lethar's like any other art. There has to be a focus. A mind, a woodheap, a horse. When you try to change the Dream, Los Velandryxe is where you look."

The torch popped, water dripped. He stared back at me, not trying to soften the significance.

"Yes" he said. "In the wrong hands—with the wrong intent—it could be the most terrible thing on earth."

"But—why didn't you take it when she—"

"No!" It was violent. "In Math you do only as you must. The temptation to alter things, to—" The sweat sprang on his forehead. "If you did master the Well, it could rot you as easily as power. Easier. Especially if you follow Math. The hardest lesson I ever had to learn is not to act. To let alone, if not well alone. To have the Well. . . ." He shuddered. "No, I can't—I won't think of it!"

"So," I was still catching up his line of march, "she offered it to you for evil. Ammath. Is that it?"

"She doesn't know what she's doing, Alkir." It was almost pleading now. "Four knows how she came by it, it was lost in one of the upsets three generations before Berrian, and he was my ninth forefather. Fengthira thought it was lost forever. She told me about Wreve-lethar, but just in explaining Math. Moriana doesn't know. She's aedric blood, but she's blind ignorant. She's learnt to tinker with a few things," again that adept's scorn, "like slowing time to keep herself young, and mastering Assharral—she picked the rest from my thought. She's a child. A child playing with a wound-down catapult."

I caught my breath. "With the world sitting in its target eye!"

Then Assharral's bondage, ten guard captains, my ignoble subjection, his defeat by his own integrity, all burst in my head at once. "A child! No child would—no child could—have you mislaid your wits?"

"Now don't start feeling your wounded vanity all over again." The grin revived. "Mine's a lot more wounded than yours."

After a moment I said, "What do you mean to do?"

His face wore the strangest look. Airy, willful, save for the lack of malice it might have been the Lady's own intransigence.

"Oh, I intend to . . . wait."

"Wait! You—she—I—what will your Fengthira say to that?"

He chuckled. A resonant, acerbic feminine voice snapped, " 'I told thee naught but trouble would come of tha gallivanting. Tha wast ever one to stick tha hand in a hornets' nest and wonder that t'was stung.' No," he resumed in his normal voice, "distance means nothing to Lathare." Ruefully, "And she's probably right. I couldn't resist teasing Moriana at the end, and look where it's landed me."

I ignored this last frivolity. "She won't help? What sort of a friend—"

"Alkir, Alkir. She follows Math. Do only what you must. If she came raving in here firing thunderbolts, who knows what she might spoil?" The chuckle answered my thoughts. "No, this isn't bad enough for a Must. Not yet. What can you do? Um. You were allowed down here once, so . . . I could do with something to eat. And something to sit on. And—most definitely—something to throw at the rats."

Part of me must have outmarched my chaotic thoughts, for as I blinked onto the street a black flash at one eye-corner spun me round with a fistful of surcoat and my sword at an unprotected throat.

"Eh, ow, Cap'n, whoa!" Sivar's heavy face was twisting ludicrously above my grasp. "I ain't done nothing, sir!"

"Oh." I let go. It was all triggered and light, as in a battle's heart. "Yes. I—what are you doing here?"

He squirmed. Then he addressed the pavement. "Sir . . . is it true? Our wizard—he's been chained up in there?"

Our wizard. I hardly noted it. Nor did I marvel anew at the wonders of barrack espionage. I was merely thankful for them.

"Walk away. Normally." We paced downhill. "It's true. The Lady—" I stopped. *Our* wizard. But how far did that go?

"He's detained." An eye-corner on his face told me all I

needed. "You're off duty? Buy some food, and something rat-proof to put it in. No, it's not the lap of luxury down there. A stool. Candles. Water-bottle. If you can find it, some," I all but said Everran, "Sathel wine. Keep things small. We'll have to lug it past the whole Treasury. Meet at my house. You know it?"

He nodded, eyes glistening. Intrigue, illicit intrigue, and with an officer. He would glory in it till his dying day.

Callissa was posted in earshot of our door. At my footstep she flew out, face transparently thankful at seeing me alone. "Thank the Lady, he's gone! It's all over. Now we can—" She stopped.

Taking her elbow, I made for our living room. Unsurprised, I noted it was already evening. Soon the twins would be in from play.

"Do we have a couple of spare blankets? And where's my campaign cloak?"

She did not move. "I thought it was finished," she said.

"He's in the Treasury vault. In chains. Can I just walk away?"

Her face was flint. I had never seen such a wall in it. "You should."

I opened my mouth. She cried, "You're Captain of the Guard, Alkir!"

"So?"

"So leave it alone! Let the Lady see to—"

"Callissa . . . listen! She told us to arrest him. He could have killed us all." She went white. "He told me he would never save himself by killing innocent men. Can I walk away from that?"

"You should! You must! If she chained him he's bad! I knew it, I knew he was, mad and bad and—"

"Callissa, she ordered us to arrest him! She wouldn't have cared if we had been killed!"

"You'd be doing your duty, wouldn't you? You always said that was what mattered. That it was all a soldier would ask!"

"Yes. But. . . . Obey orders, yes. But how if they're not right?"

"Not right! They were the Lady's, weren't they?"

"Yes, but—suppose they were still wrong?"

"How could they be wrong? What are you talking about?"

"If they were . . . not good?" Ammath, he had said. How could I explain, with only the vaguest newborn notion of what its own disciple admitted to imperfectly understanding, this intangible, unintelligible Math?

Her face was brittle with scorn and strain and hostility. "I don't know what you mean."

"Callissa. . . ." Never had I so desired the gift of words. "He's an aedr. A wizard. He has powers. Magic, if you like. But he won't use it, unless he thinks it's right. He—"

"Right! Oh, you're besotted! He's sorcelled you! He can't help you, you can't help him, he's just a mad magician and he'll ruin you, you'll lose the captaincy, the—"

"I don't want the captaincy!"

"Oh, Alkir! No money, no house, no rank—the disgrace—the wives whispering—the whole school jeering Zem and Zam—"

"To the pits with the wives, and the brats as well! Do you tell me you're afraid of that?"

"No! No!" Suddenly she screamed it, gabbling at me. "What about the Lady? She'll never forget it, she'll take you like the others, you'll go up there and never come back—"

"Then I'll have done my duty! My real duty, for once!"

"And what about me? What about the boys? A criminal's widow—evicted—begging—stoned—the boys—" Her face crumpled. "Oh, I wish we'd never left Frimmor! I wish we were home and s-safe!"

With shame I admit she cried a good ten heartbeats before I could reach out for her.

"Be easy," I told her hair. Bitterly I envied those who had no hostages, no bonds to shackle their honor at such a pass. "Don't worry. I won't . . . leave the Guard. Only—where's my campaign cloak?"

She drew away. At the beaten apathy in her face I made to draw her back. But she said, "No. What does it matter? You won't listen to me."

Our passage drew scared glances but no opposition from the Treasury scribes. As we unloaded, the prisoner raised his brows at Sivar, grinned, "Don't tell me you've never been in cells?" turned to me, thanks clearly on his lips. And stopped.

"We'll be back tomorrow." I ignored his expression. "The Treasury's locked at night." You were allowed down here once, he had said. It was pure but determined assumption that we would be allowed again. "We'll bring more candles. I'm sorry about the bucket, and the straw. So late, we could get nothing else."

He merely nodded. The pity had grown clearer. Then he said quietly, "We all have our own choices. Don't blame her for putting your sons first."

I opened and shut my mouth. Then I felt an easing, as when a bandage is slacked over a swollen wound. Tossing out the blankets, sure he would read the mock-taunt rightly, I said, "Sleep well."

A Guard Captain has duties, whatever his allegiance. Parades, inspections, escorting the Lady abroad. The old world engulfed me, emphasizing the change at home, driving in the knowledge that I am not made to serve two masters, and that a choice would have to be made. I almost welcomed the furtive meetings to enlist more of the escort as provisioners.

"Cheerful, he is," Sivar reported at the third noon-watch, face knotted in wonderment. "Been killing rats by the hundred.

Reckons he'll charge mouser's fees to cover stabling the mare."

"The mare!" I had quite forgotten her. "I'd best go down and pay something before they turn her out in the street."

I entered through the long post-house yard with its ranks of seemingly disembodied horse-heads, meaning to inspect her first for myself. But the whole inn force was moiling about out there, ostlers, tapsters, scullions, cooks and hysterical chambermaids. I paused to retreat. Then I saw the red streams oozing amid their shoes and tore into the crowd as into a battle-front.

The mare lay flat on her side on the cobblestones, neck outstretched and belly mounded up in that pathetic posture of a horse's death. The blood was on their shoes, in the cobble crannies, in her shimmering gray coat, on her unshod hooves. A slash behind the jaw had all but beheaded her. Cleaver at least, said my soldier's past, before I saw the human body pinned under her, the mashed mess that had been a face, and the weapon beyond. A cleaver it had been.

I had no need to ask. They had already fastened on the black surcoat, the badge of succor, authority.

"Went mad she did—quiet as a cow 'n then kicked down the door—put us out o' the yard! Clean up the waterpipe—Tem had at her with a pitchfork, savaged him—yah, over there, near to—not the street, the kitchen—maids screeching fit to bust—she went right in! Kicked over the spits 'n the cook had a giggling fit—two barons o' beef, clean ruined! Roosting on the drainpipe—Tath there back from the butcher—'Watch out,' I said, 'she'll butcher you!'—'Butcher!' he says, 'n off for the cleaver—join the army he was going to—at her full tilt—swipe—no, she knocked him flat—never, he got her first swing—'n then. . . ."

They all went quiet at once. Battle, murder, sudden death. It was too alien to their little world. I looked with them at the dead. I should have grieved for the man, my own kind, my own breed, my own blood. But I could only see her on the road, gay and docile and beautiful, and I grieved for the mare.

A portly aproned person was forging up, outrage well in advance of sorrow in his eye. I heard myself promising reparation for damage done by the beast of an imperial prisoner, arranging a funeral, someone to tell the family, check their finances, provision for the savaged groom. And the mare. "Get the knacker's mules," I was saying harshly. "I'll show him where to go."

She left a long smear of blood down the hill among plunging horses and scandalized carriage folk, through the gate, along the harbor, into the forest quiet. I grieved for the damage that the dragging did. In a clearing amid the helliens I made the knacker's man help with all the familiar details of a field-pyre. Then I poured on a whole jar of hethel oil and waited, as an honor guard should, till only embers remained.

At the Treasury I caught the last porter and bullied the keys out of him. Then I went, slower and slower, into the tunnels below.

The vault was in darkness, total, impenetrable. As I checked, aghast, a sharp green flare became a candle-flame. When he said, "Over here," the tone told me he already knew.

He was hunched on his stool amid the straw, my old campaign cloak's faded brown and field-green blotches bizarre over the blue robe. The candle displayed his face. Deep-lined, drawn to the bone. But quiet. Perhaps the touchstone of an aedr is such acceptance of hard reality, but I knew it had not been easily won.

I sat down in the straw. Water ticked. Presently, in a voice remote beyond sorrow, he said, "Thank you, Alkir."

Words were still superfluous. Queries remained. At last, he answered them.

"She used the Well. Broke my Wreve-lan'x. I was a fool not to expect something like this."

"You mean, you're not vicious enough!" I could not help myself. "Do you still say she's a child? That this isn't a Must?"

He shook his head. Our common pain made me lash at him. "What will your Fengthira say to this?"

He looked up. His eyes told me he had broken his own news, with a hurt to which mine was trivial.

"She said, 'Tha'lt have need to think on the words. *Vengeance is sweet. But wisdom chooses salt.*' "

"In the name of—" I found I had shot to my feet. "Are you both mad? An innocent beast! That never asked to be brought here! That trusted you! That—and you made a song and dance over Gevos!"

He did not protest or retaliate or excuse himself. He merely bent his head.

"All this talk of Math," I raged, "and you can't protect one poor poxy beast! If I—" And then the straw fell out from under my feet.

"Oh," I said. "Oh. . . ."

"No." He did not look up. "That was all true, yes. It wasn't unjust. It was what I'd already told myself, yes. It's no harder because you say it again. Don't blame yourself. No, don't." He raised his head. The candle defined that laughter's resurrection, painful, unquenchable. "There's been enough blaming around here."

What could even begin to make amends for such crass, blundering imbecility? I had a vision of the night ahead, alone with nothing to do but think. I sat down again in the straw, hauling my own cloak closer round my ribs.

"No," he said. "Go home. And don't argue. Callissa will be expecting you." It was an order. A general's order, permitting no demur.

★ ★ ★ ★ ★

When I woke the mare was in my mind, like a bruise, more hurtful the morning after the blow. I went on duty because there was no alternative, and Sivar met me by the guardroom, saying for the benefit of a passing pentarch, "Sir, about my leave. . . ." The pentarch receded. Worry mushroomed in his face. "Sir—something wrong. He wants another blanket. Made it a joke, said no exercise. But I don't like the look of 'im."

My heart sank. Parade, guard-change, recruits, a mess dinner that night. "Buy the blanket." I disgorged fendellin. "I'll try to come down sometime."

"Sometime," was late afternoon. The tunnels were dank and chill as ever, I felt the cold invade my flesh as I went. He was hunched on his stool again, but now the candle was lit, he had all three blankets over my campaign cloak, and before I reached the light I knew he was shivering.

"Killing rats with Axynbrarve," he said ruefully, "doesn't keep you very warm."

"The Morhyrne's forge wouldn't warm you down here." His arms were huddled close, the classic pose of a man in cold too bitter to remedy. I could see the fine, continual tremble of his shoulders under the rough gray wool. I doffed my parade cloak, black velvet with the moontree stitched in silver. He shook his head. I said roughly, "Don't be a fool," and he forced a laugh.

"I doubt," he said, "it will do much good."

After a moment I said, "Look here."

His face fairly jerked up. Then he gave a somewhat shaken laugh.

"Nothing. That's just how Fengthira begins a Command." His eyes were a little puzzled. "What is it, then?"

"Fever." Though I am no physician, Phaxia had shown me that glassy, slightly unfocussed look too often to err. "Pains in your joints?" He nodded, taken aback. "Headache?" Another nod. "And cold. Or you feel cold." To be sure, I touched his temple. "And you're hot enough to shape horseshoes on. Swamp fever. From Lisdrinos, probably." Silently, I groaned. A physician, sickroom gear, the care such fevers demand. . . . Scrambling arrangements in thought, I took some time to absorb his words.

"Probably not." He sounded diffident, apologetic. And quite, quite sure.

"Eh?" I said.

He shifted his right arm. I did not have to be told that slow, forced movement had hurt.

"Hawge . . . the dragon . . . left a sting hole in my ribs. Sometimes it aches, swells up, that sort of thing. It's aching now. But—I don't think that's all."

A cold knot formed in my belly. "You mean. . . ."

"It would be logical." He was carefully calm. "First the mare, then me. And with the Well, anything's possible."

I swallowed. Hard. Then, feeling hunted, I said, "We have to start somewhere, and it looks like fever to me." I took up the water-bottle. "To begin with, you can drink this. All of it!"

We would need more water, I thought. Heat. A couple of braziers, coal, someone to stand watch, lay him down. . . . Looking at the chains I groaned again. They were fastened side-running, left wrist and ankle to the left, right side opposite. To lie straight at any angle was impossible. Smith's tools, then. A physician. "I'll see to the rest. Don't worry—Well or no Well, we'll get you through."

"Sir," he said dutifully, and produced the ghost of a grin.

It took a long time to organize help, heat, cudgel my brain for other sickroom needs, browbeat a night pass out of the Treasury. It took so long I was waiting by the mess when Evis returned, splendid in full-dress uniform, a frown joining his thick black brows.

"Sir." His manner warned me what to expect. "There's not a leech'll touch it in Zyphryr Coryan. By the end they wouldn't let me in their doors."

You should have expected it, I told myself. "We'll have to do without them." He shot me a dubious glance. "I'll have to do without them." I gave the thronged mess a rather wild look. Candlelight, armor, decorations shimmered back. The moon-tree's silver orb had developed a leer. "Did Amver find the smith?"

He said blankly, "Smith?"

"To knock those shackles off. I told you. Did he find one?"

Evis put a hand to his brow and looked decidedly odd. "Sir, I . . . remember you told me. Now. But I'd—forgotten it."

With breath drawn to scour him I stopped. Evis was a second wasted on the Guard. In the six months of my command he had never forgotten anything, from horses' tail-ribbons for a big parade to the details of a route-march's provisioning. "No matter." She, I thought viciously, saw to this as well. "We'd best get this over with."

If a dinner took longer you would be eating in your grave. It was moonlight when I finally tore through silvered streets to the black hulk of the Treasury. The gate was just ajar. From inside, Amver's voice demanded, "Who goes there?"

"Me." I was flustered beyond recall of our password, but his reply held relief. "Oh, it's you, sir. Sir, I beg pardon, I forgot them tools till too late. I can't unnerstand it! I went soon as Sivar tole me, an'—an'—"

"Never mind. I know what happened." I hurried past him to the silent scribe-shop within.

Two braziers at full heat barely tickled the vault, but within their range it was like noon in Phaxia. Sivar rose hastily from the straw, stripped to a drenched under-tunic, sweat shiny on his wide red face. But the prisoner, hunched on his stool, wrapped in cloak and blankets, was still shivering.

He raised a sort of smile. I could smell the fever stench, see the glaze in his eyes, already sunken into parched, waxy skin. The fever would burn him up, the shivering flog his muscles to exhaustion, as I had seen with men in Stirsselian.

I asked sternly, "Have you been drinking?" And he nodded.

"Three water-bottles." His voice was slightly blurred. That was familiar too.

Sivar looked nervous, as well he might, no physician, lacking even my experience. I looked from the chains to the straw to the wall, steaming torridly. "We'll get you loose tomorrow. If you could lie down—even against the wall—"

"I'd burn a hole in it." However reduced, the grin was there. "Don't worry, Alkir."

"Worry!" I nearly had at him. "Wait—this happened before, you said. What did you do then?"

His brows knit. He had to struggle to marshal his mind, and that was familiar too.

"Poultices—wild honey. Thassal will know—oh. No. Thassal's in Everran. But she's dead." He put a hand to his brow. "I keep forgetting . . . we live longer than you. . . ."

"Who was Thassal? What would she know?"

"Nursed me. After Coed Wrock—Hawge, I mean. But—there was no fever. At least . . . perhaps there was. I never knew. . . ."

Desperation winged my wits. "The past-sight. Could you see?"

He gathered himself together, or tried to gather himself. Already the fever had frayed not only wits but will. After a moment he let his hand fall, mastered a flinch, and said in that woolly voice, "I'm sorry. Can't . . . focus properly. . . ."

"Never mind," I said in a hurry. "Poultices. Wild honey." We would have to break the irons and strip him first. "Sivar, I'll relieve you." He, too, would have duties elsewhere. "Tomorrow morning, get some honey. In the market. And smith's tools. Can you find Amver a relief?" Never had the staples of command seemed so chaotic, so unmanageable. The coal was low. Callissa would be expecting me. There would have to be a nursing roster. Evis must take command. . . . I ripped my cloak off for the heat and the shine of armor made the prisoner cover his eyes. I knew that symptom too.

In a stronger voice he said, "Can't play nurse and captain both, Alkir."

"Amver'll stand watch tonight," Sivar butted in eagerly. "He's off duty tomorrow. 'N I c'n muster some more."

"Do it then," I said with relief, looking back to my charge. He had raised his head, but I could tell focusing was an effort too.

"Go on," he said. "They'll look after me."

At dawn I was making back for the Treasury. Cocks crew in distant rosy farmlands, late fishermen and early merchantmen moved on a harbor of pink and silver and wonderful azure blue, the city was full of fresh dawn air. But belowground was dark and dawnless, and the stink of fever and coal smoke had permeated the whole Treasury. The scribes will be pleased, I thought—then Sivar hurtled up the steps at me with blood on his face and water on his surcoat, white-eyed and blind as a bolting horse.

Clutching a fistful of cloth I swung him round, bawling, "Halt!" and he bleated like a girl. Then he caught my arm and hung onto it. "Sir—s-sir—sir, he's gone mad! Crazy—like the mare!"

My heart turned a somersault. "What do you mean?" I

snarled. "Talk sense!"

"Amver—c-come up at first watch—I been to the market—honey—took such a time, I—weren't five minutes we left him, sir! I go d-down." He shook all over, I shook him too. "H-he didn't know me, sir. I'm just through the door. He starts—not yelling. Like a snake. 'Get out,' he says. 'Go!' I—I'm not all pudding, sir, whatever you think. It's the fever, I reckon. 'Easy,' I say. ' 'S only me. Sivar.' I start walking. He—" He quaked again. "J-just threw me, sir. Like a ball. Slam into the wall, I—winded me, sir, 'n there's a lump big as eggs on my skull. 'N when I got up—he threw coal." He felt gingerly at his bloodied face. "I ran, sir. 'N he chased me clean upstairs! Great lumps of coal, rattle, whack, bang—" He was on the verge of control again, teeth chattering, eyes rolling. "He's crazy, sir! Right out of his head!"

"Shut up! Stand still!" I grappled for a point of contact. "Did he say anything else? Anything at all?"

"I—I c-can't—" I shook him till his teeth clacked. "Something about, 'I know what you are.' Some word I dunno. Like 'He'veh.' But it was the *way* he said it. Not like a man at all!"

Terror clenched on me. Fever. Delirium. I had seen men go mad in Stirsselian, break bonds, fell orderlies, chase physicians with half a tent pole, or just run screaming out in the swamps where the demons in their minds drove them to die or drown. And this was a wizard. Burning up with the fever; we had to get to him. But if ordinary men in delirium were capable of such things, what could a wizard do?

Sivar was still goggling. Fit for nothing else, I thought. And was undeceived.

He said, albeit shakily, "I could get Amver—Karis—Wenver 'n Zyr—if we rushed him—"

"No." Mere suggestion showed me the impossibility. "He'd kill us before we were in range." My mouth was dry. The alternative loomed, inevitable, terrible. "I'll have to—try it myself."

Sivar fussed worse than Callissa would. We were still wrangling when the first scribes appeared. Furiously I said, "If you won't go and you won't let me go, you'll have to come with me. If I—" I swallowed hard. "If that happens—oh, I don't know! Come on."

We wobbled down the stairs, me with helmet pulled down in case of missiles, Sivar quaking at my back. Nothing happened. There was no sound. But the very air was thick with menace, choking as the miasma of a Stirsselian swamp.

We turned the second-last corner. Faint red light dyed the walls. Then came a crash, a ricochet, a shower of pattering fragments, and as we flew back coal shards spun and tinkled about our feet.

"Stay here." I dug Sivar's fingers from my surcoat. "Here, you puddinghead! I'm armed. You're not."

I stepped from cover. Another shot whistled past my ear, a third thumped into my right shoulder and I stumbled back under its force. Recovering, I advanced. A rain of missiles pelted me, quite like catapult fire, except it was too fast. He has, I thought grimly, to run out of ammunition sometime.

The arch appeared. Flattening to the wall I got my head, eyelash by eyelash, round the jamb.

Light tore up in a huge ragged blaze, a hedge of fire across the wet stone floor. I shrank back, and in the movement understood. He had swept the straw into a ring and kindled it, walling himself behind the flame. I peeped again.

Red tendrils leapt and lashed toward the upper dark, smoke coiled everywhere, catching my lungs, blocking my sight. Then he spoke.

My spine turned to a rod of ice. Sivar had been right. He did not sound human. It was a snake's voice, low, sibilant, inflectionless. But charged with more than serpent's malignity.

"I see you," it said. "I know what you are." He hissed. Fire leapt almost to the roof. "Come, then. Come and . . . meet with me."

When Sivar's hand plucked my surcoat I was more than ready to heed. We shrank down the passage and the firelight pursued us, red, ravening tongues of flame. We were at the stairfoot before I reclaimed my wits.

"It's only straw." I held Sivar by the collar. "It has to burn out sometime, however it's lit."

Luckily Krem arrived just then. We bolstered ourselves with each other's presence till the fire-glare began to wane, then I pulled off my surcoat and cloak. Sivar said desperately "Sir, he'll be worse now—" But I had had time to think.

"If he's out of his mind," I said, "it's not how you mean. He's delirious. Seeing things. More frightened than we are. If I can just make him recognize me. . . ."

This time I did not slink, I marched straight down the tunnel into the waning fireglow, boots grating on the stone, and as I passed the arch I used the name he had given me.

"Beryx!" I said.

The blaze had died to embers, the coal heaps were beyond his chains' radius, and he must have exhausted himself beyond reaching them by magic. He had been trying to hook a lump over with the stool. When I spoke he leapt in the air. Then he sprang backward. Then he seemed to freeze, limb by limb, staring at me.

"Beryx," I repeated.

He started to back. I took a step. He came up against the wall, and rammed it as if to push himself clean through. A lesser man, I knew, would have been climbing it by now. I took another step.

"Fylghjos," he said. He must have been almost paralyzed with terror, for his voice had lost power, evil, even its natural authority. It had a note I had heard in battles, when you have broken your opponent's will. He was still fighting, it was his nature, but it was a mere gesture, drawn from the lees of spirit in some overwhelming defeat.

Not understanding, thinking only that he had recognized me, I said, "Yes," and took another step.

He said, "It was before my time." I took another step. He shook so the chains clinked like hobble rings. "You were never one for revenge."

Quickly, I thought, get it over with. I came on, and he thrust out a hand. "Helve." It was not a command. It was a last gesture of despair. "Imsar Math, Fylghjos." His voice nearly got out of control. "It was not I who murdered you."

Something clicked in my head. Fylghjos. But not me. A namesake. Someone else had borne that name. My voice came out in a drill-ground bellow and I roared at him, "Beryx, will you stop being a benighted fool!"

His head jerked back, I charged through the coals and grabbed him by the shoulders. "I'm not your poxy Fylghjos, I'm Alkir!"

At my touch he collapsed as if his bones were gone, eyes shut, probably still sure I was a ghost and beyond resisting it. We landed in a tangled heap. Something warned me to keep hold of him, so I shook his shoulders, mere bone and scorching heat, saying wrathfully, "I'm not a ghost, you can feel me, can't you? Open your eyes. You're delirious, that's all!"

Either I pierced the delusion, or the very fear produced a spell of lucidity. He did not open his eyes. But he took hold of my arm, if take is the word when his fingers nearly bent the bones, and hung on, choking as if half-drowned.

It did not deceive me. Anyone else would have been in full hysteria. When his breathing eased I said severely, "Now remember who we are, for all love, and don't do that again."

Then I yelled for the others with an impatience that was the backwash of my own fear.

"That's Sivar," I announced as they tiptoed up. "You nearly stove his skull in." He winced. "And you've pelted me black and blue. Can't you give yourself an order or something, so you'll know us if this happens again?"

He shook his head. His face was ravaged now, wasted by the fever and his own power's extravagance. My skin shrank from the heat of him. "Not strong enough," he said in a husk of a voice. He rubbed his face, groping for coherence. "You'll have to blindfold me."

Instinctive repulsion made me hesitate. "You must," he whispered. His eyes had glazed again. "Now. Before I . . . lose hold." He reached out for my wrist, as if it were the one rock in a boundless, raging sea.

Chapter V

When Karis came down to announce nightfall, I was still there. That first relapse had proved neither of the others was capable of reaching, let alone calming him. I lost count of the times I said, "It's all right. I'm here." I still feel his fingers, a red-hot manacle, clamped with terror's force as he fought whatever had invaded his mind this time. One of us only had to move to make him go rigid, then start to shake instead of merely shivering.

The fever was still there too. We had tried cooling the braziers, fanning, drenching him, pouring water down his neck in bottlefuls, then in desperation we reefed blanket and cloak away, but he shivered so frightfully I feared it would exhaust him altogether. I had sent Amver, Sivar, Karis, Krem, Zyr, Wenver for smith's tools, only to have them return in empty-handed bafflement. After his third attempt, Sivar paused by me, and at last asked, "Captain . . . what is it?"

By then I was past considering the risk if he ran shy, if they all deserted me. "The Lady," I said flatly. "That's what it is."

He put his knuckles to his mouth like a frightened child. Then, like me, he swallowed hard. Then he said with false bravado, "Guess I'm already in no-man's-land. Gimme that fan, Krem. You couldn't raise a breeze on a windy day."

I did get a message to Evis, deputizing him as commander. He came down at some stage. "I'm sorry," I said. "I know you wanted to keep out of this."

He eyed me, crouched in the straw, Beryx twisted up against my knees with a stranglehold on my wrist as he wrestled whatever had been conjured by a strange voice. "Looks," he said wryly, "like I'm in whether I want or not." He took the water-bottle. "This needs filling." And vanished up the stairs.

Around second night watch the delirium grew patchy, leaving him conscious for five minutes at a time. In one such spell he said in that thready voice, "You'd best go home, Alkir. While you can. Math knows what's coming next."

My heart sank. Then I said, "Very well." I had purposes of my own to pursue.

A lamp burnt low in the hall. In the living room Callissa sat red-eyed over her sewing. She did not run to welcome me. Just said dully, "You're all right. I kept some supper. . . ."

I ate it, reflecting there was need of strength. Then I said, "Callissa . . . I want to ask a favor of you."

Her eyes were full of fear. I said, "We can't get a physician. And I'm only a field-butcher. I need help."

She put the needle by. Her look grew almost accusatory.

"If we weren't allowed down there. . . ." I did not want to pursue where that thought led. "If he was meant to die, none of us could get near him. So he might live—if he were only well enough nursed."

She bit back words. I said, "You're the only one I can ask."

Her eyes went to the door. Returned. Sounding spent and listless she said, "I suppose Rema would mind the boys. What must I bring?"

Her entrance routed Sivar and Amver outright. Karis tried to don four garments at once, Zyr dropped the water-bottle by Beryx's head, and Beryx himself wound his chains in a cocoon it took five minutes to undo. By then she had absorbed the impact of our sick-room, and like any woman in authority was throwing her weight around.

"Alkir, I want those clothes off. You, fetch this honey you should have used. You, tear this sheet for poultices. You, get some more water. Phew!" She took the fan and began energetically stirring fetid air. "Come on, Alkir. Never mind the fever. The wound."

Detaching two blankets, I eyed his over-robe. "Cut it," she ordered. Beneath was a buttoned, once-white shirt. "Pull that back," my commander bade. Dragging it off his shoulders, I caught my breath. "Sit him up." Then she also caught her breath.

The dingy yellow of scar-tissue covered his right side from waist to armpit, almost from spine to breastbone, pitted with cavities I knew meant a surgeon seeking splinters after the main wound closed, gnarled and knotted where flesh had healed and bones knit awry. One rib in the middle could never have knit. It was severed by the biggest pit of all, a livid plum-red crater deep in swollen flesh, deep enough to plumb beyond the bone. I have had broken ribs. With such inflammation, every breath must have been agony.

Callissa recovered first. She bent closer, reaching carefully; but not even fever, delirium and exhaustion could erase the reflexes that wound had taught. Her hand was six inches away when his midriff and belly muscles stiffened. The rib cage shrank, his face clenched. Callissa withdrew, saying, "I'll wait till the poultice goes on."

We put one poultice on. Another. A third. Upstairs, night was cooling into dawn. Callissa's face had grown sharp. When we lifted the fourth one she looked from the wound, more inflamed than ever, to his rigid face, and said, "We're paining him for nothing. We'd best stop."

"Then what," I asked rather desperately, "are we going to do?"

My words must have touched some deep chord, for Beryx

opened his eyes. Glazed, deep-sunken, colorless, they wandered over our faces. Reached Callissa's. His muscles twitched, he tried to sit up.

"I beg your pardon, ma'am." His voice was thick, vague, but full of open dread. "I am going. I—it was just for a moment." He strove to get a hand under him, the wound pinched, he caught his breath. ". . . know this is a respectable house. But I don't have plague. I'm not drunk." His head must have spun, he tried to clasp it and prop himself and ended in a heap with a silent gasp as the wound quite winded him. In despair, he dragged the good arm over his head. The words came from under it. "Only a wound . . . promise. If you could wait . . . just a moment more."

Over him Callissa's eyes met mine. My feelings must have been plain, for she ducked her head. Wondering savagely what woman had thrown him out of her "respectable house," I took him by the shoulder and said as gently as I could, "You don't have to go. You don't have to go anywhere."

After a while he relaxed, or at least lay loose in the chains. I said rather wildly, "That's something we can do. I'm going for that key."

I set out up the hill, I clearly remember that. The pure light of false dawn on the first three streets, early workers going by, I saw all that. I am not precisely sure where fact and perception diverge. The fact is that the sun rose to find me, empty-handed, back at the Treasury gate.

I tried again. I think I tried five times in all, before I gave in and went raving back downstairs, to find Beryx raving too.

To me it is fever's most loathsome aspect, worse than the physical indignities, because it breaks the locks of the mind and breaches the last privacy, leaving you without so much as awareness' censorship. Beryx was no exception. He tossed and turned and cried out at the wound's stabs and tumbled his life out before us whether we would or no.

Some was incoherent. Some was unintelligible. Some was history. I caught names I knew, Th'Iahn, Lossian. But most centered round Everran, the dragon, his wife, and someone called Harran who had been involved with them. His wife's name was Sellithar. Sometimes he called Callissa that, sometimes Thassal, sometimes he thought she was the innkeeper who had thrown him out sick. A woman of Everran. That was what had burnt it in. Sometimes he thought I was Harran, sometimes a certain Inyx who must have been the phalanx-commander, for Beryx had still not forgiven himself for letting the dragon massacre Inyx's men. Sometimes he thought I was the dragon itself, and that was worst of all, for he confused Everran and Assharral and tried to bargain with me to save us from Everran's fate.

Three days it went on. The wound was still swelling, big as an apple now, and Callissa wadded his armpit, for if his arm brushed the swelling he would scream uncontrollably. The watchers came and went, and gradually they assumed the look I knew I must be wearing. A grim, unresigned despair.

The third night he was still tossing, muttering, shivering, as he had when we covered him, cooled him, fanned him, tried to feed him broth, to speak to him. But words and movement were little more than intention now. Callissa sat on her heels over him a long time, her haggard, sharpened face a copy of his. Then she muttered, "It can't be worse," and looked up at me.

"Alkir." Her tone scared me. I had heard commanders go into a lost battle sounding like that. "Boil water. A lot of it. Get some clean cloths. Send somebody for linseed oil and oatmeal, and find me a knife. A very sharp knife."

I gulped. She snapped, sharper than her face, "I'll draw it up with hot poultices. Then cut it." Her voice assumed the common note of repressed despair. "It won't stop the fever. But it's all I can do."

For the linseed oil and oatmeal I went myself, expecting to be turned back before I raided our own house. It felt alien, part of another life. I regained the vault to that sound most evocative of battle mornings, the whit! whit! whit! of someone whetting a knife.

Sivar's dagger had been selected as the thinnest. Krem was watching a big pot on the brazier while Karis tore up cloths. Callissa mixed the meal and oil, directing us in curt, brittle sentences to drag the brazier closer. "He'll kick," she warned. We ended with me kneeling on his wrists, Sivar, the heaviest, clutching his ankles, and the rest twisted somehow in between.

Tight-lipped, Callissa took the cloths from Zyr. Plunged them in the boiling pot. Wrung them out, wrung her hands. Slapped one on Karis' shield, turned the oil and oatmeal onto it, whipped the other atop, came swiftly across, and more swiftly pulled the steaming bundle tight over the tumor of the wound.

Given time, no doubt he would have kicked. Luckily for us all, he fainted instead. The first time, that is. And by the last he was too spent to struggle much. With open nausea Callissa hurled away the poultice, rapped at Amver, "Knife," and knelt at his back, frowning thunderously, hand trembling as she positioned it for the stroke.

The blade shivered in the shaky light. Her brow came out in sweat, the frown became a grimace. I thought she had lost her nerve. But then she drew a long breath and slashed.

It was a good cut. Horizontal, plumb from the swelling's forward edge to end plumb with the other side, dead center across the pit, with the rib to stop it going dangerously deep. I remarked all this later. At the time all I saw was a thick yellow jet that spurted up in the firelight before Beryx's convulsion all but threw me off his wrists.

Callissa dropped the knife to fling her weight on his shoulders, Amver landed on his hip. When the brunt of it passed she panted, "Turn him . . . flat."

It would have been easier to turn him inside out. Then she made us bend him to and fro till I thought we would break his back. But every twist sent another ooze of yellow matter into the straw and made her growl with relief, so I kept quiet. And at last one particularly noisome clot vomited something black and she fairly squeaked, "That's it!"

Everyone but me deserted their posts. I knelt panting on Beryx's wrists while she extricated it from the pus, gripping it in a scrap of cloth. Long as a thumb-joint, it was wickedly serrated, the blunt end jagged like a snapped arrowhead, coated in some secretion grainy as lizard-skin.

"That's it." She was hushed this time. "It must be . . . the dragon-sting."

There was a pause filled only by the braziers and deep-drawn breaths. If we never saw a dragon, we had had an illustration of their powers. Now, here, tangible, was part of the thing itself.

After the cleaning up I went outside. It was second watch, almost midnight. Tramping across squeaky marble floors to the gate I looked down on Zyphryr Coryan, idyllic under a full-blown moon, tranquilly asleep. Only from the Morhyrne's shoulder stared a single, unblinking light.

"He's asleep," Callissa greeted my return. I hugged her, starting to babble, and she cut me short. "The fever hasn't changed."

I recall feeling insulted, outraged, incredulous. "It must have!"

"It hasn't." Her hair was wet strings, her face sagged, she was almost trembling with fatigue. "I can't help it." Tears were very near the surface. "I've tried everything I know."

He was doubled up under a blanket, motionless, but his face

was a death-mask, and I needed no touch to feel he was still burning unquenchably as his own mirth. Around me was silence. Hope deferred is not so sickening as victory snatched from between your very hands.

I said stubbornly, "We'll wait a while."

I think I slept, for I was sitting in the straw when Sivar's touch recalled me to a muted, "Sir? Morning watch." His tone told the rest.

I stood up, looking to the roof as men do when earthly resorts fail. Where, I thought, is this Math? Or his own Sky-lords? Will nothing, nobody give us any help?

I turned to find Callissa at my elbow, a fanatic glare in her eyes.

"The witch. Fengthira." He had raved of her as well. "She might be able to do something. She must!"

Looking at Beryx, I thought, This is surely a Must? Then I remembered.

"She's in Hethria." I was too tired to snap. "Too far."

"Then think of something!" she nearly screamed at me. "Think!"

I rubbed a thumb over my brows. Something nagged in my mind's depth. Thinking. Speaking. Lathare. Mindspeech. He had spoken to her from Assharral. But he was an aedr. We were not.

Callissa's stare was a needle-point. "You have," she said fiercely. "You've thought." The others clustered behind her, tense and mute, but only she knew me well enough to read by expression alone.

"It won't work," I said. "He could speak to her. We can't."

"Oh, rot you, Alkir!" She stamped her foot, tears on her cheeks. "Try it! Try at least!"

Helplessly, I scanned the vault. "I don't," I said feebly, "know how. . . . What to say."

"It doesn't matter what you say!" She could not have been more passionate were it Zem or Zam's life at stake. "Ask what we do, how we break the fever, will she come, anything! Just get through to her!"

My eyes returned to the roof. Then I shut them. "To speak you have to be taught." Despairingly, I thought it, a forlorn signal into space: *Fengthira, how do we break the fever? What do we use?*

Amver shrieked and spun like a top, Beryx almost left the floor. Karis and Sivar fell writhing, clawing their ears, Callissa dropped as if heart-shot, the night burst open on a cacophony of screaming children, dogs, fowls, birds, horses, cattle, cats, the very city tottered, my head exploded and I had no perception of what might have been a very Sky-lord's signal, only a residue of meaning as the aftermath resonated shatteringly in my skull: *<SALGAR, THA DOLT!>*

Groaning, gasping, praying, we picked ourselves up. My mouth had not shut before Callissa was shaking me, reeling drunkenly, babbling unmindful of all else.

"Salgar, she said! The trees down by the harbour, at Tyr Cletho, you know, you know! Alkir, wake up! The clethra bark, you *know!* You told me about using it in Phaxia! Oh, wake up, you great gawping clot!"

No doubt I woke. I must have, for later there was horse-sweat on my trousers and salt mud to the top of my boots. So I must have been to Tyr Cletho, the tiny inlet where no boats moor because of the knotted, ever-encroaching arches of the clethra roots which clamber out over the reeking mud under their mushrooms of olive-green foliage and slippery, splintery, mud-gray trunks. Clethras which are the only trees to grow in fresh water or salt, whose bark was accidentally found to be a swamp-fever cure during the last months of the war. Too late, for most of us.

I have an image of Callissa babbling to a breathless audience as she stews it on the brazier, the bitter reek that infiltrates the sweat and smoke and fever-rancid air. Of our first tussle with Beryx, when we tried to make him drink, and with the dregs of his strength he kept whispering, "Yeldtar. No," and pulling his head away until Sivar held his nose, waited for the gasp and tipped the cupful down his throat. Which nearly ended it all when some found the windpipe as well.

At some time I see Evis enter with a face steeled to confront death, saying, "Second day-watch." Remaining to watch, on tenterhooks with the rest. And then Callissa weeping quietly in my arms while Sivar and company hover grinning stupidly, patting her back, saying, "There, there," and Beryx lies in the straw behind us, wraith-like and limp as ever, but with the first dew of sweat beading his skeletal face.

His recovery was nothing short of supernatural. Conscious that evening, eating like a young morval in two days, on his feet in a week, back to health long before we had regained normality. I thought it was his aedric will, for what he had survived would have killed a normal man. But when I knew him better I found I had been misled by his maiming, and the impression he gave of a big man past his flower of strength. If he was thin, he had been honed by the very arts which demanded such fearful physical exertion. The thinness of the triple-tempered sword-blade, which can dispense with mass.

After two days of behaving like a wildcat with a litter, Callissa calmly abandoned us, saying, "You won't kill him now." I rediscovered my troops. The watch dwindled to a night sentry and daily visitors, the bonds forged by crisis gradually relaxed. Only I was uneasily aware that, however we scattered, we had become a cadre of sedition in Assharral's docile midst.

It did not keep me from the Treasury, if I waited my turn on watch. I remember that night he had shaved himself for the first time, and was ridiculously prideful over this small feat. When we settled down I asked one of the many questions simmering in my mind.

"Who was the real Fylghjos?"

His eyes stilled, midnight green. Presently he said, "An aedr. Of the Stiriand line. Th'Iahn's time. One of the first followers of Math."

When he did not continue, I said, "You thought I was him."

His eyes went quite blank. No doubt it was pastsight, for he revived with a little grin.

"I was out of my mind, after all. And coming in without that surcoat, you looked the image of him."

Not sure I relished that, I prodded, "How . . . why—"

"Did I say he was murdered? He was. Killed by raiders at Ker Stiriand's gate. He made a tactical error. Sent his troops after raiders across the range, and another lot stormed his citadel. Why were the Heagians to blame?" I sensed an abridgement. "Because he believed in Math, he tried to protect others before himself. And Th'Iahn was the bringer of Math."

"Oh." More of that awesome accepted responsibility. "But why should I look like a—a Stiriand?"

"Coincidence, perhaps." His manner told me he was withholding something. But before I could ask, he answered the rest in his old style.

"You didn't remember bitter-bark because Moriana stopped you. More abuse of the Well. And for the same reason Fengthira couldn't tell you till you asked. There's a virtual Ruanbraxe over Assharral. We have to bawl to hear each other, and she had to bawl harder for you." His eyes crinkled. "And she was a little—er—anxious. Which is why she deafened the whole town. You didn't actually use Lathare. She was reading your thoughts. On stand-by, so to speak." He grinned. "If your dignity's sore at being called a dolt, be easy. She's called me a lot worse."

For the first time I grew curious about the being herself. "What is she like, this Fengthira?"

"Sounds short-tempered and has the patience of sand. Prefers animals to men, because men's bungles tempt her too much. I know how she feels. That's why she lives in Hethria."

"And what does she look like?"

"Gray eyes. Gray hair. Face. . . ." He considered something and abandoned it. "Oh," he said blandly. "If you meet her, you'll know."

He was a good convalescent. "Practice," he told me. "I was hot-headed before, and I had a vile time paying for hotheadedness." Nor did the continued confinement fret him. He spent hours absorbed in farsight, to confound me with remarks on parts of Zyphryr Coryan I never knew existed, let alone the rest of Assharral. Its races gave him unending delight. "All those peoples under the one roof." When I thought uneasily of the future, he just quirked a brow. "Strategic offense, tactical defense. I'm here. She has to attack. All I need do is wait."

She did not make him wait for long.

It was a high day, so the Guard turned out to help control the temple crowds. Having seen off the first reliefs I had set out to check the guard change at Ker Morrya when the court met me in the street.

They came with the usual fanfaronade, beadles with silver staves to clear the way, then the ensign-bearers' huge black silk pennons almost sweeping the stones, the censers who swung perfumed smoke from silver bowls, the road-sweepers, the court-jesters, then the advance guard tricked out in their ridiculous regalia and sporting badges of office more ridiculous still. Warden of the Perfume. Keeper of the Soaps. Scullion-commander. Bath-master. Jewel-holder. Lord of the Plate. Ruler of the Cups. I noted a dull corselet among the puff-chested guards, rainbow heads amid the Lady's escort of notables, Chamberlain, Mistress of the Maids, Steward in Chief, Holder of the Chair, Carver, First below the Throne. I saluted as the Lady herself approached.

She was in red again, a superb wine red in some fluent cloth that made a second skin down to her hips, then flared into a monstrous plume of train that needed six small pages to keep it from the dust. The thillians on her wrist and throat sparked brilliantly, but they were dull to the gold meteors in her eyes, and warm to the malice in her bell-cool voice.

"How timely, Captain." She was smiling. "Now you can show off your handiwork."

My throat dried. Dumbly I fell in as that curved finger bade, behind the potentates. Our destination I already knew.

The court made outcry at the dark, the tunnels, the filth and wet. There was much wielding of scent balls and shielding of sleeves and raising of skirts and shrieks at mention of rats. There was more surreptitious simpering and whispered mockery when they had crowded into the vault and formed a ring at a safe distance behind the braziers.

Beryx must have been very far away indeed. He had risen, but when the whole court had deployed and the Lady herself swayed into the forefront opposite him, his eyes were still quiescent, wells of tourmaline, bent on something far removed from her.

Her own eyes widened, slowly, black as the vault's lightless upper dark. A tiny smile strung her lips. In that limpid voice she remarked, "Manners to match your palace, I see."

The court giggled. Beryx's eyes woke. Then he inclined his head. A royal courtesy, unburlesqued. Throwing the onus for chains, wet and rats straight back on her.

"And quite recovered too."

He did not accept the false sacrifice and retort, No thanks to you! He did not poker up. He grinned openly and bypassed the attack with one quicksilver thrust. "This audience will have to hear what you mean."

Her eyes gave a tiny flare. Cooled. She turned to the court.

"This," she cooed, "is an aedr. A sort of magician. They have great powers." One graceful hand swept the vault. "As you can see." The court hurried to laugh. "You'll have to excuse its looking rather like a . . . a . . ."—she studied Beryx with elaborate distaste—"sort of ragamuffin. Or is it a scarecrow?" Callissa had replaced his ruined clothes with a calico gown sewn up on him. Certainly, it was not elegant. "Perhaps a bear. Yes, I think it might be a tree-bear. It looks as if it should go on all fours. Only, of course, it doesn't have four legs." The court thought this hilarious. "And it's rather ugly too. Not—quite—one's taste in a pet, hmm, Klyra dear?"

This was a creature at her elbow, got up in strips of gold and ruby tinsel that revealed fishing net hose, and a headdress like a fairground guy. It tittered. I felt a hot ball of rage in my throat. After one swift glance at Beryx, the Lady pursued her assault.

"It comes from a place called Everran. Somewhere in the west. A little smaller than Axaira, I believe, and much more primitive. But we must allow for vulgarity over there. And once . . . once . . ."—the tone said, Would you believe it?—"it called itself a—king."

But for face-paint the court would have laughed itself to tears. Those who could trust the costume-seams slapped their thighs, others held each other or their own ribs. The Lady's silver peal overrode it all.

"And," she called as they subsided, "it couldn't even keep its little kingdom. You see, it's barren, my dears."

My teeth snapped together. I looked at Beryx, in dread.

He was leaning on the wall. He had folded his arms. I looked, and looked again, and then rubbed my eyes. For his eyes were dancing with what I incredulously realized was enjoyment, and his mouth had curved, a grin that widened as I looked.

"So," the Lady proceeded, "it was expelled by a dragon. And it fled to Hethria. Into dudgeon, if not dungeon, you might say."

My mouth opened in ungovernable rage. You lying bitch, I wanted to howl, you know, you know he killed the thing! My breath went in and a general's bawl chopped it in my throat.

<Keep quiet!>

I fairly shot to attention. <Hold rank!> he rasped. I had just recognized mindspeech when the Lady began again.

"Hethria being a desert, it was quite apt. Barren to barren, you see." They did. "It even found a mate. But our gethel grew restless. Though not for trees. It came to Assharral. It wanted—listen my dears—it wanted to see the sea!"

This time several of the more advanced sycophants had to be held off the floor. One actually rolled on it, to the great detriment of his balloon-shaped cloth-of-gold breeks.

"And when it arrived. . . ." The Lady elaborately wiped a tear from one perfect cheek. "Dears, do wait a moment, you haven't heard the cream. When it arrived, do you know what it did? It fell in love—no, only wait a moment! It fell in love . . . give me the fan, Klyra. . . . And it wanted to marry—you'll never imagine—It wanted to marry—me!"

I hoped those in need of smelling salts would choke on them. I memorized several faces for an alley some dark night. I solaced myself by noting how like a zoo they looked. A bedlamite, boot-licking zoo. I acknowledged, with chagrin, the masterly way she had converted a mortal insult to a prime weapon of offense. Do something! I raged at Beryx. Say something! Finally, with shame and reluctance, I looked at him.

The grin had fairly split his face. He might have been handed a whole battle on a plate. When the uproar sank to speaking level he said with quite fiendish glee, "Do go on . . . dear."

For one glorious moment I thought she would lose control. A red spot rose on each cheek, furnaces burnt in her eyes. Then she turned back to the hiccupping crowd.

"So I thought this—exhibit—might amuse you a little. Being demented, it has to be chained up, but it could still be quite diverting. Come, Thephor, don't you know how to bait a bear?"

Thephor was the favorite. In scarlet today, with a preposterous feathered hat, he had kept his ox-goad stave. He smiled gaily at the Lady, at a total loss. With honeyed venom, she smiled back.

"I'm sure," she cooed, "you'd all like to see a magician's powers?"

This was much more to Thephor's taste. He clapped as enthusiastically as the rest. "Don't worry, darling," she assured him. "It can't hurt you, I've seen to that. Why don't you wake it up?"

My spine went cold. Remembering that catapulted coal, I wondered, Does she know what she's fooling with?

Thephor had entire faith in her. He minced past the braziers, hove his staff up two-handed, and made to prod with it.

Beryx did not move. But the staff head veered aside and grated down the wall by his left hip.

The crowd laughed. A couple jeered the bad aim. Thephor tried again. This time it was a distinct thrust, impelled by most of his scanty muscle, I should think. The staff end shot up past Beryx's motionless face, described a slow circle, and dropped to earth with Thephor clinging as if it were too heavy for him to the middle of the haft.

Into the hiatus came the Lady's tinkling laugh. "Dear me, Thephor!"

Thephor had lost his smile. He re-hefted his weapon. This

time he swung it cudgel-wise, sidelong at Beryx's chest.

The staff twisted from his hands, described a graceful parabola over the audience and disappeared into the dark. From somewhere down the vault came a heavy, thudding crash.

Beryx looked at his assailant. His eyes were not roused. After A'sparre, I had seen that. There was just a crystal whitening, an intimation of power roused.

Then it became something like pity. He said, "Take someone your own weight, Thephor."

Thephor half-backed, glancing round. The Lady's eye made me pity him too. In the pause the woman Klyra gave a shrill laugh, then pulled the gilded scent-ball from her wrist.

Wonderfully for a woman, the throw would have been straight. But six inches from Beryx's face it rebounded, sailed lazily back to Klyra, turned a loop and vanished with diabolical accuracy between her amply exposed breasts.

He burst out laughing at her leap. The court laughed too, but with malice. A moment later missiles sailed from every side, scent-balls, hand-mirrors, fans, bracelets, smelling salt phials, ivory engagement books, the kind of play that verges on blood-sport and needs a feather to tip the scales.

Beryx's eyes shot a salvo of white flashes so fast they seemed continuous. The missiles sprayed away from him, not back to the thrower now, they were too thick for that. The crowd laughed, the Lady's smile stopped my breath. The bombardment dwindled. In the lull Beryx gazed blandly back at her, and cocked a brow.

"Did you ever," she cooed, "try juggling for your bread?"

He gave her a dazzling smile. Then he said in absolute earnest, "Moriana, give it up."

"You've forgotten your audience."

"It's the last thing I'd forget. Look at them. You—Thephor—heir to Climbros' first house. If you were one of my nobles you'd be governor of the province now. Instead you're a bed-boy headed for the chopping block. You—Klyra—Mistress of the Wardrobe, aren't you? Wife to the biggest cattle-lord in Darrior, and you wouldn't know a stud bull if it kicked you in the face. You—Femos—your flocks graze half Kemrestan. What's your wool worth? All you can tally is the Cups. You—Kreo—your land marches with Phaxia. Have you seen one border fort? When the raiders cross you're squabbling with the Jewel-keeper over privy precedence and paid soldiers die to save your loot. You—Ashon—the biggest merchant bank in Assharral. You'd be my Treasurer, not keeping my soaps. You—Hazis—own half the merchant fleet. Ever inspected your books? You—any of you—do you manage your estates? Lead your army? Govern your provinces? Guide Assharral? No. Do you know why?"

His eyes whipped round them. For one moment I saw awareness of his point, vision of what they should have been. Then, from the right horn of the circle, commanded or voluntarily, someone hurled a chunk of coal.

Whoever it was had a good eye and hate to power his arm. It took Beryx under the ear with a sickening thud. He staggered, his head jerked, and instantly the whole court was screaming like a pack of foxhounds on the scent of blood.

I sprang into the rear. A surge of sickly-sweet satin bowled me away as they rushed the coal. I charged again. The press was solid. I dropped a shoulder and smashed into backs, and something brushed my mind, feather light. Next moment I was over by the arch, watching as if the whole abomination had nothing to do with me.

Even in my trance I wondered why Beryx did not resist. He could have repelled the projectiles. He could have struck down the throwers. Instead he staggered to and fro under that brutal, battering rain and made no attempt to fight. He only tried to shield his head. Then his body. Then he dropped in the straw and made to curl up, while the coal kept thudding into his ribs, shoulders, neck, head, with that vile sound of a catapult load striking flesh, and the screams grew less human with every hit.

By the end they were all quite rabid. The women danced up and down while the men ran round and round seeking more ammunition, and I stood, and Beryx lay horribly unmoving in the straw. And the Lady watched, immobile, with a small, gloating smile.

"Dears, dears," she chimed at last. "We don't want to demean ourselves, do we?" They ran down, and stood gawping, their finery thick with coal dust, stupid, sated bloodlust in their eyes. The pages wheeled her train. The court fell in. Passing me, she murmured with a daggerish smile, "It seems, Captain, you'll have to pick up the pieces all over again."

They must have left the building before she turned me loose. This time I did not rage or puzzle, simply tore across to grab his wrist, and when the pulse throbbed, I gasped in relief.

The worst blow was the original, under the left ear. The rest were bruises, except one splendid purple graze on his right cheek, but the first was already egg-sized, oozing blood into the straight black hair, and when I tried to swab it he flinched so badly I stopped. But then he groaned, wriggled, and tried to sit up.

Propped against my shoulder, he said thickly, "Ow."

I was still too furious to speak. He felt the nape of his neck. More strongly, he said, "Blighted idiot." I gasped. "Not you. Me."

He fingered his cheek. I kept silent, since I agreed. He said with asperity, "You ought to know better. I'd have ended by killing them. Or worse."

"Eh?"

"Gave her the battle. She diverted me to them. And I went.

Through instead of Round." He grimaced. "And she nearly trapped me into fighting for command of them. Then she'd have used the Well and . . . it would have got right out of hand. Fengthira'll rake me like a garden bed. Ouch—and she'll be right."

A movement caught my eye's edge. I jerked my head up and the boy Thephor was standing over us.

Beryx's grip pinned me. He did not speak. Just looked up at the fair, shallow, handsome face, the incongruous finery, the fidgety be-ringed hands, until the boy spoke with a jerk, mixing defiance and defensiveness.

"I didn't throw it. It wasn't me."

Beryx wore an attentive, neutral look. He said, "I know."

The boy eyed the coal-strewn straw, the overset braziers. Again it came with a jerk.

"What did you mean—your nobles would be provincial governors?"

Gravely, positively, Beryx said, "That's what you're for."

The boy fidgeted anew. Argument, uncertainty, distrust, yearning fleeted across his face.

Beryx shifted. Met a coal lump, grunted, "Four!" With complete naturalness he used Axynbrarve to toss all the coal back into its heaps, plucked up the stool, set it by Thephor's leg, and said, "What are you shying for? You had the prodding stick. Sit down."

Thephor sat, thump. Beryx watched him as if he were a raw battle-line.

Then he said, "The lords of the land are not bred to fritter themselves away at court. They are the ruler's shield. Sword. Eyes. Hands. They have obligations. Did you ever hear the word?"

After a moment, Thephor shook his head.

"Fealty to the ruler," Beryx said quietly. "Duty to your folk.

They make you a lord. They keep you a lord. You owe them. Just like a king. If you were one of my lords, you'd be taking that responsibility."

For a moment naked yearning was in the boy's eyes. Then he averted them. With hostility he demanded, "What was all that about a chopping block?"

"Don't they have morsyrs in Climbros? How long have you been favorite? How long did the one before you last?"

This time it was plain fear, growing to despair. He said, "This is Assharral."

Beryx's eyes flickered like schooling fish. I could not guess what calculations passed in that flash. But when he spoke, I guessed how much hung on the words.

"Do you want to get out?"

Thephor turned up his hands.

"You can."

I looked at Beryx then and could not look away. His eyes were in flux, swirling, gyring, a vortex of green upon green upon green that sucked like earth itself. Yet his mind was not even bent upon me.

"Think carefully." His voice was low. "No money, no rank, no comforts, no servants, friends, kin. Mortal danger on the way, and a rough welcome at the end. Not Thephor, the Lady's favorite. Nobody. In somebody else's world."

Thephor had straightened. Now his shoulders slumped again. "So what? It can't happen . . . anyway."

Beryx squared his own shoulders. His face daunted me. He said softly, "If you want it, it can. Do you want it?"

The vault seemed to have grown still. Thephor twisted his hands. At last, just audibly, he answered, "Yes."

Beryx said, "Look here."

Thephor's eyes rose. Flickered. Widened. Emptied like those of the dead. Beryx exhaled, driving the breath till his stomach went concave and his back arched like a bow. His lips drew back. The inhalation lasted forever. Sweat did not spring, it ran in rivulets down his face. His eyes were blind, incandescent. I thought to see sparks shower from them as when the smith strikes red-hot iron. They were furnaces, sun-cores, searing, blinding, burning my own eyes away.

Vision revived. Amid dancing red spots I found Beryx, a hand pressed to his side, breath whooping as he tried to regain his lungs' control. The calico gown was plastered to him, making barrel staves of his ribs. And Thephor, staring in bewilderment, sat limply on the stool, intact.

" 'S . . . it." A grass-scrape whisper. "You . . . can go."

He recovered before either of us had managed to move. "Don't just sit there." He sounded irritable. "Get some proper clothes. Make up a message, anything that'll get you post-horses. Then ride for the Hethrian border like Lossian's on your trail. Find the Sathellin. Say Thorgan Fenglos sent you. Go on, boy!" Thephor shot to his feet like a twitched puppet. "I've broken the Command. She can't hold you now."

It seemed a long time before the patter of the boy's feet died away. It was far longer before Beryx's eyes awoke and he lay back, with a soundless sigh, into the straw.

"He's out of the city." He sounded quite weak. "On his way."

I set up a brazier, kindled it. Fetched the water-bottle. I would not have asked, but he answered anyway.

"Not worth it? Nor is anybody, if you judge like that. Why? A Must. At least, to me." He pushed limply at his hair. "Math knows, I'm no Velandyr, but sometimes it's like war. You have to go on your own judgment and hope for the best. What did I do?" A wry smile. "Broke that permanent half-Command of yours. Yes. Took on the Well. Don't start a victory dance, it was only one weak mind. Then I gave him a Command of my own to shield him. But it's a long road to Hethria. And they'll be waiting all the way."

His face grew bleak. "Maybe I've killed him. But . . . I had to give him a chance."

I heard myself say, or rather croak, "All anyone could ask."

His eyes turned to me, tired, trusting, indeed reliant, and I thought: You can take on the Well, breach your strategy, expose your flank to a deadly enemy, all but kill yourself, for a fribble. And then have courage great enough to admit you might be wrong. Sometimes the fixing of a loyalty can feel palpable as if it were done with nails. I knew then, with perfect certainty, that my choice of masters had been made.

After that internal defection it surprised me to find myself still Captain of the Guard next day. Returning from parade I was more surprised by a figure in the crowd, a tall man with a magnificent snowy curling beard, a blue velvet robe worked with golden symbols, and a rod topped by the sign of Axvyr, infinity, a horizontal 8.

Phathryn come from Tasmar and seldom visit Zyphryr Coryan. Thinking of Beryx, like the escort with their bulls and butterflies, I made haste after Dismissal to catch the seer before he set up his pavement booth.

It took a high price to halt and double price to lure him, but at last he made his stately way downstairs. I said, "Beryx," for the first time using the name easily, "this is how we foresee in Assharral."

Beryx glanced up sharply. Then his face became a mask. Politely, he rose, while the Phathos eyed his surroundings askance. I said, "It's not what you're used to, but I can settle that. Will you make a forecast now?"

At length he deigned to seat himself on the stool, with my cloak spread for table on the straw. Feeling in his robe he drew out the cards, and Beryx's eye showed something close to distaste.

"Ystir," the Phathos intoned. Beryx twitched. "Imsar Losvure. Pharyn, latharyn, ystryn." He abandoned priestliness. "Is this reading for you, Captain, or"—his nostrils curled—"for him?"

"Him," I answered before Beryx could object, and took the tendered pack.

"Cut and shuffle three times," the Phathos ordered, eyes closed, hands on knees. "Hand me the top card. That will be the Seeker's sign."

I shuffled the heavy cards with their cryptic, haunting images. The four corps, Cups, Stars, Vines, Staves. The ruand cards, Priestess, Empress, Wise-man, Hung-man, Devil, Sun, Star, Wheel, Chariot, World. Without looking I handed over the pack. He took it, started, gave me a bristly stare. "I am not," he said, "amused. Again."

The Emperor, Fortitude, Judgment, Moon, Destruction, the High Priest. I handed it back. He glared and rose. "But wait," I stuttered. "What have I done?"

"That"—he held it distastefully by a corner—"is the Sage. Not a Seeker's card. You have given it to me twice. I can only suppose you have your own reasons for this knavery."

"But it just came up! On my word! Wait—let me try once more. Watch, this time."

After another price rise I shut my eyes and shuffled again. He watched like a basilisk. I held out the pack. There on top, standing at his altar, clad in his red-and-blue cloak and white gown, holding his staff crowned with infinity, was the Sage.

He looked at me. Then at Beryx. His eyes narrowed. Rather dryly, Beryx said, "Ystir. Truth indeed."

The Phathos drew a breath. Beryx said, "Your cards don't cover that?"

As if flurried, the Phathos flicked them out. Above, Beneath, Behind, Before, Cross, Crown, Hope, Fear, House, Gate. They stared up from the black velvet, an omen that lifted the hair on my neck.

There was not a corps card in the cast. It was pure ruands. Above: the Moon, triple-faced, shining blandly between her towers. Beneath: the Hung-man, pendant upside down. Before: the Devil, cloven-hooved, horned and hideous. Cross: the Priestess, veiled, enchanting, inaccessible. Crown: the Lovers, hand in hand beneath the Tree. Hope: Justice, blindfolded, holding her naked sword. Fear: Destruction, the lightning-riven tower. House: Death, cackling from his ass beside the noble knight. Gate: the Fool, dancing blithe and blindly to the precipice, eyes full of empty air.

Beryx was shaking with silent mirth. "Your face!" he spluttered at me, and the Phathos rose in affront. "The Ystryn," he thundered, "show the truth! They are not a matter for jest!"

Beryx controlled himself. "Of course," he agreed solemnly. "If I d-don't . . . laugh again . . . will you say what they mean?"

"The Moon," the Phathos began dourly, "is your present influence. It means crisis, deception, enemies and risk." He sounded pleased. "The World is behind you. You have lost supreme happiness, the achievement of a life. Before you is the Devil. Bondage, insensitivity, revolution, carnal desire. Also dishonest wealth. You have no cause to laugh. Beneath is the Hung-man. The meaningful past. Sacrifice, renunciation, abandonment." I too saw no cause to laugh. "The Lovers, the Crown, are future events. They show trials ending in success. Marriage. A problem solved by wisdom's light." I started. "The Cross, opposition, is the . . . Priestess. . . ."

He looked at me, at the chains. His hand crept out to the pack. Beryx said wickedly, "Go on. If the Gate's what I think, she's more likely to make you rich."

After a splutter the Phathos snapped, "The Priestess signifies enlightenment, wisdom's quest. In opposition she is a blighted future, bewilderment." He eyed Beryx with sour pleasure. "Your hope is Justice. It means just that. Your fear is Destruction. Patterns snapped, unexpected shock, catastrophe. Your House, your nature, effect and function, is Death."

"It's not as bad as it sounds," I struck in hopefully, and the Phathos snorted.

"It symbolizes the soul's death. And," he added reluctantly, "its regeneration. It means," he revived, "the death of kings. Also revolution." He gazed balefully at me. "As you sow, you will reap."

Beryx had grown thoughtful. Now, hunched forward over his knees, he glanced at the Fool and his eyes lit with vivid hilarity. "And," he asked demurely, "the Gate?"

"The outcome," the Phathos almost snarled. "The Fool symbolizes divine wisdom ignoring the lower world. It means a vital choice requiring"—his eye sneered—"great wisdom. But the Fool also contains elements of anarchy, recklessness—and improper levity."

Beryx crowed with delight. The Phathos tore the cards to his bosom, kicked my cloak, hissed, "Your silver is accursed!" and took the steps like a cavalry charge with me plucking vainly at his elbow while Beryx rolled in the straw, quite gagged by mirth.

"Did you have to?" I asked ruefully, coming back. "I thought you might be interested. And—and some of it seemed to fit."

"Oh, dear, I'm sorry, Alkir." He wiped his face. "But . . . ! The Moon, the Devil, Death, the Fool!" He calmed. "It's like a bad mirror. Real things made unreal. I suppose they inherit it? Some must have known Velandryxe once. Ystir. *Truth it is.* That's the Great Tales' opening. And Imsar Losvure. *In the Sky-faces' name.* But—Alkir, he's a charlatan! He uses pictures! Four! Now I know why Th'Iahn would say 'bastard sorcerers' and kick them out of the house."

I kept silent. I am an Assharran, raised with the cards. To me a pure ruand cast was portentous enough, without the recurrent Sage, that sinister Cross, and the still more ominous Fool jigging in the Gate.

"Never mind." He twitched up my cloak. "Math does say, 'The wisest mirror shows a fool.' So you can console yourself by—" He broke off.

I spun round. The Lady Moriana, in a ruby-red gown marbled with white striations, a gold coronet on her ebony hair, a single torch-bearer at her elbow, had halted just within the arch.

Chapter VI

My back went stiff. I stood like a stock. But in one glance Beryx construed the hesitation, the lack of escort; dropped my cloak, lifted the stool by Axynbrarve beyond armslength, and with a royal gesture invited her to sit.

Slowly, never taking her eyes off him, she advanced. Her eyes were bigger than ever, and dead black. Depthless, motionless. With honest goodwill he smiled at her, and said, "This is my hearth."

My ingrained fear became stupefaction, turned to rage. She had chained him, slain his mare, nearly killed him twice over, made a guy of him. Now he welcomed her when she had the gall, the effrontery, to risk herself alone within the compass of his powers.

Then, rather bitterly, I thought that she knew him better than I. *My hearth.* Whatever her perfidy, he would never stoop to foul play against a guest.

He was watching her, openly, as I had never dared, without so much as a shred of wariness. Startled, then resignedly admitting he would always startle me, I decoded his expression. Candid, unoffensive admiration: any decent man looking at a beautiful girl.

She sank onto the stool. The torch-bearer hovered. Not turning, she gave a tiny dismissive nod. Then, tacitly admitting her trust in the host, she looked about her. When her eyes returned to Beryx he held them long enough to make his message clear.

Then he sat down in the straw and expectantly raised his brows.

Leaning back, graceful as a browsing deer, she linked both hands about a knee and without warning offered her greatest challenge yet.

"Tell me," she said, "about this . . . Math."

The chain clinked as he rubbed his chin. Marshalling thought, not reconnoitering for a trap.

"It began with a vision," he said, "in Los Velandryxe Thira. The very Well you have. It was seen by our ancestor Th'Iahn." His eyes crinkled. "Your line began with his grandson Lossian. Mine came six generations later. Your foremother was a mistress, mine a concubine. I can't tell you about the vision, because that was between the Well and Th'Iahn. It doesn't show in Phathire, and the Well itself couldn't reproduce it. I can deduce the bones from what Th'Iahn said and did, but there have been seventeen aedric generations since. Math now is . . . like a building started to Th'Iahn's design. A great many minds have left their mark on it."

"But," I blurted, "I thought the world changed as soon as you saw—"

I bit my tongue. He answered, unruffled, "When the first smith forged an iron sword-blade, everyone else didn't do it next minute. But once it was forged, that smith had changed the world."

He turned back to the Lady. "Whatever Th'Iahn saw, he set out to end the Xaira, the separation of aedryx and men. He was a great aedr, but also a practical man, so he didn't go off to live on locusts in Hethria and hope his idea would travel on the air. He began at the beginning. To spread an idea, you need it to travel. To cause travel, you must offer profit—or expose a need. To carry them, you need an instrument. So Th'Iahn built a road."

"Eh?" I forgot my place again.

"A road from his keep to his country's annual market. Then roads all over his lands. So trade improved, and everybody profited, and the market expanded, and they did better still. But they also, both aedryx and men"—his eyes were white-green, crystalline, thought's combustion made visible—"came in contact with the idea."

Roads are for carrying ideas. I heard him saying it, in Kemrestan.

"Pharaon Lethar—the land—was jammed with aedryx, most at loggerheads if not open war. Th'Iahn's arch . . . enemy—rival—other half—was an aedr called Vorn. When he saw what came of Th'Iahn's roads, he started building too. There's a saying about that, supposed to be Delostar's—Th'Iahn's son. 'When Ammath seeks, Math finds.' So Vorn grew rich, but the idea entered his lands. There were other aedryx, especially in the north—Stiriand—who suffered from foreign marauders just as Th'Iahn did from corsair raids. When they came to the market Th'Iahn spoke about alliance, linking shields against enemies. The Stirianns listened. So did Vorn. He knew that to miss trade was crazy, but to be left outside an aedric alliance would be plain suicide. It was all coming together when Th'Iahn's only daughter eloped with Vorn's eldest son."

After a moment I whistled. But the Lady had already laughed, a crystal, cynically delighted peal.

Unaffronted, Beryx gave a sorrowful nod.

"Oh, yes. Th'Iahn was aedric to the marrow. Away went the alliance, into the cupboard went Math, and the feud was on." He sighed. "There's a great deal of history, much like any other history. Mistakes and bungles and bloody-mindedness wrecking good intentions, and insults wiped out in other people's blood. Somewhere on the way Th'Iahn's idea became a council of the eight aedric lines—the Tingrith. In theory it was to ward Pharaon Lethar without and within. In fact it was always disintegrating in another bout of the feud, invasions, bloodbaths, all but destruction of the aedric race. But the Ruands, the council leaders, always kept the Well, and in it they sought for Math. And some of them were very wise."

The Lady spoke at last. The tale's tragedy had left her untouched. "But what is this Math?" she said.

"Um." He scrubbed at his hair. "Th'Iahn must have meant to end aedryx' abuse of their powers and men's fear and hatred of aedryx, but all he ever *said* was practical arguments for his alliance. That peace brought profit, and so would conserving humans' lands. That the alliance protected its members, and to protect humans would be profitable too. His son Delostar, first council Ruand, took another step and said aedryx should unite with men—the northern invasions were at their worst in his day. Then Ruands from Stiriand decided aedryx' power should be used for the good of both aedryx and men. Then somebody decided power should just work for good. And then they tried to riddle out how, and now Math is a chain of precepts, like Respect that-which-is, Do only what you must . . . The full saying is, *The fool reasons, and does as he thinks he should. The wise man does only as he must.* But the proverbs are all negative. 'Who sees Math does not speak. Who speaks of it does not see.'—'The Math that can be named is not the vision of Math.'—'Math is not Velandryxe. But Velandryxe is Math.'—'Say, Math, see Ammath.' The best I can do is that it's not a thing at all. It's a way of seeing. Seeing everything."

"Then what use is it?"

He looked at her under his brows.

"Before Math," he said evenly, "aedric law was, As I Want, I Will. And they had aedric powers. The greater the power, the greater the risk of corruption. The greater the corruption, the greater the ruin. They ruined themselves. They ruined Pharaon Lethar. Cycle after cycle of wanton cruelty, murder, brutality, wholesale destruction. And they thought it was normal. Natural."

I said nothing. It was so little time since I had thought nature, normality, was the state of Assharral. But the Lady arched her brows and retorted, "Isn't it?"

"Certainly. Without Math."

Her lips parted. And closed again.

"When Th'Iahn brought Math from the Well, he changed the world. He gave aedryx—and humans—a choice. A chance to escape Ammath. Maybe they refused, maybe they misunderstood, maybe they tried and failed. But never again were they doomed to remain below the level of beasts."

"You cannot," she said incisively, "choose something that cannot be defined."

"Oh, that's much easier. You need only define its opposite. Ammath. Cruelty. Waste. Destruction. Pleasure in misusing power. Math says, Respect that-which-is. Because"—his eyes held hers—"that-which-is is reality. Ammath distorts it. And the greater the distortion, the greater the havoc when reality is restored."

She was silent.

Very softly, he said, "It does happen, you know."

Elaborately, insolently, she yawned. "So we're back at that. You want me to renounce everything for the sake of your 'Math.' "

"Not 'my' Math. And not for Math's sake. For yours."

"And what good will it do me?"

After a moment he said, "Turn it round. What bad will it do me if I don't? Sooner or later, the distortion will collapse. And the later the fall, the longer and bitterer the memories of Ammath. Assharral's a big empire. And only the wise say, 'Vengeance is sweet. But wisdom chooses salt.' "

Inexplicably, her eyes turned to me.

Then she straightened up, that flowing water motion that was so beautiful. Rose. Strolled between the braziers. His eyes followed her, and now the admiration bordered on longing, indeed open desire.

She turned. Watching him under her lids she said sweetly, "Why?"

When he did not answer, she probed, "For love of 'good'? Because you want to redeem me from my vice? So you can feel righteous and pure, having done your tiny bit for 'Math'?"

Suddenly he grinned. "Because I hate waste," he said.

"Or suffer from want."

"I am rather a bear, yes."

"More of a bore."

"I thought you loved your beasts in Assharral?"

This time I recognized that tingle which had informed the air by Los Morryan. Just so Callissa and I had sparred in our first courtship bout.

She stretched. A hint of tantalizing, of display. Lazily, but quite finally, she said, "Poor beast."

"Poor beauty."

She raised her brows.

"You are beautiful." The sparring was done. "Going to waste. Like your powers." The pity was clear. "An aedric empress. And you twist it into Ammath."

"Powers?"

"You could have them. Speech, the Sights, the Commands. Mastery of beasts, weather, fire."

Aghast, I thought, he's taken her in good faith! Has he forgotten everything he ever knew of war?

"You could have Velandryxe," he was saying. "Wisdom. Understanding how not to act. The most important of all." He looked at her as if in pain. "For the Four's love, Moriana, can't you see what a waste it is?"

Her head tilted. Sounding half-swayed, I was sure in whole falsity, she said, "And this Well of mine? That brought the vision of Math? That changed the world?"

I shut my eyes. Don't, I prayed. Show her through your armory, explain your tactics, but you can't be such a fool as that!

He could. "The Well didn't bring the vision," he said. "Th'Iahn and the Well made it between them. In Wreve-lethar, the highest aedric art. To alter the Dream. Change the Universe."

"Why," she asked innocently, "did he need the Well?"

"Because it's the focus. You can't do Wreve-lethar without it. That's what the Well's really for."

He looked at her eagerly, sure that truth was invincible, she need only hear it to yield. Nothing is so vulnerable as good faith. And she, I thought in blinding fury, she had known it.

Her mouth curled. "Thank you." The triumph was almost obscene. "Now I see why you called me incompetent. But of course, I didn't know."

Horror ripped across his face. He plunged to his feet. And stopped.

She was poised for escape. His eyes were writhing flares of moss, leaf, laurel green, laced with dazzling white. But they were turned inward, upon the forge of thought.

He put a hand to his brow. Very slowly, it dropped.

Making it a prayer, committing all to a wholly unsure gamble, he said, "Imsar . . . Math."

Then he looked at her.

"Then," he said, quiet as fate itself, "you know it now."

For one instant her eyes flickered with what could have been fear. Then they swung on me.

"My trusted captain," she purred. "Who let a traitor walk out of this prison. Under his very nose."

"Who had no choice," he cut in quick as lightning. "I'm an aedr too."

The meteors flared. "Who ate my bread. Took my wages. Swore my oath of fealty. And schemed to suborn my guard."

I flinched. Beryx's voice slashed, "Moriana, let him alone!"

She spun on him. "Why?"

"Because"—and contempt appeared at last—"you're giving a perfect demonstration of Ammath. From devilry to pettiness. You couldn't bait a bear, so you want to skin a mouse."

Her skirts made a white and ruby comet in her wake. She whipped round in the arch. "It may interest you," she hissed, "to know your smuggling failed. They caught him in Darrior. He's dead!"

It was a long time before I dared look at Beryx, and when I did, I dared not ask the question that hovered on my lips.

He was still watching the arch. His eyes were quenched, not merely opaque but dulled black, and there was fatigue, discouragement, a poignant sorrow in his face.

At last he turned away. Slowly, he brought the stool in reach and sat down, shoulders bowed. Finally he looked at me and said with that courage which can admit mistakes, "It's true."

I could not, did not want to reply. He gazed past me, into a distance beyond my reach.

"They tortured him," he murmured. The pity was strong as pain. "Poor little fop."

Into my mind rose a sharp, concrete image of a city gate, shreds of a body dangled on the wheel, morvallin circling for carrion above frustrated dogs. Perhaps it came from his Sight, but it was enough to sting me into speech. Pain for him, Thephor, myself, became wrath that had to be assuaged.

I said harshly, "Why?"

He did not fence. He answered wearily, "Math says, Keep

faith even with unfaith. Could I have turned her away?"

"You needn't have—" The full enormity recoiled on me. "The biggest baboon who ever wrecked an army knows better than to blab like that! And to tell her about the Well—I thought you meant to *help* Assharral!"

He made a little throwaway gesture. "I don't think I can make you see." It was fatigue, not rancor. "When Ammath seeks, Math finds. If you—"

"To the pits with Math! I'm talking plain commonsense!"

"You can't. Not in this. I—Look, Alkir. She tried to kill me with that fever, and it rid me of Hawge's sting. That I've carried seventy years. She sought Ammath, I found Math. Don't you see?"

"No—all I see is that you blindly—insanely!—took her on trust, and she rolled you up. Horse, foot and camp!"

He straightened, summoning strength to deal with me among the rest. I should have pitied him, but I could not. "Explain that!" I said.

He sighed. Then he said, "I had to take her on trust. Or break trust myself. I had to tell her the truth. Because lies are Ammath. If you don't hold to good, you become evil. That's the real defeat."

"So she flogs you off every field by using your beliefs against you! You're hamstrung by the very thing you're fighting for!"

"Perhaps," he said heavily. "But she does know, now, about Math."

"And about the Well! All about the Well!"

"Yes. I . . . I can't explain." He sank his head in his hand. "Velandryxe . . . the sayings tell you, over and over, that it seems madness. The supreme wisdom looks like foolishness."

"The foolishness I see. The wisdom I don't."

"I had to tell her about the Well. Or deny truth. And once she knew, I couldn't wipe it out. Or fight it. And I know it looks like a disaster, so in the end I had to take a monumental risk, and hope Velandryxe will bear it out."

"How?"

"Ammath has to end. And with such power as the Well—that I can't master—perhaps the only thing that can end it is the Well itself."

"What? How?"

"Math fears to act. Ammath doesn't. Now she knows what the Well can really do, she might try something so vile that—it will be the one thing too much. That will break the Well's power. It would fit with Velandryxe. The supreme foolishness. Admit the truth, do nothing, allow her to misuse power. So Math refrains, and Ammath acts, and Ammath too great to be destroyed overreaches and destroys itself. Just like the sting and the fever. Do you understand?"

"No!"

His shoulders bent. Quietly, humbly, he said, "I suppose not."

I looked at him sitting there, worsted in battle, blood on his hands, betrayed by his own good faith, patiently accepting recrimination and abuse and desertion, and a mountain fell on my neck. Gevos, the mare—and now a third time I had upbraided when I should have upheld, wounded when I should have salved, broken faith I should have kept.

In bitter pain I said, "You should know better than that."

His head came up. The smile was almost tender. "Fylghjos," he said, "you're too like me. You blame yourself worse than anyone else."

I could not speak. He was still smiling, giving the comfort I had refused, ungrudging as if I had never wounded him.

"Yes," he said, "crazy, and the remotest chance, and pure blind hope. But that's Velandryxe. Inyx—a friend of mine—used to say, 'Lose every battle but the last.' " The smile became that indomitable laughter. "We're doing pretty well with the rest."

Feeling raw, hunted and desperate, I went home to Zem and Zam's inevitable. "When is Sir Scarface coming back?" then passed a night of fearful dreams in which the Lady flung Beryx from the Morhyrne, or I drowned him for her in Los Morryan, or Callissa chased me with a cleaver for letting him die of cold, or I tried to light the brazier and the entire vault collapsed. It seemed an uncovenanted mercy when I crept out next day to find Zyphryr Coryan apparently unaltered, quite intact. I would have sacrificed, if I still had anywhere to offer it.

Three days passed, by which time I half-wished doom would fall and be done. Third night was my vault sentry-watch. I left after supper, to Callissa's silent protest, but as I closed the garden gate a woman's voice hissed, "Captain! Alkir!"

I whipped about. A hand beckoned, the moon sparked on thillians. I backed. A mincing court accent chattered, "It's all right, quite safe. . . ." In anguish, "Oh, *come* over here!"

Hand on sword, I sidled cross-street. The moon flashed on eyes painted like targets, a grotesque pole of hair. "It's me, Klyra. You know me. I have to talk to you!"

Instinctively we both looked behind. She gabbled under her breath, "You're in with him and you'll be able to tell him, straighten it out . . . if she knew she'd—I don't know what she'd do, you mustn't breathe a word—"

"Don't babble," I muttered. "What am I supposed to tell who?"

"Him. The wizard." Her hand twittered on my arm, I felt the talon-like nails. "About the Lady. These last three days she's been impossible. . . ."

"Come to the Treasury," I said, "and tell him yourself."

Before shifting a woman I had sooner try to dislodge Phaxian skirmishers. We compromised, amid squeals and frou-frou to wake the Morhyrne, on a bench under the garden keerphar. When she finally subsided, I asked, "What is it I'm to say?"

"The Lady." She clutched for thoughts flyaway as her frivolous gold-mesh bag. "She's . . . she's been summoning all the governors. Poor Havath, he's Nervia, he was quaking, I had to lend him smelling salts. . . . When he got in, the Lady says, 'Do you approve my orders? Have I ever given you cause to hate me? Are you happy in your post?' I ask you! As if you'd dare say otherwise, not that she isn't a good mistress and I'll not hear a word against her, but—well, you know what I mean.

"And the chief priests, she had them up yesterday. 'Do you approve of my worship?' she says. 'Of course,' they say. Or in so many words. 'You don't think it's bad?' They have conniptions. Well, I mean, they would, wouldn't they, it's their life, and can you imagine not worshipping the Lady, I'd not know what to do with myself, and the high days, the people love them—she had them up too. A fish-gutter and a tanner, you couldn't credit the stink. . . . 'Do you believe,' she says, 'I am immortal? Do you think that's wrong?' I tell you, the poor boobies hadn't a clue.

"And then she calls Mavash and Zabek, and she says, 'Do you think we need a Council?'—'Council?' they say. 'So you can advise me,' she says. I ask you, Captain, have you ever seen a general look faint? Then she gets Kreo and Tamon, Cup-bearer and First below the Throne, and she says, 'Do you want to go home to your estates?' And Kreo just appointed, and everyone knows Tamon can't *bear* Gjerven, all those swamps. . . . Then I'm watching the dressers, you wouldn't credit how they treat those gowns if they're not stood over—she comes up behind me, I'm sure *I* needed smelling salts that time.

" 'Klyra,' she says, 'are you happy here?'

" 'Happy?' " I say. 'Why, ma'am, whatever—whyever wouldn't I be? Highest women's post at court?'—'You wouldn't,' she says, 'rather be in Darrior?'—'Darrior!' I say. 'You think the court's worthwhile?' she says. 'You don't think I'm wasting your life?' Well, really, I could have hugged her, she looked so forlorn. 'Dear Lady,' I say, 'of course not. The court's my life.' She gives a sort of nod and goes away. But. . . ."

She paused for extra drama and leant forward. "That's only the shell of the egg. Yesterday, high banquet, Kreo's on her right, I was next to him. When the oysters come in, she loves them, she didn't touch a one—'Kreo,' she says, 'if you wanted to marry me, what would you do?'

"Well, the poor man nearly falls through his chair. Says the proper things, too unworthy, never think of it. 'But suppose,' she says, 'you were—Zass of Phaxia—how would you go about it then?'

"Of course, he has some wits, or he'd not be where he is. 'Most high,' he says, 'I would begin with gifts. The best spices of Eakring Ithyrx, the most precious gems, the rarest rarities. Then poets to hymn your beauty. Musicians.' He's getting into the swing of it. 'Painters. Jewelers with lovely things. I'd ransack Phaxia. Then I'd—I'd make peace, and arrange a court visit. Balls, masques, entertainments, dress up the palace fit for you.' Dreadful barrack, I've heard it is. 'I would worship at your feet. I might abandon Phaxia, if you were heartless, and become a beggar at your gate—'

" 'Yes, yes, that's enough,' she says. I'd have been pleased, I'm sure. Then Timya, she's chief tiring Lady, she told me, when she was taking off the coronal, a proper puzzle that one is—the Lady looks in the mirror like she's never had one before.

" 'Timya,' she says, 'I *am* beautiful. . . .' Running her hands up through her hair. 'Yes, ma'am,' says Timya, wondering if she's in her wits. *Every*-body knows she is, she's never had a thing to fear from anyone that ever came to court.

"But she sort of smiles at herself. Mocking, you'd say. 'Too beautiful,' she says, 'to change.'—'Ma'am,' says Timya, thinking, Sakes, what's the matter with her? 'You won't change, you know that. You're immortal.'

" 'Yes,' she says after a while. You'd think she'd only just been told. 'I am.' Now wait a moment Captain it may sound tittle-tattle but if you knew the Lady like I do. . . . We were up in the bower, I like going there, the difference, only a minute and whoosh! time to change. . . . The Lady, she's not like I've ever seen her. Can't sit still. Tramping round, really, I couldn't set a stitch. Then out of the blue she says to me, 'The wizard. What did you think of him?'

" 'Think?' I say. 'I think he's the crudest, most brazen—'

" 'Oh, yes.' And she giggles. 'It was your scent-ball, I forgot. Phera, what did you think of him?'

"Phera's chief maid. 'Ugly,' she says. 'That awful scar. Just like you said, ma'am. A bear.'

" 'Ugly?' she says. Sounds quite startled. Phera knots her tongue.

" 'Yes,' the Lady says after a bit. 'He is. Ugly. Insolent. Arrogant. Preposterous. How dare he!' Captain, I've been at court a dozen years, I've seen her rages, but this was all different. Most times nothing shows, you just *know.* But this time . . . she starts storming round, then she catches up her sleeve—Nervian silk, best Tasmarn work, hazian sewn, oh, that dress was the pride of my heart—in her *teeth!* Rip! And her face red as lythian leaves and, 'How dare he? How DARE he? I'll have him strangled! Crucified! I'll—' Rip! I tell you, we didn't know whether to run or pray. 'Preach at me!' Her fan's on the seat, she snaps it in half, crack! 'Sanctimonious beggar! Pious fraud! . . . *Oh, I might even marry you!* How dare he! How *dare* he! I'll, I'll. . . .' Off down the stairs like a whirlwind, we didn't know where to look. And Phera—too big for her shoes, that one, someday she'll trip—she says to me behind her hand, 'If it wasn't him, and wasn't our Lady, I'd say, It's a case with her.' "

She nodded, vindicated, at my speechlessness, and tapped my arm. "Then today it's ten different dresses and boxing Timya's ears and a pet to rebuild the loggia, there's been workmen in all day and none of the designs'll suit, she tore one to shreds and the architect, well, he's . . . disappeared. You know? And this afternoon she comes in the wardrobe. Slates this, rips up at that, I thought I'd vanish too, but, 'Come in the boudoir,' she says. Makes me sit down. Won't do it herself. To and fro, to and fro. 'How,' she says, 'can anyone know? Klyra, do you know what's bad and what's good?'—'Ma'am,' I say, minding the decanter, it's that lovely Thangrian crystal, 'what on earth do you mean? Good's to make the sacrifices and do your duty, like the rest of Assharral.'

"She looks at me, sharp as needles. 'And what's bad?'—'Why, ma'am,' I say, 'displeasing you.'

" 'Ohh!' she says and spins like a top. 'Ma'am,' I say, all of a creep, 'if I've upset you. . . .' 'No,' she says. She pulls at the drapes, that lovely gold velvet—oh, you wouldn't know—'I won't,' she says. 'It's stupid. Plain insanity.' She starts to get angry again. Then she spins round and—Captain, if I didn't know better, I'd think she was scared.

" 'Oh, Klyra,' she says, 'I don't know what to do!'

"Well, I've been here a dozen years and she still seems a girl. 'Sit down, pet,' I say, 'and drink some of this, and don't worry. You just do what you want.'

" 'I can't,' she says. Crying. I've never, ever seen her cry. 'I don't know what I want! Oh, damn him to the fiery pits, I don't know!' And out she goes in tears, Captain, believe me, in tears!

"Then this evening Tannis makes a bear joke and she *rends* him. He's disappeared too. Oh, Captain, you just don't know how it is up there." She gripped her hands together in genuine distress. "I've thought of it all day and I couldn't bear anymore.

I slid out, I thought I'd come to your house, you can tell him—make him stop. He's got the whole of Ker Morrya in such a turn-out, and the Lady . . . let be I'm terrified, I can't bear to see her like that. It ought to be stopped!"

She stared with those grotesquely ringed eyes while I tried to muster my wits. All I found was the conviction that Beryx must know. At once.

"I'll tell him," I said. "You'd best be off. Be careful." We both caught our breaths. "I—think he'll be grateful. But I can't promise it will stop."

As I should have expected, Beryx's reaction was unexpected. At first he did look pleased. The tantrum produced a gleeful chortle. But then he sobered, and by the end there was pity in his face, outright distress.

"Yes," he said, staring into the brazier. "Yes."

This time I kept quiet.

At last he said, "If there was hope, this is what I'd expect. But. . . ." He bit his lip. "Math isn't teaching, or coercion. You have to find it for yourself." He got up and began to pace. Sounding quite tormented, he said, "There's nothing I can do."

Nevertheless I slept better that night, waking in a crystal morning to a sea wind fragrant with salt. As the new guard marched up to Ker Morrya I thought wistfully of bygone days when Callissa and I had sailed a racing dinghy out near the Heads on days like this. . . . We rounded the curve onto the gates. There on a pole before us, bloody and hideous with that bizarre paint over the death scream, was Klyra's head.

I fought in Phaxia. Yet I cannot blame the guard who toppled in a faint. My belly turned over too. People were everywhere, scuttling by with furtive looks, the duty sentries were fish-white and gulping continuously, my troop lost rank, broke step, never was habit such a lifesaving rope.

Somehow we managed the change. The old guard almost flew downhill, I took one step after them, and stopped. I did not know why. Until a moment later the Lady Moriana swirled in a black whirlwind out the gate.

"Captain." A true viper's speech. My eyes shut instinctively, I cringed with eyelids printed by the glare of gold in burning black. Her words pierced, a stiletto, cold, thin, certain death.

"I thought," she said, "that you would wait." My feet moved me after her, willy-nilly, down the street.

The crowds melted from our path like dust. She swept them away, a black silk tornado, more fearful than a tornado can ever be, for when it razes and shatters and rends it does not will the ruin. For that you must go to men. Terror pierced even my trance. The Well, I thought. She was evil, and now it was beyond spite, rampaging, out of control.

How Beryx knew I cannot tell, but he was standing before she entered, his face formed, a battle-line. As she whissed into the vault he said, "She did it from loyalty. Because she cared for you."

She stopped. Her skirts swirled, black froth broken on a rock. Something swept me like a blast of poisoned ice.

He said, "It was embarrassing, yes. She shouldn't have spoken." Again pity was in his face. "She wasn't wise enough not to act."

She was standing quite still. An immobility more fearful than any paroxysm. Almost gently, he said, "I know how you feel."

Her back stiffened. The ripple of an adder rising to strike.

His face snapped taut. "Moriana, wait—"

She pivoted on her heel and her eyes traversed like a catapult. My vision shattered in a hail of golden darts, her teeth showed, the grin of a fury, between those perfect lips.

I was moving forward, toward the closest brazier. Its red mouth filled my sight, its bed of coals needed my touch—

The brazier bounced as if struck by a catapult bolt, flew high and crashed in smithereens, spewing a fiery fan of coals. Beryx nearly shattered my head. *"No!"*

I had staggered half a dozen strides back. It was irrelevant. The other brazier remained.

Something let go, abrupt as a snapped rope. Again I staggered back. They were both on tiptoe, she arched to strike, her eyes black fire that distorted her face, he bowstring taut, and his eyes were white-starred burning green.

"Very well," he said. It grated like crossed steel. "If that's what you want."

How to continue? Words, physical metaphors fail to convey the immaterial, and my memory is crazed by the blast, my own pain. I remember their eyes which seared like branding-irons pressed relentlessly into flesh, that it was like being caught between two suns' hearts, consumed by both. Images of a sort. Black lava tides that clash with tides of green and white, my mind withered in the turmoil's heart. Molten black and white sword-blades that snicker in and out my eyes, hurtling gouts of gold-black, green-white fire that explode on collision in my head. Blindness, and the fire still consuming me. Torn apart, not limb from limb but will from will, sense from sense, thought from thought, fragmented in some vacancy, and the fragments re-torn between two wrestling, rending entities that could not win them and would not give them up. You suppose feeling stops, when pain deprives you of wits, but I have known otherwise. I have been a myriad particles spattered in nothing, and each one had its consciousness.

Shattering was nothing to the re-assemblage. Later I found my surcoat plastered with mud, dirt under broken nails, bruises on palms, knees, skull. And that was only the flesh.

When I stopped voicelessly screaming, and pain cast me up on its further beach, I was sitting on the floor. The Lady stood over me. She was panting, each breath straining the black gown at her breast, her face bathed with sweat, still fixed in its battle grimace. Her bracelet had snapped. Thillians lay round me like fallen drops of ice. And in the straw Beryx was on his knees, doubled over, muscle and bone and mind buckling in company, over-matched.

Given free will, the sight might have made me run about and shriek. Instead I stood up. There is no conveying the sensation of your limbs moved by another will.

The Lady smiled. At that too, given liberty, I might have shrieked.

With a fiend's triumph, she said slowly, lingeringly, ". . . Math."

Beryx stirred. Twisted. Made a pathetic attempt to rise. Fell prostrate. After two or three trials, wedged an elbow under him. Levered it straight. It shook as if palsied, and when it bent he slid helplessly back into the straw.

Then he simply lay there, for an uncounted time, until some shred of body or mind's strength returned. Back humped, still trembling in every muscle, he managed to sit up. Raggedly, he wiped at his face.

The Lady waited. Finally, he looked at her.

She said, "You lost."

He answered, in the whisper of exhaustion, "Yes."

Her eyes turned to me. In the same thread of a voice, he said, "No."

I was beside the brazier. Its red heat held my outstretched right hand, my face. Behind me, he repeated, "No."

She answered, pitiless. "Would you do it yourself?"

My hand poised before the coals. Five, ten, fifteen tallied my heartbeats, in casual interest. That jagged, shaky voice said, "If that's what you want."

She did not reply, but I found I had left the fire, turning, able to see them both. She was still grinning. He was looking up at her. Not in a plea for mercy, but with a kind of wonder that such creatures could exist. Then, effortfully, clumsily, he got himself on his feet and shambled, bear-like in his exhaustion, toward the fire.

She watched. He shook his sleeve back, the bizarre action of a man not wanting to wet his shirt. Not the vilest Phaxian torturer would extort such a price, such a voluntary price, from a one-handed man.

He did not hesitate, plead, look back in a last hope of clemency. He walked straight up to the brazier and thrust his left hand in among the coals.

It must have been the aedr's will. His body flew back like a tight-wrenched bow, his face contorted. And his hand did not stir. He did not make a sound.

The fire crackled, the vault filled with that loathful stench. I heard his teeth grate together. She must have waited to be quite sure she would be denied the final pleasure of screams and writhings and total breakdown, before she said, "Yes."

As his hand met the air he dropped, with a screech of jerked chains, face down in a tangle on the stone. There was no other sound. When he did not move, the Lady, with a gorged, ghoul's satisfaction, turned away. And she chose that I should follow her.

As I tore back from the harborside my mind had divided again, one part raging, The last twist of the knife, the filthy whore, she knows about burns, that's why she sent me so far. . . . I shot across the market, snatched a pot and hethel oil, strewed coins, the other part of my mind cursing, And if you could think when you're snatched, were prepared for it, could fight. . . . I skidded downstairs, across the vault, and with frenzied haste sloshed oil into the bowl.

It must have been some sort of swoon, but also an aedric art. Or wish. After the first stupor he had thrown himself around. The straw was ploughed, he was wound in an impossible knot, blood on his rasped wrists, the left arm twisted somehow in midair, his face driven into the straw. He was making slow, senseless sounds at each hoarse breath, twisting in time with it, grinding his cheek into the stone. But he was quite unconscious. When I jammed his hand in the oil he only gasped, then whimpered again.

I clung to his wrist, fighting to keep the burn covered and the bowl upright. It was too late, inadequate, I knew what was needed, and could not go for it. . . . It seemed the very incarnation of Math when I looked up to find Sivar hovering cravenly at the door.

"Run to my house!" I yelled. "Someone, anyone, get them to give you the Xhen plant, the whole pot! Go on, man, run!"

He excelled my wildest hopes. When the big clay pot of spiky, dull-lime, cactus-like leaves came bumbling down on Sivar's legs there was a white, terrified but obdurate Callissa in its wake.

She knew what to do. She threw down a cloth, ripped off one soft foot-long spike and split it to scour out the translucent green jelly within. "Come on!" she snapped at Sivar.

In less than a minute they had a mound of it. She rapped, "Ready!" I took a good grip, whisked his hand across, she scooped the pulp over it, pulled up the cloth, he had barely time to sob before she was saying, "Other rag. Tear a strip. Tie this on." Then, shoving back her hair. "I'll hold it. You untangle him."

By the time we unthreaded him the Xhen jelly was at work. He was still unconscious, but the terrible writhing had eased, muscles shuddering as they relaxed, and he lay back with sheer exhaustion rather than agony in his face. Xhen. Burnt. I have no idea of the herbalist's name, but in Frimmor it has been Xhen, the burn-plant, time out of mind, and nobody making a garden would leave it out. For soothing and healing burns it is the sovereign remedy.

"Thank you," I said at large, trying to convey all I felt: for the help and for the courage that offered it.

Callissa said nothing till Sivar, eyes whitened at the clay shards and dead coals and thillians, began to edge away, muttering, "Get 'nother brazier, sir?" Then she reeled off a list of provisions long as my arm. Looked at the head on my knee, said, "Water, too," and followed Sivar.

When Beryx came round he lay a good while before, eyes still closed, he whispered, "Sorry . . . Alkir."

"Sorry?" I tried not to explode. "You?"

"My fault." The lashes lay on his ashy cheek, long and black, as if too heavy to lift. "Had to go and fight her. Act. *Blighted* fool. And you had . . . worst of it."

"Not by much." I had carefully ignored the full import of that defeat. "If I could have fought for myself. . . ."

"Don't be—idiot. The Well. Nothing you could do."

Callissa brought the water-bottle in and began, somewhat brusquely, to lave his galled right wrist. Then a thillian made her notice the debris. Her eyes widened. As if we were the twins' age she demanded, "What on earth have you two been doing?"

"The Lady," I retorted. "Not us."

She dropped the bottle. I pointed to his hand. "That should have been mine."

"But," she stammered. "Why? Why you . . . ?"

"Hostage," Beryx whispered. "Should see point . . . Fylghjos. Stayed in the Guard. Why?"

I saw. "You'd do better," I said grimly, "if I'd stayed on her side."

The rudiments of a grin emerged. "Get stupider . . . with

age, Fylghjos." At which Callissa, rallying, exploded, "Well, I don't see! What is this? What do you mean?"

He opened his eyes. "Would you rather," he said weakly, "burn your own hand, ma'am—or let it happen to the boys?"

She shrank. Then she whispered, "But you. . . ."

His face grew mulish. "Nobody shall suffer . . . in my place."

"Did it occur to you," I asked in some indignation, "that I might feel the same?"

His eyes flew wide. "Oh, Four!" And at that Callissa boiled right over.

"Stop being so stupid and heroic and honorable and talk sense, the pair of you! If somebody had to, it's better that—I mean—at least—" As she foundered, his eyes opened on a quite impish glint.

"Quite right, ma'am. Better me than him. No family . . . for a start."

She turned so red it could have burnt. Her eyes flinched away. After a moment she began, "I didn't mean to—I shouldn't have—" And decidedly but gently he cut her short.

"Then call it a debt from the fever. And leave it at that."

He refused the soporific of yeldtar juice, declaring, "This stuff's the best pain-killer of the lot." Recalling he had been burnt before, I added that to the Lady's conduct sheet. But even with Axynbrarve he could not fend entirely for himself. The nursing watch re-enlisted, Sivar endured tirades on his barbering, Zyr became an expert bandage-man. I tried to act a Captain of the Guard, and felt the sword poised over us all. But nothing happened, at least in Zyphryr Coryan. About Ker Morrya, it was no longer possible to tell.

Not until I found myself ascending its marble steps.

Panic burst clear through the trance. Never considering it was mere thought, I yelled as ignominiously as any school-brat.

Beryx, help me! Stop her! Get me out of this!

And was answered, to my total disbelief.

<I can't stop her, Fylghjos. But if I can, I'll help.>

I knew my feet's direction, and I was right. Los Morryan bubbled mirthfully, uncaring. Never had I loathed beauty before. The Lady Moriana stood beyond its spray. In black again, printed with huge ember-red lythian leaves whose long broad dagger blades clashed across my sight.

No doubt I cowered like the veriest worm. The memory of their handling in the vault was still painfully clear.

She laughed. My spine froze. She came forward, rustling over the flags.

"A big brave sword-swinging soldier." She flicked a fingernail across my cheek. "Don't swallow your tongue, Captain. I've brought you here to talk."

My will was released. I leapt back. She laughed again, a cascade of ice. "Do the Phaxians know you're as brave as this?"

That stiffened my spine on its own account. Almost gobbling with fury I said, with the rudest inflection I could manage, "So talk."

She strolled beyond the fountain. Round again. Her eyes touched mine and slid away. Gaining bravado, I rasped, "What do you want?"

She dabbled her fingers in the cascade. "How is your bear?"

"Better," I said through my teeth.

"And does he hate me now?"

"You should know better." With bitter irony, I used his own words.

"More fool he, you think."

I did not have to speak. Her lids lifted, swarms of golden motes adrift in night. "Because of himself, or because of his Math?"

"Eh?" I was past manners, and glad of it.

"Because," she said impatiently, "he's not allowed to hate me, or because he can't?"

"Anyone," I ripped back, "who didn't hate you now could only be someone crazy enough to follow Math."

Her fingers stilled in the silver froth. "Oh."

"Yes, oh." I merely saw a weakness, and was vengeful enough to charge at it.

After a moment, sounding oddly reduced, she said, "You don't believe in Math?"

I opened my mouth. Thought of his burnt hand, the coal throwers, the fever, Klyra, Thephor.

"I believe in justice," I said.

"And your bear only hopes for it."

Beryx might have matched her. I could not. I said sullenly, "If you know, why ask?"

Her eyes came up, steady, straight. "You'd like to see me dead."

No doubt mine replied. She smiled, a small, bitter smile. "Were you ever as loyal to me?"

I could not, dared not reply. Restlessly, she moved away.

"What did he say—afterwards?"

"Don't you know?"

She whirled, her eyes shot an ebony flash, fear melted my bones. "Don't," she breathed, "tempt me, Alkir."

"He said," I mastered my voice, "that he was a blighted fool."

"Nothing else?"

"That it served him right."

"Nothing else?"

"Nothing important."

"Nothing about me?"

I answered with satisfaction, "No."

Again I had an elusive sense of dashed hopes. She was toying with a perridel spray. Gold dust puffed, powdering her hair. She said abruptly, “Why did he tell me about the Well?”

“Because,” I answered wearily, “to lie is Ammath.”

The blossom stilled. She was looking down, a hint of dreariness in the turn of her lips. Truculently, I said, “And why did Klyra have to lose her head for opening her mouth?”

Her eyes came up. Endless, depthless stellar black. “You,” she whispered, “have said more than enough. Walk.”

I fought. That is, my mind kicked and squirmed like a puppy held by the scruff of its neck. My feet continued to advance inexorably toward the parapet and the empty air beneath. Mentally I also screamed with rage and terror more ignobly than before, but I suppose it was an improvement that I could scream at all.

The compulsion broke. A clockwork toy reversed, I ran back almost to the wall, choked a yell, spun for pointless flight—but the Lady Moriana had forgotten me. She was up on the seat, on the back of the seat, skirts clutched high, naked terror in a white naked face. A darre, a full-grown coffin-snake, six satiny pinkish-brown feet of reflexes faster than light and venom that kills within five minutes of the bite, was reared up, its coffin-shaped head weaving as they do when roused, in striking distance of her feet.

Even then I might have helped her. Protective urges in a man, a soldier, any human faced by a serpent, are ingrained deep. But as I wavered Beryx’s voice said in a rush, <Don’t just stand there, get out!>

I ran clean down to the vault, stampeded for the only sure sanctuary. As I burst in, he let out a huge breath and sank back, sweat dripping everywhere, against the wall.

When he could speak, I ventured, “The Lady . . . the snake. . . .”

“Illusion.” He was still breathing hard. “You’d—say. Pellathir. A high art. Had to get you out—somehow.”

But he did not seem relieved. His face was taut, almost bleak. An awful intimation burst on me.

"Don't," he said after a minute, more easily. "I couldn't have put words in your mouth. If she called you there instead of coming here, it was her choice. She had to take the consequence."

"Consequence! Oh, if I'd thought—remembered—only shut my cursed, useless mouth!"

He said with affection, "Clot." I groaned. "So you offended her. So she might have come round if you'd said something else. So I jumped right in on your tracks. Come on, Alkir." I could hear the general, met with disaster, tying a knot, carrying on. "I've blundered worse myself."

But when I looked back from the arch he was staring into the fire with that same braced, bleak expression. A general facing a blunder that will cost more than a battle, more than a campaign, more than an entire war.

As I lay beside Callissa's softly breathing back, that face looked at me from the dark. Don't worry, he had said. Shielding me from catastrophe, refusing to allot the blame I deserved, when Assharral, his life, the very world lay in the scales where I had cast the fatal speck. I writhed. Tomorrow, I vowed, I leave. Quit the captaincy, pack the family, tell him he'll do better without me, it's justified desertion. Leave Zyphryr Coryan, pull out.

As always, the crystallized decision brought relief. Turning over, I went slowly if not easily to sleep.

And woke with a plunge that made Callissa squeak, his voice in my ear as it had been in Lisdrinos, but this time with a grim, controlled urgency that bit like a lash.

<Alkir, wake up.>

Chapter VII

<Wait!> He caught me half off the bed. <Don't let her yell.>

I clapped a summary hand over Callissa's mouth. The orders came in a steady spate.

<When she's calm, tell her to dress herself and the boys for the road. The servants—the cook, a maid? She must get them too. Any more?> The gardener, I recalled with dislike, lived out. <Math be praised, if you don't like him he'll be all right. Your neighbors? Just acquaintance?> I could hear the relief. <I'll rouse the guards. Evis. You value him? I'll wake him too. Fetch every living thing you ever felt a moment's affection for out of that house. Tell your wife to hold them in the garden. As soon as you can, come down here.>

Leaving a disrupted household under the helliens I tore into the streets. The moon was low. It was third watch, civilian small hours, the wagons had come in, the revelers gone home, the peep-o'-day workers were not up. At the Treasury gate I recoiled from a shadow, and Evis confronted me across our naked swords.

"Can't explain," I hissed. "Guard this gate. Anyone doesn't give the password Tingan, chop them. But quiet!"

Words on the boil, I fled down familiar steps. The sight of Beryx stopped them in my throat.

He was on his feet, facing into the wall. Coiled, immobile, the stillness of a wound-down catapult. The air pulsed, the vault seemed to be contracting round me, drawn by the suction of some gigantic mouth. I almost looked to see wind beat the gown about that tall, blade-thin shape.

Tighter and tighter grew the clench. I could not draw, let alone catch my breath. Then his body whipped, lash and recoil. With a blinding green-white flash, a horrendous screech and a shower of sparks, he stumbled backward and all four plated, riveted, deep-set fetter rings tore bodily from the stone.

<Blankets,> he commanded as I reached him. <Never mind me. Muffle these cursed things. No time to cut them now.>

Slashing up blankets I wadded the chains, draped them round him, helped him up, wrapped my cloak over all. We labored upstairs. Across the squeaky marble floors. As sweet fresh air welcomed us into silvered black immensity I heard him draw a long, long breath.

A knot of shadow hovered at the gate. <Thank the Four your guards are scallawags, Fylghjos. Know the tomcat roads.> I could hear the grin. <Send four of them with Evis to the post-house, he can throw rank, can't he? We need fourteen mounts. Two spares back here, the rest to meet at your house. Come on.>

The familiar, groggy, bewildered voices dispersed. Eons later, hooves sounded shatteringly in the street.

Sivar jittered at the bridle while I helped Beryx up. Settling astride with the automatic ease of a cavalryman, he whispered, "Drop the reins on its neck. I can manage now."

More eons later horses fidgeted by our wall. A breath of challenge came. Hissing, "Tingan," I slid to earth, Beryx after me, whispering, "A spare uniform, Fylghjos? I'd better look the part."

In black moontree cloak and surcoat he vaguely did so. Some outmoded caution made me pull the door to behind us. He had lumbered on into the faded hellien shadow, whence I heard his clear, calm, decisive whisper.

"I can't explain now, but we all have to leave. Callissa, you can ride? Sivar'll give you a horse. Yes, Rema, you and Zepha too. You can double up behind Krem and Zyr. Zam, you go with your father. Zem—will you come with me?" Zem's ardent whisper, " 'Course!" and he was propelling Callissa gently but irresistibly down the path.

Off at last, through still-empty streets, my lungs aching with suspense. <Fylghjos,> he said, <tell me at the last corner before the gate. Just think it. I'll know.>

At the corner, feeling a zany, I told myself, *This one.*

Something like the Lady's command closed on my mind. I found I had reined in, heard the others copy me.

<Six guards,> he observed. <Keep yours quiet, Fylghjos.> Then came the just audible, endless, feathery whistle of an indrawn breath.

Heartbeats ticked by. A horse shifted, tossed its bit. Zam was pushed, a small scared puppy, against my heart. The night rang with that seashell murmur of quiet deep enough to hear the blood in your own ears. Beryx breathed out, on and on.

<Go. Lead my horse.>

Fuddled, I reached for a rein. Hooves clopped into motion, loud as a charge. We rounded the corner, here was the empty breadth of the gate square, glow of the guardroom brazier, two surcoated figures, colorless in the moonlight, leaning negligently on the leaves of the open gate.

Evis gasped. I snarled voicelessly, "Shut up!" I could fairly hear the horror of the rest.

Our horses paced forward. One sentinel was propped with folded arms, one grasped a grounded spear. Their breasts moved, their eyes, black hollows in the pallid moonlight, gazed at us. Through us. My mind reeled. I thought, We are invisible. The Arts.

Horse noise unrolled under the arch. We were on the harbor

road. Oblivious, unaware, behind us Zyphryr Coryan slept. An eygnor was in song, deluded by the moon. The road dipped. Beside me Beryx released another superhuman breath and leant forward on the withers of his horse. “Keep,” he said faintly, “going.”

In a minute or two his breathing eased. <You can let go the rein. I’ve got him now. Before you burst, it was Fengthir. A secret Command. We weren’t invisible, I just forbade them to see us. In the morning they’ll swear we never passed. Another check for the hounds. . . . >

Beyond Rastyr he swung us north, but not onto the great highway of Stirian Ven. Instead we took to the forest, committing ourselves to that hidden voice which chuckled, “I probably know Assharral better than any of you. Do you think I slept down there?”

Single file, eyes strained for a bob of the blur ahead that would signal a low bough, we serpentined through forest depths that should have been in uproar with the thump of startled lydwyr, lydyrs’ fff! and rattle in the undergrowth, birds roused to squawk and clatter broken leaves. None of it happened. As at the gates of Zyphryr Coryan we seemed invisible, a dream traversing a dream.

The moon died. Selionur, whitest of stars, blazed down on us as he raced in his brief winter course at the Hunter’s heel. The dew settled, the enchantment of all night journeys lapped us round. Valinhynga topped the horizon, a glittering aerial Well, the sky shallowed, the air assumed that piercing purity which heralds dawn; before a thick shadow copse Beryx said, “We’d best breathe the horses and sort ourselves out.”

After the dismount’s confusion settled I found Callissa pressed to my left side. I put an arm about her and recoiled from a furry third breast, only to realize it was the cat. Zem’s arm circled my right leg, Evis cleared his throat beyond, Sivar wheezed at my back. Further on, Rema was muttering the prelude to one of her formidable complaints.

Before me an invisible Beryx said mischievously, "This is what the military manuals call a strategic withdrawal. In other words, get the devil out of it while you can." Fatigue lay close under the levity. "And if anyone still doesn't know, the devil is a lady this time."

Evis spoke up with the apologetic firmness which meant he would not be denied. "Sir, I can understand you might need to make a—a strategic withdrawal. But what am I doing here?"

"You're here for the same reason as the rest. Because you mean something to Alkir or me, and I've just played a trick the Lady will repay in blood, or worse. I'm glad you brought that cat, ma'am. I wouldn't like to think of an animal flayed or roasted alive just because it belonged to the family of a man who gave me help."

There was a chorus of gasps.

"Oh, yes. Have you never heard of reprisals? If any of you had stayed in Zyphryr Coryan, you would have died. Tomorrow, or the next day—or the one after, if you were really unfortunate." This time nobody gasped. "Now I'm out of reach, she'd mangle anyone even vaguely connected with me." His voice grew somber. "She probably will."

Sivar said in a tight, strange tone, "Sir, these fellers are all outlanders. But my family's back there."

After a moment Beryx asked, "Fisherman, is he? Your brother? Would that boat make Eakring Ithyrx?"

"Probably, sir, but—that's overseas! Foreigners!"

"That's the only chance. Just be quiet."

Silence marched on his heavy, protracted breaths. They eased. Sounding tireder, he said, "I've woken them. They don't understand, but they'll sail on the morning tide."

Sivar mumbled combined protest and thanks. Amver ventured, "Sir, once we helped with the fever, we reckoned we'd all have to run if it came to the worst, but—just what happened, sir?"

A horse behind us uprooted a tussock, mouthed and jingled its bit. I heard the muffled clank as Beryx leant back on a tree.

"The Lady and I," he began, "are having a private war, over what she's doing to herself and to Assharral. To me it's evil, and I'm fighting to have it stopped. Unluckily," it came with wry amusement, "there are many weapons I won't use. I won't lie, I won't withhold truth, I won't break faith or let others suffer for me or kill innocent men for my own ends. So I keep getting thrashed because she will. The Mistress of the Wardrobe told Alkir and me some of the Lady's private affairs. She was so furious it wasn't enough to behead Klyra. She brought Alkir down to me, and she would have made him put his hand in the fire."

I heard men's grunts, Rema's guttural squawk.

"I tried to stop her in a wizard fight, and lost. So I said, I'll burn mine instead. I don't like torture better than anyone else, but it hurts me worse when someone suffers in my place. Call it crazy if you like." That mischief teased me. "It's part of—my beliefs. If I deny it, I've lost the war. That paid for Klyra, but she'd seen a flaw in my guard. Yesterday we upset her again, and I was worried, so I did some scouting, aedric style. Read her thoughts. It's just an art." His voice grew bleak. "She had plans, sure enough. This morning, she meant to torture Alkir's wife and sons in front of me. And now she knows I'd rather suffer than let others do it, there would have been no substitutes."

Callissa gave a throttled sob. Zem's arm about my leg became a tentacle. Evis began thickly, "Love of—" and snapped it off.

"So I had to run," Beryx went on tiredly, "and take you with me. It was what we call a Must."

Dawn whitened behind the trees to reveal they were vyxians, scaly umber monsters lancing up sheer to a cloud of foliage. So that, I thought, as cold horror squeezed my heart, is a Must.

Beryx was staring south, with a haunted, wretched look. In disbelief close to exasperation I thought, He didn't want to go!

A honey-eater gurgled in the scrub. A saeveryr responded, chickle, churr. Callissa's small, high, hostile voice asked the question that was paramount to us.

"Where are you going?"

His face set. The crisis had arrived.

"Phaxia," he said. "Nowhere else is far enough."

He let them shout themselves out. Then he said, "Yes, it's four hundred miles, yes, we have to cross the Stirsselian swamps, yes, we'll be slow as a baggage train, yes, you're technically at war with Phaxia. Yes, we're not prepared for a journey, yes, it's a huge wrench to step out of an entire life. I know. I've done it before. Is there any choice?"

Slowly, among the guards, I saw grim acceptance creep over each face. Evis still looked balky. Rema's bottom lip stuck out like a shelf, Zepha was in tears, Callissa holding her fire. Beryx looked wretched too.

"I'm sorry," he said. "It's a cruel sort of joke. If you were evil, you wouldn't have helped me, if I were evil, I wouldn't care. But you did. And I do. Some of you weren't even directly involved. It isn't just." Pain stirred in his look. "Life isn't just. I suppose that's why we aim for justice above all, and never fully accomplish it."

"To the pits with your philosophy!" Callissa's control snapped. "You've wrecked my husband's career, you've outlawed us all, you've hauled us out here without a fendel or a loaf or a spare stitch between us, you want us to die as foreign beggars in Phaxia, and all you can do is talk philosophy! Well, I won't! I want my house back! I want to be safe! I want my life—like it *was!*" And she burst into tears.

Rema's grievance burst too, Zepha howled in sympathy, the men shifted and looked everywhere but at us. All except Beryx. He watched her weep, as if this were one more penalty he had no right to evade.

When her sobs eased at last, he said tiredly, "There's no answer that will satisfy you, ma'am. The best I can say is—if you go to Phaxia, you may come back. If you stay here, it's certain death."

Evis had made his choice. Looking stark and resolute he squared his shoulders, said, without looking, "Sir, permission to carry on," and went past me to Beryx. "Well then, sir. Do you have any plan? Route? Tactics? Provisions? Those fetters will have to go. And our surcoats. Have you considered disguise?"

"The Lady sees through it." Beryx was regretful. "And every Assharran will be her hands. Haven't you ever caught a 'rebel'? How did you know he was? She told you, of course."

Evis deflated. Beryx grinned. "Cheer up, there's one thing in our favor. Me."

Evis did not look reassured. Beryx said, "We'll keep the surcoats a while." He gestured north. "The highway's just over that knoll. A post-house. You and Sivar could liberate some shoeing tools. Throw your badge around, spin a tale. Valuable beast, has to be re-shod on the spot. . . . A sledge and chisel would do."

They did. With a good deal of trouble the manacles were chewed through on a convenient stump, the left one with blows that must have jarred his burnt hand to the bone. But though white and sweating, he rose with a spring. Shook his arm, sighed, "Math! That's good." Scanned the horses with a cavalryman's eye, and turned to consider Rema, planted broad, bulging and balky on a fallen log, Zepha drooping in her arm. A twinkle dawned.

"We need speed. And if we're not built to make it on

horseback. . . ."

Rema said flatly, "I'm not going. You can turn me inside out with your magic, I'll not budge." She patted Zepha. "Nor will she. The poor child, walking out she is, they'd be wed next new moon. . . ."

The eddy in Beryx's eyes was the image of the weighing, planning mind. Then he said, "Yes."

As Rema's jaw dropped he said, "I'll give you a Ruanbraxe. A mind-shield. It may not block the Well, but you can stay in Assharral. Not in Zyphryr Coryan, do you understand? You must go under cover. A new name, a new past, a new place. If you contact anyone you know, it will kill you both." He forestalled her despair. "It won't be forever, Rema." A pledge, for a dawn he could only hope to see. "I can't explain, but . . . it's the best I can do."

Then he sat on his heels between them, eyes on the ground as he drew those huge straining breaths, until the sweat patched his surcoat and his muscles shuddered as they did in the throes of the other arts.

Rema too was horrified. When he relaxed, whispering, "There," she burst out, hostility forgotten, "Eh, sir, you've near killed yourself! If I'd known—I didn't mean to—"

"I'm used to it." He rose, forcing a smile. "Off you go. I'm sorry to bring you so far out of your way."

After the farewells he watched them leave with anxiety, concern, veritable tenderness, and the insight burst on me like a signal flare: there is the definition. Apologizing to a cook because you cared enough to save her life and it took her out of her way, still worried when she leaves the shelter of your care. That is the reality. Math.

We remounted with Callissa mutely recalcitrant and Zem now on my saddle-bow. From the knoll Stirian Ven showed beneath us, its walkers' and horsemen's lane set between the double-paven carriageways, dotted with traffic, shivery with mirage pools, leaping into the blue northern hazes like the image of unswerving thought.

"She'll expect me to make for Hethria," Beryx said. "We need speed. Traffic's light. Come on. I can use Fengthir to handle that."

Before the noon change of horses I had held his rein a score of times while his eyes went blank and he put forth the fearful effort needed to send carts, carriages, wagons, traveling herds, groups and solitary pedestrians or riders past as if we did not exist. If we trusted the magic by then, we still found it eerie. And none of us was reconciled to its cost.

"Sir," Evis urged as the post-house came in view. "I know we have to change, but I can make up a story. Love of—sir, you'll kill yourself!"

Beryx forced his back straight. Wiped his face. "Story's no good," he muttered. "Got to cover tracks."

We rode in unquestioned. In the same dreamy blindness of ostlers, post-master, pay-scribe, changed our beasts. Mounted. Rode out. I led his horse away down the empty road, while he flogged himself to fulfill the last terrible demands of the art.

When it ended Evis determinedly rammed his mount in and held Beryx up until the worst was over. Though his eyes remained shut, a hint of pleasure showed in his face.

"Did it," he murmured. "Forgotten us. The whole lot." A workman's pride in the conquest of a supremely difficult technical task.

As he said, "Can let go, Alkir," Zam gathered up the bridle and announced in a small but determined voice, "Sir Scarface, you do the magic. I'll manage the horse." And with a tiny, tickled grin, Beryx murmured, "All right."

By late afternoon I had had enough. Over a rise one of Morrya's swift coastal rivers appeared, sparkling khaki and olive under its high-arched bridge, and I said belligerently, "There's cover down there. We'll halt."

He did not demur. Merely whispered, with the sketch of a smile, "Headstrong as a general. And only a captain of guards."

In the upstream shrubs and canebrakes a little glade opened on the bank. While we watered the horses Beryx, like Callissa and the twins, lay flat and immobile on the grass, but as I came over he began to sit up. I cut him off. "We're going to forage. Don't worry. We may not be aedryx, but no one'll see us to forget."

The forage was motley. Two hens, corn-cobs, a helmetful of eggs, a burst waterskin which Sivar, with astonishing resource, had knotted up for Uster to fill, with more surprising skill, from an unsuspecting she-goat. Beryx hiccupped over the story. "Milked . . . upside down!"

He eyed the hens. I said, "I've savaged more of these with a dagger than you've got arts. We'll spit roast them—oh."

"Oh," he returned smugly. "At least you'll have to let me light the fire."

"Flint and tinder," Evis ruminated over a drumstick. "Spoons—pot—cups—salt—mint-tea would be good." He was his old provident self. He eyed Beryx's bandaged hand. Few of us had yet outgrown the fascination of watching him eat with Axynbrarve, fowl fragments flicked deftly into his mouth.

"Good practice," he informed us. "Just needs delicacy. Which I lack." Now he followed Evis' eye to the grubby linen, and shook his head.

"We'll do all that in Frimmor." He lay back, head rubbed sensuously into the grass. "How I wish I didn't need sleep. I want to look at the sky."

At sunset, to our unbelief, he woke fresher than we did. "You bounce back fast," he explained, "when you're used to Ruanbrarx." And night travel was easier, with only the post-house people to demand his arts.

I soon grew anxious about Callissa instead. The boys were all right, dozing in our arms at the walk, bouncing grimly stoical at the trot, but she was still taciturn, the cat clutched in her arm, her face growing more pinched with every mile. Such a ride was arduous enough for fit, healthy men. For a woman, used to the house. . . .

Second watch came and went. The traffic had vanished. I had grown jaded myself. When I glanced back, Sivar was shadowing Callissa's beast. Beryx slowed his horse on her other side, and I heard his almost humble, "Ma'am, will you let me help?"

"How can you?" Fatigue. Unflagging antipathy.

"If you let me, I can give you a Command."

"Do something to my mind?"

"Ma'am . . . I won't read your thoughts. I won't—do anything you'd dislike."

After a moment she said ungraciously, "If I must do this, I may as well save trouble for the rest."

There was silence, while we all listened fearfully for another of his magic's punishing variants. But Callissa just asked fretfully, "Is that all?" And he returned with a smile in his voice, "Until it finishes, and you fall apart."

When Valinhynga rose he called a halt. Too weary for talk we followed him from the road, crawled off our horses, picketed them and collapsed.

I woke with the sun in my face and a root in my back. Having remedied both, I found myself in a green-and-gold precinct, a clump of huge old kymman trees gone wild, their low-slung branches and thick ferny foliage completely hiding us from the road. I could hear it, though, within bowshot. Grind of wheels, bellowing calves, herdsmen's shouts. The low sun struck under the trees to catch a bit, a horse's eye, a dewy spider web, silver on a mounded back. I lay luxuriating in rest as you do only when very tired, idly counting the kymman's brown peanut-shaped fruit, feeling Callissa curled behind me, still asleep. The twins, I saw, somewhat startled, had burrowed into Beryx's cloak, into his very sides, I should think. He himself was awake, and looking past me. I rolled over, at the feeling in his eyes.

All over Frimmor and Morrya lythians grow wild. Acquainted with them from childhood, I hardly noticed. Now it seemed I had never seen one before.

It was a big bush, man high, twice as wide. The thin sappy stems and glossy serrated dark-green leaves were lost against other foliage, but the blossoms were staring bright, shaggy crowns that spread from the curly upper tips to the broad daggers of the petals' foundation, splashes of jagged vermilion, indescribably brilliant in sunlight upon a blue dawn sky.

Unplanted, I thought. Untended. Unwished for, undesired. And undeterred. I turned to Beryx, feeling for myself the joy and wonder and gratitude for earth's off-hand magnificence that had made his eyes glisten with tears.

After a moment he spoke. Even in mindspeech it was hushed. One word, but now I knew a fraction of what it meant.

He said, <Math.>

We breakfasted, fully if not fillingly, in somebody's ferroth grove. The head-sized, green-and-orange-streaked fruit with their rich yellow pulp and black, loose, jelly-coated seeds, should really be eaten with a spoon, and the twins emerged daubed from head to foot, but much refreshed by the delightful task of assisting Beryx, the worst off of all, since he could not even grasp the piece he tried to bite. But hilarity faded swiftly on the march.

Evis had pressed for a wait till dark. Beryx replied, "No time." We were in the Cessala, the unbroken thirty miles of caissyn farms that produce the spear-high purple sweet-grass whose stalks are crushed for sugar juice, and it was harvest, every farmer cutting or carting or burning off. Billows of black smoke severed Stirian Ven, the roadside fields were going up to heaven in red and yellow ranks of flame, or full of sooty harvesters who swung long hooked knives in the van of numberless pickers-up, stackers, and haystack-high bullock carts. The road itself was one long stream of them. The fires' heat distressed us all, but for Beryx they must have been purgatory itself.

After five miles I saw a lane that offered cover and veered my horse. He snarled, <Curse you, get on!>

In another mile Sivar had annexed Zem. In a second Evis was holding Beryx on the horse. After another two a post-house came in sight. Evis began, "Sir, we must tell a story this time, you can't—" and got a savaging of his own, a straightforward, brutal, <Shut up!>

How he managed it I do not know. But he did, drawing one breath of triumph rather than torment before we were back in the flood.

That day if ever I profaned Math, for I cursed those bullock-drivers' simple existence, and they were innocent men. The sun climbed, reinforcing the fires, we were all awash with sweat, and still they came, one after another without so much as a breathing space as they plodded along beside their tall white teams, plenty of time to look about. Whistling, some of them, the final maddening iniquity. Blithely unaware that they were putting Beryx through a torture that would make kindness of the rack.

Around noon we found a farm track that ran into an unburnt field. This time I simply swung the troop aside and ignored his furious, <Alkir! Curse you, stop!>

Round the first bend we halted, Amver and Dakis leaping off to catch and lower him, still impotently spluttering, into the meager shadow of his horse. The tall ranks of caissyn rustled overhead, the sun weltered in the narrow track, while we stood over him and mutely paid our dues to Math in the knowledge that this was borne for us.

For a good five minutes he simply lay there, every muscle limp, the scar staring purple in a bloodless face. Zyr clumsily wiped his forehead. Evis beat off flies. At last his eyes opened, dull black, drained dry.

Fraction by fraction, the green returned. His breathing crept up to the audible. He blinked. Then the thunder burst upon our heads.

If you ever doubted he had led an army, you would have known then. At the mere preamble every drillmaster I ever knew would have wept and confessed himself hopelessly outclassed. For range and scope and unfaltering flow of invective I never heard its equal, but it was the tone that put it far beyond a drillmaster's scope. Sheer awful authority, descending to annihilate us in god-like wrath.

When the pulverizing finished, he had finally got his breath. Then his face changed. With ludicrous horror he exclaimed, "Oh, dear! Oh, drat! I've done it again!"

The contrast was too much. We held our ribs and fell about. With tears of laughter in his eyes Evis gasped, "Oh no, sir! Don't regret it—just hope I can remember a bit!" I could feel the grin stretch my own face as I added, "No, sir, I'm grateful to be taught my place. I'll never call myself fit to chew out a defaulter again."

"But," he wailed, "I'm not supposed to do that anymore!" At which Evis patted his shoulder, saying kindly, "Never mind, sir. It was an education. Now you just relax and get your wind."

It was all he would delay for, and afternoon was worse. Never have I been so thankful as when the carts thinned and the caissyn fields tailed off into the foothills of the Frimmor range.

There is an inn at the pass foot. Since he fainted clean away after the final cart, Sivar was free to dart into its kitchen and annex a fistful of cups and a mighty kettle of mint-tea, from which we all recruited our strength. As we rode off I glanced back to see a sooty child, clearly a scullion, gaping after us. I glanced at Beryx, and kept quiet. One child could hardly prove dangerous, and he had driven himself hard enough.

Frimmor range is just a winding climb among the tawny coastal hills, and traffic was blessedly light. Beryx reached the crest with strength in hand for a last view of Morrya, patches of opulent black soil, lush cultivation and lusher natural greenery spread into the smoke haze, steaming under the humid sun.

"So rich," he said under his breath. "So much potential. How could you want Ammath, when you owned a province like that?"

"Isn't Everran," I asked, "like that?"

He came to himself. "Everran was poor land," he answered. "A lot of it desert, most only fit for hethel trees and grapevines. Nothing like this."

"Was," I thought. Everran, supreme happiness, had been deliberately, irrevocably put behind him. A sacrifice. At least two of the Phathos' cards had spoken truth.

We changed horses at the post-house on the crest. This time he wobbled out in the yard and personally chose every horse, the selections of a cavalryman. And chosen, I noted with foreboding, for stamina above all else.

<Yes,> he agreed without looking at me. <We won't be changing these for a long, long time.>

Frimmor is just high and dry enough for grain, chiefly fed to the ubiquitous milking herds and more ubiquitous pigs. Most of Assharral's cheese and bacon come from us. The crops patch into the rolling red-and-yellow-green landscape with its dirt tracks to each whitewashed farm, the earth tank and cultivation and selected groves of shade-trees, the paddocks grazed by phalanxes of red or roan milking cows. A quiet, prosperous, mellow land. I had never coveted its kindness, till I saw it through Beryx's eyes.

Sunset, fading golden to prettify our stubbly faces and mistreated clothes, found us at the bypass for Tengorial. Stirian Ven makes no concession to towns. In its path, it goes through, otherwise it goes past. Callissa eyed the faded sign with her first show of life. Evis eyed it too. Hungrily.

"Sir," he suggested, "if we asked for dinner at a farm . . . couldn't you make them forget?" Evis is not one to let weapons, however unusual, rust in his hand.

Beryx weighed it. Then he said, "The next useful cover, two of you can go and ask a farm for whatever they'll give. If it's not enough, don't press them. We'll try somewhere else."

On or off the road, Frimmor has little cover. We ended under a stand of tall silvery hisgal whose boughs offered little more than midday shade, and the very grass beneath had gone for travelers' fires. Beryx slid off and lay flat, leaving it to us. When Karis and Krem brought back a bucket of milk, a cooked ham and a wheel-sized cheese, he roused to blot their tracks, but then he lay back again, a shadow in the dusk. And we were so hungry it was a shameful time before we remembered him.

"No," he murmured, waving away Evis' fist-thick wedge of ham and cheese. "Later, perhaps. Not yet."

In consternation we coaxed and begged. To no avail. Evis gave up in patent distress. Callissa had been supervising the twins, with brittle severity. Now she muttered, "I've had enough of this!" snatched the disdained food and bore down on him.

"Sit up!" There was no kindness in her voice. "You have to eat, and you will, if I push it down your neck." She cut off his answer in her no-appeals nursery voice. "Don't say, Can't, to me." She broke a piece of cheese and prepared to make good her threat. "Open your mouth!"

"Oh, Math!" he lamented. Then he struggled onto an elbow.

"All right, ma'am. I know when to do as I'm told."

We were still resting on our stomachs when he said apologetically, "I know you're all very tired. But . . . tonight may be the last time we can use the road."

The silence was more eloquent than words. Then Zyr said grimly, "If you c'n do it, sir, so c'n we."

Few Frimmans travel at night. After a time we adapted the long-distance cavalry mode, half an hour ahorse, five minutes afoot, while Beryx nursed us with the skill of the born cavalry commander, who senses just how much beast and man can bear before he must slacken the rein. Once I recall gazing up at the constellations learnt from so many campaign watches, drowsily telling him the Assharran names. Tirstang, its five stars rolled over by the passage of the night, the sparkle of the two bright Ethryn pointing in to it. Firkemmon, its crooked scourge sweeping across Ven Selloth, the stars' own highway, the golden eye of Heshyr shepherding us from the west. And at last Selionur, as he rose at the Hunter's heel to bring the morning watch.

I woke with my head on a curb and dew on my cloak in what resembled a battle's aftermath. Loose horses browsed in the ditch, men lay with an arm through the reins, propped on each other, on curb or gatepost, oblivious. Sivar was actually upright, his horse's neck in an affectionate embrace. At my back Callissa's arm pinned a restive cat. Beyond her the twins had been laid out straight and rolled in a cloak. Beryx sat over them, finedrawn and pale, watching in the sun.

Looking past him, I started to see a gate known all my life. With a dogged grin he asked, "Think they'll feed their wandering boy?"

"We had to hurry," he said as the rutted track led us past the five black-butted morgars where I cantered my first pony after truant cows, past the sorghum patch, the milking yard, the orange orchard fence. The dairy rose ahead, the red house-roof, I could hear the squeal of dining pigs. Then his last words caught up. ". . . take them a while to pack."

Reason was sluggish. We topped the last rise. I said, "They won't go."

"What!" he sounded alarmed.

"My father's been here from birth. Like my grandfather. And his father. Even for . . . the Lady . . . I doubt he'll go."

Callissa struck in vengefully, "They won't. They're pharraz. Like my people. They don't leave their land for flood or fire or drought, or any trouble on earth."

Beryx shut his eyes. I saw that until now I had only thought him tired.

Callissa pressed on with rising triumph. "And if they would, Alkir has three brothers and two sisters, I have two of each. They're all married. With families. Are you going to uproot them all—not to mention fifteen or twenty uncles and aunts?"

Beryx said with unutterable weariness, "Let's have breakfast first."

He did his best. After my father had kicked a dozen truculent dogs, tilted back his ancient hat, drawled, "Ah, Alkir. You back?" After my mother kissed me, and we had devoured an entire milking, a side of bacon, three days' eggs and a week's sorghum porridge, when Callissa had fallen asleep on her plate, the twins had been borne out and the rest succumbed on any vacant floor, Beryx argued with conviction, urgency, unflagging energy, and unfailing respect.

My father, a little thinner and more stooped than I remembered him, sucked a sorghum stalk and said, "Ah," in the right places. At the end, he announced, "That's all as may be. But this is my land. Whatever comes, I'd as lief it found me here." While my mother smiled at Beryx and said, "I'll warrant that's made you dry, young man. You'd best have another drop of tea."

Then I did my part. They listened with slightly more interest, exclaiming, "Well, well!" and, "Fancy that!" Then my mother enquired mildly, "But, son, what on earth would the Lady want with us?"

Beryx put down his cup. He did no worse, till an unlucky mention of his wizardry woke my father up.

"Are you, by'rLady! Then just you come and look at this cow. Two heifers the goodwife had from me, and she's drier than when I asked. . . ." Beryx was swept off, to return still protesting his ignorance of cows, and so seal his rout. My father retired on the sorghum. Beryx sat on the doorstep, head in arm, shoulder to a jamb. I propped the other side, taking and I hoped giving comfort in defeat.

"They have to come," he said into his arm. "They're the first ones she'll—and we've killed ourselves getting the head start to—it can't be much longer. Alkir, can't you—"

"I stopped arguing with my father at fourteen," I said, "and joined the army to find someone I could beat."

Evis, who had vanquished sleep, came up demanding, "Sir, can't you make them? Give them a—a Command?"

Beryx lifted his head. He was red-eyed, with that strung air of a man functioning on pure will. "It would not," he said flatly, "be right."

I said, "Not even as a Must?"

"No."

Evis fell quiet. I looked at the filthy bandage and said, "We should do something about that."

My mother was helpful, though palpably shocked by the wound. But when she said, "However did you do this, young man?" and he retorted, "Put my hand in the fire to save Alkir burning his," her eyes merely rounded, before she said, "Very kind of you, I'm sure." Frimmor is too far from Zyphryr Coryan to credit city barbarities.

As she tied off the bandage Beryx gave a jaw-breaking yawn. Then he said, "We'll wait for dark," rolled himself in his cloak and the cloak in a corner, and plummeted into sleep.

At Rise-and-shine I caught a maternal reprimand for dragging Callissa about the country like a thief—"what would her people say?" Callissa, scrubbing viciously at the boys' noxious coats, supplied the rebuttal in a toneless voice. "He won't leave the wizard. The boys won't leave him. And I can't leave the boys." I withdrew before I said something to regret.

Evis was assembling his commissariat, while Beryx checked hooves and backs. After one glance at his brisk bright eye I asked, "What have you planned?"

"Magic," he said cheerfully. "Phatrexe and Pellathir."

"Translate."

"Phatrexe. To write a message, on a gem, a chair, a horse, a man, keyed to the right receiver's mind. Yes, it would be the cipher of the world. I'm going to write on this whole farm." I gasped. "A big job, yes. I don't think it's been done before. I'll write in Pellathir." His eyes danced. "If anyone comes here meaning harm, they'll trigger what I write."

I gulped, gasped. Rallied. "But will a—an illusion . . . ?"

"Imagine if you ride up here bent on mayhem and lightning strikes in front of you—darres wriggle out—demons charge your flank—" He was chortling. "Then a wizard materializes overhead and says 'Get the blazes out!' You think that won't work?"

"Uh—uh—I suppose it might! But—can you do it?"

"Oh, yes. It might take a little time."

The understatement of all time. It took perhaps half an hour and cost him more than the whole day in Cessala suffered at once. I was quite sure he had killed himself. I could not hear a breath, find a pulse, I held a drenched, boneless corpse. Then his lips parted on a single silent breath.

<Saddle—up.> The very mindspeech was a thread. <Ready . . . by then.>

He was. Erect, revived, saying with patient emphasis, "Yes, sir, but *if* anyone offers harm to your or Callissa's family, you must bring them all out here. I can't guarantee it, but I think the magic will protect you. It's important, sir."

"Keep the weevils off the sorghum?"

"No, but—"

"Urrhum. Thought magic'd at least do that."

Beryx cast his eyes up, then retorted with restraint, "I'm not a weevil-master, I work with minds. Point taken, Alkir. Let's go."

Of the two hundred miles from Frimmor range to Gjerven we covered forty that night. Cross-country, zigzagging to farm gates, skirting dog-ridden homesteads and towns, off and on secondary roads, cantering more often than not, swift and unseen as ghosts. "I always did like," Beryx remarked, "to get along. And this is easy. Just have to find the way."

"Oh, yes," I said politely. It was barely starlight, we were in a maze of ploughland, I had no idea where, how we had got in, or how we would get out. "You can see in the dark?"

"No need. I'm using Phathire. And I scouted in the light."

His high spirits were infectious. Valinhynga rose as we bivouacked in someone's old hay-shed, and while we watered the horses I heard Sivar emitting noises that could only be an attempt at song.

We dined palatially with mint-tea in cups and hot porridge spooned from a pot. That night was dark of the moon. "Lovely," said Beryx. "Black as a morval's heart. No need for cover.

And the Lady's still waiting for a nibble on her Hethrian lines."

That night saw off another thirty miles. Amid general satisfaction we halted in what must have been Frimmor's last uncleared tarsal scrub, and set a watch on the horses, knee-hobbled to graze. Uster woke me at noon. Couched in the maze of shadow, silver leaves, subtle gray boughs and boles and fallen timber, bathed in the warm broken light, idly scanning the horses' abnormal blotches of color and the sleepers in their artful tangle of boughs, I watched a ploughman snail up and down his chocolate-red ridge, not half a mile away, oblivious.

When I woke again, shadows at every possible angle barred the golden light of evening which flooded the scrub. Beside me Beryx and Zem, unbreathing, watched a lydwyr buck, his doe and a youngster feeding up to us. A patch of fallow red, a black nose, a long dragging tail, melted and reformed in the sun's windows, only movement flawing their superb camouflage.

The wind yawed. The buck jerked up. The doe bounced. All three bounded away, jiggering wildly as the horses blocked their path. Beryx and Zem shared a silent laugh. A moment later the camp was astir to what was already routine: gather firewood, assemble food, saddle up. The easy efficiency of a seasoned patrol early in the campaign. Before the battles and the losses start.

Sometimes a mere thought can tempt bad luck. I was still feeling complacent when I noticed Krem.

He had been bringing an armful of wood. Slowly, deliberately, yet with a weird unnaturalness, he came to a halt. His arm opened. The wood fell out. He drew his sword. Then he about-turned to advance on Beryx, perched on a nearby log, blank eyes turned south in his own reconnaissance.

Instinct forced my shout, caution throttled it. But Beryx had already spun to hurdle the log with one hand flying out as his eyes shot a green flash and he hissed, "Stop!"

The bustle shattered as everyone woke up. Some ran in, some back, Callissa gagged her own shriek to snatch the twins behind the fire, horses snorted in contagious fright. Krem was still walking, sleep-slow, arrow-straight. Beryx dodged wildly in the timber so for one corrosive instant I thought he was in flight. Then a sun-patch caught his eyes, jade laced with lightning, and I changed my mind.

The chase went on, a nightmare pursuit, Krem angling through the obstacles while Beryx circled and zigzagged in wild jerky motions that resembled abject rout. I saw Karis' and Evis' faces move to disbelief, rising contempt, and wanted to bawl, You're wrong!

Then Beryx's eyes shot a gout of pale green fire that dulled the sun. He whipped upright and froze, muscles set like adamant. I heard the first huge intaken breath.

Krem was still coming. Fifteen feet. Ten. An automaton, a puppet's mechanical, mindless advance. Beryx was gasping, heavy cough-like grunts jerked out by an exchange of blows dealt with all his aedr's might.

They were five feet apart. Krem waded, as in thigh-deep mud. Beryx's eyes brightened intolerably, his body arched to some stupendous stress. As Krem's arm began to swing Evis ran in behind him and swept his sword two-handed in a swipe that all but took the head clean off.

As the body spun with head flopping sidelong from that thick red jet and the limbs flailed in their hideous dance I lunged at Callissa and whirled her into the twins, roaring, "Behind the horses! Till I call!" I had no mind to afflict my sons with the memory of such a death.

Krem finished on the rim of the fire. Sivar gulped, "Thank the—" We all stood shaking at the supernatural's assault, the escape. Only Beryx was still locked in his fight.

The fulcrum must have been a shaven second before Evis struck. Now he was shuddering, jerking, with a barbaric grin of triumph slamming home blows to seal the enemy's rout. His shoulders arched up, he laughed aloud as you do in the field upon the killing stroke. Stepped back, gasping, a raw jubilance in his sweat-drenched face. And saw Krem's corpse.

I had time to think: I saw Gevos die. I should have warned Evis.

"B-but sir," he was stammering. "He would have killed you! I couldn't . . . Sir, I didn't mean—I only thought—I didn't *understand!*"

Beryx's eyes were still on the body. I saw the anguish become that quiet, desolate despair he had shown over Gevos. The words burnt in my mind: *Velandryxe. The ultimate wisdom is not to act at all.*

Evis cried, "Sir, I'm sorry, I shouldn't have—please don't look like that!" He too had sufficient Math to suffer for a mistake.

The desolation faded, willed into abeyance by greater imperatives. Math demanded that he console the destroyer, not mourn the destruction of another part of Math.

"Don't worry, Evis." He said it gently, no touch of sarcasm. "I know you did it for the best."

The burial party returned, wiping earthy swords, just as I finished kicking dirt round by the fire. Callissa crept back. I felt two small arms lock round my legs, and sat on a log to embrace them instead. Beryx dragged his eyes round the hushed, daunted group.

"She's found us," he said.

He sank slowly on his heels. With a stab of guilt I wondered if my scullion had shown the trail.

"That was the Well. I might—not have broken her Command in time." I knew he had changed his words to spare Evis. "So to be sure of ourselves now, if of nothing else—I'll free every one of you." A brief glimmer of amusement. "From the spell, you might say. Zem, will you come here?"

Like Thephor, when my turn came I wondered, Is that all? Just looking into his eyes, into that incandescent green that burnt furiously, magnetically, while he put forth another gigantic effort, and I felt nothing at all.

He sat back, wheezing, and retorted, <I hope nothing's enough.>

Evis flapped, saying, "Sir, you must rest—" He shook his head and looked at Callissa, the only one left.

Callissa backed around the fire with a sharp, panicky "You're not touching me."

My forbearance failed. I addressed her like a ranker for the first time in my life. "Come here and do as you're told!"

"No!" She backed faster, in a moment she would run, at full stretch I just caught her elbow and yanked her round with a harshness wrung from my own taut nerves. "Come here!"

She struggled, I subdued her, one hand over her mouth, she fought in a frenzy as Beryx struggled up and approached. Yet there was only concern and shame and affliction in his look.

"Ma'am"—it was entreaty—"please don't distress yourself." I sensed her fear had opened an old wound. "I don't want to harm you. You mean as much to me as Alkir." He lifted his left hand. "If I did this for him, how can you think I'd mean ill to you? Please think a moment. If I leave this, you're open to the Lady. Like Krem. And she won't turn you against me. She'll use you against Alkir. Or the twins."

He waited, a suppliant. Once more I thought bitterly how powerless is power that binds itself in goodness' chains.

Callissa's muscles loosened. I let go her mouth. With a different sharpness she said, "The twins?"

"What it can't best," he said, "Ammath will do its utmost to hurt."

Another pause. Then, steeling herself, she said sourly, "If I must."

Chapter VIII

There was no sparkle in that night's ride. Oddly enough, Krem's absence depressed me most of all. Odd in such a peril, odder because he had been a purebred Gjerven, black to the whites of his eyes, so the one time I should not have missed him was at night. . . . I berated my mind back where it belonged, with my horse. If Beryx had been "getting along" before, he was now in downright haste.

Long before dawn we were installed in a tumbledown abandoned milking shed. Blundering over the debris of bails to feel through the acrid scent of ancient manure for each salt-caked shoulder, steamy back, drooping neck, I thought grimly, If this keeps up. . . .

"It can't," Beryx said at my elbow. "We must have fresh horses tomorrow. It's still sixty miles to Gjerven as the morval flies."

"Sixty! It can't be!"

"We veered west tonight; tomorrow we'll go east. Try to lose her." The cloud lifted a moment. "You'd never think, would you, that the one thing to foil an aedr, even with the Well, would be simple dark?"

I could not share his frivolity. "But the horses—"

"Alkir, do you know where we are? Five miles west of Vendring. What's a mile to its east?"

I thought, remembered, was deprived of breath. I sat down precipitately on a broken bail. "You wouldn't—you couldn't—even you wouldn't—not the imperial stud!"

"Oh?" He was snickering like an urchin. "Why not?"

"Why *not?*" Then it got the better of me. I let out a guffaw. "You madman, if the Lady doesn't crucify you, Zabek will!"

"Then," he said solemnly, "we should get the fastest possible beasts." And we both folded up.

Every soul in Assharral knew the imperial stud, the light of the Lady's heart. Its stallions were the cream of field and track, its mares sprang from an old pure line that was every other breeder's despair, its cast fillies went to the knackers, its cast colts sold as geldings for an outrageous price. Its champions carried the Lady's colors, its other progeny were the pride of the cavalry, which was the pride of Zabek. Once, back from a posting in Gjerven, I rode past, just to look. The huge immaculate stables, the lush green white-railed paddocks, the gloss of a farm free of an empire's purse, all paled before the stock. Mares with foals at foot, playful yearlings, two-year-olds walking out for the breakers, stallions bugling from their pens. And for any single one a horseman would sell his soul.

"We go in," Beryx squatted under the fallen door-beam, "about middle of first watch. After night round, before they check the heavy mares. You, me, Zyr, Evis. We're in luck. The cavalry draft goes next week." I practically heard Zyr's mouth water. Like all Axairans, his true god is a horse.

"Er—" Evis cleared his throat.

"Evis," Beryx reproached him. "Have you never lifted a horse? Blanket boots. We'll make them today." He twitched his cloak. The crowning insult, to hide the theft of the Lady's treasure in her own guard's gear, blazoned with her crest. "I know the way. And I think I can still control a horse or two. Someone will see us? Evis, you positively wound me. Don't you think I'm a wizard at all?"

The four of us left the rest at the brood pasture end, under a huge kymman clump, horses solemnly commanded to "Keep it quiet." Snaking up the pasture, Beryx clicked and murmured to shadows that snorted or leapt, then stood with spellbound serenity in our wake. Past the exercise yards. The stables snorted and rustled and sighed, the human quarters shone with blithely ignorant lamps. Beryx strode down the long aisle as if he owned it, lightning selections, a low "Stand, child," and we slid in to the sniff, the shine of a liquid, curious, tranquil eye, the still more amazing docility with which they let us tie on the blanket boots, lead them out. Twelve colts we lifted, and never a one so much as jibbed.

Quite speechless, we slithered outside. Back across the pasture, never a nicker heard. Trembling with tension and unbelief we saddled up, the colts steady as old cavalry mounts. Swung up. "Come on," Beryx bade beasts and men. Our old mounts fell in like dogs. An owl called in praiseful derision as we rode away from the most brazen, impossible horse-theft ever perpetrated in Assharral. Ho-ho-o-oke! Ho-ho-o-oke!

Three miles east Beryx called a halt. "Good lad," he murmured, bandaged hand rubbing behind his old mount's ears. "You did so very well. Off you go." They all melted away. "And now," he bubbled into gaiety, "let's get out of here."

"You do know," I cantered beside him, reveling in the colt's effortless rake of a stride, "that if all Assharral wasn't hunting us before, by the pits, they will be now!"

"Might as well annoy her," he answered blithely. "You know the saw: Lost temper, lost fight."

Thirty-five miles later we found the outbuildings of a disused inn. "How," I wondered, "do you ferret out such. . . ." and he laughed. "I had ample time to look."

It dawned on me then that every step of this journey had been minutely, meticulously planned. The horses were still willing to go, but he shook his head. "Save them. Tonight we'll need every ounce of it." He grew grim. "If not before."

No one asked his meaning. Nor did anyone cavil at clambering in turn to the musty hayloft where we stood to crane through a skylight at the four dusty roads that converged upon the inn, while the others slept amid our splendid loot. Zyr would rather have used the day to worship his tall lean yellow-dun colt. "Magic!" he said over and over. "If this is magic I'll—I'll turn wizard myself!"

Beryx grinned and retorted, "Partnership?" But his sleeping face, slack, stripped and spent, revealed the foray's cost. Wrevelan'x on not one but twelve horses, first at the stud, then over forty fast-ridden lightless miles, had exacted a price beyond even the value of the prize.

I plunged awake to Sivar tearing at my shoulder with awful urgency in his face. "Sir, cap'n, save us, there's dogs 'n hoes 'n pitchforks 'n I dunno what 'n half the country headed this way!"

Up the ladder I shot. He was right. All four roads bore a turbulent cloud of closing dust, too irregular for troops. My eye made out the gleam of domestic weaponry, the uniform of farmer, cowman, roadman, cook, Krem's purposeful dream-like advance. Not an enraged but an enlisted mob.

We fled forthwith, straight north between two roads at flat gallop to outstrip the pincers instantly thrust from each flanking crowd. As we drew clear I glanced back. The vanguards had slowed to a stop. Spilt aimlessly. Were gaping at each other, at their weapons, clumped in bewildered groups, scratching their heads.

Beryx laughed aloud. "It'll be the riddle of the century," he called. He steadied his horse. "Hang on, ma'am." His bay rose to a sagging gate, I heard Callissa squeak as hers sailed over in his wake, and wondered how she was holding him. I was hard put to do that myself.

Across a cow pasture we poured, Beryx slowed, and with prideful expert's riskiness Zem leant far out to slip the gate chain. Beryx glanced at the sky. An hour after noon. Flushed out, I thought, and the hounds running on sight.

It was a harrowing afternoon. We ducked and dodged erratically to avoid farms and mask our route, pursued with vain zeal from Kenath and Imarval, with three gallops to evade those menacing puppet crowds which sprang up full in our path. It cost time and distance and horse-flesh, yet I could see we were still making what could be called a dash. And that however zigzag, our general progress was north.

The inn, I judged, had been twenty miles from Gjerven as a morval flies. We must have ridden more like thirty, but in third watch the horizon bulged, and my heart leapt. Every soldier back from Phaxia hails them as homecoming's seal, the rank of crooked, thumb-like pinnacles which line the Frimman glacis. The Fallers, they call them, though they remain upright. The Gazzath.

By then we were deep in Gazzarien district, which grows the rhonur whose white bolls spin a finer thread than wool. In every direction rank upon arrow-straight rank of chest-high bushes marched off to clash across the next farm's ranks, the sun weltering down on their humid greenery while the Gazzath swam in a blue murk of heat. Somewhere to the left was Veth Gammas, the best and chief way down the two-thousand-foot drop known as Gazzal, the Fall. I was still squinting for it when Evis, the tail-scout, let out a yell of dismay. "Sir! There's cavalry behind!"

No mistaking them. At least three troops, the flicker of armor, the geometric formation so different from civilian riders however purposeful, retained even at the gallop. As these were.

Beryx checked, Callissa went white. Zyr's eye flashed. Amver groaned. Evis shouted, "Sir, we can't waste a moment, we have to reach the road, we'll be pincered on that cliff—" Beryx rapped, "Quiet!" in a voice that shut us all up like traps.

"Math," he said, wheeling for one quick scan. "I didn't want to do this." He licked a finger. The wind was vigorous, from the north. "Waste. Wanton waste. . . . Hold your horses. I said hold them, not put them in leading strings!"

Quelled, we each took an iron grasp of the bit. He drew one protracted stertorous breath. Then his eyes spat green fire and the length of the rhonur rank behind us went up simultaneously, a half mile of tinder-dry white bolls that exploded in fusillades of eager flame.

Wrestling my colt, I saw his eyes' second flash. Another rank went up to the left. Traverse. Flash. Another on the right. Two, three miles of fire took hold and swept enthusiastically away before the wind, pouncing on the uppermost bolls and hurdling to the next rank as if the six-foot intervals did not exist.

Beryx's breath escaped on a single concussive sob. He collapsed on the bay's wither, it spun and reared and in horror I slammed my own beast in to back up Zem's brave snap on the bit.

The colt dropped and stood, Wreve-lan'x restored. Beryx straightened, as if crippled, face dripping sweat. Croaked at Zem, "Good lad." Took a last look at the fire. Three long-drawn breaths. Then he wheeled his horse. "Now," he said with that general's intonation, "sit down and ride!"

We parted the rhonur bushes like a stampede, rushing them breast-deep, cramming the colts to prevent a balk, we jumped whatever divided their formations, gate, ditch or fence, we took gullies as they came, we scattered a division of rhonur pickers and a hundred frantic dogs. Nursing my green and fiery steed to keep rank and survive obstacles, I wondered if Veth Gammas were garrisoned, what we would do if the cavalry overcame the fire in time to cut us off, how we could stop them following us down. Glanced at Beryx, and did not ask. The flared eyes, blind to all but the land ahead and poised for lightning-swift choice or change of course, the taut face warned me. You do not distract the pathfinder of a cross-country cavalry charge.

The rhonurs ended at a fence, a road-ditch, and we right-wheeled thunderously onto paven carriageway, Beryx roaring, "Whoa!"

Plunging, foaming, protesting colts cavorted everywhere, my chestnut passaged uncontrollably into a vertical yellow flank, Zyr still crooning "Oh, you beauty, you dream, you pearl. . . ." We looked back on a boiling black wall laced with red twinkles of flame, a diagonal swathe that bisected twenty rhonur fields, and a mob of farmers coming pell-mell with bawls of honest murderous rage.

Sivar let out a cracked laugh, but Beryx looked ashamed. "Didn't want to do it. Such a good crop. And ripe for harvest, too. But we can't explain. Come on. At the trot!"

Under the flank of the gnarled thumb nicknamed One-up, every soldier knows why, and Gjerven lay two thousand feet below us, a motley green of rice field and yam patch and pig wallow and swamp, broken by clusters of stilt-legged conical grass huts. Down to the left went the road at a steady one-in-four gradient, and Beryx pulled up.

"That'll do." He fore-armed sweat from a white and purple face our career had not flushed. His eye was on a cluster of granite boulders that overhung the road. "If I can . . . just manage it." And for the first time there was a flaw of doubt.

As Zyr and Karis whooped I thrust my colt against his bay and ordered, "Give me the bridle. Evis, carry on. Don't let them trot, they'll kill themselves!"

The clatter faded. Bloodthirsty shouts echoed from above. With an air of near desperation, Beryx shut his eyes and propped his wrist on the withers of the dancing colt.

Abruptly, it stopped. They are trained to halt at a double leg-squeeze. His torso had gone rigid, if his leg muscles spasmed the same way he must have near cut the colt's barrel in half. His face pulled out of shape. Then his eyes flew open, he gave a tremendous jerk and his lungs emptied in one explosive grunt.

The boulder clump disintegrated. Four small supports opened like an orange, the topmost monster tilted, tipped, slid, landed with a sonorous crunch that sank it a foot deep amid splintered paving stones. The road was completely blocked.

"Axyn . . . brarve." It came on a long-drawn sob. "Not . . . unusual. 'Cept . . . the precision. Easier . . . tip it right down hill." I jerked the bit viciously to still the skirmishing colt. He lay with his left arm on my shoulder a moment longer before he straightened up, and said on a breath of relief, "No hurry . . . for a while."

There was no garrison, there was not a shadow of traffic on the road. Half an hour later we walked sedately out into Gjerven's steamy, marsh-rank atmosphere, and as he slapped off the first mosquito Beryx observed, "That's a good-looking swamp. We'll spell the colts."

Walked, cooled, watered and caressed, they fell eagerly on Deve Gaz's famous earnn grass, we fell hungrily on the last Frimman provisions, and the mosquitoes fell ravenously upon us. Beryx grinned as he caught my eye. "Feel at home?" Then Evis produced Xhen leaves from his bottomless pack, and Zem and Zam lost the worshipful stupor that had lasted since the fire and burst out in chorus, "Sir Scarface, I'll do your hand!"

The burn had filled in and was drying. Soon it would be fit to meet the air. Gingerly flexing the wrist, he remarked, "I'll be glad to have this back." He glanced at Callissa, stonily packing cups. Then he asked suddenly, "Ma'am, does that brown horse pull too hard?"

I saw surprise, a fleeting softness in her eyes. Then they hardened. Chilly courteous, she replied, "I can manage, thanks."

With a silent sigh Beryx turned his eye on the colts. When he said, "We'll give them a bit longer," my heart sank, for I knew we would go on that night.

He lay back in the grass. A series of shuffles edged the right arm under his head. The twins moved closer, rancor woke in Callissa's eye. Parceling up his medical kit, Evis glanced at those drowsy green eyes, still open, absently content. Paused. With sudden decision put by his pack and hunkered closer too.

"Sir," he began. "Krem—why—did it upset you so much?"

I closed a mouth open to call him off. An aedr's resilience is more wonderful than his arts, and I had seen those green eyes wake. Resigning myself to the mosquitoes, I lay down and drifted off to Evis' first steps on the road I was traveling myself.

If that night's going was safe, it was woefully slow. Gjerven is far wilder than Frimmor, and most of its cultivation is rice, which means paddy fields, which mean irrigation channels and mud. Which is hard on any horse. Moreover, we had ridden hard on a half-day's sleep, and we were flagging ourselves. I doubt we managed ten miles' actual advance before Beryx called a halt.

"No use overdoing it," he said softly, while I waited to see the current lair. "Yet." Despite full night vision I could find only the vaguest blur ahead. He clicked to his horse. We waded one more slushy channel, mounted an earthen dyke. Grass cones bulked against the stars, I caught the cluck of sleepy hens, a pig's grunt, hissed in horror, "It's a village, we can't—" and he cut me off. "It belongs to the ferryman. He's sleeping on the other bank."

"For the love—you mean there's a river here? What if the

Lady finds us? If we're caught against that—"

"Alkir, Alkir." He was laughing under his breath. "You just magic up fodder and stabling for these colts."

It was actually a Gjerven farmstead, five or six huts in a stockaded compound, hens and pigs loose on the bare-trodden earth, even that rarity, a Gjerven cow, which we instantly milked. The horses were dispersed in a couple of lean-tos with liberal helpings of the ferryman's doubtless precious earnn hay. We climbed into a hut, lit the usual Gjerven mosquito repellent of two dung-cakes on a clay saucer, and after staring fixedly across the sluggish brown ribbon beyond the stockade, Beryx came in and remarked casually, "The punt just broke its tow pulley. No crossings today."

Despite his confidence mine was an uneasy sleep, ended near sunset amid the bustle as the others ate, packed or went off to saddle up. "Have a kanna," said Beryx, cross-legged beside me, and took another bite at the creamy crescent of peeled fruit hovering before his mouth. "All we could find."

Then the physicians descended. As Zem untied the bandage and Zam opened a Xhen leaf, Callissa materialized to snap, "That bandage wants changing. Isn't there another one somewhere?"

Evis gulped and delved hastily in his pack. Callissa tied it on, cut short Beryx's thanks, and stalked away, just as Karis tumbled up the steps.

"Sir, sir, she's found us! There's half a hundred savages out there with nothing on but their hats!"

Beryx's face showed a hint of vexation. "Drat," he said, as I bounded up. He let the kanna drop and strode to the door. Then his shoulders shook. Strung for instant perilous action I was enraged to hear him remark, as if at a parade, "I love those Gjerven helmets." Pure mischief entered his look. "I wonder if. . . ."

His eyes fluxed, crystalline green and white. Reaching the door, I was in time to see the enemy breast the stockade, an unexaggerated fifty Gjerven warriors, complete with wooden spears and warpaint and towering white and crimson headdresses, a most impressive battlefront. Before the forehead band of every headdress snapped.

"Best battle I ever won," he chortled, as the phalanx disintegrated into a yelling gesticulating wreck. "Come along. It now behooves us to depart."

We cantered with expedition east along the river bank, back into the mud and the enveloping dark, unlawfully requisitioned another ferry punt somewhere downstream, and again turned north. "I like Gjerven," Beryx announced into the splashy, mosquito-ridden dark, and laughter tinged his voice at my grunt of disgust. "Zyr, if that pearl of yours really can outrun the wind, you might try to catch a pig before we camp."

Zyr did not catch a pig. He did find Vyrlase, the end of Stirian Ven, whence the highway fans in a score of tracks to the border forts. "Excellent," approved Beryx, headed for the easternmost path. "Now we can get along a bit."

At that I found my voice. "But surely we should go west? The further east the wider Stirsselian gets, and the worse—"

I stopped. The guards had never crossed Stirsselian, but barrack-tales would have painted it luridly enough.

"Alkir," he chided, "you're getting old. How did you last go to Phaxia?"

My jaw dropped. Evis muttered, "I'll be—" Obsessed with crossing at the narrowest possible part, I had forgotten the Taven, the engineers' marvel whose creation Mavash decreed when we invaded Phaxia: fifty miles of timber-cord causeways and pontoon bridges set just where Stirsselian turns salt, spanning tidal channels and clethra sloughs and evil black mud in one bold slash. The road that had borne an army into Phaxia, supported and provisioned it and brought its survivors back.

Evis asked eagerly, "Sir, will it be safe? It's been a good six years—"

Beryx replied calmly, "It looked all right last week." Evis, recovering, burst out, "Then all we have to do is ride!" With a chuckle, Beryx agreed. Adding a silent parenthesis, <I hope.>

Sometime in third watch it began to rain, a steady Gjerven downpour that would probably persist for days. While I thanked providence we were off Frimmor's open uplands, Beryx said, "Good cover," and Sivar grumbled, "Wish I'd kept me cloak." But it had no bite. Recalling that night in Thangar, I almost managed to find a smile myself.

Chafed, sodden, chilled, we finally stowed the horses and snugged down in the thick Gjerven regrowth to wait for dawn. We were on the edge of the Astyros, the stringently maintained mile of cleared land that provides a glacis for the border forts. I said in Beryx's ear, "If I remember right, Salasterne's about three bowshots to the left. The next's Colne Clethra, about five miles west. Three-hundred man garrisons. Watch-towers every half mile." I felt him nod. "The Taven began about halfway between those two forts. There was a big heagar tree just by the first causeway." I could see it still, a glossy green hulk that shaded a hundred yards of ground, bastion-thick trunk supported by secondary roots dropped from the boughs, wounded or resting soldiers in their nooks, trunk aflutter with hundreds of votive rags. "We'd stick a trophy there when we got leave, to be sure of getting it again."

The gray light was broadening now, creeping horizontally across a shrunken world under a low weeping sky. As Stirsselian itself hove into view I felt a familiar sourness in my mouth.

You could not see much. The curse of Stirsselian is that you never can. There are no landmarks, no lookout heights, nothing to raise you above the swamp miasma for so much as the illusory relief of a view. From where we lay, the Astyros' tumbled stretch of stump holes, dug-out roots, newly slashed or uprooted regrowth, ran head on into an olive-green and jungle-gray wall. Clethra trees, so uniform in height that not a head topped the rest to give you some estimate of their depth, so thick no light picked out the groves, straight-ranked and impenetrable as a close-order phalanx front. It does not show hostility. It has no need. It rests upon its strength.

Beryx blew a mosquito off his nose. Evis parted more leaves. Then he twitched, showering us all. "Sir . . . sir, you did say watch-towers? Then what in heaven's name are those?"

A trumpet had called in Salasterne, lowering dark and idle behind its lofty stockade under the moontree's limp black dangle of rag. At the sound, the desolation before us came to life.

"Ten . . . fifteen . . . twenty." Imperturbably, Beryx tallied them up. "Must be cursed uncomfortable, roosting out there."

He was not looking at the watch-towers. He was studying the troop-cordon, posted in pentarchies less than twenty yards apart, right along the Astyros. They had been masked by the rubbish. Now they rose, beating hands, huddled into drenched brown and green field cloaks, cursing the weather, the fire, the orders and each other with the fine munificence of disgruntled soldiery as they struggled to make their breakfast fires. When they moved I could see the tent-like protuberance above each left shoulder. They were archers, and they had slept with their bows.

Facing calamity, Evis was mute. Beryx blew another mosquito away and gazed on, eyes unreadable. My stomach was a cold, flat pit.

"No wonder," I said at last, "she didn't worry about pursuit."

"Mm." That sounded cryptic too. He squirmed back into the

scrub. "No point in rousing that yet. We'll post sentries and wait for dark."

I drew some comfort from the thought that sentries would conserve his own strength. We huddled under the trees while the rain poured down to seal our wretchedness. Callissa, mercifully, said nothing. The twins were big-eyed and mute, but when Beryx woke they converged on him. "Be my guests," he smiled, tucking one under each arm. "Driest rooms in the house."

From his left armpit Zem asked with desperate composure, "Sir Scarface, you did kill the dragon, didn't you? In the end?"

"Of course." He sounded reassuringly matter-of-fact. "That's why I'm an aedr, you know." Zam's head emerged, I saw others' interest. Anything to occupy them, I thought.

Beryx evidently agreed, for he went on, "Magic was the only way to kill it, you see. So I had to find an aedr. Someone"—he looked sidelong—"who'd teach magic to me."

Zam popped up too, eyes wide in gorgeous awe. "Fengthira?" He did not, I noticed, stumble over the name. "She taught *you?*"

"She did." He was smiling faintly. "Yes."

Zem was nearly bouncing in place. "So once you knew magic, you killed the dragon."—"And then Everran was safe."—"And you could be king again."

The smile faded. "Not quite," he said softly. "Once I was an aedr—I couldn't go back to being a king."

Puzzle pieces showering into place, I sat stone still lest I break the thread. Zem and Zam were thinking with their eyes. I wanted that thread intact too.

"Aedryx aren't kings," he told them lightly, smiling again. "It isn't right."

This digested, Zem asked a strange question. "But—an aedr could be a soldier—couldn't he?"

"I don't see why not," Beryx agreed. The query that woke in

his eyes was never answered. Amver pelted up from the southern sentry-point with a face shouting ultimate catastrophe.

"Sir, sir! There's half a phalanx coming up behind us—'n they're beating the timber on the way!"

Beryx's voice slashed the tumult to bring Amver up as on a rope. "How far?"

"Sir, a mile, less'n a mile—"

"And how fast? How fast!"

"S-sir they keep halting, they gotta wait for the flankers, the timber knots 'em up—"

"Stand to your horse!"

A crack that lifted the whole camp. He was all aedr now, irises writhing in the heat of calculation swift as light. He glanced at the sky. Whatever he saw there, the resulting expression turned me weak with fright.

I had no time to ask. His face twisted in denial, conflict, distress. Then it set.

"Not Math," he muttered. "But. . . ." And was on his feet with the lunge of a rearing snake.

"Sivar, take Zem. Karis, take Zam. Alkir, you know your tree? Be sure, man!" His eyes skewered me. I nodded, praying it was truth. "When we go, make straight for that. Lead my horse. Don't talk to me, and whatever you see, don't stop! You hear? Don't stop!" He took six huge strides to the bay and swung himself up.

My hand shook on the wet clammy rein. Behind was the hubbub of panic half unleashed. Beryx shut his eyes, propped his left wrist on the bay's wither, and drew the first harsh extended breath.

Nothing happened. His face contorted, his muscles shuddered, the bay backed under the merciless pressure on his ribs, crueler and crueler grew the battle for each riving breath. And nothing happened. A wizard tearing himself apart while we stared helplessly, doom closed on us, and the gray rain dripped from a bleak gray sky.

Only when I cast a desperate glance across the Astyros did I realize with shock that the rain was pelting down out there so hard its ricochets jumped from the mud, so hard that visibility had shrunk to a scant quarter mile, outposts, forts, watch-towers all lost in a sheet of solid white. My heart leapt, and sank. What use was cover, with guards posted twenty yards apart?

A surge of wind hit the trees. Behind it came the rain, beating clean through the foliage, pounding on our heads. The colts began to spin and plunge, it was pummeling us like fists. I heard the front wash on across the timber in one huge airborne wave. Overhead growled the fruity, thick-throated thunder that escorts deluge rain.

Beryx gasped and dropped, face down on the bay's neck. With terror's severity I jabbed the bit to restrain the horse. He was shaking as if every muscle were unstrung. I could just hear his words.

"Count . . . five hundred . . . or wait for yells. Then go. Fast as you can ride." He straightened, head bowed into the deluge, black hair streaming waterfalls over a bloodless face. His back arched. As I counted ten I heard the resumption of those racking breaths.

Two hundred. Three. I was choking with tension and fear, not least that I would lose the count. Four hundred and fifty. Fifty-one. Evis bounced and gasped. "I heard something! From Salasterne! Sir—"

"Four-sixty—wait! Sixty-one . . . two. . . ." And tearing the rain like paper came the scream of Salasterne's trumpets as they sounded the Attack, the Alarm, General Stand-to, Alarm, Alarm!

"That's it!" It came out of me in a grunt as the colt, mad with waiting's tension, fairly fired us into the rain.

How we got over the Astyros at that pace, in that downpour, I conceive to be a direct mercy of whoever-you-like. There was no visibility. I galloped for a stump I had laid in line with the heagar, picked another beyond it and bucketed on, praying that if Beryx's colt tripped without a firm hand on the bridle he was long enough in the rein to gallop himself up. From behind came the dead thunder of hooves in mud and the yells of men too crazed to think what they were saying, over all was the cavalry rumble of the rain. . . . They'll never see us from the road! I was yelling it in silent manic delight, And we can ride the cordon down—

With shattering instantaneity we burst out of the rain and tore in virtually clear air and full view of the forts across the last quarter mile of the Astyros, we would be atop the archers in twenty strides, my hand leapt for the bit as my mouth opened for a frantic futile Halt! and Evis' black jammed its shoulder into me while he screamed and howled like a man watching his horse take out a close-run race, "Come on keep going it's all right it's all right!"

My eyes shot left, a smoky breakfast fire flashed under us and was gone with not an archer by, my eyes shot up and they were running, running like madmen, but not for us, they were bursting their hearts to reach Salasterne and nobody there would think about us, the trumpets were still shrieking and up every side of the stockade poured a flood of little bandy-legged men in spiked helmets and fish-scale armor and mud-brown cloaks whose color was more familiar than my own eyes. The colors of Phaxia. A surprise attack.

War reflexes are burnt deep. Even then my heart made an extra pump, my bridle hand leapt automatically for the wheel that would fling us to their aid and Evis nearly deafened me. "He said don't stop, he said don't *stop!*"

Before I could argue Stirsselian leapt at us, unmoved, inimical, blank, fresh terror stopped my breath. Then there it was, a midnight cloud above the clethras, the giant heagar.

I would undoubtedly have swept the whole unit clean past it onto the causeway without attempting to draw rein, I was too crazed to think of anything else. But as we tore round the tree's buttress Beryx twitched and almost burst my head. <Whoa!>

We ended half on the causeway, horses going mad in the same tranced drive to run as ours. He literally fell off the bay and crumpled in the mud, I abandoned both beasts to dive and catch him up. Hooves flailed about us while he jittered convulsively in my arms, far gone and driving himself to get out the last crucial commands.

<Horses—let go! Tell them dismount! Quick, quick! On causeway—run. Never mind me, go!>

I bellowed the orders and enforced them by sheer manic will. The colts fled broadcast, going like bolters, the humans stumbled past us onto the slimy, treacherous logs, he was pushing me with a nerveless hand, choking, "Go, GO!" Disobediently I lifted and dragged him with me, aware even at that pent-in moment of some change in the outer world. Then I realized what it was.

The trumpets had fallen quiet.

At the clethras' brink I could not help one backward glance. Rain blotted half the Astyros. I could hear its tidal roar. Salasterne loomed black and distinct against that curtain of white. But no fiendish little knife-fighters capered in triumph on its catwalk, no bodies, Assharran or Phaxian, lay writhing or moveless in the mud. There were no Phaxians at all. Just a crowd of archers and garrison who confronted each other over arrow and sword-point, motionless, too thoroughly confounded even to scratch their heads.

We were on the first bridge, with Evis helping Beryx to stagger between us, before I finally understood. Then I yowled like a cat-a-mountain and pounded bruises into his back.

"It was Pellathir, it was Pellathir, wasn't it? You lovely crack-brained lunatic, they were never there at all!"

He was reeling, white and wet and spent beyond all but an attempt to laugh. He answered in mindspeech, <Alkir, you *clever* soul!>

Then we both laughed so hard we fell over, and the others had to rush back in fresh panic to pick us up.

<Pellathir for the archers,> he said, as we tottered off again. <Wrevurx for the rear attack. It's still coming down in waterfalls. They won't have seen a thing.>

"Wrevur—" It slammed back at me. "Weather-work! You mean—you didn't just conjure the Phaxians? You made the rain as well?"

<Shouldn't have done it.> He sagged on my shoulder, eyes falling shut. <Twisting things that far . . . not Math.>

I literally hugged him, still too delirious to care for anything but the stupendous splendor of the trick. "It got us out, didn't it? When any mortal general would have sat down and cut his throat? Who gives a tinker's ill-wish about Math!"

It was a long time before we sobered up. What if we were penniless, provisionless, horseless, shelterless, faced with a fifty-mile walk in pouring rain over an unscouted road to Phaxia? We had escaped Assharral. Foiled the Lady. Shared a stratagem that would have made military history, if any historian could ever be brought to write it down.

"And," added Beryx proudly, "it didn't kill a single man."

We congratulated him as we trudged, contented except for Zyr, who was engaged in a wake for his colt. "Why," I asked, "did we leave the horses behind?" At which Beryx shook his head. "Too dangerous out here. Besides, I hope it might—er—mitigate the crime."

I could not see it mattered, now we were forever beyond the Lady's power. Sivar had just asked with not-quite-pure facetiousness, "Sir, whyn't you send all this rain off to Assharral?" when Evis, tail-scout as usual, called in a carefully wooden voice, "Sir! I think there's something behind."

Beryx stopped in mid-stride. He shut his eyes. I heard him whisper, "Oh, no." He called without looking round.

"Are you sure?"

A pause, while we all strained our eyes. Then, yet more woodenly, "I'm sorry, sir. I'm sure."

Beryx still would not look. "Can you tell what it is?"

There was a change in the rain-smeared umber length of the Taven, that stretched blade-straight back to the Astyros' open light. I knew the answer before Evis spoke.

"Troops."

Silently, Beryx groaned. I wondered why he had not used far-sight, recalled he had still leant heavily on me as we went, saw he was using it now. He spoke again.

"How far?"

"I think . . . two miles—mile and a half."

"Mile and three-quarter," interjected Sivar. I realized where Beryx had been looking when he said, summoning strength, "Hurry then. It's a mile to the next bridge."

We hurried, and they gained, though their pace was not fast. There was something dreadfully familiar about that steady, smooth advance. Once Beryx himself glanced back. His eyes dilated, and he began to scurry faster, with jerky, un-coordinated strides.

It was a major bridge over the first tidal channel, six pontoons anchored by a web of cables to the clethras that flanked a muscular, dirty-chocolate stream, tree-trunk bridge-spans floored with planks. Cat-footing in the slime, we crept across.

The troops had closed to three-quarters of a mile. "Phalanx," said Amver, superfluously. We could all see the broad white shields, blazoned with a black moontree, as they shone dully in the rain, the fitful shimmer of helmet or mailcoat or the gleam of a sarissa head, fifteen feet above.

Beryx cast a hunted glance at the clethras, deep in fluid mud, at water's shine between the mud-coated tussocks in the marshes ahead. Evis said, "Sir—sir, we'll have to cut the bridge. No cover up there. And the children—"

No need to finish, They could never keep ahead.

For the first time I saw overt indecision in Beryx's face. The troops had closed to half a mile. Evis said tentatively, "Sir, if you—could you—"

"I could. . . ."

And did not want to, I could hear. I said roughly, "We can do something for ourselves. Sivar, Dakis, Uster, don't just stand there—you do carry swords!" Beryx opened his mouth, then let us go.

We hacked with strenuous haste, concentrating on the third pontoon. But those cables were set by good engineers who meant their work to last. We still had two uncut when Beryx called, "Come out of it, Alkir! I'll do the rest."

The troops were inside three bowshots, still coming, steady, unhurried, a whole taxis, two hundred phalanxmen, their rank kept with remarkable skill, in quadruple file for the track. Beryx gave them one last look, then turned to the bridge.

It was less summons than a supplication. He said, "Imsar . . . Math." Then he clenched his fists, arched his back, and his eyes fired like a multiple catapult, flash upon searing flash.

The cables snapped. The planking jumped in the air. The two tree trunks cartwheeled majestically and went seaward in the pontoon's wake with a resounding splash, and Stirsselian's noisome waters swirled hungrily under a twenty-foot gap. With sighs of relief, we turned our attention to the troops.

It took some time to accept. Then Sivar's voice cracked in shock and disbelief. "Sir, they're not gonna stop!"

"Clear the bridge," Beryx snapped. "They may try to throw—though what they expect to hit with sarissas," he echoed my thought, "I can't think."

We retreated thirty yards up the causeway. The troops came on, unhesitant, unhurrying, tramp, tramp, tramp.

They were in bowshot. Fifty yards. Amver shifted uneasily, some premonition showed on Sivar's face. I glanced at Beryx to find him deathly white. I caught what may have been an actual thought fragment, for it did not sound like speech. *She wouldn't—she couldn't—she can't!* Then he yelled in mindspeech, nearly pulverizing my skull.

<Moriana, don't be such an imbecile! We're out of reach! You could surrender with some *grace!*>

We released our ears. The troops came on.

<Moriana, what in the pits are you playing at? Pull them up!>

The troops came on, thirty yards now, tramp, tramp, tramp.

<Moriana!> Panic had adulterated the wrath. <Let them stop—they can't get across!>

The troops came on.

<Moriana, I won't fight you for them, you know I couldn't free two hundred men! Let them stop!>

Twenty yards. Tramp, tramp, tramp.

<Moriana—for the love of heaven! They can't reach us, do you want to kill them all for nothing, pull them up!>

The troops came on.

"Oh, Math!" he said aloud. Sweat stood in great drops on his face. He yelled again, sounding desperate.

<Moriana, please! Let them stop!>

The troops came on. I could see the front-rank faces, set, stern, expressionless. Tramp, tramp, tramp.

<Moriana, you can't slaughter them for nothing, they're innocent men!>

The troops came on, tramp, tramp, tramp.

"No!" he said in anguish. "Moriana, listen—" He changed to mindspeech, deafening my ears as well.

<Moriana, I beg you, *let them stop!*>

The troops came on, forty feet from the bridge, tramp, tramp, tramp.

<Moriana!> Tears were streaming down his face. <You can't do this! You can't!>

The troops came on.

<Moriana, listen, listen to me . . . ! I'll do whatever you say, I won't go to Phaxia, I'll come back, I'll give myself up!> He had moved forward, my hand shot with motives I had rather not analyze to snatch his arm. <Anything you want, but for pity's sake, let them stop!>

The troops came on, up to the bridgehead, he was tearing at my hold, yelling, <Anything, Moriana, anything! I swear it! For the love of Math!>

The troops came on, faces still blank, wholly expressionless. Onto the bridge, tramp, tramp, the front rank's gaze was fixed on us, seeing but unseeing, I too wanted to scream madly, hopelessly, Stop! Stop!

But it was too late. They were past the first pontoon, the planks rumbled, the bridge bucked wildly to their unbroken stride, the second pontoon plunged under them and he screamed in pure agony, "Moriana, *NO!*"

Instinctively I jerked him round and hauled him up the road and slammed a shoulder into Callissa as I panted, "Get the boys away!" He fought my hold with the whole remnant of his physical strength. I put a headlock on and literally ran him off with thanks to someone that my arm was over his ears, so he at least would not hear that awful repeated sickening splash.

In a hundred feet he collapsed. I picked him up and carried him, driving the rest. Zyr was about to throw up. Dakis was in tears too, Evis whispering, black stricken eyes in a papery face.

"Why did I look, oh, why did I look? They went straight in—all of them—two hundred phalanxmen—not even trying to stop!"

His voice shot up and cracked. I thumped an elbow in his ribs and snarled, "Thank Math they were phalanxmen, in that armor they'll drown, would you rather they smothered trying to climb up on the mud? Or got out and we had to kill them afterwards? You blind imbecile, get on!"

When Beryx came round no one dared speak to him. After one glance, I hardly dared to look. Eventually we camped, cutting open surcoats to drape over branches on a relatively high spot, then huddled cold, wet and supperless while the rain came down and Stirsselian's stinging flies helped the mosquitoes crown the misery of the night. Beryx spoke only once, when I thought of setting a watch.

"No," he said, and there was death in his voice. "There's no need for that."

Nor did he speak next day. There was no forage of any sort. We drank swamp-water and struggled on, leading him like a sleepwalker in our midst. Two days later the rain stopped, the sky cleared, the clethras shone silver-bright, and a brisk wind blew snowy clouds down over sharp red mountains behind Phaxia's umbrella-roofed border forts.

At Stirsselian's edge Beryx roused himself, and in a lifeless voice bade us cut and peel a clethra bough to make a herald's staff. Too tired and starven for fear we watched him plod forward with it to the nearest fort. Sentinels challenged. He parleyed. An officer appeared. He parleyed again. After what seemed hours, he turned and beckoned. We crept forward, steeling ourselves.

Small bandy-legged slit-eyed yellow soldiers surrounded us, jabbering frenziedly. Beryx said, "We have safe conduct to Phamazan." Then he handed me the staff and quietly fainted clean away.

Chapter IX

After they recovered from twelve Assharran refugees' appearance over a border uncrossed in living memory, the Phaxians were kind enough. They tried to stare no more than was humanly possible, and to Beryx they were more than kind. Doctors, the best quarters, any necessity, no expense or trouble grudged.

It was needed. For three days he did not stir out of that swoon. The chief physician did his best, tapping my belt buckle, whose height was most convenient, as he assured us, "Is quite all right, sir captain, only exhaustion, is no cause for alarm," in that sing-song Phaxian accent which makes all sentences end in midair, but we still found it hard to believe.

Meantime they fed, clothed and housed us, causing drastic upheavals in the fort, and asked not a single question about our flight, even about the state of the Taven, which in a Phaxian general's place I would have had out of us forthwith, manners or not. After Beryx revived we had only to walk about like visiting lords, while we adjusted to the four layers of Phaxian clothes, the pointed felt hats, the wildly spicy food, and admired the well-kept, well-designed, well-sited fort with a catapult under each of the four-storey tower's overhanging roofs, the skirmishers' ponies for sorties, and the clean, keen, five hundred troops.

Zem and Zam were adopted by a patrol and almost deserted us. Callissa kept close. The others, like me, were troubled that we could not repay so much kindness with trust.

I have never understood our primeval antipathy to Phaxia. It is not their barbaric customs, skull-top drinking cups, prisoners of war sacrificed wholesale to Ahlthor, ruler chosen by death duels, his bodyguard pledged to slay their horses along with themselves upon his grave. Not even their taste for fricasseed dog. Odder customs occur in Assharral. Nor is it that we are usually at war. Nor a difference in race. Our little band was a perfect sample of the Assharran stew: Sivar and I were white-skinned gray-eyed Frimman stock, Evis a swarthy hook-nosed Nervian who shaved twice on parade days, Zyr pure Axairan, red as his canyons with the same facial planes. Amver, like Krem, was all Gjerven, frizzy hair, midnight skin, squashy nose, while Karis' yellow hide and dropped Morryan eyelids could have been Phaxian. Uster and Dakis were bronze-black high-nosed Kemrestanis, Ost had the dun Tasmarn skin and coarse horse-like black hair, and Wenver was a golden Darrian. We never noticed our differences. Yet one sight of a Phaxian would have us hackling like dogs with an intruder in the pack.

After a week Beryx courteously but adamantly left the physician protesting by his vacated bed. Physically he seemed recovered, and he was brisk enough; but we all knew the memory of that Taven bridge had not healed. His once incorrigible, often infuriating merriment had vanished, and we grieved for its memory, as you do at sight of some great swordsman with a tendon shorn.

In another week he had intimated to the commandant with the invincible charm of high nobility that he wished to be on his way. Little Phaxian horses were produced, and amid exchanges of esteem and a fifty-man guard too respectful to be called an escort, we set out for Phamazan.

Phaxia's capital is a bare fifty miles from Assharral, but safe enough, for most of that stands on end. It lies on the high arid plateau beyond the even higher Azmaere range, where you boil in summer and in winter freeze. Less hardy rulers summered in mountain eyries and wintered among Gevber's palm-lined coves, but Zass stayed in Phamazan all year round. It is a good indication of his character.

That was written, though, on every mile of our road. Phaxia is more populous than Assharral in far less space. Small yellow people swarm in the most barren and inclement districts, compensating with industry for their poor material. The Azmaeres are terraced to the very summits, minute fields that plunge dizzily down the mountainsides, ploughed by tiny sure-footed donkeys where no Assharran would dare to hoe. The Veldisk plateau is irrigated by channels from the great northern river Othan, and the narrow coastal strip of Gevber is cropped for rice three and four times a year.

All this the escort officer told me with unassuming pride. He had no need to tell me the point of the arms drill in every village, the profusion of troops on the march, the endless pack-trains of arms coming from the big northern cities of Vyrne Taskar, the bustle of supply collection and levy enrollment in every sizeable town. Steadily, purposefully, by a long-prepared program, Phaxia was winding up for war.

Natural enough, I thought. His last trouncing would rankle in Zass's militant mind. No one could wonder if he meant to even the score, but I felt no happier now I was technically on his side. Those wicked little jungle fighters in Stirsselian had scarred and scared me far too much.

At Phamazan we were billeted in the palace itself. As Klyra said, it is a barrack of a place, sullen yellow sandstone, stuck on a hill outside the town like an oversized citadel: no concessions to the site, treeless without and few gardens within. Most of the courts are bare pavement. Fountains are rare. And everywhere wide windows offer a sentinel's prospect over miles of glary sandstone-studded landscape, where the dust smokes from the zealously worked fields to the rienglis that circle patiently in that thirsty upland air.

When we arrived Zass was watching cavalry maneuvers from the balcony above the mile-long practice field that serves as the palace's great court. Dust whirled above the sandstone battlements, and the chamberlain, ushering us into a vestibule, murmured, "The master is with his army. Never to disturb." We sat on long felt cushions, tried not to grimace at the bitter black tea, and declined the services of pages with huge paper fans, until the chamberlain shepherded us into an audience hall.

At the far end Zass sat enthroned under the hall's sole ornament, a trophy of Phaxian swords. They are lovely things, curved shimmering blue blades of the finest steel I know, hilts that include every extravagance of fabric and workmanship, gold, silver, ivory, gems, all fantastically carved. Tall copper-colored drapes were half drawn across the windows behind, so the light showed the faces of petitioners and masked Zass's own. I made out he was in cavalry boots, trousers and over-tunic, standard issue and liberally floured with dust, his only signs of rank a truly outstanding sword and a scarlet pointed felt hat.

Like most Phaxians, he is small, bowlegged and wiry, inexhaustible. Unlike most, he has high cheekbones, barely slitted eyes, and a jaw undercut so extremely that his mouth resembles a shark's, set straight between nose and neck. The chamberlain made obeisance. Silently, Zass crooked a finger. Then he made a pushing motion as we all moved, leveled the finger at Beryx and crooked it again.

Beryx stepped forward. His arm was in a silk sling, the fort commandant's one victory. Since no ordinary size would fit, some hastily conscripted tailor had made him Phaxian clothes, and he carried off the baggy trousers, voluminous shirt and close-fitting mud-brown tunic well enough, though the tailor had closed his eyes at the sight. But as he stepped toward Zass his bearing set a royal cloak swirling at his heels. He was no longer a fugitive wizard. He was a journeying king.

Zass had read it in the first stride. The finger crooked again. Stewards flew like hail. A state chair materialized on the dais to the right of the throne, an inlaid table set with ornately enameled jar and cups for Phaxian rice wine followed it. Beryx inclined his head and seated himself with the same regal air. Zass swiveled sideways on his throne. I saw his hawk-yellow razor eye, and knew that if a sword had made him, he had no swordsman's mind. Then a steward plucked discreetly at my sleeve. Our presence was no longer required.

To our relief we were quartered together, in the eastern wing. Forbidden to explore, Zem and Zam resorted to making cushion castles and sliding down to flatten them. Evis prowled. The others were out of their depth and showing it. A hundred questions about our future hung in the air.

There was time to ponder them. Being mere chattels, we were left to cool our heels while Zass gave Beryx a conducted tour of Phamazan, then had him to dinner in the royal rooms. Bugles had called the Phaxian Lights-out from a hundred different barracks before he came to bed.

He still wore the polite mask of a diplomatic duel. It melted far enough to assure Sivar and company, though without his former gaiety, that they were not yet for the rubbish heap. Then he quirked a brow and asked, "Fylghjos, can I degrade you to body servant? I'll never worm out of this tunic alone."

His room was furnished with the usual austerity, though with a few additions: a splendid silver ewer, a silk quilt on the low wooden bed, a conspicuously posted scarlet hat. Eying it, he observed with a trace of his old self, "Show your rank, or else."

As he sank rather heavily on the bed, I essayed his own tactics and asked, "Shall I start with the boots? My squires always did."

He answered in mindspeech, without looking up.

<It's no good.>

It was sheer incomprehension that muzzled me.

<Zass would be delighted to give me asylum. I'm a king, I have manners, I'd set off his court. The trouble is the board. I'm also an aedr. The weapon to end all weapons. With me he couldn't just settle his score and give the Lady the bloodiest of noses, he could conquer Assharral.>

Confusion whirled in me. *Wasn't that why we came, it's better than beggary, did you mean to forget the whole thing, surely you wouldn't mind a little of your own back, won't conquering Assharral remove Ammath?*

He lifted his eyes, black-green in the lamp glow, revealing the fatigue of Zass's interview and the stresses beneath.

<I don't want to invade Assharral. I certainly don't want it invaded by Zass.> He shuddered. <The bloodshed, the waste! I've done enough damage there myself.>

But it would overthrow the Lady, I thought.

His face sharpened. <To replace her with Zass.>

I sat limply on a tathrien stool. *Will you leave Phaxia, then? You can hardly stay, if you refuse Zass!* With sinking heart I contemplated fresh flight to some wholly foreign place. *Will you go back to Hethria?*

<No.>

Then . . . ?

He pulled himself up. "I don't know," he said. "And I'm too groggy now to find out. Skin me out of this tunic, Fylghjos. I might turn up something in my sleep."

It did not show at breakfast if he had. He was composed but inscrutable, and soon left at a summons from Zass. We had resigned ourselves to another day's idleness when a chamberlain entered to announce that the foreign lord desired his retinue. Looking unsociable, Callissa muttered, "I'll stay with the twins."

The great court does have a colonnade, a promenade for officials, nobles and idlers. As we appeared Beryx rose from a stone bench by the main gate, saying, "I thought you'd like to see the great court. Thank you, Fen, that will be all."

Chamberlain dislodged, we paced out onto the hot, dusty, hoof-beaten earth, dutifully noting the myriad slender pillars of the balcony, a princelet flying a merlin in jesses, the dusty emerald flutter of a forgotten cavalry mark. When other strollers were well clear Beryx said without preamble, "I'm sorry to tell you this, but I can't stay in Phaxia. If I do, Zass will expect me to conquer Assharral for him."

I looked round on blank dismay. They too would have preferred a fixed exile, it seemed.

At length Evis asked hollowly, "Will we—go to Hethria, sir?"

"No."

"Vyrenia's not bad," Sivar offered half-heartedly, " 'cept that blighted rain every day."

"Vyrenia?" Beryx stared. "Why would I go to Vyrenia?"

"But sir—you can't stay in Phaxia, you gotta go somewhere!"

"To go to Vyrenia won't stop Zass invading Assharral."

"Let him," said Dakis. "Who cares? Not our affair."

Beryx said flatly, "It is not what Assharral deserves."

There was a discomfited pause. Then Karis asked, "How're we gonna stop it, sir?"

He studied our faces. A hint of the old mischief flickered, overlaid by worry and remorse.

"Zass knows my powers," he said. "If I weren't in his camp, he'd be very wary of crossing me. And he'd think twice about invasion if I were anywhere I could interfere."

Zyr pulled a copper plait. "Yes. But, sir, where?"

"I thought a long time about that. In the end, there was only one choice. Only one place it could be." He paused. Plunged. "Stirsselian."

That is the closest I ever came to outright revolt. No, I thought in instinctive refusal. Bad enough to be homeless, penniless and futureless in Phaxia, but not Stirsselian! The mosquitoes, the quick-mud, the fever, the clethras, the whole nerve-fraying reality washed back over me. *No,* I cried before I could help it, *Not again! Not with Callissa and the twins!*

My eyes cleared. Beryx was watching me, with sympathy, understanding, absolution. <I know,> he said. I know, that look added, exactly how you feel.

Hearsay alone had given the others pause. He turned to them.

"This is something I have to do," he said. "But I have no claim on you. I've already made you exiles. If you want to go to Vyrenia—Hethria—I'll do my best to see you safe."

There was some hard gulping and grimacing. Then Sivar set his jaw.

"I been in this from the start," he announced. " 'N Stirsselian or no Stirsselian, I don't reckon I wanna pull out before the end."

Amver set his teeth. "Or me."

"Or me," Karis came in.

Others followed. I was not aware of the choice. I only heard myself say, sounding distorted, "Once is enough." They looked at me in puzzlement, but Beryx understood.

He looked around us. Swallowed too. Then he said, "I wish I could give you more than thanks."

Feet were shuffled. Evis was already deep in plans, the others facing up to the plunge. Then Wenver spoke up.

Like most Darrians he seldom wasted words, but he was something of a tactician in his methodical way. "Sir," he began, apologetic but not timid, "if we want to stop Zass . . . we can do it just as well . . . probably better . . . and a lot more comfortably . . . from Vyrenia."

Beryx considered him. Then his eyes pulsed, shimmered, turned to white-flecked jade. With joy, with intense foreboding, I saw the old impishness return at last.

"Yes," he said. "It would stop Zass if I sat on his northern border. But it wouldn't help with what I want."

"Then what," I demanded, "do you want?"

He said, "Assharral free of Ammath."

All our mouths fell open. He stared at us. And then the laughter sparkled out at last, alive, wicked, fountaining like Drytime sun through leaves.

"When I called this a strategic withdrawal—that was exactly what I meant. I may have shifted my ground. I haven't ceded the field."

"B-but," Dakis out-spluttered the rest, "we thought—"

"So you did." The laughter had become an outright grin.

"But if we ha'nt pulled out," Karis burst forth, "whyn't you stay with Zass? If ever there was a chance to smash her, it'd be here—"

The mischief was full-blown now, provocation giving it fuel.

"I don't want," he said blandly, "to smash her. I want to free her too."

My jaw hit my collarbones. His eyes danced at me. "Yes," he said. "Yes."

"You—you. . . ."

"Yes. Oh, yes."

"You are impossible!" I was beyond manners, let alone respect. "Turn up these crazy, these lunatic ideas and laugh. . . . Laugh! Is it the magic? Did the Lady rot your brains out? Or were you always like this? Heaven pity your phalanx commander—he probably lost *his* mind as well!"

He was simmering like a kettle, his whole face alight. It did waver at mention of his phalanx commander. But in a moment the sparkle revived.

"Inyx," he agreed, almost demurely, "did use to say things like that. . . ." I threw my hands in the air. "But I think I was probably born this way."

I got my breath. Carefully, I said, "You mean—you don't just want to free Assharral—you'll go on trying to reclaim, reform, convert, whatever you like to call it—the Lady? To—to—"

The simmer had become sparks of sheer delight. "Actually, I don't mean to do anything," he said, "except follow Math."

I would have flung my hands up then, had I been capable.

"Madness, yes." He chuckled. "Pure insanity. But—"

"But you can't—you won't—what can you do!"

The light spired, spiraled in his eyes, dancing as in that vision by Los Morryan.

"I shall sit in Stirsselian . . . and block Zass . . . and infuriate Moriana . . . without doing a thing." The dance intensified. "Zass is a canny general, with nothing personal against me. When his agents report from Assharral, he'll decide it's worth his while to wait. But Moriana . . . Moriana has a grudge. So . . . I shall let her make herself into Math."

For an instant the laughter spilled over so it seemed to clothe him in light, summer-green, riotous, reveling. Then the dancers stilled.

"That is," he said unsmiling, "if she doesn't make Ammath out of me."

As we trooped back to quarters I reflected that the most daunting part of it would be to tell Callissa, and I was right. The storm evicted the rest and terrified the twins. I wished fervently for Beryx's help, but it did not come. In the end I was reduced to the flat statement that I was going, and the boys with me, "and if you want to stay in Phaxia, that's up to you."

After Zyphryr Coryan we had no doubt that an aedr could get us out of Phamazan. He did it that night. Doors opened, horses materialized, underlings helpfully fulfilled our needs and washed us from their minds, we rode out the city gate past a blithely oblivious guard. After he recovered, Beryx glanced back at the rowdy lamplit streets and said rather guiltily, "I hope Zass doesn't roll any heads for letting an aedr slip." Then he flexed his hand, two days out of bandages, glanced at the rising moon, and said, "We don't have a lot of time."

We were down that vile switchback road and over the Azmaeres by dawn. The sun met us in the foothills, staring copper-red on the few unploughed rocks, spreading a tender blue-and-green haze toward the distant sea and more distant Assharral. But directly ahead it fell flat and impotent on the olive-green-and-gray band of Stirsselian, and my stomach knotted at the sight.

"Sir," Amver pushed his pony into the van. "I been thinking. About Stirsselian." Beryx nodded. "We might do better going west. See, sir, it's fresh water then. 'N it widens out a lot. Better for hiding." This is true. In places the basins are two hundred miles across. "What's more. . . ." He grew ill-at-ease. "There's—wild Gjerven up there."

Unless driven to it, no civilized Gjerven will so much as admit they exist. They are too close akin. Beryx said, "You think they'd help us?" And Amver wriggled on his wooden saddle.

"Well, sir—it'll be worse'n impossible in there if they take a dislike to us."

I had never seen one, but the tales were lurid. Little naked men with stone spears and poisoned arrows who were there and gone in a blink, who could set an ambush six feet from a path, who signaled on drums and were wont to eat their prisoners. Amver offered the supreme sacrifice. "We lived on the edge of Stirsselian. In fact—I was sort of—brought up with them."

Nobody ostracized him. Evis said in relief, "Best news since Frimmor." Beryx carried briskly on, "Thank Math for someone who might know what he's doing. Amver, I've been thinking too. The best way to move in there wouldn't be horses, or on foot. It would be boats. Do you know anything about. . . ."

"Sure, sir!" Amver shot up ten feet. "You want a swamp punt. Two, three, maybe. We'll make 'em on the edge." He grew pensive. " 'N . . . we better boil up some salgar as well."

Around noon we abandoned our ponies, took a final backward glance to be sure no zealous Phaxian had sighted us, and tramped, with varying shades of reluctance, across the last soggy field, over the first swamp branch, and into Stirsselian.

It was much as I remembered. Steaming wet, peculiarly airless, not only because of the smothering trees and the sun that stewed miles of water, jungle and mud, but with a listening pressure that is the most unnerving of all. It is as if Stirsselian itself were sentient, and resentful, and at any moment the ambush will be sprung.

The mosquitoes struck instantly, backed by stinging flies, sticky flies, leeches, and some odd bees that like the taste of sweat. Our march flushed an army of birds, gray hisyrx, the northern heron, black and white waders, all kinds of duck, red-billed slithillin, pouch-billed pelicans, tiny water-runners and tree-dwellers as well, which attracted the raptors, morvallin, rienglis and so on. Once a perrilys glared from a whitened stump, gold-rimmed eye, mottled white and brown six-foot wings, but he was a fish-eater and little concerned with us. The morvallin were another matter. They thought it a hunt, and expected scraps, and in the end Beryx needed Wreve-lan'x to be rid of them.

By then we were on an eyot conveniently infested with emvath bush and hooky quennis vines, with a small fire to boil up the first salgar infusion while Amver supervised the making of punts. This meant wading, often thigh-deep, to the stands of smooth pole-like thrithan trees which are the swamp-dweller's staple, and which were inevitably barricaded among helmyn clumps. They are palms whose leaves grow in spirals, are lavishly barbed, and when stepped on rattle like the drums of a general alarm. Amver, however, said we would grind the nuts for flour.

He also treated the quick-mud patches with cavalier unconcern, merely bidding us prod with a stick if we left others' tracks. A wide slide-mark down a mud bank made me shy in real alarm, but he discounted that too. "Fresh water sort. They don't eat men." Resolved that Zem and Zam would be confined to camp, I struggled on, wrestling my queasy stomach, picking off leeches, and finally, like Amver, repulsing the mosquitoes by daubing all my exposed skin with mud.

The punts were festooned with vine-ends like a botched haystack, almost unmaneuverable, but they floated, they held two or three people, and they had a bare six-inch draught. Amver took command of the first. Sivar, on the strength of his brother the fisherman, was allotted the second, and Beryx, boasting, "I may be one-handed and never have sailed in soup, but I can bully you lubbers around," installed himself in the third. The twins promptly joined him. Callissa, still red-eyed and bitterly mute, gave them a savage glance and pointedly made for Amver's craft.

I let her go, since there seemed no alternative. We renewed our mud masks, downed our salgar draft, manned our paddles, and blundered away west into the labyrinth.

I must admit that to tackle Stirsselian by water, with a competent pilot, is far better than to wallow along in an army patrol, with the nerve-wracking chance of a Phaxian ambush round every bend. Before camp Amver reckoned we might have made eight miles, and since we had struck west on land, this put us near Kerym Cletho, the first of the gigantic basins that fill Deve Gaz's rift from march to march. We camped among helmyns over a deep channel. There were no mud slides, but fish showed in the amber water, and also lilies, anchored flotillas of a deep vivid pink, closed for the night. Beryx gazed at them a long time, with an expression of revived and poignant if not happy memories.

Stirsselian soon routed the past. We had hardly lit our fire when Evis cocked an ear. Amver stopped, listened too. Then nodded. "Drums," he said.

They muttered on in the hush, a just-audible irregular pulse. Zyr looked behind him. Zem and Zam closed up on me. Beryx raised his brows to Amver. "Do we make a peace sign? Or leave it to them?"

Amver pulled his wide lower lip. He sounded a trifle unsure. "I think . . . we just go along quietly and wait. When they're ready . . . we'll know."

Beryx nodded. "Like Hethox. Look you over first." And he turned to choosing a bed-spot, unperturbed.

For three days we paddled deeper and deeper into Kerym Cletho, the only sign of other human life those evening drums. We acquired a helmyn nut grinding-quern, a net of pounded vine fibre, a bow built by Evis to shoot arrows with fire-hardened points which eventually, amid general triumph, felled an unwary duck. Like Zem and Zam we began to replace clothes with mud, more practical for wading, easily repaired, far more leech and insect proof. No crocodiles, Phaxians, or quick-mud appeared. At times, as we wobbled down some convoluted deep-water channel, roofed by a mesh of sun-shot clethra leaves, walled in arches of clethra roots, pleasantly cool in the watery shade, with white dashes of sun on amber water, helmyn fronds dangling harmlessly overhead, lilies sliding safely underneath, mud to foil the mosquitoes, Amver to steer us, and Beryx, if necessary, to get us out, I almost enjoyed myself.

It was not mosquitoes that roused me the fourth day. It was a sound that hurled me back to those awful dawns when the Phaxians made a surprise assault: the grunt of a man struck down and out.

Plunging from my cloak I clawed for a sword—or would have, had a vise not pinned my hand and Beryx rapped, <Keep still!>

I sat, every muscle over-taut, tightened further at what I saw.

The camp had been overrun. A ring of small coal-black men with helmets of mud-packed hair watched us from behind drawn arrows with dull, smeared heads. My blood ran cold. More were among our baggage, at the punts, the smoored fire, watching the rest wake. Zyr, the sentry, lay face down, motionless, while a nuggety warrior with cicatrices on his breast tucked a short bludgeon back in a twisted hair belt. It was impossible to deduce anything from those small, shut, wildcat faces. Thankfully, I saw Amver rouse.

His mouth sagged open, but he kept his nerve. After a moment, still supine, he spoke to them.

It was some Gjerven dialect, too corrupt for me. He sounded conciliatory, but like a man among strangers of his own blood. None of the archers reacted; but at length the sentry-feller approached.

There was an exchange. I caught, "Assharral," and, "Phaxia," and, "alsyr"—peace. Then, rather impatiently, the small warrior asked something else.

Amver's face changed. More talk. His surprise became wonder, incredulity, something near to awe. He gestured at Beryx. The warrior glanced round, then issued a command.

Amver rose. They both came over to Beryx, still seated in his cloak with his empty left hand prominently displayed, and in a very queer tone Amver said, "He wants to know if—you're the rainmaker, sir."

Beryx did not hesitate. "Tell him, Yes."

The warrior had understood. He squatted down in that boneless way, knees in armpits and hands dangled between, staring into Beryx's face. His small eyes were pitch-black, bright as coals, and as intense. He might have been trying to read the mind behind the face as well.

Silently, Beryx looked back at him. His own eyes were barely awake, just a hint of motion in the irises, the twine of deep currents in a green-stained stream. But no human eyes move like that.

The camp was dead quiet. For a moment I wondered if they were exchanging thoughts. Then the warrior reached out one small pink-palmed hand and delicately, but without timidity, laid it to the scarred side of Beryx's face.

Beryx did not move. Withdrawing his hand, the warrior looked at the crippled arm. Beryx shrugged it from his cloak. The warrior put his hand on the wrist. Carefully, withdrew. His eyes moved. With a small grin Beryx murmured, "I'll end in my skin," and began to unbutton his voluminous Phaxian shirt.

It was half-open when the warrior, with that same intent, unoffensive decision, intercepted his hand, kept the grip an instant to be sure it was not misunderstood, then gently eased the shirt back until he could see the edges of the scar.

Beryx waited. Even more gently, the warrior re-adjusted the shirt, then watched closely as ever while Beryx did it up. After that he squatted a long time and once again studied Beryx's face. I could not decide if any change showed in his own.

Finally, not turning his head, he addressed Amver in a level, dead-pan voice.

Amver's brows shot up. He wrought with emotions. Then he said, "He thinks, sir, that our fishing net must have been made by a—a—sheep-butcher from Kemrestan."

I had just worked out that this came to an insult when Beryx showed me its real nature by replying in the same straight-faced formality, "Tell him that should please him. We'll miss more of his fish."

Amver translated. A sparkle warmed the black eyes. A silent laugh rippled round the perimeter, and before I knew it the warrior was talking full gallop to Amver, hands flying, emphasis in his face, Beryx was saying, "Take it quietly, all of you," and a crowd of small, respectful but thoroughly searching rank and file were all over us.

Ulven are not content to use their eyes. Pink-palmed hands tested our bow, assessed our cooking pot, felt the texture of my cloak, my sword-hilt, my hair, my very fingernails. Zem and Zam got on famously, for they touched with equal freedom in return, but after Callissa's first shrink and squeak they avoided her. In any case, it was Beryx who was the real cynosure.

They clustered round him six deep, putting out their hands with that odd, intense concentration that held neither fear nor captor's insolence, but was not, as with us, plain curiosity. It was as if they already knew what he was, and were driven to make the closest possible contact with what they saw.

His dialogue over, Amver forged into the crowd, more agog than anyone. "Sir, they know about wizards—aedryx, I mean!" Beryx nodded, unsurprised. "Lisbyrx, they say, rainmakers, there are old stories handed down, so when you made it rain at the Taven they knew what you were, they've been trailing us since Phaxia, that was the drums, of course, because there's a prophecy—I've never heard it!—that a crippled lisbyr'll come to Stirsselian, this is the headman's son and the old folk sent him to find us because," with rising urgency, "there's troops coming in from Assharral!"

Beryx's look of confirmation had become a kind of wariness. Now it sharpened. "How far? How many?" He was the general again. "On our track?"

"Nossir, there's four or five patrols at the end of Kerym Cletho but they're just probing 'n in trouble with the swamp, the Ulven're shadowing 'em all 'n they reckon no problem to get rid of 'em—if you want. . . ."

With a glance at the bows Beryx emphatically shook his head. Amver nodded as if he had expected it and was off again. "So they came to warn us and they'll hide or help us or whatever we want because you're a lisbyr and because"—he assumed a thoroughly mystified tone—"the prophecy says the crippled wizard will end the Assharran drought."

Beryx sighed in candid relief. "Just so long," he said, "as I'm not expected to make yams and kanna fall from the sky."

"But what's it mean, sir? There's no drought in Assharral. Unless they mean Axaira, 'n it never rains there anyway."

"No?" Beryx shot him a piercing glance. "How long have they been 'wild'? And why? Not been hunted, by any chance? Nobody thought they were dangerous animals and tried to wipe them out?"

Amver stammered, confounded. "B-but—we—they—it's always been like that! They are dangerous! They raid crops—kill cattle—burn farms, sometimes! My father sort of knew them 'n he still had to pay a bullock a year peace price 'n—everybody thought we were low going near them at all. . . ."

He tailed off, finding, as I had, shame in what had once seemed reputable. Beryx nodded sadly, his eyes on the naked crowd.

"Primitive," he said. "Driven back on poor land, then punished when they couldn't live on it. Made more backward by the hunts. Just primitive, and the stories warped to a cross between demons and beasts." There was pity in his eyes.

He looked back to Amver. "Not your fault," he said more gently. "You were bred to the thinking. But . . . no wonder they want to end the drought."

Amver rallied a little. "But sir, the prophecy. How did they know?"

"They don't. It's a hope. A lot of us live on them. Or perhaps there's a foresighted strain, there often is with people like this. And your headman's son doesn't know Ruanbrarx, but he could follow my mind. He only knew about this"—he touched his side—"when I thought of it." His smile was wry. "Empathy. Like a higher form of beast."

Amver retired hastily on the tangible. "Do we go with them, though? 'N what about the troops?"

"Go with them, yes, if they can get us round the patrols." He frowned. "But not to their village. When Moriana gets serious she might destroy it. I don't want any surplus hostages."

"No problem, sir." Amver's face cleared. "They don't have a village, just season camps. They live on the move, in their boats."

Beryx's face cleared too. "At least," he said, smiling, "they might teach us how to fish."

They taught us we were babes in Stirsselian compared to them. That first morning, giving their tacit opinion of our punts by ignoring them, they loaded us in their own craft, single log dugouts without so much as an outrigger, kept upright by the paddlers' balance and skill, no deeper than the punts but immeasurably swifter, handier, water-tight, able to knife unchecked into the thickest undergrowth. Their fishing nets are finger-sized meshes of twisted human hair, they use tiny bird-bows you can draw in elbow-length, bone sliver knives and needles kept in their hair, woven cane tents that fold down into a dugout and can be pitched anywhere, stone spears and axes patiently chipped and ground from raw flint. They are immune to swamp fever, insensible to mosquito and leech, swim like fish, see safe mud at a glance, move with shadow speed and silence afloat or afoot, know their territory to the inch, and have positively uncanny communication on the road or in the hunt. The dugout fleets veer simultaneously, like starlings in the air. Nor are beaters or archers instructed for a hunt. They assemble at the boats, reach the run, melt away, flush the game, and rise at the precise spot for the equally silent, uncelebrated kill.

Silence, indeed, is the watchword of Ulven life. Babies never cry; even at play children do not shout; adults consult, gossip, mourn, exult, in a permanent undertone. No doubt, like their impassiveness, it has been bred in by generations of outlawry.

What their race numbers I have no idea. Normally they live in family groups which rove a particular territory, but we had caused a general mobilization of the most tenuous sort. Some fifty warriors had mustered to scout or meet with us, from which I guess there are perhaps three hundred in the Kerym Cletho tribe, but we never saw them assembled. On a low islet whose sole sign of occupation was its bare-trodden earth, we met the headman, whose one badge and function of office seems to be the maintenance of four wives, and the rest of the Old Ones, men and women as inscrutable as their envoy. They studied us all, gathered to touch Beryx with that same deep constrained respect, then dissolved, leaving the warriors to act as escort, commissariat and guides.

There was also an entourage of families, brotherhoods, hunting teams, who would join us for a day or a week, then melt away and be replaced. Perhaps it was because we were in their runs, but chiefly, I think, it was that they wanted to be near Beryx for a while.

They were never extravagant or importunate. There was just the silent, intent gaze, the compulsion to touch, the repression by their people's discipline of an emotion close to reverence, that yet contained affection. A hunger for bodily contact with something legendary, a prophesied deliverance that was also flesh and blood.

It neither embarrassed Beryx nor went to his head. I daresay he had been schooled to a lesser scale of such treatment when he was a king, but his use of the arts certainly did nothing to discourage it. We landed one day in a stand of huge nerran trees where a work-party were hewing with stone axes at a dugout-sized trunk. Two days' labor, and the cut, dimpled like embossed hammer work, was barely three inches deep. Beryx took one look and sprang to life.

"Four! They'll be there for weeks." A swift glance raked the terrain. "Amver, tell them to stand—over there. You others too."

The Ulven obeyed, impassive as ever, but every eye was riveted on him. He swung to face the tree. Stiffened, drew the first familiar extended breath.

Pressure built up. The air seemed to vibrate. Then his body whiplashed, there was a lash of green-white fire. With a deafening crackle of shorn wood the giant snapped at the cut, tilted, gathered momentum and thundered to its earth-shaking fall.

Leaves, twigs, and frightened birds erupted everywhere. Beryx stood back, getting his breath, with a contented smile. "Not the biggest I ever cut," he said to us. "But it's something I can do for them."

The axemen, nailed down till the last echo faded, had finally crept up to look. There was none of the outcry you would find in Assharral. Just small hands creeping over the shorn butt, and a look behind them, whites vivid in those masked Ulven eyes.

Beryx smiled at them in turn, and made the gesture for "It was nothing." The eyes grew wider. They were still watching two hours later when we paddled away.

That swelled our entourage over the next days, especially at the midday halt, when we Assharrans, to the Ulven's puzzlement, would insist on brewing mint-tea. Since his art was quicker than flint or tinder or even coals from an Ulven ember-flask, Beryx had got into the habit of lighting the fire. A crowd would inevitably gather for it, quite silent and mannerly, those ranks of unwinking eyes patiently expectant for the green flash, the flare of flame; after which they would melt off to let us rest in peace.

Callissa usually made the tea. Having managed to muster us all in the one place at the same time, she was pouring out that day, while we sat cross-legged round the fire like any patrol brewing up. The twins were ensconced at Beryx's elbows, also as usual. He had just taken the first cautious sip when Zem piped up, "Sir Scarface, why is Mi like a Quarred fyr?"—"And what is it?" added Zam.

I saw Beryx pole-axed at last. He choked, the cup flew from his hand; but instead of being caught with Axynbrarve it dropped plumb in the angle of his crossed shins amid a scalding flood of tea.

"Oh, you stupid boys!" Callissa broke out crossly. "Stand up, quick, before it burns you." More tartly still, "I don't want that again."

She might not have spoken. Beryx had got his wind. Absently he shook out his wet trousers, but his eyes were turning from one to the other wide-eyed, guileless face. He answered with conscious casualness.

"Quarred is a country with a lot of sheep. Fyrx are the dogs that work them. They're red and small and clever, and very quiet. And I was thinking your mother was like a fyr, because here we all are, going quietly along together in the right direction, while she rushes round out of sight, doing twice the work. Just like a Quarred fyr with a mob of sheep."

They nodded as if they too saw nothing odd. Callissa was torn between unwelcome pleasure at the compliment and insult at the comparison to a dog. I sat speechless. I had noted his choice of verb.

Still intent on them, he asked casually, "How long have you been hearing me, Zam?"

Zam replied with equal nonchalance. "Ever since you came. But with most people we have to really listen. You're much better. It's quite easy to hear everything."

"Everything," Beryx repeated. He sounded a little faint. I knew he was torn between consternation and mirth.

Mirth won. He let out a splutter. "Served with my own sauce!" And sobered. "Do you listen to everybody?"

"We listened when you first came," Zem explained, "like we always do with new people, to be sure they're all right. Mi and Da don't often make mistakes, but it's harder if you can't hear."

"Thank you!" I said. "You pair of—of—" Beryx grinned without looking round.

"So I suppose you've heard me talk to your father, and the Lady as well?"

Zem nodded. "And we heard you fight for him." I cringed. "We didn't like you then, till Mi explained what you really did. To herself, I mean." He added conscientiously, "We can't always hear Mi and Da properly either, unless they're stirred up, but they're better than anyone except you." He looked disapproving. "That Fengthira nearly deafened us. And she called Da a dolt."

"She's no diplomat." Beryx's shoulders shook. "You've always been able to hear?"

They nodded. Zem squirmed. "At school—we used to—but nobody understood—or liked it—so now we just use it for ourselves."

"I see." His eyes were in flux, lightened to crystal green, but this time it was not the rise of power. Then it altered to amused percipience.

"So now," he said blandly, "you thought you'd make some real use of the thing?"

"Yes!" they chorused. "We want to talk."—"And see."—"And light fires."—"And manage horses."—"Like you."

"And you want me to teach you?"

Their eyes lit up. "Yes, please!"

"Well, I won't." He did not mince matters. "Not because I don't want to. Because it wouldn't be right. You'll know why, later on."

He gazed at them with longing, and the nervousness of someone handed a fragile, potentially dangerous yet precious living thing. It was not their paralyzing innocence that he feared, I understood, but his own inadequacy.

"Dismiss," he commanded. "Case is closed. Go and talk to the Ulven. And don't listen in!"

Dashed but obedient, they departed. His eyes lifted across the fire to mine.

"Yes," he said. "You've bred a couple of aedryx. Or aedryx-to-be."

"But—but—" I spluttered. "What—how—"

"Oh, your side of it's easy. I thought the moment I saw you, That's a perfect gray-eyed stiff-necked granite-honest Stiriand."

"I am not!" I said in revolt and fear. "We're farmers, we've always been farmers—"

"I don't mean your blood's pure or that you're even in the direct line. Some branch of a branch probably drifted east, so long ago they've lost the very memory. Or were driven underground, the way they were in Everran when the aedryx were wiped out. You're just a throwback to the looks, and maybe you carry the power's seed. But. . . ."

His eyes turned to Callissa, whose face revealed protest, abhorrence, scandalized horror and outright mutiny.

"What was it, ma'am?" The question was gentle, but not to be denied. "Bee-master, water-finder, soothseer, witch? With such a strong show as this, the blood couldn't come just from one side."

Callissa went white. Then her eyes shut. It was a bare whisper when it came.

"The sight . . . my mother's people." She might have been confessing descent from an army whore. "We never talked about it, but. . . ."

"You've no call for shame," he said gently. "In fact, you should be proud."

Her eyes shot open. He did not notice. He was gazing after the twins.

"You may not think it, but—you've mothered something beyond the greatest hope you ever dreamed." An immense distance entered his gaze. "Something that couldn't be manufactured by Velandryxe itself."

"Eh?" I said.

He woke up. "The aedryx before Math lived in cycles," he said. "A cycle would start, they'd increase, then they'd exterminate themselves. Then a new founder would appear, and it would start again. The last cycle was Th'Iahn's own, and Fengthira thought she was the last of them. Until I came along. I am the first new aedr for eleven human generations." His quiet voice kept the import of the words. "I was made, not born. And I can't found a line. But. . . ." Now it was sheer reverence. "They were born. A natural blending of aptitudes. And when they learn Ruanbrarx . . . they'll grow up with Math. Not, like every other aedr who ever came to it, have to graft it on." A brief, depthless, ungrudging envy crossed his face. "It'll be in their lives' grain. And if a new cycle starts . . . for the first time, it will begin in Math."

And, I thought, as my heart moved in unflawed joy for him, you will have found your sons.

Callissa took breath. Knowing what she would say, I cut in first.

"If that's so, why won't you teach them? The sooner the better, surely, and who better—"

"No," he said flatly. "Ruanbrarx must go plough-track. Between opposites. Man to woman, woman to man. I don't know why, even Fengthira doesn't. The old aedryx didn't always follow it, but they knew perfectly well that when they didn't it brought Ammath. I was lucky that when I learnt, the last living aedr was a woman, so I came to it the right way. No matter how much I wanted, I wouldn't teach them. Not run the risk of—warping a thing like this. If only—"

He fell silent. Then he shot a glance at Callissa, and said abruptly, "Somebody called Math a river because it finds channels where no reason would expect. I'll just have to hope it finds a channel for this."

Callissa would not talk about it, and for the boys' sake I was reluctant myself. The others took their cue from me, so by evening the revelation might never have come at all.

It did make me more conscious of where the boys were and with whom. Next midday, or the day after, we halted under a big heagar, and, waking from a catnap among its roots, I thought as usual, Where are the twins?

There was no sound of them. Beyond the buttress at my back Callissa stirred and murmured. Then she started up with a mew of alarm, and somewhere further away Beryx said in quiet reassurance, "Swimming with Amver. Quite safe, ma'am."

I heard her breathe in, wholly enraged. "And if they got caught in a snag, the lilies, a man-eater came—just what could you do?"

"I could get them out, ma'am," he answered softly. "Even then."

Leaving Phaxia had made one of those long-term rifts in a marriage which time had only just begun to heal. But from the day we left Zyphryr Coryan her coldness to Beryx had been as dogged as his consideration for her, his patient, indomitable and constantly rebuffed offers of peace. So I was startled to hear her answer. And more than startled by the raw note of jealousy.

"No wonder they come before all the rest of us. You knew all along that they'd be sorcerers too."

I could not have tackled, much less resolved such a mare's nest. He took the unspoken grievance first.

"Ma'am, even if you weren't their mother, weren't Alkir's wife, had never lifted a finger for me, I couldn't care more for them than I do for you."

She said stonily, "Why?"

"Because you are."

"What?"

"Because you are reality. Living reality. A human being. And there can't be—degrees of caring for reality. I have to feel as much for every one of you. Else I might as well not have lived."

"What do you mean?"

"I was born a king. To safeguard anyone in my keeping was bred into me. I built my life on it. Now I'm an aedr it's more binding still, because I have more power, and everything that is has a claim on me. So I have to do my utmost to—keep faith. I follow Math, and Math says, Respect that-which-is. All of it. If I made differences between you, I'd break faith. I—I'd destroy myself."

Why, I thought, does he lay himself open like this, where it can do no good? And found the answer in his own words. Keep faith with Math, or destroy yourself.

Callissa was saying with perverse relish, "So I mean about as much to you as a tree? Or a—a dog, I suppose?"

"Not quite, ma'am." A shade of laughter woke. "It would take a Sky-lord to be so just, and I'm not perfect by any means. I still feel more for people than for trees. Or dogs, if the truth be told."

Shadows shifted on a stir of wind, dappling trodden chocolate earth, bringing the cool of afternoon. Her silence was unappeased.

When he spoke again it was entreaty, the last resort of power shackled by its own will.

"Ma'am, whatever I say to you I can't make you believe. I can only say that I never intended harm to you. I've never wished you ill. Whatever unhappiness I've caused you has been greater unhappiness to me. I never have and never will hold you cheap. And however you've treated me, I don't bear a grudge." He sounded suddenly spent. "But I'm only flesh and blood. When I have doors shut in my face, it hurts."

Surely, I thought, breath held, she cannot shut the door on that?

The silence seemed endless. Then she said, wretched but no longer inveterately hostile, "If only we'd never left Frimmor. . . ."

"Ma'am. . . ." He had recovered. Respectful but indestructible, the laughter was awake.

"If you'll forgive me saying so, those are the most pointless words anyone ever spoke. You can't reverse time. Not if you're an aedr with the Well, not if you were a Sky-lord Himself. And if you could, and if you remade it from the first waking of the first idea of the creation of the world in the first of the Four's minds, it still wouldn't satisfy everyone. If you'd never left Frimmor. . . . If my line hadn't interbred till one of us turned up sterile, I wouldn't have come to Assharral, because I wouldn't have been an aedr, because there would have been no dragon to kill. I'd have lived and died a king. In Everran. With. . . ." He broke off. I could barely hear the rest. ". . . sons of my own."

"But it happened," he resumed. The grief, however mortal, had been veiled. "We can't go backward. Wherever we are, we can only go forward. And make the best of it."

When Callissa did not speak, he said meekly, "I'm sorry, ma'am. I've been talking philosophy at you again."

She cleared her throat. She still sounded brusque, but the ground-note was different.

"My name is Callissa," she said. "There's no need to call me ma'am." I heard her scramble up. "And those boys should be out of the water. They've been wet far too long."

Chapter X

We were still making circles round Moriana's wretched patrols, who indeed we never saw. It was all done with the drums. Zem and Zam never tired of watching our drummer squatted between his two hollow wooden pipes with their lydwyr hide heads, polished and blackened by decades of sweat, his palms fluttering like butterflies as he beat out the signal, so soft at close quarters, carrying for miles on that soggy air. He would stop. Listen. Speak to Ygg, the headman's son. Ygg would relay to Amver, who would ceremoniously repeat to Beryx, who for form's sake would consult with me before returning the ritual reply, "I will use Ygg's eyes." And Ygg would launch us into another maze where I had to wait for sun or star-rise to orient myself.

Our routine was already formed: breakfast and salgar at dawn, drum-talk, march and hunt, brew up. Catnap, march, bivouac, drum-talk, bed down. To the Ulven it was normal life with a spice of danger added, and soon it seemed so to us. Then Amver listened with mounting excitement to the morning report, and burst out, "Sir, they're going back! The patrols've pulled out!"

A wide grin split Ost's muddy countenance. Karis pounded Zyr's back. But Beryx lowered his eyes and said nothing at all.

"Sir?" Evis prompted at last.

"Yes," he said. His eyes were unsmiling, midnight green. "I just wonder what she'll try next."

Our fears eased when she had tried nothing by noon. Evis, however, had been speculating on his own lines. As we lay watching the barbed helmyn fronds scratch and whisper overhead, he asked suddenly, "Sir, the Lady . . . who—what is she, actually?"

"She was born," Beryx answered presently, "of aedric stock. A branch from the same tree as mine." His eyes crinkled. "And across the blanket like us. Her father came east after one of the aedric collapses. A bloodbath, as usual. Nearly—eleven of your generations ago." Evis caught his breath. "Part of that's the Well, of course, but aedryx do live longer than men." He spoke without apology, but without pity either. It was a fact. Reality.

"Eleven generations." Evis had taken it another way. A slow, vengeful anger woke in his voice. "Of enslavement for Assharral."

"Not all her fault," Beryx demurred. "She was the only child of an aedr with non-existent morals and hair-raising vices. He died when a boy his pet darre was chasing in the snake-pit threw it out on him. She was left the heir. A fifteen-year-old girl with four equally villainous uncles, a brood of hell-hound cousins, and a grandmother who could put the fear of death into them all. The uncles expected her to be a puppet. If she got too uppity, one said, he'd marry her.

They took her ten years to remove, not exactly by honest means, and by then they'd done a fair job of brutalizing Assharral. When she poisoned the last, five provinces were in flames, three in arms, and the last two were hardly models of fidelity. That's when she discovered the Well. I think she crushed the revolt so drastically because she was new to that power. And young. And . . . afraid."

The silence disagreed.

"At any rate, she made such a job of it that you've never risen again. That left her with the cousins, a viper's nest of trouble and intrigue. She arranged a family banquet and made a clean sweep of them. She still had her grandmother to survive. Five years 'regency.' If you could call it that, with the old harpy thwarting her at every turn, and always the danger that she'd provoke another revolt." It was near sympathy in his voice. I knew he looked from a fellow sovereign's point of view. "In the end, the old lady pinched at her once too often. Moriana walked her over Los Morryan's parapet."

When nobody spoke, he went on himself.

"So then she was on her own. The Well in her hands, an empire under her yoke. Unlimited power of both kinds, no knowledge of Math, a bad upbringing, a worse heredity, and some cruel experience to reinforce them. All in all, it's a wonder she didn't rot far worse. After all"—his eyes turned, teasing me—"Assharral has been wealthy, peaceful, orderly—and fairly safe."

It was Evis who supplied the rebuttal. I had never heard such savagery from him. "And bewitched."

"Well . . . yes."

Evis sat up. "I think," he said with grim emphasis, "the Ulven are right. It's time to end the drought."

Beryx was looking unhappy. "Yes. There must be an end to Ammath. But . . . you must be careful how you manage it."

"I know how to manage it." Evis' teeth showed. "We ought to make her walk over that parapet herself. But a gibbet will do. It did for my grandfather. And he was never a 'rebel' in his life."

"Yeah," Dakis came in, the blood light kindled in his own eyes. "And there's a few others'll hang with her. They reported my uncle—just for keeping one cow undeclared."

"No," Beryx broke in, almost desperately. "Can't you see, if you do that, you've changed nothing? You're as bad as what you destroy. You'll just re-create Ammath."

Evis turned on him. "Then do we walk out with our hands

up, sir, and say, 'We forgive your sins, come and commit a few more on us'?"

"No, of course not. But you can stop wrong and not renew it. Not load it onto your own backs."

"By the pits"—there was a slow blaze in Wenver's golden eyes—"not them that come for my father's folk—"

"Let off scot-free?!" yelled Zyr. "Those boot-licking—"

"Never!" shouted Karis. "Let 'em pay their debts!"

Beryx's dismay vanished. He shot upright and his eyes were crystal white.

"If you do that you are more abominable than the wickedness you destroy. There is no absolution for those who go into evil having knowledge of Ammath."

He glared at us. It was not simple wrath. It was the threat of justice, more pitiless than the evil it will suppress. Only Evis dared to retort.

"If you say so, sir. But whoever's let off, there shouldn't be any mercy for the witch."

The white threat vanished. His eyes danced green, his mouth turned up, he was suddenly mischief incarnate. "Oh," he drawled, "I do have plans for her."

But though we waited expectantly, it seemed that was a quite private jest.

Next morning the drums reported all clear. In an almost lazy atmosphere we packed up, and the twins were helping me cart the first load to the dugouts when Zam dropped the pot. He clutched his head. Zem cried out. Then he said, "Sir Scarface!" And they both bolted for a tangle of lianas beyond the camp. In my own alarm I hurried in pursuit.

Beyond the vines sun struck bright on a little inlet's gloss of olive-green water and root-gnarled banks and the spiny green of helmyn fronds. Beryx must have been on reconnaissance too.

He was perched on a leaning helmyn trunk, his back to me. The twins were within armslength, silent, motionless, strained forward yet not touching him. Some quality in his stillness halted me as well.

It seemed a long time before he turned. He was white, the scar livid as a brand, with a numb blankness in his eyes. He looked at the twins as if he had never seen them before.

Zem swallowed, Zam gulped. His eyes came past them to me.

"Rema," he said dully. "And the maid—Zepha, wasn't it?"

My mouth dried. He hid his face in his hand.

"The Ruanbraxe . . . she couldn't break it. So she hunted them. Family . . . informers . . . spies. . . ."

I heard myself speak. Needlessly. "Dead?"

His head moved. I could just hear it. ". . . tortured them. . . ."

A helmyn frond crackled down. His fingers were crooked over his temple, white among the raven hair. I swallowed too. But what could I do or say? I knew where he would lay the guilt.

At last, trusting he would know it was tact and not desertion, I turned away. Like a new-dealt wound, the news moved with me as I went back, told Amver to postpone departure. Braced myself, and disclosed the rest.

When Beryx reappeared it was left to Callissa to give the only practical aid. With her own magic she had kept the fire up, the pot on the boil, and brewed tea the instant he appeared. Wordlessly she took the cup over and put it in his hand.

He nursed it against his right palm, staring into it. A ring of Ulven had formed, taking the sense of the tragedy with the empathy he ascribed to them. He drank the tea. Then he looked at me and said dully, "I suppose . . . we'd better go."

★ ★ ★ ★ ★

Next morning I woke in a dread Beryx did nothing to allay. He looked ill, almost cowed, and when he woke, sat a long time huddled silently in his cloak. We were packing up before I saw him take a deep breath, stiffen his shoulders, and turn his gradually emptying eyes toward the south.

The camp movement ebbed away. One by one we turned to watch him, waiting, with a pang of fearful anticipation, for what his vision might reveal. The Ulven had gathered behind us, silent as ever, but with a shade of expression in their midnight eyes.

Heartbeats ticked by. Were left uncounted. Their passage grew stressful, painful, and still he stared . . . Then he gave a violent jerk and wrenched back, clapping the left hand over his eyes. His shoulders twisted. He said something incoherent, and buried his face in his knees.

It was an act of sheer willpower when he straightened up. After another endless moment, he began to speak.

"Your sister. . . ."

My eyes flew up, Zyr had blanched a mottled whiteish pink. Beryx's eyes were black in a bloodless face. I knew what he wanted to say, and that no words were adequate.

He got up, tottered up, a hand to his head. "Think," he said thickly. "Must think. . . ." And walking through us as if we were not there he vanished into the scrub.

The sun climbed, the Ulven appeared and dissolved and reappeared. The day crept on. We offered our futile sympathy to Zyr, and he wrought with his grief. Zem and Zam, looking scared and queasy, had drawn in close to me. Recalling their gift, I could not stop myself asking, "Can you. . . ." And Zam nodded, and gripped his lips together. But he did not speak.

It was mid-afternoon before the scrub rustled, and Beryx,

slow and bent as a cripple, made his way out.

His face was pale, with shadow-like bruises round the eyes, he had that shrunken look of a critically wounded man, and he moved as if he had met some adversary beyond even an aedr's strength. His eyes found Zyr, and flinched away. Then he came slowly to the middle of the camp, and nerved himself to speak.

"I put a Ruanbraxe on . . . all your kin. All I could find." He forced his eyes back to Zyr. "If I'd thought . . . if I'd done it sooner . . . I'll never forgive myself."

And that, I knew, was gospel truth.

Zyr answered very steadily, "Not your fault, sir." Iron came into his voice. "It's hers."

Beryx shut his eyes a moment. A cold rill shot down my spine. I could tell he was steeling himself for other, more dreadful news.

"Rema. The maid. Your. . . ." His voice was ragged, just audible. "I had it wrong. . . . Not revenge." He dragged in a breath. "It's the next . . . offensive. In here . . . we can't be reached. So—we have to be brought out."

We stared. He seemed to shrink on himself.

"By—by—using . . . hostages."

Understanding, then vivid horror, then an altered horror showed in every face. The conclusion none of us dared to voice.

"I thought about it." The mere consideration must have been torture. "I thought of—everything." His face twisted. "And—I have no choice."

I heard Callissa choke a cry. Amver was gray, Evis white. The image of Klyra's head, Thephor's remains, burnt before my eyes. But not the twins, I thought desperately. Not the twins as well!

Then bitter, helpless hatred blazed in me. Witch! I raged. Hell-hag, diabolical whore . . . she knew he could not have borne the murder of innocents, his followers' kin, blameless in every way. That he would sacrifice himself first. And us. Once again his own good, that should have been a shield, had been made a dagger inside his guard. With fists and teeth clenched I prayed, If I could just get my hands on her . . . oh, to the pits with this useless, crippling Math!

My eyes cleared. The acceptance of certain, horrible death was on every face. Sivar spoke for us, his voice just recognizable.

"Well, I—I'll go with you, sir—at least."

Others murmured. Beryx stared. Then more excruciating realization woke. His voice shook worse than Sivar's.

"No . . . You don't understand. I mean—I can't go out."

For a moment I doubted either my ears or my wits. All of us were speechless. He faced us, a man caught between his own integrities and being pulled apart.

"If I stay," his voice shook almost uncontrollably, "she'll hunt out your families . . . farthest kin . . . friends . . . anyone so much as linked with you." The sweat was standing on his face. "One by one . . . While we watch. . . ."

"Sir, can't you stop it?" Evis broke in wildly. "Fight her! Do something! Surely—"

"She has the Well," Beryx said flatly. "I'm not strong enough."

The silence yawned like a grave. We had seen the scope of his power, however leashed. For the first time I really understood Los Velandryxe' threat.

Wenver was stammering, "But s-sir, if we went back to Ph-Phaxia, if we didn't try to—"

Beryx's eyes blackened like smoke-stained glass.

"She planned it . . . while we were in Phaxia. I saw. . . ." He thrust a hand over his eyes. "She let me see. . . ." It was the barest whisper. "She'll go on with it . . . wherever we are."

Beside me Callissa spoke up in a small, unsure, wholly well-wishing voice. "Fengthira . . . did you think to ask . . . ?"

Beryx's face clenched. "I can't see her. Or speak to her. I don't know if . . . Moriana's stopped me. Or—"

My blood ran cold. That the Well's malignity might reach so far as Hethria, affect Fengthira, who had been in my mind, an unexamined hope of reserves, superior force, was almost the worst of all. And for him, to find his own mainstay gone. . . .

He wiped his face. There was a shake in his hand. "But the worst is . . . if I . . . give myself up. She'd . . . she won't kill me." He struggled to go on. "She'd corrupt me. The Well . . . I couldn't hold out. I'd—" He actually gagged. "I'd become—Ammath."

I understood. Death, torture, betrayal of us and our innocent kin, all would pale beside the threat of being not merely defeated, not merely enslaved, but perverted. Himself become the evil he feared and shunned and fought against with all his living might. There are worse destructions than to simply die.

He was flinching at some further horror, the most unbearable, because it was already familiar to him.

"She'd make me . . . the bane of Assharral. And I can't. I couldn't . . . not again!"

That broke us all. Evis blurted, "No, sir, you mustn't, love of—That would be the worst that could—" Amver, stiff-lipped, cut in, "If we gotta go, our people gotta go, all right—but not that!"

We had not eased him in the least. "You have no right to decide that—I have no right! To spill innocent blood—whatever the reason, it's Ammath! Whatever I do, it's Ammath!"

He had reduced us to his own helplessness. It was Callissa who went across to take his arm and say with frail control, "Then you have to take the lesser of the two. If some of us suffer . . . it's still better than—than the worst."

He looked blindly down at her. "I thought of killing myself." She turned white. "But that solves nothing. You're left in her hands—and Assharral as well."

"You can't do that." She spoke with fright's command. "You must think of something." I caught my breath. With just such blind faith she had bidden me "think of something!" in the vault. "There has to be a way out. You'll have to find it, that's all. You must!"

Incredibly, that steadied him. After a time he stopped trembling. In a quieter if still hopeless voice he said, "I can only see one chance. And even that. . . . It's pure chance. Blind trust in Velandryxe. But . . . if I don't . . . give in. . . . No matter what she does. . . ." He shuddered again. "She'll go on trying—worse and worse. And perhaps . . . she'll try the one thing too much. Overreach herself. Break her own power. And do what I can't. Destroy Ammath."

He looked at her without hope of understanding, and I thought how I had failed him at the same tactical crux. But whatever her sense of the theory, Callissa had a better grasp of the emotional point.

"Then that's what you must do." She sounded quite matter-of-fact. Her lips trembled, but she mastered it. "No matter what happens—what it costs. At least there'll be a—hope."

I saw him swallow. Then he set his teeth and took a long deep breath. His eyes looked past us, drained of power or vitality, but I knew he was mustering resources for the worst battle of his life.

It is hard to assemble a picture of that campaign. As in battle or nightmare or by Los Morryan, time grows distorted; memory jumbles under the impact of stress and distress, and, as in all crises, the past shrinks upon itself. I suppose we drank salgar, made and broke camp and traveled in Stirsselian, but like eating after a funeral, we took no note of it. Our real life was in the waiting, like citizens of a plague-stricken town, for the axe to fall on us.

Beryx's strategy was not all passive. In those first days he scattered our kin across Assharral, commanding them to flee if without certainty of escape, doing his very best to thwart the Lady's pursuit. "Neither of us," he said, "can See everywhere at once. If I concentrate on anyone, she'll just raise more and more hunters till she smothers me. But she can't hunt a hundred packs as one. . . ." So he shifted his attention between fugitives, making this one zigzag, another double back, blinding or disturbing un-Commanded pursuers or guard-posts to help a third, bringing others to shelter or a horse. And abandoning them, with bitter anguish, when the Lady took command of the chase.

Sometimes he succeeded. When Karis' father sailed a dinghy out of Zyphryr Coryan we celebrated with more joy than I felt returning from Phaxia. When his cousin reached Stirsselian, Amver egged the Ulven on to raid a caissyn farm and concocted a brew that laid out the whole camp. When Evis' mother found the Sathellin we lit a bonfire and danced. To a Sky-lord the whole thing must have resembled a chessboard in the heat of a ferocious contest, each player striving to deceive, anticipate or wreck the other's assault. But this chessboard was a whole empire, with a hundred scenes of ploy and counter-ploy, and one player was determined not to damage the pieces, while the other was bent on savaging him regardless of cost. And the pawns were not wood or ivory, they were living, breathing flesh and blood.

Beryx actually said it to me once. "It's like Thor'stang. Aedric chess. Only she doesn't know how to read my mind or use a hidden Command or mesmerize me, and I can use all the arts. But she has the Well." His face stiffened. "And we're playing with pieces of Math."

The mere sustained relentless deployment of his arts would have been draining enough, even if, unlike the Lady, he did not care for the pawns. And of course he did. Every loss wounded him triply, for the dead, for the bereaved, and on his own account. It was a breach of faith. A culpable negligence. A failed responsibility.

At the beginning he asked us, with rare awkwardness, "Would you rather know—or not?" Feeling a pale echo of his own choice, we decided we would rather know, so he had the task of telling us atop the rest.

That is one of the clearest memories, printed deep by repetition and the crescendo of that helpless, expectant fear. A morning fire, among helmyns, in a heagar shadow, amid some eyot's scrub, baggage stacked on the bare earth that is the only sign of an Ulven camp. Callissa crouched over the boiling pot. The Ulven perimeter. And the faces, stiff, strained, trapped in idleness, even at times betraying the vile hope that this time it might be you, to have it over with.

Until Beryx emerges from his reconnaissance, haggard and white with more than simple defeat. Then that searing endless moment while he nerves himself to deliver the blow in one or another waiting face. And the hideous knowledge that however deeply you suffered, it was still not over. That it would not be over, until your whole family, down to the remotest marriage kin, had been wiped out.

He flatly refused to say what happened to them. From the nightmare look on Zem and Zam's faces I guessed they sometimes heard, and the Ulven must have shared it too. After the first really cruel reverse, when Wenver's brother and all his family were taken on the very march of Kemrestan, Beryx was crouched on a stump, more shattered than Wenver himself, when Ygg came over. He did not speak. He merely laid a hand on Beryx's shoulder and left it there.

After a moment Beryx looked up at him. He was silent too. Support was offered, and accepted, and gratitude returned, in an understanding that did not look for words.

The ordeal took a fearful physical toll. Weight melted off him, and he went off his food to compound the effect. Most of his time was devoted to the arts, but the breaks did little to revive him, for he could seldom sleep. If I roused from my own broken rest he would more often than not be pacing the camp, a silent, unseen focus of distress, and when he did sleep his nightmares were worse than mine.

That is another image driven deep by repetition and stress: Callissa's face over re-woken embers, thicker shadows of sleeping men in the outer dark. Beryx crouched over a cup beyond the fire, so the light exaggerates the jut of bones in his wasted face, images more dreadful than reality haunting his eyes. Sometimes they talk, the trivia of such moments. And sometimes a fire spurt catches the gray glint of Zem or Zam's wakeful, watchful gaze.

All this time she and I had been waiting for our own swords to fall. We knew we must be prime targets, yet the days passed, and still the blow delayed. Reason told me it was only a matter of time, or a refinement of the rack. Reason has little sway over what is neither mind nor flesh and blood. It follows its own senses, and is never ready for the smash.

The first warning was when Beryx did not return from his reconnaissance. The waiting, always a torment, became unbearable. We shifted and looked at each other, not daring to ask, What is it this time? Or is it he, himself? In the mind below thought, I think I already knew. When the Ulven began to wriggle and eye the sun, I went to search for him.

He had found a tangle of clethra roots on the water's edge. His back was turned, bowed, so for one frightful moment I thought that stance betokened final disaster, surrender rather than defeat. Then I understood.

I recall thinking, with vicious outrage, that the greatest of all injustice was that Math's servants should suffer less from their enemies than from themselves. That it would cost him less to discover the atrocity, than to make himself turn around.

He looked up at me, eyes all black in a deathly face. His lips moved. When nothing emerged, he used mindspeech instead.

<I can't tell her,> he said.

A great calmness came on me. "How many?" I said aloud. "Who?"

He hid his face. <Her parents. Everyone . . . with them. At the farm.> He added a rare detail. <It was burnt.>

As I steeled myself, for Callissa's sake as well as my own, he was driven to fill the pause. <After everything I've cost her . . . I can't face it. Not this.>

Looking down at him huddled on the clethra roots, his nerve gone, when he had not hesitated to put his own hand in the fire, I reflected with still more bitter irony that it took kindness, not cruelty, conscience, not coal-lumps, to break the courage if you followed Math.

There was a rustle behind us. I knew it was Callissa before she spoke.

"Who is it?" She sounded calm. Steeled to meet the worst.

Beryx shrank like the most arrant cur. I put my arm round her, led her back into the scrub, and told her what he could not.

She did not break down. She did not so much as weep. She listened in silence, eyes bigger and bigger in a shrinking face. Then she left my arm and went back through the scrub. Beryx literally cowered. Standing in front of him she said quietly,

"Don't. You said it to me. 'Wherever we are, we have to go forward. And make the best of it.' "

Fugitives were coming by then, in ones and twos found and guided by the Ulven into camp, shattered by the hunt, utterly baffled by its motives or those of their flight. Amver's cousin, one of Karis', Dakis' brother-in-law. I never admitted, and could never stamp out the last stupid flicker of hope that one day my parents would appear like that. Everything I knew of them, of the situation, told me otherwise, but hope is not a reasonable thing. It persisted till the day Beryx emerged from a thrithan clump looking even more flogged than usual. And this time his eyes came to me.

At such times instinct demands solitude. I do not recall going, but when he found me I was huddled into the cover of another heagar, beyond sight or earshot of the camp. Only when the van of the grief had passed, begun to alter into the will for revenge, into unslakeable hate, did he break in upon my thoughts.

<I can't dispute your feelings. I know it's unforgivable. But, Alkir>—the very force of his will dragged my eyes up—<I beg you, I beg you. . . .> I knew he felt it was hopeless and that only integrity compelled him to go on. <Don't let it drive you to Ammath.>

My eyes must have answered. His grew almost translucent.

<It can't be forgotten. But if you give in—if you start to hate>—even in mindspeech I felt his anguish—<then she's really won. The only fight that counts.>

My expression cannot have changed.

<I know it's . . . I know. . . .> He did not have to say, I too would find it all but impossible. <I just wish you could . . . try.>

I was within a hairsbreadth of turning on him as I had in the vault, I could see the expectation in his eyes and knew that even now he would not fight back. I understood then that there are bloodier battles than those where armies massacre each other. And what a conquest is demanded of those who claim so much as the tithe of a right to say, "I follow Math."

If I did not choke, it felt so. My very flesh seemed to boil with pain and hate and the need to hurt. When it subsided, I put up my hand and found, with no surprise, that there was sweat on my face as I had so often seen it on his.

He was smiling at me. A shaky, exhausted, radiant smile. I knew then that I had just won him his greatest triumph. That I had redeemed my past betrayals, that if the Lady finally vanquished him, I had bestowed his victory crown.

How much longer did it go on? More distortion of time. I remember, though, that the swamp began to dry, mud margins widening, trees shabby, sun staring from an ever-more-torrid sky. Then the first battalions of soggy, long-based silver clouds massing in the north, the heavier sultriness, and Amver saying, "The Wet won't be long." I recall that because it was the day before the Lady opened her next charge.

Beryx could not look at us that morning. He would not even speak until Callissa, divining a crisis, half ran to him with the usual cup of tea and thrust him down on a rolled-up tent. It was to the cup that he finally spoke.

"She's . . . changed targets." We all froze, half reprieved, half in deeper fear, for the new atrocity was plainly worse. He did not look up. "Your old corps. . . ."

All the eyes jerked to me. The words jerked in my throat.

"What about them? What?"

He put the cup down. His hand was steady. I do not know if it was control, or the torpor of being struck too much.

"She executed them. All of them. Last night. In the main

square . . . Zyphryr Coryan."

For a moment I shared his pain for innocents slain on my behalf, crueler in some ways than kinfolks' loss. They had done nothing, nothing at all. Merely served with me. Faces filled my mind, troopers and seconds and brother-officers, honest, loyal, blood-bound comrades with whom I had hammered out trust in so many battle lines. Now hung on gibbets like traitors, deserters, criminal dogs. For a moment it was too much. I learnt then that the battle is never over when the enemy is Ammath.

I came round with the taste of blood in my mouth and the nails driven clean through my palms. Beryx was watching me. With compassion, with comprehension. And now with the praise of a fellow-fighter who understands your victory. The most precious garland on earth.

"She's learning," he said at last. "A clean sweep, because otherwise I'd have got some out. At night. And not kinfolk, because she knows this is worse . . . once you're bound by Math."

It was Evis who exploded. "Then for the love of your cursed Math why don't you stop it! Fight her! Do something!"

Beryx came off the tent in a single bound and his eyes went green-shot white.

"By the Sky-lords' faces, you squalling pup, do you think I don't ache to tear the whole thing apart and stamp all over its guts? Do you think I want to sit like an owl on a stick and bleat to a bunch of ninnies about 'Math'? Do you think I don't have to fight myself every mortal second not to go out there and take her on, here and now, and to your pits with the consequence, to the pits with everything so long as I can act!"

Evis nearly fell over. The rest of us recoiled, cowered, fled outright. We had seen him vexed, we had seen him touchy. We had never seen him in unbridled wrath.

He was breathing like a racehorse, face distorted, hand driven into his side. For a moment I saw what an aedr could be, as Th'Iahn had been, uncurbed by Math. Then I realized that this strategy had crossed not only his beliefs but his nature. A king, a general, it was born and bred and schooled into him in the face of disaster to react. To refuse had galled him so bitterly he had lost control not merely from stress, but in the revolt of instincts too long and too savagely denied.

The rage had already collapsed. "Oh, Four," he groaned. "Oh, Four . . . I'm so sorry, Evis." The remorse became despair. "Oh, when will I ever learn to follow Math?"

Though still fiery red, Evis was over shock and fear and struggling to swallow the rest. He answered unsteadily, "Sir, I should have known better. Don't blame yourself."

They looked at each other. Then a wraith of humor woke in Beryx's eye. "I think," he said with irony, "you'll have plenty of chances to get it right."

The Lady worked through the army as she had through our kin. Every rankmate, fellow officer, friend, barest past or present acquaintance that she caught was executed in the basest way. Beryx saved some by the exhausting maneuver of tracing all our careers with Phathire, then breaking her command over possible victims and sending them off in flight, but they were heartbreakingly few. The chess war resumed. Some did escape. The others supplied another turn to her knife, but this time injustice mingled rage into our grief. And at times I mourned the Asharran army, in which I had been proud to serve, for whatever its allegiance it had been a fine service, and I sorrowed as for any skilled craftsmanship wrecked in wanton spite.

As that phase closed we all began to wonder what she would try next. Where humans can live is less miraculous than where they can laugh. We met our losses with silence, our wins with vicious delight, and we speculated on the future with that black wit you find in lulls along a sore-tried battle front. Beryx's condition was the one thing about which we could not jest.

He was skeleton thin, unable to eat. He still slept badly, recovering more and more slowly from his bouts of Ruanbrarx. And, we noted with silent apprehension, his physical strength had begun to fail.

By the third day after the army's release the tension had gone beyond jest. When Beryx retreated with lagging steps into a clethra stand we waited with a keener version of the old dread. We knew her capabilities now. We did not know her choice.

We had underestimated. He came out of the clethras like a bolting horse, halfway across the camp before he got control. "Oh, Four," he said, turning in circles. "Oh, Four, I don't think I can handle this."

Terrified, we rushed to calm him, sit him down, fetch tea. He would have none of it. He strode up and down as if driven by whips, raging to the indifferent air.

"How could she? How could she? Four, not the lousiest bandit, not the dirtiest mountain rat with four troopers in his tail and a half a yoke of Gebria to terrorize would—" His voice rose in anguish. "It's worse than incompetence—it's—it's—bestiality!"

"But sir," pleaded Sivar, scurrying in his wake, "what's she done?"

He spun round. His eyes were crystalline light green, distilled rage.

"Tengorial. She turned the whole town out on the farms. Worse than an invasion—killing, wrecking, raping, burning—their own folk! And then she turned them on each other." His eyes narrowed, fairly spitting. "Tengorial's ablaze and the citizens won't fight the fire, they're butchering each other in the streets. Etalveth's the same—but she used the garrison there." He choked and whirled on his heel. "Four, the bloodiest usurper ever crowned never made his people tear their own country apart!"

"She must have gone mad." Zyr was stunned. "Lost her wits."

"Oh, not in the least!" He began to patrol with the same huge frenzied strides. "This time I can't do a thing. I can't anticipate, I can't prevent, I can't interfere. If I do, she just moves somewhere else. They don't have to mean something to us. Anyone will do. They're all Assharrans. All innocent. All her own—oh, Four, Four, how could she ever think of it!"

Words were on Evis' lips. They were on mine, but I held them there. I had said too often, Is this not a Must?

Wenver said it for me. "Sir, mightn't this be—the one thing too much?"

"No!" Beryx rounded on him. "It hasn't broken her power. For that she has to misuse the Well so completely that—I don't know what will happen, it'll shatter, blow up in her face, I can't guess. No, Four help me, this isn't the one thing too much." The gale collapsed. "Except," he sounded strained, "it may be too much for me."

After that we watched him like a fever patient at crisis point. I have to confess, with shame, that Assharral's woes meant less than they ought to us. We had been through the fire. We felt for his pain, and we feared he would break, and we earnestly desired to live. Not only for survival, but because, despite all he had said, we wanted our revenge.

There was no march that day. The Ulven crept about the perimeter, Callissa made endless brews of tea, and the rest of us kept in earshot but beyond the thunder's range, while he scoured up and down, more than three quarters out of his wits.

A dozen times he checked to stand staring south, with rage, with grief, in an agony of opposed compulsions, only to wheel and start pacing again. Once he burst out, "Cursed woman!"

Once he cried, "Oh, if only Fengthira was—" More than once he cried, "No!" and spun like a top, but what he was refusing we could not tell.

He brushed off Callissa's attempts to make him eat or drink, with his nearest ever approach to brusqueness, and presently I found the anxiety had acquired a sharper tooth. I knew now what Math required of a conqueror. It is not enough to defeat your enemy, or to forego retribution. You must also worst Ammath in yourself. Even if he did not crumple under the pressure, she had broken his guard. Outraged his ruler's instincts, the deepest sanctities of his life. He was perilously close to losing what he had called the real battle. Of succumbing to hatred. Falling into Ammath.

It was late afternoon before the tempest waned at last. Yet again he halted, staring south. But this time I saw the tension slowly drain away. His shoulders relaxed. Then they firmed, the stance of the ensign-bearer that proclaims, Here I am, and here I stay.

Presently he spoke. Very quietly, a final commitment, he said, "Imsar Math."

Then he came over to the fire. His eyes were translucent, sheets of heaving green shadow like the aftermath of storm swells in their depths, his face loked almost pure bone. As he sank down by the coals Callissa silently poured yet another cup of tea. This time he took it, saying in a rather slurred voice, "Thank you, ma'am—Callissa, I mean."

It was only a lull. Next morning he had to reconnoiter, and by noon he was fighting the whole engagement over again. By nightfall his fingernails were bitten to the quick and he was pacing to and fro, to and fro, with eyes that patterned the inner tumult, swirls of lime and viridian, fluctuant, vivid and fascinatingly spectacular. Only this time the dance was not power but distress.

The Ulven crowd had increased that day. I had the oddest feeling, as their eyes followed him about, that unlike us they were not in search of reassurance but poised to offer help. Just on dusk Ygg came up to Amver and drew him aside. Then they summoned Callissa. Then she beckoned me.

She held two or three sprigs of some unknown plant. "Ygg says," she began without preamble, "this is a sleep-maker. I'm going to put some in his food. But Ygg wants your consent."

"I know the dose." She was impatient at my blank look. "But he says Beryx won't like it. I don't know how he knows, but . . . anyway, he says you have to agree."

I could not see what my consent had to do with it. Then I looked again at that driven, easeless face and said without hesitation, "Yes."

It took more coaxing than a virgin's seduction to get the fish down his throat, but the result was all we asked. He fell asleep over the plate. Not breathing, we rolled him in his cloak. He did not stir. Feeling happier than for weeks, I set the watch.

Dawn was past before he woke. First he rubbed his eyes, then his head. Then he stared about, at our carefully disinterested faces, Callissa making business at the fire, the Ulven audience. His eyes flickered. He got up.

"I'll have some of that tea," he said, walking up behind Callissa, who nearly joined the pot in the coals. "And this time, see it's not doctored." He glared at us, an attempt to look baleful foiled by a twitching lip. "Confounded impudence!"

Since we knew better than to repeat that, we tried feeding him instead. Some mornings he would end like a temple idol, heaps of every known or unknown game, vegetable and fruit piled at his feet, and a score of Ulven pleading in dog-like silence behind. Since he could not bear to disappoint them, that had limited success. The one thing he did express a wish for we could not provide. None of us played an instrument, few of us could sing, and all lacked the nerve to try. "Never mind," he said wearily. "I just thought. . . . But this is Assharral. You don't have harpers here."

How long? Again I cannot tell. We did not ask about the torments of Assharral, though we knew he watched them all. Frimmor, Darrior, Climbros, Thangar, Gjerven, Kemrestan, Axaira, Tasmar, Nervia, Morrya. When the wind set southerly, smoke would pierce even Stirsselian's humid shroud. Sometimes a particularly wanton ruin would make him cry out, as at some precious possession of his own smashed before his eyes, but we did not ask. It was enough to know that if, beyond our refuge, Assharral was malignly tearing its heart out, it had not yet succeeded in breaking his.

The weather grew heavier and more sultry. In the shade, at night, you were still oppressed by the stifling air, the weight of thunder coming to the boil. When Amver called me for middle night watch I was usually awake. I recall the night he whispered, in a tone of revealed miracles, that Beryx was actually asleep.

"Sat down just now and dropped right off. Worn out."

The ever-present, unacknowledged fear was in his voice. Trying for silence myself, I tiptoed off to the sentry post by a thrithan clump. Ygg materialized beside me, and we sat watching Beryx's shadow against a clethra butt, head fallen on his breast, breathing softly, motionless. Then Ygg's hand took my elbow, and in the same moment I heard it for myself: the first low longdrawn growl of thunder, far in the north.

With a blood-curdling yell Beryx turned inside out and bolted as he hit his feet, my own rush collided us head-on and he punched and kicked and clawed as if tackling Hawge barehanded. I just had time to pray he would not use the arts, before he woke.

Sobbing, shuddering, he hung on to my wrist, while I got

him to the fire. Hushed the camp, made a hash of brewing tea. He was still shaking so badly that he dropped the cup. Blessed with nightmares of my own, I did not ask, "What woke you?" But Ygg came and crouched beside him, one hand on his crippled wrist, and presently, like a horse at a calming touch, he grew quiet.

"Nothing," he said at last, both answer and denial of my thought. The thunder had died. He looked off into the south. When he spoke my heart jumped, for the tone was no longer torment; it was abysmal, yielding weariness.

"Four," he said, "let it not be long."

The next night was hotter than ever, and alive with fireflies. For a long time I lay on top of my cloak, ears full of the mosquitoes' perpetual whine, thinking that the Wet could not come too soon, while I watched the clouds of tiny torches wake and swirl and prick out again against the stars. When I did drop off, it was to dream that they had become the Lady's golden meteors, and were sucking me off into space that was not space but the inner distances of her deadly eyes.

But the nightmare did not wake me. I came to sitting up with the camp bolted upright round me, all of us flung straight into battle readiness by the sound.

It was in the air, the jungle, the water, the earth itself. My sleeping ears had recorded its inception, a blast to split the sky. My woken mind perceived the sequel, a protracted ground-shaking thunderously sonorous drumbeat that rumbled on and on and on, till it sank to a floodhead roar that never completely died.

Evis tugged my arm. Twisting in my cloak I saw his face, but not by the glow of our little fire.

The clethras on the camp perimeter were cut out in silhouette, stark and precise, every bole, branch, twig and leaf. A red glow had opened the horizon behind them, a vermilion fierce as sunset, lightening to lurid crimson and then to a diluted scarlet that crept, even as I looked, toward the zenith sky. But it was not moonrise, not even a stupendous sunrise. For I was facing south.

I got up and went over to a gap in the clethras. Without surprise, I found Beryx already there.

The fire dyed his face blood color, and showed its expression. It held no triumph, however innocent of Ammath. It held sadness, and the serene, drained languor of a man in long and excruciating pain who has finally been released.

The red mounted to the zenith, illuminating the whole land around. I could see the dugouts, the tents, the Ulven's ruddy eyes, every shrub and branch. And hear that distant growl, shaken occasionally by a deeper throb, as of some spasm in the heart of an expiring beast.

"She was trying to use Wreviane," he said. "With the Well. Before the Wet came. To burn the whole of Stirsselian over us."

I caught my breath. His eyes were still on the south.

"And," he said softly, "it went awry." That peace, too spent to be called triumph, remained in his face. "The Morhyrne's blown up."

I was deprived of speech. He remarked, "It always was a volcano, you know." Though his gaze had not moved, the bloody light showed decision, quiet, sure purpose, crystallizing before my eyes.

"There it is." He murmured it, with calm, almost elegiac vindication. "The one thing too much."

With action permitted he knew how to act. Dawn found us on the edge of Stirsselian, uneasy in our mud gear for the first time, farewelling Ulven who had not seemed to need explanation. Beryx embraced Ygg, smiling into his face. "Yes," he said, not waiting for an interpreter. "No thanks needed either side. We're off to end the drought." And Ygg lifted his hand, and watched us walk out into the Gjerven rice-fields, and melted quietly away.

"Stirian Ven," Beryx said as we tramped. "I'll get horses, but it may take time. The whole country's in chaos. And we must be careful. She was lucky with the Morhyrne, the cone blew out at its southern base. So Ker Morrya's still there. And so is the Well. She'll have a good deal on her hands. But not enough to forget us."

We were in striking range of Stirian Ven just before dusk. Halting us in a well-isolated kymman stand, Beryx grinned at me with a resurgence of his old blithe authority. "Want to add horse-catcher to your trades, Fylghjos? Get down by the road and wait."

I slid into a thrithan clump above that familiar double-paven carriage way, and ensconced myself, gazing down those empty swords of distance into the south. Except for the distant perpetual rumble, it was deathly quiet. No human voices called, no axes rang, no beasts cried or birds sang. Indeed, none had sung all day. The air smelt as if a gigantic forge had been overthrown in mid-fire, and greasy black smoke had spread over the whole sky, so at high noon we had moved in an eerie dusk. But now the sun was going, and the dusk was topaz, golden wine, lilac, royal crimson, a dome of glory over the broken earth. An ironic splendor to have sprung from ruin.

As I thought that, my ear caught the sound of hooves.

I leant out of the thrithan stems and jerked in surprise, for the beast was nearly on me, coming at a smart collected walk. Then it moved out of silhouette, off the road's skyline, and the hair prickled on my scalp.

It was a gray mare, shimmery as moonlight, built like a war-horse, well-boned, long in the rein, with a fine if placid carriage of the head. And a Sathel rider, blue desert robe, black turban, no stick in his hand. The mare clipped quickly up the carriage-way, she was abreast of me, I was still wondering how she had got so near before I noticed, when she checked.

As in a dream I rose among the thrithans, looking up into a pair of almost rectangular, black-lashed, rainwater-clear gray eyes. The mare blew gently through her nostrils. Shadows wove in those gray irises, and then I knew what I had met.

"Fengthira," I said.

CHAPTER XI

Those gray eyes raked me, one swift compressive glance. Yet I had the unnerving impression that Beryx himself had never seen me so completely; that for a moment I had been no more than a sheet of glass against the sun.

She answered, "Ah."

"Best not stand jawing here," she went on. Her voice was decisive, resonant, yet utterly feminine. "Come tha and stop them trying to take my head off at the camp."

The mare cleared the road ditch in one easy spring. Her rider seemed to know the way, for I found myself hurrying to keep up.

"Save tha questions," she said over her shoulder. "Not that tha askst many." A note of wintry approval. "And needst not pother about his beasts." She slowed the mare. "Come tha in front."

I went past her, with a warning whistle that raised bellicose figures everywhere. My "Stand easy" hardly reassured them. Beryx alone did not move.

He was cross-legged, his breath slow and effortful, eyes blank, deep in trance. Wreve-lan'x, I thought. Then a warm horse breath touched my elbow and above me Fengthira said, dryly amused, "Nay, t'is only the Hethrian witch."

She slid down while they were still dumbstruck and went up behind Beryx. Evis lunged forward with a warning growl. She glanced at him, and he seemed to freeze in his tracks.

"Calm thaself," she said, the mockery sharper yet, before her eyes dropped to Beryx. "T'is not Velandryxe, but. . . ."

With delicate care she brought her hand in contact with his neck. Her breathing slowed to match with his. Then hers altered, his followed, and she stood back while he sat blinking, rubbing at his eyes.

"What . . ." he said. "How. . . ." He twisted round. Then his face burst open in almost ecstatic relief.

" 'Thira!" He came up with a leap and hurled himself, clutching her in his left arm and trying to do it with his right. "Oh, thank the Four—if ever I needed you it's now!"

Her turban emerged, well down his chest. Her hands, a light, affectionate clasp, were either side his waist. "Ah. Hast been through the crucible this time, I see." Her head came clear. "Daft looby. I'd to use a Ruanbraxe, si'sta? No sense letting the filly kick us both out of the yard."

He was laughing, somewhat shakily. " 'Thira, I could strangle you, if you knew what I've been thinking. . . ."

"Ah. No way to guess if she'd know it too."

He nodded, briefly sobered. Then the joy revived. His arm tightened on her shoulders. "How did you—when did you—what did you—how should I—oh, Four, I'm too full of How and What and Why to have a hope of First!"

Her eyes were dancing. I knew the turban masked a smile.

"A month on the road. Act as tha'st planned. And art in good truth a looby. I tell thee Through is sometimes worse than Round, and when it does sink in tha ironclad skull tha must needs fetch a circuit round the back of Selionur."

"Oh." He sounded so dashed I could have boxed her ears. "Four, 'Thira, I didn't know what to do, I—every choice was Ammath." His head drooped. "I might have known I'd make a botch of it."

"Botch?" Her eyes were sober, but there was quiet emphasis

in her voice. "Didst the only thing tha couldst."

After a moment his look became understanding. Then a solemn acknowledgement.

"And *I* might have known," she added tartly, "when tha tookst a prentice tha'd choose one twice as hard in the mouth as thaself."

If I had thought Beryx could no longer startle me, I was wrong. His eyes flew wide. Then the color flooded his face from brow to chin and he blushed like the veriest boy.

Fengthira merely stared, the hard laughter sparkling. "Ah," she said.

He got his breath. "Drat you! You horrible inquisitive—I might have known you'd—"

She chuckled outright. "T'is a change," she said with wicked airiness, "to see the filly put the breaker through the hoops. But we'd best be off now, before she breaks a leg in the rope."

Beryx assumed an awful dignity. "When I was interrupted, though you may not have noticed, I was in the process of assembling a few essentials for that. But of course, such a mighty Velandyr—"

"Half a mile down t'road. Twenty head. Didst not wonder why tha hadst such trouble finding any, then?"

"Oh, you. . . ." He flung his left hand in the air. "Then you can cursed well double me down to them. And"—an obvious quotation—"don't say Can't to me."

"Mare'll never notice. Clown? Art more like a Manuighend scarecrow. Couple of forked sticks tied in the middle with string."

He was laughing as they reached the mare, arm still over her shoulders. The crinkle of those gray eyes told me she was laughing too.

"I don't suppose you'd care to do anything so normal as be introduced? Of course you know them, but they might feel a little happier if it were made, um, legitimate."

"Ah, I know them." Again those penetrating eyes ran over me. "T'is wonderful how ignorance undoes itself. Were I a Morheage wishful to snare thee, the last living soul I'd use for bird-net would be a son of Stiriand." Her eyes warmed as they shifted. "Hast had a fine time with him, ah? 'I won't eat this, I don't want that, canst not see I'm bloated with mighty matters of wizardry?' " Callissa's mouth opened like an empty bag. "Shouldst have made him wash up. T'is wonderful how that takes the fidgets out." The smile chilled. "And couldst use that lesson elsewhere too."

Her eyes moved on. The smile vanished altogether. A deep absorption held the surface of her gaze, but gray patterns moved, an echo of the thought in Beryx's eyes, through the depths beneath.

Zem and Zam gazed solemnly back. Once one parted his lips, but neither spoke. At last that amusement, so like yet unlike Beryx's, for his never had an edge to it, resumed its silent dance.

"Ah," she said. "I'm like to call thee something worse than dolt."

Zem drew a breath that I saw, with shock, was pure ecstasy.

The gray eyes twinkled. "Hast a small matter of a mother to suit with first. I'll not lift a foal where the dam's like to kick in my head."

I was quite lost, and could see they were no more so than Beryx, watching with a small, eager, anxious grin. For an instant the four of them did indeed seem beings of an alien kind.

Then Fengthira nodded, clicked to her mare, said, "Must wait on the filly," and shot Beryx a glance. "Shall I lift thee up?"

"Femaere," he said, going round to vault up on the off-side. He looked down at her, a glint in his eye. "I should make you walk."

She cocked her head. "Dost think tha can?"

They both spluttered. He held out his hand, she came lightly up, the mare turned on the spot, and her words floated back.

"Ye need not stand there like a row of barley stooks. Should be broke to aedryx by now."

The horses were in a half-burnt deserted post-house. "And now," Fengthira remarked as Stirian Ven clattered under us, "tha canst well 'get along a bit.' "

They must have used the arts on us as well as the horses, for the night passed in a smooth rapid dream, whence I dismounted at dawn feeling we had hardly traveled at all. Strolling past, fresh as a daisy, Beryx grinned, "Easy with two," and Fengthira, doffing her turban as she strode toward the kitchen of another empty post-house, threw over her shoulder, "Make me some eggs, if tha thinkst it so easy. That'll stint tha cackling."

She made him eat them, too. Then they resumed work, and we came out to find a fresh change assembled in the yard. "Assembled" is the word, for one wore harness blinkers, one a set of broken hobbles, one a snapped halter, and most sported no gear at all. When we mounted, Beryx said, "I'll do the first turn." Fengthira nodded. Apprehensively, we trailed after them onto the open road and the light of full if bleary day.

Nobody saw us. Aedryx' doing or not, there was no one to see. There was only the smoke, and the ravaged countryside, and the road that unrolled till I began to feel myself a parcel whisked along by aedric messenger post. Beryx was tense, distracted, naturally distanced by the presence of an equal. And acquaintance with Fengthira did not breed familiarity.

We still felt umbrage when she addressed Beryx like a small unruly boy. Nor was it comfortable to be called by name when she hardly knew us in the flesh. Moreover, Fengthira was far more the usual idea of a wizard than Beryx had ever seemed.

Once accustomed to his arts, you saw through to the man, a man whose courage and mirth and humility made him impossible to dislike, and then liking deepened, unable to resist his deep and unforced warmth for all humankind. But around Fengthira was a distance that never closed, something that went far beyond an awareness of her nature and her origin. Her mirth had an edge; her care was impersonal. There was an aloofness that, before meeting Beryx, I would have taken as the essence of an aedr's difference. She was like some wild thing that will come to share your bread but never share your life.

We were cantering along Tengorial bypass as I thought this. Early morning, horses going easily, only the scarred land and the stifling gloom to bring your spirits down. Then a gray shimmer crossed the tail of my left eye.

"Si'sta," she said. "I'm not overfond of men. Horses come first, with me."

I tried not to gulp.

"Thinkst me impertinent?" She always seemed to laugh at rather than with you. "I made him an aedr. Dost salute tha recruit-boys? And I've seen a stud-book's worth of kings."

I recalled the Lady's gibe at Fengthira's age. Without her turban she did indeed looked an old woman, silver hair, deeply seamed skin over those haughty bones. But now, giving whippily to her mare's action, eyes full of that ageless aedric laughter, she seemed the merest girl.

"He," she went on, "was made. Men are in his bones. I was born. Makes him softer than me." She glanced ahead, and her own eyes softened. Then they came back, with the stab of a rapier. "Wilt need to remember that, up there."

"Eh?" I was startled into speech.

"Art well enough, thaself. Loyal to tha backbone, upright as old Granite-eyes. And as hard." I spluttered. "Think'st tha's fathomed Math. I don't say tha's not well begun. But"—her eyes fairly skewered me—"Math's no set and surveyed highway with every by-road wrong. We all see it for ourselves, and every seeing's right. But I doubt tha seest like him."

"What," I said, "do you mean?"

"Spell it out, ah? Then don't look, in Zyphryr Coryan, for him to lead you over the palace gate yelling, Justice! And, Burn the witch! Don't expect a halter for her, let be a block and axe. T'is what tha praised in him as against me. Soft-hearted, clear to daftness. Ah. T'is his way in Velandryxe. 'Vengeance is sweet, but wisdom chooses salt.' "

I opened my mouth to snap, I understand that. Perhaps I would have boasted that I had chosen it myself a time or two. Then my parents' memory roared over me like a running fire. My vision went red, my fists clenched. I did not have to bawl it aloud: Not this time!

Fengthira had seen already. I surfaced to find it in her eyes. She gave me one quick jerk of the head.

"For all but tha own blood, ah? And how many more to say the same? But si'sta. He will not."

"I—" I did manage not to blurt total inanities like, Even he can't be that crazy! But if the rage fell back, reason endured.

"And just how," I said through my teeth, "can he stop it? Aedr or not?"

She gave a slight, all but one-shouldered shrug. "T'would take a Velandyr to answer that. And happen not a seer either, before t' time. But hearst tha this. Whatever haps, he'll not belie Math. Unless tha dost the same, when the pinch comes, t'will be fare-thee-well 'twixt him and thee." Her eyes were agates. "So I warn thee, to ease it. Whatever he owes thee, even those with thee, even Assharral—he'll put the filly first."

The next morning, we rode out on Rastyr's cliff.

If I knew the cliff when I saw it, that was all I knew. Tyr

Coryan had shrunk to a bowshot of scummy gray water. The city was gone. The world was hot and throbbing, throttling full of smoke and dust-fine ash, the forge-stink had become a stench of brimstone, like a fireball shop in full career. As we reined in, Beryx glanced at Fengthira, who glanced back to us.

"Let them come," she said. "Safer for them, and chance help for thee." She added with mordant humor. "They think they're here to see it end, and surely, they will."

She glanced at Callissa. "Tear a strip of shirt-tail, child, and make a mask. Else tha'lt choke in this brume." The gentleness remained as she turned to Beryx, who had grown stiff and a little pale. "Lead on, lad. T'is tha road now."

Along the harbor they repelled two ambushes, not the steady, menacing puppet advance of a Commanded attack, merely villagers or fisher-folk crazed with fear and recent mishandling. Beryx knocked the club from one man's hand. Fengthira rolled another head over heels. He chuckled, "Should see me eat with Axynbrarve." She retorted, "Assharral's taught thee manners, then." Hearing them jest like sword-mates in the filthy fog, knives about them, an unknown calamity looming ahead, the very atmosphere rank with Assharral's ruin, I found the whole thing uncannier still.

People remained in some villages, but at our approach they fled. Zyphryr Coryan was still veiled in the murk. The earth vibrated steadily, unfalteringly, to that distant roar.

We were near the gates when the air suddenly grew scorching, a glow lit the left-hand fog, and then, rising into it like some vast slanted branding-iron appeared a shaft of incandescent golden red.

Both aedryx checked. I heard Fengthira say, "That's new." And Beryx, more sharply, "It must come right down through the city—" then in sudden panic, " 'Thira. . . ." And her brusque, "Bah! Starts below the palace, as tha'd know if tha'd matched Phathire."

I was aching to demand, But what in heaven's name is it? when she answered me.

"Lava, ah? Hill's opened this side too. There'll not be much to vaunt in Zyphryr Coryan now."

Beryx took her up with decisive urgency. "If that's moving like it seems we'd best hurry or we won't get in at all."

Choking worse than our horses, trusting our leaders' eyesight, we cantered forward into the gloom. The heat grew ferocious. I smelt things burning, live trees, furniture, leather and aged wood, the harsh stink of old building stone purged by flame. Over them, drowning them, came a different smell, so hot it was a mere searing sword in the lungs. Till you breathed out, and your palate kept the tang of conflagration fed on no common fuel, the taste of molten rock, of earth's own fiery core.

I glanced aside and barely a bowshot from the road a fiery cliff loomed over me, dispelling the smoke like steam from a heated iron. Fire without flame, a wall of heat and light that was its own sufficient food. Blinking away the red-hot after image, blurred in defensive tears, I knew I had seen the front of the lava flow, poured down across Zyphryr Coryan like the wrath of Math itself.

The gates were unguarded. There was uproar in the city, distant screams and shouts and death-cries, the clash of arms. Corpses littered the gate-square, some stabbed, some trampled, and Beryx said tautly, "Must have been a stampede." He turned his horse for Treasury hill. "We should be able to go up the spur. The lava heads just under its neck."

Just under its neck. As my horse dived sideways from a mansion spilt out in rubble and I ducked a hanging beam, my mind's eye placed the spot. Almost directly below the parapet of Los Morryan.

The streets were a cross between earthquake and sack, blood

and rubble mixed, fire and looting, murder done by or among the scavengers. I wondered where the remnant of the army was. Then came a crescendo in the subterranean roar, a spasm in some unimaginable heart. Heat spewed up, the smoke rose with it, and before the curtain dropped I saw Zyphryr Coryan clear.

We were halfway to Ker Morrya's gate. Below and beside us the city sank away between spur and harbor down the Morhyrne's flank, once a mass of mansion, temple, tower, park, garden, colonnade. The buildings looked as if a stick had been swept across a flowerbed. The city wall was flat on its side. The trees and grass were fire-blasted brown. And clear down the Morhyrne's side lay that lava slash, so bright it did not seem part of the earth it flowed upon, so bright it must surely have extruded from another, more intense, scaldingly vivid world. The heat of it lashed across our faces, once. I was thankful to fall back with coughs and splutterings into the murk.

"Take the horses up," I heard Beryx choke, and Fengthira, "Safer for both." We forged on up the cumbered street.

The Treasury facade was down, columns rolled out in heaps of drums whose diameter exceeded a man's height, gates crushed beneath. I spared a thought for the scribes. Then it occurred to me that guards, more loyal than I, might remain at Ker Morrya's gate.

"Amver," I snapped to the wraith at my elbow, "take Zam. Evis, give Zem to Wenver. Come on, you others. They can't use farsight in this."

As we closed up on them Beryx gave me a quick distracted smile. Fengthira also glanced about, a wintry gray flash. "Kindly thought on," she said.

The gate square was devoid of life. Live beings, that is. Bodies were strung in a row under the arch, men and women, naked, vilely mutilated, and before my eyes winced away I saw the tatters of what had been court finery on the cobbles beneath.

"Ah," said Fengthira, sliding down, with another scythe of a glance. "Dost feel like vengeance now?"

Nobody replied. Her eyes rose to Beryx, sitting his horse with the guise of numb horror I knew so well. She tapped lightly on his foot.

"Wake tha, lad." It came with rough kindness. "Hast work to do."

They walked among the horses, bidding them stay, then he turned to us. "Alkir, will you hold the gate? And the horses." With an almost trusting look, he stepped between Callissa and the arch. "You'll see the twins don't see too much?" He turned back to me, and I took the words out of his mouth.

"Evis can handle this. I'm coming with you."

I am still not sure what made me say it. Concern for him, remembrance of Fengthira's prophesy? One last bloody determination that if Moriana escaped him along with Math, she should not escape the requital of Assharral?

I did have the wits to suppress that. I said, "Assharral needs a witness," and stared him straight in the eye.

He looked away. Aedric reflex, his own habit, to protect human fools. His eyes and Fengthira's crossed. She gave me one south-wind stab of a glance, and then, abruptly, turned to Callissa. "I'll," with a nod to me, "look after him."

Callissa stared, then nodded too. For an instant I almost thought they had exchanged a conspirator's glance, but I had no time to consider it. Beryx must have received his own message. He was bracing himself to face the gate.

This time the palace had not been upturned by its owner's will. The signs of sack were everywhere, the ruin that is more than greed, more than callousness, the demon that possesses men at such times, here spurred on by revenge. There were bodies, too. If the court had fled for asylum, it was in vain.

"Foh!" said Fengthira, weaving down the colonnade, and shook her head at Beryx's mute, sickened glance. "Every breaker to his beast. I know horses can be vicious. Which way now, Alkir?"

Smoke had rimed the fretted walls of the green vestibule, the floor was ripped up by something like picks, the jade plaques bore foul scribbles in fouler ink. But no mark of traffic, let be rapine, showed on the rough-hewn steps.

"Curs," Fengthira coughed. "No guts for the stallion. Make do with t'heavy mares." She glanced at Beryx. "What art waiting for?"

He turned. I was stunned to read uncertainty in his face, apprehension, outright timidity. Her eyelids crinkled, but she spoke with mock impatience.

"Art such a mouse's heart as that?"

" 'Thira. . . ."

"Get on with thee, man. Tha prentice. Claim her, then."

"But. . . ."

Her eyes mocked him. "If th'art fearful, trust tha silly heart. One thing'll not fail thee is tha foolishness." But it was a good luck pat with which she pushed him to the steps.

As the fog swallowed him she glanced round, and her mirth become open hilarity. "And art gnashing tha teeth to come so far and miss all at the last. I'll have mercy on thee. Look here."

Her eyes flared. A gray world sucked me in, leaving behind her last words, ironic with self-mockery.

"I doubt I'd bear to miss it myself."

I do not know what she did. But one moment I was gazing at her across a rumpled pavement, the next I was a pure faculty of vision, soaring over the rivannon trees to view the bower of Los Morryan.

Chapter XII

It must have been like a furnace down there. The plants and perridel leaves were scorched brown, dust lay on the shriveled moss. I saw with shock that the fountain's basin held a mere residue of heat-crazed mud. No water, no sweet heedless melody. I hardly mourned it, for I had seen the Lady herself.

She was poised, balanced, atop the porphyry parapet. Her hair had been pinned up under some sort of coronal, but it had come loose, so thillians spurted white fire amid the ebony coils, and free strands wove on the lava's updraft like snakes about her neck. She was wearing black. Fine black sendal in some tight-waisted robe whose floating skirts furled and shifted like huge black fluid lily petals, black that left her throat white as marble but no whiter than her bloodless face, black that paled against the inky depths of her eyes where the gold meteors blazed like battle-flags, black that could not tinge the dewdrop purity of the great globe she clutched with both hands to her breast. The lava glow spurted up behind her, livid red through the leaden smoke, and her head was back and up, the pose of the cornered darre that sees death coming and yet rears to strike.

"Ah," said Fengthira, doubtless in mindspeech. "Whate'er the Morheage lacked, they ne'er had craven hearts."

A moment later, I heard feet.

Beryx paused between the rivannons. Their eyes flew together. I could feel the lightning snap. Then her lips lifted back. If she had lost the power, she retained the hate.

"I knew," she said, "you'd be here for this."

Beryx was looking stern. Mostly from nervousness, I suspect.

"Not going to produce any catchcries? 'I told you so'? 'Incompetence'? 'It serves you right'? How 'good' this is for Math?"

When he shook his head the grimace became a snarl.

"So *kind.*" It came like a poisoned dart. "But then, you always were. No matter what I did—you'd never hit back."

His silence made her eyes flare like golden hail. "And now I shall repay it a hundredfold. But you won't have the last laugh. Oh no! You can have my splendid 'empire,' my loyal 'subjects'—or what's left of them, ha-ha! And plenty of patching up, won't you love that! But you won't get me to drag round the streets on a rope! And"—her voice went shrill—"you won't get this!"

She jerked the Well. Its surface shot a red sheet of deflected light.

"And, my fine virtuous friend, do you know why? Because we're both going down there!" She jerked her elbow to the inferno and her voice shot up in a shrilling laugh. "Let's see what you do about that!"

She glared at him, breathing in quick short pants. Like her eyes, I guessed her pupils would be dilated, but they were lost in that single night.

He waited till her laughter was quite finished. Then he said, with no inflection at all, "I don't want Assharral."

"To be sure!" A shriek of truly witch-like mirth. "Is it too much damaged? But I thought that would appeal to you!"

He waited again. His eyes were steady now, the nervousness gone.

When she had calmed, he answered, "I never wanted Assharral. That's something you know you knew."

"No, Assharral would have been gift-toll, wouldn't it? What you really wanted was this."

She spun round, my faraway heart stopped. Over her shoulder she taunted him, the Well poised above the abyss.

"What will you bid for it this time? Don't tell me you don't want it, that's a lie. No offer? Oh, so sad. It's going first. I want to watch your face when your precious Fount of Wisdom, your wizardly pride and joy, your chance to change the universe goes flying down there, phut! If that's the last thing I see, it'll be worth the price. And it will be the last. How very, very sweet!"

She shook the Well. Beryx's face was empty. He did not so much as twitch. When she paused, he said, "Throw it, then."

She was the one off-balanced, this time. Her mouth half-opened. Then she turned to face him, the Well clenched to her breast.

"Don't try to cozen me! I know what it is. You told me. I didn't think even you could be such a fool as that. There'll be no more Wreve-lethar when this is gone. No more supreme art, no more making Math. Not one of your warlocks that ever lived wouldn't weep blood at the thought of losing it. And you're no different!"

"No." He sounded quite casual. "I know what it is, and what a tragedy it would be to lose it. I'd sooner you destroyed all Assharral, yes. But"—and for the first time a gleam of humor showed—"that's not what I want."

She stopped laughing and stared at him, her eyes narrowed as if to see over a great distance, blazing black slits. He did not look away. And suddenly I knew with fear and outrage and sheer exasperation that she was reading his thoughts as well. And he was permitting it.

"Bah!" she cried. "It's a lie!"

"It's not."

"Don't try to hoodwink me!"

"I'm not."

I saw her breath stop. Then her head reared back and up and if she had blazed before she fairly erupted now.

"So even the Well and even Assharral wasn't enough! Not for you, you upstart little—king! And if there was no other way you'd have crawled there up my skirts!"

I heard Fengthira choke. I saw Beryx's chest rise and hold, and knew he was struggling with all his might: not to curb anger, but to contain a laugh.

"No," he answered, straight-faced. "At a pinch—I could have foregone the skirts."

She very nearly threw the Well at him. Her forearms jerked, it flared red light. She hissed between her teeth.

"Get out! Slimy, cackling, hypocritical whoremonger, *get out!*"

He sobered. Quite gently, but inflexibly, he answered, "When I get what I want."

As her head reared again he went on softly, unhurried, unstressed.

"I don't want the Well, I don't want Assharral. I don't want to mend your wretched country or turn you into an aedr, or even try to save you, for your own sake, from Ammath. I want something else."

Her hands trembled on the Well. A chaos of reactions battled in those enormous eyes. Outrage won.

"So you think now I'm beaten you can stroll in and snap your fingers and say, 'Here, dog,' and I'll come crawling all over your feet? Because it's my only hope?" Her teeth bared. "I'll see you blinded first!"

He clicked his tongue. "You should know better. You do know better. If I were so boorish as to snap my fingers, the last thing I'd want is you crawling over my feet."

Her cheeks flamed red as the spasming fire. "Thank you!" She could barely hiss. "Then just what do you want?"

He smiled then, outright. A sweet smile, full of mischief, with something hotter underneath. "A token of your thanks?"

"OH!" It was too much. She did throw the Well, but she did it without malice to mind her of the lava, she hurled it in sheer ungovernable outrage straight at his head. And it missed.

There was a crash, a spray of vivid white sparks. The Well rebounded, leaving, I saw in total disbelief, a dent in the black native rock. Struck the pavement, left another dent, and rolled slowly, lazily, to his feet.

He did not look down. He watched her with the tag-end of that smile, while she teetered on the parapet, quite literally gnashing her teeth.

"You ape! You bear! You dancing bear! So now you have it, don't you? All of it!" Tears of pure chagrin spilt on her cheeks. "But I'll tell you once and for all, you won't get me!"

She went up on her toes to spin and leap and he took one swift step and shouted, "Stop!"

It physically wrenched her head around. I wanted to hide from her eyes. They were actually scorching me.

"Moriana," he said. Quietly. And more quietly, "Don't. Please."

Her teeth bared. "Why not?"

"Because," he answered softly, "I ask."

The lava steamed, the earth roared. A dead branch rattled on the perridel. Then, fraction by fraction, she turned her back on the abyss. Now the glitter in her eyes was ice.

"Why," she said, "not?"

"Because I love you," he said.

She was so stunned she almost whispered.

"What?"

"Because I love you." It came now without plea or passion or stress. "I don't care if you chained me or gave me fever or burnt my hand or drowned two hundred phalanxmen or murdered innocent people or tore your country apart to blackmail me. I don't care if you're queening it up here or running like a pi-dog with every Assharran out for your blood and nothing to your name, not even skirts. I love you. You're what I want."

Her eyes dilated, flared and narrowed, a sequence of passions flew across her face. Shock, hate, fury, triumph, a torment of conflicting spites. If he had the Well she had, now, the ultimate weapon. To wound beyond remedy this foe who had just delivered himself into her hands.

The tumult passed. A vicious glee succeeded it.

"That will make me truly happy," every word a stab, "when I go."

He gave her the pleasure of pleading. "Moriana, please—"

She laughed in his face. "Just what is left for me? Deposed, thrown out—lynched! Or crawling round some hovel, turning to a hag, in debt to your—mercy—for what's left of my life!"

"Moriana—"

"I'd sooner die and be done!"

She whipped about and he shouted, "No!"

It was panic. More than panic. I felt it as she must, she whirled back, teeth bared, fists clenched in her skirts till the black ripped under her fingernails.

"You hypocrite! Preach about love and use your filthy arts on me? To be sure, you'll ask!"

The laughter had gone. Under the dirt and travel-dust he was completely white. He lifted his hand, one gesture that tried to say it all: I would never enforce it, I never meant it to happen. I would never compel anyone like that. Least of all you.

Her eyes burned like the lava behind her, her head came forward as if to spit. I wanted to cover my own eyes. To cry, No, don't let me see.

His face said it all. Final destruction, defeat. Loss of the one thing that might have balanced the wreckage. His own dreams.

His wildest hopes.

But he stood there and watched her, and then he made the slightest shift of his good hand. So brief, so simple, a child could read it, yet an aedr's gesture: If it was a command, I revoke it. You are free. If you choose it, go.

She understood that. Her lips drew back in that vampire smile. The lava pulsed below her, a red flare in the smoke, she tossed her head up in response. "Changed your mind?"

Just audibly, he said, "No."

"Had wiser thoughts?"

For a moment his face took me back to the clammy dark of the vault. Then he turned his hand out in that little, assenting motion and I knew that once again he was committing everything to a gamble. To the chance that she would remember his own beliefs and tenets. What he had said about Math.

"The choice," he said, so quietly, "is yours."

The choice of death or life, and more. The surety that, whatever he felt for her, he would not interfere. Not even for this.

She froze on the parapet, poised like a fallen leaf. For an instant I knew that, to her bones' marrow, she had understood.

Then those black depths slitted. The gold meteors stilled.

"So. . . ."

It was barely breathed.

He must have stopped breathing too. I wondered the lava itself did not stop.

"If I. . . ." The hand-wave finished it: did not go down there. "If. . . ."

Go on, his eyes said. Torture me if you choose.

"If I stayed. . . ."

It must have been easier to fight the Well than to let her finish. To stand, the length of that hesitation, and simply wait.

"If I stayed . . . you'd . . . protect me?"

In the flesh I would have shut my eyes. Would have yelled, Don't believe her!—Listen to me! It's not wariness, it's calculation, nothing else!

But he had already replied. Clenching his fist, his shoulders, to keep the words steady. Pledging himself with his eternal lunacy that would deny truth and caution and common sense for the sake of impossible hope.

"Yes."

"You'd stop my—loving subjects'—revenge?"

No, I could not bawl! Not even for Math! I did shut my eyes, or at least the faculty of sight. Through whatever passed for ears the word came. Steadier than before.

"Yes."

I looked again. She was staring, those black gulfs of eyes starred with golden darts. The mouth was set, no softening there. The face of a gambler. A predator.

"You'd save me from my—just deserts?"

He answered as evenly, a little faster.

"Yes."

"Save my life?"

It went up a little at the end. Perhaps even she could not master that disbelief.

Like his eyes, his voice never faltered.

"Yes."

Her hand turned in the sendal's black. She drew a visible breath.

"You'd—marry me?"

Perhaps she had expected him to balk there. He answered as if she had asked him how the weather looked.

"Yes."

Smoke whirled in a breath of wind, the dead leaves hissed. I felt my own lungs choke on the brimstone fumes, could feel the sweat trickling on her temples, her jaw, into the pure white curve between her breasts. I could not read her face at all. Not triumph now, not fury, not mockery either. But the blackness of her eyes had hardened. The shift was in her voice.

"After I've whored with 'ten lives' favorites'?"

He answered as if nothing had changed.

"Yes."

"If I lost Assharral? If I was a beggar, a pauper?"

"Yes."

"If I was old and ugly and—and sick to death?"

"Yes."

"And you'd forgive everything I've done to you?"

"Yes."

"All my—Ammath?"

"Yes."

"Not because it's right? To 'forgive me'?" Now the sneer was molten. "Because you have to do it or betray your 'Math'?"

"No."

"And if it came to a choice between me and Math, you'd put me first?"

His face moved. Clear, open anguish. But even then his voice kept control.

"I would hope it never . . . came to that."

"But if it did?"

He did shut his eyes. It came in the barest whisper.

"If I had to . . . if it was the only . . . yes."

The air, the Morhyrne trembled under me. Burn you in the everlasting pits, I swore at her. Do you know what you've just heard?

Something she must have felt. I actually saw her own lips tremble, so quickly he could not have seen before he re-opened his eyes. But the look that met him was harder than obsidian. As black, as pitiless.

"Because you're 'in love' with me? You couldn't live without me? I mean more to you than anything else?"

She made it flaying satire. His answer turned it back to honest truth.

"Yes."

The meteors blazed then, flaming into white-hot scorn. "You love me so much you'd pervert justice for me, deny your 'beliefs'—such as they are!—for me, betray your friends for me, you'd marry me on those terms—and afterwards I could tread all over you and you'd go on suffering and forgiving and refusing to hit back and doing all those bloody-minded forbearing lily-livered things, and bleat that you had to do it for the sake of"—she fairly bawled it—" 'Math'!"

His shoulders sprang upright. His eyes shot one green streak of mirth.

"Oh, no," he said with the utmost affability. "If I ever do lay hands on you, madam, I shan't suffer anything. I shall tie you to the bedpost and beat you black and blue. Every . . . single . . . night."

She all but fell off the parapet. Her hand clapped to her heart. The color fluxed wildly in her cheeks. Her eyes were enormous, there was some strange convulsion in their depths. She hiccupped for breath.

The spasm passed. For a moment she was wholly, perfectly still.

Then her lips shook, her eyes went impossibly wider, the gold flamed and crescendoed and died. And the obsidian melted. Blackness shivered and shifted, transformed to sheets of coal-black mist.

"Oh," she whispered. She was laughing, crying, both together, unable to help herself. "Oh, you are such a *fool!*"

The sun came out in his face. Looking back at her he laughed in pure delight.

"An outright imbecile! An absolute idiot!"

"I am, I am! Else I couldn't have made such an almighty bungle out of this."

"B-bungle?" She was crying, and trying to blink rather than wipe away the tears.

"What else could you call it? When I tried to propose I ended making fun of you, and you threw me in chains. When you came down to bait me I had to preach at your courtiers and you all but broke my head. And when your Wardrobe Mistress blazoned your very private affairs all over Zyphryr Coryan I didn't even have the sense to shut her up."

"Klyra! That . . . ! How would you have felt if someone—"

"Believe me, I knew just how you felt! Who made a laughing stock of my very private feelings to the whole confounded court?"

Her lips twitched. She tried to stop a sound and choked. Then, for the first time, I heard the Lady Moriana laugh without menace or malice or spite.

Their mirth died away together. She looked at him, he looked at her.

"And what," she demanded with feigned belligerence, "am I supposed to do now?"

He was still smiling. I had never seen such joy, such tenderness, such candid happiness in his face.

"You could," he suggested softly, "come down—if you liked."

She looked at the pavement. He came over, holding out his hand. For another long moment she held back. Then hers came to meet it, and he helped her down into the bower.

She stood looking up at him, uncertain, and trying to mask it in truculence. A new light, not of laughter, woke in his eyes.

"I shouldn't," he said rather thickly, "do this. But—"

He still had hold of her hand. He gave it such a jerk she literally tumbled into him, caught her with his right elbow while he transferred his left hand from wrist to waist, said, "Blast you, look up here," and began kissing her in a way that had absolutely nothing to do with Math.

Chapter XIII

I was back in my body, looking across a battered vestibule into Fengthira's face. "Ah," she said in pure satisfaction. "At last."

Then she saw me and that smile came, fey and chilling even in mirth.

"What, didst think he'd kiss her forehead and 'forgive her'—send her off to do better like one of tha mewling priests? Tcha! May be soft, but he's flesh and blood."

"But—but—"

Her eyes narrowed. "Hast paid *no* heed at all? To aught he looked? Aught he said? When even her jimping popinjay of a maid could say, T'is a case with her?"

"With her, yes! But he—" I tried to rally. "I thought he—admired her, yes, I thought—"

She gave a veritable horse's snort. "And when he said, I've plans for her, hast never wondered, What?"

"I—uh. . . ."

She snapped her fingers under my nose. "Then soften tha granite head and wonder now! For I tell thee plain, it's been in his mind since the day he clapped eyes on her. And if tha or thine tries to botch it for him, after all this. . . ."

I gulped and tried not to hold my head on. And then tried in earnest cowardice to think no further. Not to say, He has what he wanted. But at what cost to us?

And is it a prize that can be kept?

I opened my mouth. Fengthira gave me one quelling glower. "Come tha. We've eavesdropped enough."

We sat on the fern-walk's lowest step. The earth rumbled, the lava hissed, withered ferns above us rustled in the gloom. I tried to think, then tried not to think. Fengthira sat quiet, whistling softly through her teeth. But at last she glanced upward, and a small frown rucked her brows.

"I doubt," she remarked, "he's as little care for time now as if he'd twisted Los Velandryxe himself. But. . . ." Then she rose quickly as scraps of conversation floated down.

". . . use your arts, then. Act without hands. Perfect if you have no hands to act."

"If you think, you coal-eyed femaere, that I'll totter down there with you under my arm and Los Velandryxe Thira bobbing like a kite in front of me, you're a bigger fool than you think I am."

"Impossible . . . ?" A splutter. A scuffle. "Oh, mind the step!"

"I am minding it. I'm quite capable of doing that—and this. . . ."

"No, you aren't, give me that—now see what you've done!"

"Much better. You had it half down already, ramping at me up there—"

"You wretch, I'll look like a, a, haymaker's wench—"

"Are you still worrying about your looks . . . ?"

Silence, sudden, absolute. Dwindling to a sense of motion, and an abrupt change of tone.

"I still don't see how you can. . . ."

"Because I'm a fool. You told me that. Fengthira told me, your blighted soothseer told me. Once to fall for you, twice to suffer you, thrice for coming back. It's only the thought of that eternally sanctified bedpost that got me through."

"Assharral—"

She broke off short. For an instant the flaw crossed his voice as well.

"We'll deal with Assharral. In its time."

"Fengthira—"

"Fengthira what?"

"Fengthira won't like it. . . ."

"Fengthira'll do as I say." Fengthira's eyes lit in a vivid laugh. "Stop that or you'll never see a bedpost. I'll pull your clothes off on these steps."

"But when I get old, what on earth am I going to do?"

"Pour out my tonic and unearth my sticks. . . ."

They reached the top of the stair. For an instant I thought the smoke had wholly gone. His arm was round her waist, one of hers round him, her other arm cradled the Well. The light hung upon them, transfiguring their faces, making them figures of legend who walk in immortal sunlight, where laughter needs no cause but springs like water from a brimming wellhead, the overflow of bliss.

Fengthira watched them descend, an echo of that light in her own eyes. I realized, in wonder, it was Moriana at whom she looked.

Moriana looked back. Her hair had come right down in a sable haystack, her face was indubitably grimed with lava smuts. But her bones were the bones of a Morheage, and the glow waking in her eyes was cold as night in space.

"There's naught so vexing," Fengthira observed, "as to hear tha'st done better than tha deserts." Her lids crinkled. "Wilt need to keep him on the bit. Else I doubt he'll give away Assharral when the fit takes him, tha shirt as well as his."

Beryx said indignantly, " 'Thira!" But Moriana twitched and gave one cut-off gasp.

"You don't . . . you don't mind. . . ."

Fengthira snorted at her, but not as she had at me. "Dost think he'd pay attention if I did?"

Moriana's brows snapped down. Tried to stay there, and slid up. The laughter rose behind them, a sudden involuntary runnel pure as the music of Los Morryan: surprise, relief, delight.

With a quelling stare Beryx ordered, "You be quiet." Quite unquelled, she looked up at him through her lashes, gold fireflies alive in velvet black. He looked down. The light was woven in his own eyes, and now it had a softness, the play of sunshine through the tenderest new-sprung leaves. . . .

"When hast time," Fengthira said resignedly, "for aught but love-taps and bedposts, couldst lend ear to this?"

Beryx tore his eyes free. "Oh," he said in some confusion. "Oh, yes. . . ."

His glance found Moriana, who said promptly, "You'll drop it, octopus." She came forward, the Well in both her hands. Her fingers, her eyes were steady. As if passing over a borrowed needle. As if it had never meant anything to her at all.

"I think," she said, "you should look after this."

Fengthira did not offer to touch it. "Hast rushed tha fence," she retorted. "There's work for it here."

Moriana looked blank. Beryx reached normality in a bound, then astonishment.

"You don't mean—but 'Thira, can you? I thought—"

"Wreve-lethar," Fengthira said flatly, "acts on Pharaon Lethar. Since when was that just headsful of air?"

Beryx's jaw dropped. Moriana looked from one to the other. Half an hour ago, I thought, she would have died before demanding so frankly, "Will somebody explain?"

Fengthira jerked her chin out at Zyphryr Coryan. "Hast a mountain out there falling to pieces and a city melting, and Los Velandryxe under tha hand. Dost know a better time to change the world?"

Moriana's eyes went to Beryx. He pulled his jaw up. "She means—" He stopped and swallowed. " 'Thira, you did mean, stop the—eruption. Didn't you?"

Fengthira sighed and rolled her eyes. "Twenty minutes love-birding and hast lost all tha wits. Nay, I meant walk on water to Eakring Ithyrx. What else would do?"

"Stop the. . . ." Moriana gaped in turn, lovely even in shock. "You could—it can—I didn't—"

She stopped again. Collecting herself. Gathering herself. To what an effort I realized when she looked back at Fengthira and said, clearly, with deliberation, "I beg your pardon. I didn't know . . . I never learnt . . . what the Well can do."

I heard Beryx take in his breath and a stab of jealousy recalled when he had responded, with half that joy, that radiance, to a sign of Math in me.

She read his eyes. Her cheeks mantled with a light, lovely blush. She said, "It would be a—good start."

He gave her a lovelier smile. Praise, pride, joy. Then his brows knit. "But 'Thira. . . . Even Wreve-lethar can't—reverse time."

"Why dost want to reverse it, zany? Well enough if tha canst mend it now."

"Then," said Moriana with decision, "that's that." And once again she offered Fengthira the Well.

Fengthira merely clicked her tongue and jerked up her chin.

Beryx lost his fuddled air and started backing. "No," he said. "No, 'Thira. The Four forbid. Not me."

"Wilt stop going sideways like a balky colt and use tha head? Needst strength for Los Velandryxe. Tha wast ever more sledge than needle, and t'is sledge that's needed here."

" 'Thira, no! I don't have the judgment! The Velandryxe! The—"

"Needst no judgment. There's but one thing to do. As for Velandryxe—art such a clown, needst not take care for Velandryxe. T'is Velandryxe will look out for thee."

" 'Thira, I'm just not strong enough! I've fought it and I know!"

Fengthira's eyes narrowed. There was a long pause. She frowned. Her eyes turned blank, and revived.

"Cause enough to try it," she muttered. "No cause to shy, that t'was never tried before." She gave Moriana one stabbing glance.

"Tha, girl. Hast the nerve to help him—and the wish—and the will?"

Moriana caught her breath. Glanced from Beryx to Fengthira and back.

"No," said Fengthira. "Tha folk. Tha fault. And tha mate."

Moriana set her teeth, an odd expression on that lovely face. She said, "I'll try."

"Not try," Fengthira rejoined grimly. "Si'sta, I've no way to tell if Wreve-lethar works with double harness. But tha'lt not be playing this time. Knowst what the Well can do if tha only 'tries.' And this will be its proper purpose. Canst not try. Tha must."

Their eyes met, and held. Then mischief, the image of Beryx's, woke in those black depths.

"If it's a Must," she remarked demurely, "then it must be right—mustn't it?"

Fengthira snorted. "He's corrupted thee already. Stint vexing me, then, and do what tha must."

Moriana glanced at Beryx, who took a deep breath. "Where better?" he said. He put an arm round her, and with her still carrying the Well they retreated up the stairs.

Fengthira said absently, "Stand, then," recollected I was not a horse, and amended with irony, "No, sit."

We sat. This time she did not share her farsight, if she used it. When I glanced round she was hunched up, elbows on knees, chin on fists, tension in every line.

My heart speeded up. I rehearsed the risk, the effort, the Well's power. Moriana's rawness in the arts, the possible miscarriages, that daunting "must." I made my peace several times over with death. The air did not quake. There were no thunderbolts. I found myself breathing fast. Fengthira said, "Calm thaself. T'will be a good time yet."

I tried to relax, then wondered with fresh alarm if marauders had found our little party at the gate. She replied curtly, "No." I dismantled a fern-frond. She enquired acidly, "How didst last a sentry-watch?" I dropped the pieces and tried to comport myself like a soldier. She observed, "Lookst like a squatter pigeon when tha swellst up like that." I wished with some warmth that neither she nor I had ever been born. She said, "Canst not reverse time." Then with a quick chuckle she gripped my shoulder and said, "Ah, lad, I'm sorry to plague thee. Si'sta, I'm in a pother myself."

That steadied me, as was no doubt intended. I said rather awkwardly, "I know now what you meant."

Aedryx need never ask a gloss. She just nodded and said, "My father called Math and love and mercy a triad to thwart Vorn's spite. But t'will be better if tha canst give t'others a lead. I doubt they're so old in Math they'll let her walk out smelling of roses and say, 'I'll make amends.' They're more like to lock on the bit. And the filly's cost him enough."

Thinking of the dead mare, recalling she put horses above men, I reflected that she practiced what she preached. She chuckled. "T'is never easy. Sooner plait ropes in water than follow Ma—"

Her words blew away. The world blew away. Earth, air, my body, all but vision was gone. Instead I beheld Los Velandryxe Thira, poised against a ground of impenetrable black.

But instead of a crystal dewdrop it was a solid orb of crusted green and blue and black and white, the blue of compressed oceans, the green in masses whose shape I had seen on maps, overlaid by ragged whorls of white with black laid like shadows beneath. What told me it was Los Velandryxe Thira was the four hands strained about its girth: a tapering white hand clinched by a strong-knuckled hand whose ancient shield calluses were blurred in scar tissue's seamy, hairless brown, a crippled claw forced tight by an elegant long-nailed hand with the eclipsed-moon signet on its thumb.

At least, I think it was on the thumb. I still wonder, sometimes, if that thumb was there, or if I saw, face whittled by earth's shadow, the real moon itself. The hands' distortion told me what they held was heavier than mountains, that it was spinning as it hurtled with vertiginous momentum through empty space, so for one awful moment I feared that clutch would break. . . .

And then I felt—Everything is the only word for it. I felt everything bump: check: lift like a wheel to a road rut, gather and run, everything from the spin of that inlaid bubble to the course of my own blood.

My stomach swam, my ear channels staggered, my heart found itself out of step and skipped to catch up, my eyes . . . when it was gone, they wanted that image back. But I was seated in the smoke on a stone step in Ker Morrya, with Fengthira gesturing me to quiet.

Scratch of fern fronds, the pound of my heart. Blood's sough in my ears. Her husk of a whisper. "When couldst last hear that?"

My heart stopped altogether. She rose and walked swiftly out to the loggia beyond the steps.

Smoke blinded us, heat stifled us. A red-hot sword lay down Zyphryr Coryan's flank. I heard clamor from the city. I heard Fengthira say, more softly yet, "Imsar Math." Then I knew what

I could no longer hear.

The thunder in the earth had stopped.

She turned from the smoke wall. "Art a lucky man." She sounded stern, infinitely remote. "Hast seen what none other will, past or future time. Tha Striand blood perhaps."

She answered my other questions swiftly as they were thought. "No, tha dost not see the fire running backward into Haz's belly or the smoke gone in an eye-blink or Zyphryr Coryan ten years ahead. He's a good lad, and wiser than he knows. Next best to hold tha hand is knowing when to stop."

Then her eyes lit up. She laughed like a girl and flicked a finger across my nose. "Content thee, Granite-eyes. They've done it. Mountain's back to sleep." And she ran lightly, swifter than any maiden, through the loggia and up the steps.

I did not follow. I waited till they came, trooping down together, easy now, slandering each other and fighting the battle over like all soldiers, their clothes patched white with sweat, Beryx and Moriana arm in arm, the Well tucked negligently in Fengthira's elbow crook. Three aedryx with the shine of joy and magic and victory on them, remote from mortal men.

Then Fengthira tapped my elbow, asking, "Wilt wait the smoke out to be sure?" Beryx demanded with urgency, "For the Four's sake help me with these women, Fylghjos," and Moriana, that soft new sheen in her eyes brightening to a kindly mischief, murmured, "What did you do with the last surcoat, Alkir?"

I had just wit to retort, "Protected imperial bloodstock, ma'am." Before their laughter drew me into the fellowship.

As we entered the loggia, Beryx looked eagerly out into the smoke. Then he broke step, pausing, drawing in a long, long breath. "Now," he said, and I knew he was invoking that promise made to Rema, for the dawn she would not see. "Now we can start."

I followed them through the murk, half soaring willy-nilly on the updraft of that happiness, half crying in curdled hate and desperation, You can forgive her. Fengthira has. But how can we forgive all that she has done?

And then, in mouth-drying fear, How can you start, until you get past us?

We came down the last steps. Onto the threshold. Under Ker Morrya's gate. What plan, if any, Beryx had made, I have no idea. My own brain was dry. I saw the faces turn, the bodies jump, the action beginning, inevitable as the shift of a phalanx-front.

Evis and Sivar had sprung forward in relief. Zyr shouted, "Ha-ha—" and the Axairan triumph yell died in his throat. Before my eyes their faces turned to sword-blades, sharp and pitiless, all leveled on Moriana in our midst.

She had pulled from Beryx's arm, chin up and backbone stiffening, the softness gone. He tried to catch at her and she almost pushed him off. Her head went back as I had seen it on the parapet of Los Morryan. But though her eyes were huge and somber as Ker Morrya's smoke pall, the mockery, the cruel amusement had disappeared.

Before she could speak Beryx flung words out with bare desperate haste. "We stopped the fire—the mountain's back asleep!"

It barely distracted them. Evis gave a brush of the hand. Wenver and Amver had let the boys go. They were all beginning to close in.

"I said *we* did it!" He had some authority back. As their eyes involuntarily came round he caught her hand and held it despite her jerk. "I couldn't have done it, without her."

He stared around them, joy lost, all-too-helpless fear becoming something else. But this time Moriana spoke.

"I have renounced the Well," she said.

It came flatly as an ultimatum. She would not sue mercy, excuse herself, let alone offer apologies to such a reception. But, I realized, she was trying to unbend. Doing a Morheage's best to announce amends.

The stealthy, all but involuntary advance had stopped. Ost stared, Uster blinked, a moment's comprehension showed in Karis' eyes. The boys had crept forward, riveted as the rest. Quick, I besought some unknown god, let me weight the scalepan. Give me something to say.

I hesitated an instant too long. It was Zyr whose eyes slitted. Zyr whose voice, lowered to a gravel-slide, broke out, "The Well. And what about the rest? Our folk? The army? Assharral?"

"Zyr, stop!" Beryx shouted in pure panic this time. "I told you—don't let it make you Ammath!"

Evis half-checked. Zyr's eyes rolled, the glare of the berserker before he loses all control. And some great shove sent me leaping to stand braced like a shoulderman at Moriana's rather than Beryx's back.

"Wait," I cried in turn. "Wait, stop—think!"

I had no weapon. I knew no weapon would help us now. I could only try to make my eyes say it. You've followed him this far. Will you destroy him in his first taste of happiness? Will you pervert yourselves and smash all hope of a future to avenge what, however cruelly, is already gone?

If nothing else, I could not add ignominiously, if you destroy me along with my lord, don't do it in front of my sons.

"Don't," Beryx was saying huskily. The sweat was running down his jaw. "For the love of Math, Evis . . . Zyr . . . Wenver . . . wait. Think." Something told me that if they refused he would not hinder them. Would not attack them, might not even resist. But they would only come to Moriana after they had hacked him apart at her feet.

"Try to—look forward." His voice shook. "You needn't—fall in the pit. You can go on. Try to—to—"

To be more than human. To achieve what in all her time the Lady had never done. To make one giant's stride out, free, over the past, and arrive at magnanimity. Greatness of soul.

Math.

They were poised as Moriana had hung, a leaf in the wind's eye, on that parapet. But there was no mercy. No heed. Not in Evis, not in Wenver's, not in any of their eyes.

And as it all teetered to the precipice edge, Zem piped up.

He had wormed to Evis' side. I have no idea how much he understood. Probably, I fear, far too much. But he spoke with his age's single-minded satisfaction at a long-standing puzzle solved.

"So that," he said, "is what you planned to do with her."

For a moment we were all paralyzed. Then Moriana's eyes flamed. Evis' jaw dropped and Beryx yelled in awful consternation, "Zem, you wretch!"

Moriana rounded on him. He literally ducked. "It wasn't like that!"

"Oh, it wasn't, was it?" She had turned whiter than on that parapet. "You dared talk about me like a—a—and to a child!"

She swung at him, a barrack-room roundhouse. He howled, "I never said a word, I never thought, I swear it. . . ." She charged him and he actually ran, round Fengthira and back behind me, the good arm over his head like a farmer caught in hail. Moriana swept down on us both. I had no time for fight or flight. He yelled across my shoulder, panicked to the point of burlesque, "I did tell you, I had plans!"

He was cowering like the most hen-hearted recruit behind a sentry-post, holding me before him one-handed, peering past my neck. I did not have to see how it looked. That was written in Moriana's face beside me, the eyes huge, the skin white, the mouth. . . .

The mouth suddenly twitching uncontrollably. The face's mask shattering, the eyes, yet again, turning to sheets of black-shot mist. And then, bursting out like a dam gone down, the full depth of that waterfall laugh.

How could the most vendetta-crusted blood-thirst resist that?

I can see Evis crumbling behind her, the swept-away look on Zyr's face. Karis and Wenver had succumbed, it swept the circle like some new, precious plague. I felt the rocks buckle in my own memory's wall. Saw the future rise beyond the rubble at last, clear and irresistible as a trumpet calling, Stand down.

When the flood ebbed Beryx was still lurking, wringing the moment to its last. Moriana caught her breath along with us. Then she spluttered and cried, "Oh, you fool! Come out!"

He crept out, not done burlesquing himself. She gave him one fulminating, not wholly counterfeit glower. Then it changed.

"You did that on purpose." It was half outrage, half disbelief. "Ran away . . . Pretended. . . ." Her voice rose. "Deliberately!"

He looked at her under his lashes. Though in his bent head that mock-timidity lingered, the corners of his mouth had crept up. But it was not foolery, when he spoke.

He said, "The Ulven called me, Rainmaker."

Because the crippled wizard will end the Assharran drought.

I remembered, then, what it had meant. Leveled in that laughter's wake I understood, through flesh and blood's reality, what it meant now: my chest's enlargement, my blood moving, heart and spirit released. As if the hate had been not merely a wall but stasis, stagnation, the suspension of time that drought imposes. A living death.

And now it had broken. Life, water, time, could move again.

The others remembered too. But a different memory, more

than understanding, was moving like another freshet in Moriana's stare.

Then she turned her head and looked me full in the face.

"Alkir"—that lovely liquid voice was lovelier for the evil it had sloughed—"we can't go back. And no recompense would be enough. But we could go on—couldn't we?" And she held out her hand.

T'would need a Velandyr, I heard Fengthira saying, to amend that. And, unless tha dost the same, t'will be fare-thee-well 'twixt him and thee. But the choice had already been made, in my own mind. My own heart.

Her fingers curled, slight and fragile as vine stems, round mine. I heard Beryx say low and thickly, "Well done." I did not ask which of us he meant. I felt the spring of his joy waken, though, as I looked at the others. And if his eye had pleaded, I did my utmost to make mine a fierce command.

They understood. And at the last, they could not turn their backs on the liberation that had taken them, however unawares.

Evis conceded first, advancing with past hate and present disapproval and undigested laughter still mingled in his look. As Moriana met his eye an answer woke in hers. But she bit her lip ferociously, and it sounded almost earnest when she spoke.

"Whatever we say will be . . ." impossible, I supplemented. An insult, a grotesquerie, or a wound too raw to touch. "But. . . ."

She pulled her chin up in that old implacable way. But I saw her shoulders brace, before, again, she put out her hand.

Evis took it, perforce. With a pause, a gingerliness close to revulsion. Then past training rescued him. He bowed over her fingers and uttered a cliché from another life. "I wish you happy, ma'am." His eye found Beryx's suddenly radiant face and he amended with no reservation and no effort at all, "Happier than anyone could ask."

One by one the rest followed, mumbling something, clasping hands. Stepping back, with a look of woken wonder on each face. Until only Zyr remained.

He glowered at us across the shifting but persistent glacis they had all left. His narrow bronze-red face was laconic at the best of times and now quite inscrutable, but in the pause I heard Beryx suddenly catch his breath.

Moriana stiffened. She did not put out her hand. I would have prayed, if I had a god left, that the pride, the mockery, had not revived in her eyes.

Zyr looked at Beryx instead.

Beryx did not speak, but I knew what his eyes would say. Don't hold back, they would beg. Do this for your own sake. It's human, it's natural to grieve and demand punishment and thirst for revenge exacted in blood, but don't do it. Be more than human. Cleave to Math.

Zyr looked back to Moriana. He jerked one shoulder to the corpses under the arch and said evenly, "For me, you should be hanging with them." He paused. "But. . . ."

His eyes flicked to Beryx again, and that glance said it all. If I can't do this for your reasons, neither can I deny you. What you made me feel. That moment's overwhelming, cleansing laughter, when the hate broke. I will do this for what *you* mean to me.

Then he caricatured an imperial salute and took a step back. I will not touch you, said that dour glance, in reconciliation. But I will sanction your passage. Into amnesty. Into hope.

Moriana's chin came down. Beryx bent his head. Softly, huskily, and I could feel with what intensity, he said, "Thank you, Zyr."

And I remember the next advance, that evening, after a trial restoration in Ker Morrya: a dozen different work-parties to clear debris, stable horses, forage dinner, gather splintered furniture for firewood, organize quarters, succor the corpses at the gate. Barricade the gate itself.

We gathered in a cleansed piece of the great gallery, lit by tallow dips in silver candelabra, reclining on salvaged cushions or Phaxian cloaks, as we ate pot-luck soup and griddle cakes and drank barley-spirit too raw even for looters from a crystal decanter they had missed. Beryx and Moriana presided, sharing his cloak, with Fengthira on his right and me on Moriana's left; which might still have been unnerving, had she ever been aware of me. As of course she was not.

When the motley cups were charged there came a sudden pause. I had felt it happening all afternoon: the recurring tug-of-heart between hope and resurrected memory, the embers of grief and hate rousing, to be re-drowned by another deluge of their joy. This time it was clearer, simpler. The moment, the action, demanded the stamp of ritual. But was it to be a mourners' wake? Or a betrothal feast?

Fengthira glanced sideways and sighed. Neither Beryx nor Moriana heard. She looked past, with irony and mockery and the involuntary, if often wry smile forced from all who looked at them, and told me, "Tha'll do. Give us a toast."

I stood up. Cleared my throat. Cleared it again. Waited. Bellowed, "Stand to!" They leapt apart, the audience fell apart. Beryx gave me a wrathfully merry look. I gave them the toast.

"Tomorrow," I said.

In a moment, Zyr's hand relaxed. Then Evis lifted his cup. Wenver and Ost nodded, looking past me too. "Tomorrow," they repeated, and tipped their cups.

Beryx and Moriana drank with us, with fitting solemnity. But they drank to each other, which Fengthira found too much.

"Hark'ee," she said. "This billing and cooing's half-measure to ye, and no use to us. Get y'selves off to the real thing—if ye can find a bed that's fit for it."

Beryx blushed. Moriana dropped her eyelids, smiled wickedly, and pulled him to his feet. She glanced down at Fengthira, and Fengthira anticipated the sally in her look.

"If th'art foundered by morning, remember, t'was thee schooled him to do without sleep."

That routed Moriana at last. As she went crimson Beryx said irately, " 'Thira, that's enough!" and hauled her doorward before Fengthira could show just how little his orders weighed with her.

Chapter XIV

That, I suppose, was in truth their wedding feast. There can seldom have been one more bizarre or less worthy of the event, but of the happiness it launched there could be no doubt. Next day they were blazing rather than merely shining, and it was a blaze that did not cool. It warmed everyone around them, it spread through the first salvings of Zyphryr Coryan, it radiated out over Assharral, changing, softening, quickening the renewal, down to the scruffiest urchin re-mustering pigs in a Gjerven swamp. Fuelling Beryx's inexhaustible energy, his joy in doing what he was bred for: exercising all his natural gifts, not merely to maintain but to reconstruct an entire realm.

Assharral needed it all. It takes longer to build than to destroy, and longer yet to rebuild what has been ruined. Some things can never be restored. The Morhyrne's cone now sags like a hunchback's hump. They still boat round the lava on the harbor road, waiting till it is cool enough to begin tunneling. Bridges will always span it in many central streets. And south Morrya will be desolate for the rest of my life. It took the first blast's full impact: every tree felled for a hundred miles, live things incinerated within thirty, asphyxiated within fifty, the earth within seventy miles shrouded under pumice and lava clots and ash.

With time and patience the other provinces will be healed, sometimes improved. But nothing can restore the bloodline of the imperial stud mares, slaughtered with their unborn foals, nor refound the school of the Climbrian dancers, wiped out to the youngest recruit. Or resurrect the human dead, all dear to someone, who lie in so many unknown graves. And it will take longer than the reclamation of Morrya to wash the salt from fields in so many human hearts.

More than once in those first months I wanted to echo Moriana's wail of "But where do we start?" So many things crying, This first. We were lucky, for the land's sake, to begin just before the Wet, and unlucky for the sake of its folk. I cannot tally the miles I rode in the rain as lieutenant-at-large, racing the plague into squalid refugee camps, organizing shelter, food, medicine, then kicking over the wheels in town and village and farm, trying to reconcile the die-hards who abhorred Beryx with the bloodhounds who only wanted Moriana's head. Mayors and governors, fencing posts and seed corn, returned fugitives, renegade soldiers, discharged priests, town plans and ownerless milking cows; Gjerven farmers persuaded to repopulate Morrya and give the Ulven room. And I had only to tidy the edges and prepare for the great new plans: tax changes, a dismantled religion, a new government.

To Beryx it was all an incentive. "I love building," he told me once. "And I've never had such a chance. In Hethria we started at dirt, and in Everran I left before the fun really began." From which I assume he defined "fun" as twenty-five hours work a day on Assharral, with extra minutes found for Moriana, and some spare seconds allotted to such mundane necessities as food and sleep.

Moriana worked with him, hour for hour. They could rarely be pried apart, even after their quarrels, which flared over a clause in the new constitution or a civil appointment, some high-handed action in her old manner or a disputed precept in Math, his treatment of some balky underling or an unacceptable part of her aedric apprenticeship. I walked in on the end of more than one storm: the room littered with hurled books and broken inkpots, an official seal poised like a slingstone in Moriana's hand, a pile of shattered plates and an overset table vibrating from Beryx's mindspeech, at a volume that would shake Zyphryr Coryan. <*Use your HEAD, for once!*>

Sometimes she would heed. More often she would yell back. The time I recall best she bawled like a maddened tree-cat and threw.

The seal caught him on the cheekbone and ricocheted onto an intact cup. In the silence I heard the fragments come to rest, fall by ticking, diminishing fall.

Then in a foam of dusty white skirt she whirled out onto the balcony, gripping the carven lily balustrade till I thought the stone would crack. Glaring, rigid to her fingertips, over the half-patched prospect of Zyphryr Coryan.

I had the wit to stand stiller than the stone. My slanted view showed me Beryx's shoulders. I listened to his breathing, distinct as the fall of cup shards, alone amid the scattered reports and requisitions of a new order, strewn under the painted cupola of a once-formal reception room.

Then he took his own five strides to the door and slid his arm tightly round her waist.

For a moment they were both utterly still. But then I heard her sigh. Her fingers relaxed. Intuition rather than information told me she had leant back in his arms, laying her head against his chest. And I heard her whisper, barely audible.

"How can you bear this? Any of this? Anything to do with me?"

"Because you came back." He had dropped his cheek forward on her hair, his shoulders relaxing too. "Because you could laugh. After everything."

I would have withdrawn, but I feared the shift of a dust-grain under my boot would break the spell.

"Because you took the brave way. Not to run. Even at the end. Because you chose to live with it. To make amends."

She made a rueful noise in her throat. Her hands lifted and disappeared and I knew she had clasped them over his. Together, silent in the noonlight, they looked out over Assharral.

Before I could creep backward, ease away, she spoke again.

"They still hate me."

He did not reply. I did see his arm tighten, in a way she must have felt in every rib.

"They think—they say—I'm not sorry. I'm happy. Instead."

He turned his head to give me a half-profile. His voice belied what that look said.

"You have *no* need to weep and wail and put on sack-cloth. I never wanted that. I never expected it." Her body must have transmitted surprise to equal mine. He shook her lightly and I heard the smile wake beneath that determination, implacable as an avalanche. "You were and you are a Morheage. Arrogance was bred in you."

She made another sound, between a snort and a sob. He shook her again. "Crawling over my feet—or theirs—doesn't matter. What matters is what you do to fix the damage. And there, the Four know, you're filling the cup over. I see that's Morheage as well."

This time it was more laugh than sob. "So *you* say. But you've been besotted all along."

"So I have." The faint amusement faded. "But the rest will need time, Aihi. A lot of time. You know that. They have to let the hate out as well as leave it behind. They'd need that, however sorry you looked."

Aihi, my stunned mind repeated. The abbreviation, the deepest Assharran love-name, for Aiahya: Beautiful one.

Both of them had grown entirely still. I almost imagined I could hear them breathe.

I did hear her sigh, before the shift of her skirt told me she had moved in his grasp. A wind drew up over the balustrade and the smells of lava-dust and mud and newly planed timber came with it, ruffling the mingled blackness of their hair, sheeny as water in the sun.

Then, with a different inflection, she murmured, "Were you always like this?"

"Oh, no." He had caught the shift as well as the sense. He sounded just too bland. "When I was a king, I had to be serious."

"Serious?" It was nearly outrage. "You?"

"All those people, you see. There all the time. Depending, relying on you. Expecting, if there's a crisis, that you'll meet their expectations. Be twice as pompous as them."

"And of course you were?" Now laughter breathed through that lovely, teasing voice.

"Oh, dear." I could hear the grin. "I only slipped up once. Shocked my hearthbard speechless. I made a joke when the dragon came."

"Beryx—!"

"It just slipped out, I swear. . . ."

"Just slipped out, oh, yes. The way they did with me?"

She tried to turn. He pinned her firmly to his chest.

"Certainly not. Now, I'm an aedr, and we don't care what we say. The crazier the better. So, my erstwhile empress, you can forget any hopes of standing on your dignity."

The eye-corner visible over his shoulder kindled to dangerous gold flecks. She lifted her gaze and then her hand to the seal's bruise on his cheekbone. Then she said demurely, "So you really earned this, didn't you?"

I felt my own breath stop. And I felt the moment he started laughing out loud, then flung his arm wide so she fell back in his grasp laughing harder still, while I shot out of sight-range and prepared to crunch up to the doorway as they came inside, the light back on them, restored to happiness' equilibrium. Ready to work again.

Even in the Wet I could feel Assharral responding to that joyfulness, like plants when the year turns and the sun's stride lengthens, and every green thing answer with leaf and bud and flower. The rhythm quickened as the Wet receded. When the real sun fell into step with ours there were times when, bone-weary, I sang on the road.

So I came back from a trip to Darrior, head full of half-raised buildings and burgeoning plans, lungs full of the smell from burnt-out fields under short, new green grass. We were still quartered in Ker Morrya, since our old house was under the lava flow. At the door I met the good smell of stew and a riotous welcome from the twins, but from Callissa an oddly constrained smile.

Still full of euphoria, I left the advance to her. We were in bed, our feet in a swathe of moonlight, an eygnor's song on air that tingled with the newborn Dry, when she said in a small, braced, constricted voice, "Alkir?"

And when I answered, "What is it?" she said, "I—want to go away."

When I could speak, I said, "Where? How? Why?"

"Not from you," responded the voice on my arm. "And I know we're happy here and it's not that I don't want to stay and I know you do. And I don't want to go back to Frimmor. Not now."

Despite this disorderly advance I knew she had been nerving herself to this a long time, that it demanded courage, and the knowledge it would be unwelcome made her more afraid.

I drew her closer and said, "I won't eat you, love. Where do you want to go? And why?"

She took a deep breath and charged.

"Hethria," she said.

This time I was struck quite dumb. She turned over and began speaking quickly, hurrying in her attack.

"I know you'd rather stay because of Beryx and they'll soon be mending the army and they'll need you if there is a war with Phaxia and you were born in Assharral, but Fengthira told me she's going back to Eskan Helken soon, they can manage here now, and she can't bear too many men for too long, and once she goes—" She stopped dead. Then flung herself. "It's the twins."

Thinking I understood left me further confounded. The small earnest voice ploughed on.

"It took me a long time to—admit what they are. But they are. We have to make the best of it. And even if they're not as important as Beryx thinks, the start of a new cycle and the first aedryx to grow up in Math, and all that—whatever they are—they shouldn't be denied the chance to—be that. Just like anyone else. And Fengthira's the one who must teach them, we all know that." I didn't, I thought, wondering how far this had gone behind my back. "But she won't stay here. Even for them. So—so—I thought"—her voice had dwindled—"we—should go to her."

Hethria. Sand and Sathellin. No army. No resurrection and perhaps consummation of the life begun at fourteen, when I walked away from my father into a barracks, into another world. No share in my new lord's achievement as it came to flower. Idle my remaining life away, deny my nature, as Beryx had denied his when he renounced Everran. But he had Assharral now. And all to fulfill nature in my sons.

It was selfish, base, instinctive, and I could not help it. I said, "But do you want to go—yourself?"

"Not really," she said at last. "But the twins. . . ."

With thought's celerity I considered sending them and staying myself, coercing Fengthira into staying, Beryx into teaching them, refusing to let them learn at all. Now I knew how he had felt, caught between integrities and being pulled apart.

"Love," I said. "You've rather . . . sprung this on me. Could it wait a little? Give me time to think?"

I had not deceived her. It was a defeated, lifeless voice which responded, "Whatever you want."

I thought, and thinking took the edge off life. When I reported next day, and Beryx jumped up from the plans and scribes and advisers and objectors, exclaiming, "Fylghjos! How did it go?" When Moriana added in warmest welcome, "Alkir! At last!" And I was instantly embroiled in the current quarrel which thereupon climaxed in a hail of flying inkpots, until Beryx shook her by a handful of hair, commanding, "Quiet, shrew," and she said, "Shan't. Alkir can settle it." And he said, "A word from me gets us precisely nowhere," and she said, "Alkir, the standard. He wants to use Everran's stupid shield and vine and we should keep the moontree, it belongs to Assharral. Tell him he's wrong."

When I said without the old fear, "If I'm judge you can't dictate the verdict," she yelled, "Partisan!" and he shouted, "Bully!" but the resulting fracas gave me time to think. So at its end I said, "Why not something quite new?"

They chorused, "What?" And remembering that dawn revelation in Morrya, I said, "Why not a lythian?"

But even when they cried in delight, "Flametree!"—"Moontree!"—"Green leaves—"—"We're both fire—"—"And it belongs to Assharral!" When Beryx said, "Thank the Four for Alkir," and Moriana gave me the full blaze of that new smile, adding, "I knew you were on my side," there was a chill where there should have been only achievement, and belonging's warmth.

It did not thaw when, as we shared a piece of cheese and a ferroth over my report, Beryx asked, "Has Callissa said anything about Hethria?"

I nodded. And his eyes, so uncomfortably perceptive, altered from warm hope to dashed understanding. Before he said flatly, "Oh."

Moriana, who had her own ways of arriving where his arts took him, put down her cheese and said, "Pox on Math!"

His eyes turned to her, briefly amused. She said, "I couldn't command him now anyway, yazyk." It is gutter-slang for thief. She considered. "Let's conquer Hethria and Alkir can be governor—no." A wicked glance at Beryx. "That would threaten Everran. Worse than the worst Ammath."

"Femaere," he said agreeably. But the cloud did not lift. I was finding that the hardest of all to withstand when he released me, saying with decision, "You don't want to go. Enough said."

But there was plenty more to be thought. It did not help when the twins came up that night, saying, "Da, we don't want to go to Hethria either. Silly old Ruanbrarx." When even my blinkered eyes could see they were valiantly denying their dearest wish in life.

I said, "It isn't settled," and on that craven compromise fled to the labor that had been so joyful, and now had lost its taste.

Next evening I was riding home from the Rastyr, through one of those breathtaking sunsets the Morhyrne bequeathed us, which continued with barely muted splendor long after the Wet. The sky flamed mulberry and coral and crimson, a light like liquid copper bathed the land beneath. Out of it from the roadside copses came Fengthira and her mare, like a horseman of legend, steeped in the gold of time itself.

The mare fell into step. The rider scanned the sky. Then she said baldly, "If t'is fighting tha thinkst tha craves, Hethria'll give thee tha fill. Not with men. T'is the oldest fight. The one that started when the first pharraz scraped a furrow with a stick, and the wind blew in wild oats. Tha blood knows it. Just as his knows that." She gestured up to Ker Morrya, ringing the mountain with a necklet of lamps.

I sought a mannerly way to say it was not my fight, that I despised it, despised my selfishness. Thought resignedly that she would already know, and said, "I know I should go. For the twins' sake, if nothing else."

"But t'is against tha wish. And Everran's holy Sky-lords forfend that a man do anything against his wish."

When I made no reply she snorted. "He'll not coerce thee. Heardst me tell him in Gjerven, he's learnt his lessons too well. Through is sometimes worse than Round, and he was ever Through, so now he goes Round twice. He was ever, Do as I wilt, so now t'is, Take tha choice. And ever Act, not Abstain, so now t'is, Abstain, when he should act. Soft, ah. Told you it was right, didn't I? Ah. For him. But I'm another cup of tea."

My surprise became a tingle of fear. She snorted again.

"I'll not use the arts to turn or twist or force thee. Just tell thee a few truths. Not about tha boys, tha knowst they're the hope of Pharaon Lethar, and a new race of aedryx, and the sons he'll never have. Canst not make that budge tha heart, however it spurs tha head. And for thaself, I've told thee, art a Stiriand to tha granite backbone. Think now what that means to tha wife.

"Thinkst I've no right to meddle," she anticipated me. "Were I he, I daresay I'd not. Dost not think tha's treated her hardly, ah? Hast kept and honored and been faithful to her. And thinks, because tha gave up real soldiering for the Guard and then stayed in it when honor forbade thee, t'is rather she owes thee. Ah. Now think on tha waiting in Stirsselian. Pleasant, was it?" I shuddered. "And how long didst wait? A month? But when tha went whistling off to tha soldier games in Phaxia, she waited two whole years for thee. Never sure when she woke at morning that tha wast not crowbait a week already, and she left a widow with two brats on her back. Not to mention," with irony, "losing thee. Think on that, when tha minds Stirsselian, waiting to know tha folk slain without a hand's turn tha couldst do for them, and they dead by their own choice."

She nodded at my flinch. "And when th'art wanting to put her to army discipline and bearing with her poor manners and finding her tantrums vex thee and wishing she'd not build her whole life round tha sons, think thee on why she does. That t'is possible tha'st looked down tha long stone nose and let her see tha just tolerates her once too often. So she's turned away from thee, because tha wouldst not let thaself come first with her, and put them in tha place."

"I didn't! I haven't!" I could bear it no longer. "I never—"

"Hold tha peace," she said inexorably. "I'm not done. Think tha too, when th'art favoring that tender will of thine, that she came with thee from Frimmor to Zyphryr Coryan and never said a word, and then fled with thee to Phaxia, and then let thee browbeat—yes, I said browbeat, and tha'lt hear me out!—her into Stirsselian, as t'were a high-headed filly that tha'd bring to hand or make it the worse for her—no, tha'lt hear me, if I have to use a Command. And tha'd go tha merry way back to soldiering, and let her suffer again as tha didst in Stirsselian—I said, Quiet! Not once, but as often as tha canst manage it in the span of tha life. Then tha wonders why she'd go to Hethria, to have thee as well as her sons safe." Her eyes were blazing on me, cold and clear and pitiless, untinged by the sunset light. "By the bones of Deve Saedryx Korven, Stiriand, if there's granite in tha backbone, there's more of it in tha head!"

My bridle hand was shaking. I could not speak. I shut my eyes a moment. There was no room for anger or shame or outrage, I simply wanted that flaying voice to stop.

"Hark'ee." Though she spoke much more gently, still I shrank. "I know very well he'd never have cut thee so. And that t'is unjust. But t'is an easy matter to change the head, another to change the rest. If tha stayed in Assharral now, tha'd be thinking ever, I have played false to my sons. And if tha camest in tha present mind to Hethria, tha'd be thinking, I have played false to myself. So I've done what he'd not. I've taken a hot iron and fired tha conscience for thee. And if I've not changed tha head"—a gleam of mordant humor—"I'll warrant it's beaten a change of leads into tha heart."

When I walked into our quarters Zem and Zam halted in mid-rush, took one look and retreated like whipped pups, clean out to their beds. Hurrying up behind them Callissa began, "Zem, Zam, what are—why—" Then her voice changed altogether. "Oh, what is it, my dear?"

I shut my eyes, in shame that it should show so glaringly on my face. Then her arms were round me. I should not feel ashamed, I suppose, to admit I was glad of them. Old schooling dies hard. But human nature is older still. I hid my face in her hair and was thankful she had not turned from me as I so often had from her.

When I lifted my head her eyes were full of purely unselfish anxiety and pain for my hurt. I was grateful for that too. Fengthira's iron had bitten deep.

She said, "Sit down. I'll get some—" And I sat. But I kept hold of her wrist. And when I said, "You're what I want," I saw the flash of unbelieving joy before she landed, off-balanced, in my lap.

"Callissa," I said into her breast. "I'll go to Hethria." And stopped. She must not see it was the result of a flogging, not a free-made choice.

"I mean, we can go to Hethria. If"—I had to scout carefully—"you think it's best for the twins."

"Never mind the twins," she said quite brusquely. "Alkir, what's happened to you?"

There was no point in trying to lie. Whoever called love blind was blind himself.

"Fengthira—talked to me."

She caught her breath.

"We'll—we can go to Hethria." And then something changed in me, nothing to do with the mind, so I could go on in honest truth. "I wouldn't mind going. I've soldiered long enough."

She took my face in her hands. Her eyes grew bigger. Then the tears started to roll down her cheeks. In some alarm I cried, "What is it? What have I done now?" And she clutched me round the neck and sobbed, "Can't I c-cry because I'm h-happy, for once?"

It was easy after that. It was more than easy. I did not just rediscover Callissa, I truly discovered her, and after ten years marriage found myself whistling round like some just-wed lout. When I came to say, with some guilt, "I think I must ask for a discharge," Beryx's face lit up. Before he stammered, "No, I don't mean I'm glad to see you go, I mean—oh, Four, you know what I mean!" He took another look. "I'm so glad you want to." Another, with those too-perceptive eyes. "I'll murder Fengthira, one day." Yet another. Then a sudden grin blazoned joy all over his face. "Fylghjos, if you're not careful, I'll be shouting 'Stand to' myself!"

Fengthira agreed to escort us. She would have traveled faster alone, she was carrying the Well, bound for storage under her eye at Eskan Helken, "where none other can meddle with it," but prolonged coaxing from Beryx persuaded her to march in human company, rather than be called back, somewhere in the desert, to extricate strayed recruits. When an entire baggage train had been assembled, culled, packed, unpacked and packed again, horses chosen and a day finally set, only one thing remained. To see Beryx and Moriana. To say farewell.

In their usual workroom we found only the onetime lordling now prenticed as Beryx's much-tried secretary. His face lightened when he looked past his quill-store to recognize me. But when I asked, "The Lord and Lady?" he very nearly smiled. "They're both up by the fountain, sir."

It was just mid-morning, a superb morning of the early Dry, sumptuous blue sky, green things in full leafage but not yet overblown, enough damp to put a fizz in the air, with a first invigorating nip to herald the winter ahead. As we climbed the rough-hewn steps familiar sounds of altercation floated down.

"Not like that, here!"

"No, here!"

"Let go, idiot!"

"Oh, you spitfire!" Then a bubble of laughter and sudden silence, ending in a hurried "Let go!" as our heads topped the rim of the stairs.

Moriana came forward, trying not to blush, sparkling her eyes at me as she said, "You can't talk, nowadays!" There was mud all over her skirts, and mud smeared Beryx's white silk shirt as he bent beneath the perridel, resurrected by the Wet. Its gold-and-silver foliage danced above him, its shadow played on the dapple of inner sunshine in his eyes. "Come and see what we're—oh!"

There had been an almost human chuckle behind her. A gurgle, a splash. And then a crystal, wordless melody, that flowed out unfaltering over the mountainside.

"It's moving!" Moriana hurried back, we hurried after her.

Los Morryan was flowing again. The water welled up out of its black basin, sluiced away the mud, rose to bubbling silver music, spattered the rim to glittering wet, blowing spray onto the fan of newly emerald moss.

"You did it!"

"I said I would." His eyes laughed at her, a dance of thought and joy and laughter that owed nothing to the motion of the perridel.

"Don't be so smug!" She swiped at him. But he caught the hand and pulled her closer, and we all stood, watching reality's motion, the crystal water freed to clear and sing and flow.

"Sir Scarface," Zem said into the pause, "you told us aedryx couldn't be kings."

"No," Beryx admitted gravely. "That was what I thought. But"—he gave the tail of his eye to Moriana—"I could hardly leave this—er—lady—to tidy the whole thing."

Zem pondered. "Was it a Must?"

Green eyes met black. Wicked amusement blossomed in both.

"You could say," agreed Beryx, straight-faced, "that it was a Must."

His eyes turned, to scan my face with that perception I no longer had to fear. He smiled.

"Good luck, pharraz." He knew the taunt would be understood, as I had once bade him, "Sleep well," in his chains. "I won't say thanks. It's not enough. And anyway—I think you've made your own."

He came to embrace us. Moriana followed, dimpling, but her voice did not tease. She said, "I hardly expected to say this. But thank you, Alkir."

She kissed my cheek. Reflecting that I never expected that either, I returned the salute.

Beryx had turned to Callissa, who was looking like a recruit the first time the phalanx moves. With the merest spice of mischief in the laughter he reached for her hand. Bent over it, and murmured, "A safe journey, ma'am."

She did not correct him back to "Callissa." She did turn her fingers to shut them on his hand a moment, an almost convulsive grasp. Before she whispered, "Thank you," and they both let go.

What she and Moriana did or said together, I did not see. Beryx had already turned to the twins.

"Behave yourselves in Hethria," he told them. "Fengthira's not like me." They grinned in perfect understanding. He added, "One day . . . I'll have work for you."

Los Morryan bubbled on alone a moment, as the promise was sealed. Then the awkwardness of all partings overtook us. I said, "We'll be back one day. To see the lythians flower." And they nodded, growing solemn too.

From the stairhead I looked back. They stood together under the perridel, the light spangled with its inner magic in black eyes and green, Moriana waving, since she had the only free hand, and though the tree's shadow was netted over them, they seemed to stand in some unfading sun. Moriana said something. Beryx retorted. They were laughing as we went out of sight.

Four times the lythians have flowered since that season, and I did not see. Fengthira spoke truer than she knew. There is a war to fight in Hethria, fiercer than any except the contest with Ammath. When they dammed the Kemreswash and bent the water southward they upset the desert's natural balance, and though farms flourish now at all the Sathellin staging points, the salt is rising underneath. We shall be fighting indeed, through my time and perhaps my sons' time, to preserve that balance, to stop the closure of the road and renewed desolation and loss of all the water won. I may never return to Assharral. Time cannot be reversed, nor can it be wholly halted, even by the power of the Well, and that they would refuse. Like Callissa and me, they will grow old, and wither, and die. But in my mind's world they will stand forever, perdurable as the lovers on the Phathos' card, their arms about each other: waving, laughing, bright in their own sunshine, under the silver leaves and golden flowers of the perridel.

GLOSSARY

Proper names given with capitals.

Coll., collective noun

Imp., imperative

Neg., negative particle

Note for readers of *Everran's Bane* who find word variants. This glossary uses eastern spelling, while Harran's tale was written down in the west.

aedr (pl. aedryx), in common sense, wizard. In aedric usage, practitioner of Ruanbrarx, q.v.
ahltar, sun
Ahlthor, Phaxian deity. From ahltar, sun, nur-nor, white
Alkir, Assharran personal name. Lit. Sower, from kyre, to sow
alsyr, peace. From ax, neg., syre, to weep
Ammath, evil. From ax, neg., math, good
anor, song, tale
a'sparre, aedric art. From ax, neg., yn-ynx, hands, sparthe, to kill
Assharral, empire. From asshar, roof-tree.
asterne, watch-tower, outpost
Astyros, Assharran border fortification. Lit. Wide-wall, from

ax, neg. tyr, narrow, os, wall

ax, negative particle

Axaira Assharran province. Lit. No-farewell, from ax, neg., xaira, parting

axos, aedric art. To blind, from ax, neg., os, sing. eye

axvyr, infinity. From ax, neg., vyrne, last, end

axynbrarve, aedric art. Telekinesis. Lit. to act without hands, from ax, yn-ynx, briarve, all q.v.

az, blue

Azmaere, Phaxian range. From az, blue, maer, shadow

belphan, bay

ber, sea

Berrian, aedric personal name. Lit. Sea-fire or flame

Bhassan, Assharran town. Lit. smoke-place, from bhassa, smoke

brenx, peak

breve, pass

briave, to act, with sense of having power/competency to do so

caissyn, sugar-cane. From cau, stick, ais, sweet

cennaphar, sandalwood

Cessala, Assharran district. Lit. Sugar-land, corruption of caissyn, sugar-cane, q.v.

chake, aedric art. To command by compulsion

cletho, mud

clethra, mangrove tree

Climbros, Assharran province. Lit. grain-walls, from climbar, grain, os, wall

clythkemmon, Lyretail menura. From clythx, heart, kemmon, tail

Colne Clethra, Assharran fort. Lit. Mangrove Four, from clethra, mangrove, colne, four

culphan, cape

darre, taipan
Darrhan, aedric personal name. Lit. taipan-tongue. Venomous
Darrior, Assharran province. From darrith, room, space
del, gold
Delostar, aedric personal name. Lit. Wall or Eye of the Golden Flower, from del, gold, os, eye or wall, tar, flower
delryr, poinciana. From del, gold, rien, crimson, nur-nor, white
deve, valley
Deve Gaz, Lit. Fallen Valley, from gase, to fall
Deve Saedryx Korven Battlefield. Aedric oath. From deve, valley, sal, sour, bitter, korb, korven, ghost

Eakring Ithyrx, archipelago. From eakring, island, ithyr, spice
earnn, "kikuyu" grass
el-ela, coll. tree
elond, ironbark tree
emvath, lantana. From ema, poison, vath, shrub
end, apple
ensal, "quinine" tree. Lit. bitter-apple
Eskan Helken, Lit. Red Castle
Etalveth, Assharran town. From etal, sunset, veth, first, i.e. westernmost
Ethryn, Alpha and Beta Centauri. From ethyre, to point, indicate
Everran, Confederate kingdom. Possible corruption of Berrian, q.v.
eygnor, magpie. Lit. black-white, from eygja, black, nor, white, with play on anor, song

fanx (pl. fann), dog
femaere, demon. Lit. cruel-shadow, from feng, moon, fell,

cruel, with supernatural overtones

fendel (pl. fendellin), Assharran currency. From feng, moon, del, gold

feng, moon

Fengela, Lit. Moontree, from feng, moon, el-ela, tree. Matriarch of the Morheage, q.v. Also Assharran mythical being

Fengsaeva, Lit. Moon-wind. From saeva, wind

fengthir, aedric art. To command imperceptibly. Lit. to draw like the moon

Fengthira, aedric personal name. Lit. moonlight. From feng, moon, thira, light

ferrathil, bellbird. Corruption of pirra, bird, thellis, bell

ferroth, pawpaw

fing-fyng, green

finghend, emerald. Lit. green stone

Firkemmon, Scorpio. From fir, sting, kemmon, tail

Frimmor, Assharran province. From ferim, dairy-herd

Fylghjos, aedric personal name. Lit. Granite-eyes, from os, eye, fylg, granite

fyr-x, kelpie sheep-dog

gar, skin, hide

gas, spear

gastath, lancewood tree. From gas, spear, tath, wood

Gazzal, Lit. The Fall, from past. part. of gase, to fall

Gazzarien, Assharran district. From gazzal, the fall

Gazzath, Lit. The Fallers

geber, east

Gebria, Everran province. Lit. east-land

Gebros, Lit. East-wall, from geber, east, os, wall

Gerperra, whip-bird. From pirra, bird, ger, whip

Gesarre, Everran district. Lit. East-flower

Gevber, Lit. East-sea, from ber, sea, geber, east

ghend, stone

Gjerven, Assharran province. From gjer, grass, ven, way, road

gyar, foot (Gjerven dialect)

hasselian, swamp. From haz, earth, ilien, water

havos, spider. Aedric line

Haz, Sky-lord worshipped in Everran. Lit. earth

Hazghend. Lit. Earthstone, from haz, earth, ghend, stone. Aedric line. Confederate nation

hazian, ruby. Lit. earth-fire, from haz, earth, iahn, fire, flame

Hazyk, inhabitant of Hazghend, q.v.

heagar, banyan fig. From heage, branch, gyar, foot (Gjerven dialect)

heage, branch (tree) family (sentient beings)

Heagian, aedric line. Lit. fire-branch, often called Flametree

Helkents, Confederate range. Untranslatable term for red of earth or rock

hellien, eucalyptus. Coll. from ilien, water, el-ela, tree

helmyn, pandanus tree. From helym, barb, yb-ynx, hand

helve, V., imp., to go

Heshyr, Arcturus. From heshyr, shepherd, from huesh, coll., sheep

hethel, olive. Lit. desert-tree

Hethox, indigenous Hethrian inhabitant

Hethria, country. Lit. desert-land

hisgal, box tree. From his, gray, gar, skin

histh, gray

Histhira, Confederate range, aedric line. Lit. gray-light, from histh, gray, thira, light

hisyrx, heron. From his, gray, yrk-yrx, legs

Holym, Confederate country. Coll. cattle

hyrne, fang

Iahn, Sky-lord worshipped in Everran. Lit. fire, flame
idrigg, cold
Ilien, Sky-lord worshipped in Everran. Lit. water
Iliennor, Lit. water-song
imlann, prized type of wood. Poss. "dead finish" tree
imsar Math, invocation. In the name of Math, q.v. below
istarel, saltbush. Lit. salt-tree, from istar, salt, el-ela, tree

kanna, banana
keerphar, bauhinia tree
keld, mine
Kemrestan, Assharran province. From kemres, border, march
Kemreswash, Everran River. Lit. border-water. From kemres, border, wash, river
Kenath, Assharran town. Lit. sale-place, from kenar, auction
ker, house, in sense of dynastic dwelling place
Ker Morrya, Lit. Black Keep, from ker, house, morg, black
kerym, lake
Kerym Cletho, Gjerven lake. Lit. Mud-lake
kymman, tamarind tree

langu, python. Assharran semi-mythical being
lase-lash, suffix, meeting, crossroad, junction
lathare, aedric art. "Mindspeech," verbal telepathic transmission
Latharyn, Lit. The speakers. V. Ystryn. Assharran form of Tarot
lethar, dream
letharthir, aedric art. To mesmerise. Lit. to make dream, from lethar, dream, thire, to be.
lisbyr, rainmaker. From lisva, rain, byr, Ulven corruption of briave, to act, q.v.
Lisdrinos, Assharran forest. From drinos, forest, lisva, rain
los, spring, or contraction of lios, face

Los Morryan, Lit. Blackwater Spring

Lossian, aedric personal name. Lit. The Well or Face of Flame

Los Therystar, legendary spring. Lit. Well of the Purple Flowers. From theryx, purple, tar, flower.

Los Velandryxe Thira, aedric artefact. From los, well, velandryxe, wisdom, thira, light

Losvure, Lit. Sky-faces. From lios, face, os, eye, vur, sky

lydel, possum. Lit. tree-hopper, from el-ela, tree, lyde, to hop

lydwyr, kangaroo. From lyde, to leap, hop, wyre, great

lydyr, hopper. Coll. Small marsupials, bandicoot, paddy melon, kangaroo rat, etc. From lyde, to hop

ly'ffanx, kangaroo dog. From lydwyr, kangaroo, fanx, fann, dog

lyng, morning

Lynghyrne, Confederate mountain. Lit. fang of the morning

Lyngthira, country. Lit. morning light, from lyng, morning, thira, light

lythian, poinsettia. From lythe, leaf, iahn, fire, flame

maer, shadow

Maerdrigg, aedric personal name. Lit. cold shadow, from maer, shadow, idrigg, cold

Maerheage, aedric line. From maer, shadow, heage, family

maerian, opal. From maer, shadow, iahn, fire, flame

Mallerstang, Assharran town. Lit. orchid-cross, from mallar, orchid, tang, cross

math, good

Math, abstraction. Aedric equivalent of god

meldene, west. Region of Everran

morg, black

morgar, black-butt tree. From morg, black, gar, hide, skin

Morglis, Lit. black-nose. Confederate cape. In Assharral, black kite. From morg, black, perraglis, hawk

Morheage, aedric line. From morg, black, heage, family
Morhyrne, Assharran mountain. Lit. Black-fang
Moriana, aedric personal name. Lit. Black Fire
Morrya, Assharran province. Lit. Black-land, ref. to volcanic soil
morsyr, black widow spider. From morg, black, syr, widow, from syre, to weep
morval, crow. From morg, black, val, wing

nerran, swamp tree
nerrys, ocean
Nerrysyr, ocean. Lit. peaceful ocean, from alsyr, peace, from ax, not, syre, to weep
Nervia, Assharran province. From nerev, banker, money-lender
norgal, ti-tree, paperbark. Coll., from nor, white, gar, skin, el, tree

os, eye or wall
Othan, Phaxian river. Lit. strong

pellathir, aedric art. To cause illusion. From pelere, to bear, carry, lethar, dream
perra, eagle. Corruption of pirra, bird
perraglis, hawk. From perra, eagle, aglis, small
perridel, coll. wattle-tree. From per, silver, del, gold, el-ela, tree
perrilys, fish-eagle. From perra, eagle, ilys, fish
Phamazan, Phaxian capital. Lit. The Gathering
pharaon, Lit. maker, creator. Loose aedric usage for "god"
pharaone, aedric art. Telepathic vision. From phare, to see
Pharaon Lethar, Lit. maker's dream. Aedric term for (1.) The physical universe, (2.) The Other World of ghosts and shamans. Cf. Hindu concept of Brahm who creates by

"dreaming" the world

phare, V. to see. Aedric art, to "read" an entire psyche

pharraz, farmer. Lit. earth-seer, from phare, to see, haz, earth

pharyn, Lit. seers. Assharran Tarot. V. Ystryn and Latharyn

phathire, aedric art. Lit. see-being, from, phare, to see, thire, to be. Mental re-creation of the past

Phathos, soothsayer. Lit. seeing eye, from phare, to see, os, eye

Phatrexe, aedric art. From phare, to see, trexe, to write. To imprint telepathic messages on matter, keyed to correct receiver

Phaxia, country. Lit. The People

Quarred, Confederate country

quennis, lawyer cane. From quienn, hook

ras, source

Rastyr, Lit. Port-head, from tyr, narrow or port

rhodel (pl. rhodellin), gold coinage of Everran. From rho, round, del, gold

rhonur, cotton. From rho, round, nur, white

riendel, cocky-apple tree. From rien, crimson, el, tree

riengjer, kangaroo grass. From rien, crimson, gjer, grass

rienglis, red kite. From rien, crimson, perraglis, hawk

Rienvur, Mars. Lit. crimson-brow

rivannon, scented tree, possible kind of cassia

rovperra, kookaburra. From pirra, bird, rove, to laugh at, mock

ruan, mind

Ruanbrarx, aedric arts. Lit. mind-acts, from ruan, mind, briarx, past. part. of briave, to act, q.v.

Ruanbraxe, aedric art. From ruan, mind, braxe, shield. To block from other aedryx' awareness

ruand, numeral one. Also leader, head capital, etc.

saeva, wind

saeveryr, wagtail. Also Cape, "where the wind turns," from saeva, wind, ryde, rythe, to turn

Saevetir, south wind

Salasterne, Assharran fort. Lit. sour-watch, from sal, sour, asterne, lookout

salgar, Lit. bitter-bark, from sal, bitter, sour, gar, skin, bark. Assharran version of cinchona bark

Saphar, capital of Everran. Lit. delight

Sathel (pl. Sathellin), wanderer, nomad

scarthe, aedric art. Telepathic perception. Lit. to read verbal thought

Selionur, Sirius. From selloth, stars, lios, face, nor-nur, white

Sellithar, personal name. Lit. Star-flower

sellothahr, frangipani tree. Lit. Sun-star, from selloth, stars, ahltar, sun

skos, broad

slief, plateau, tableland

slithil, ibis. Lit. water-knife, from ilien, water, slith, knife

stiriand, north. Region of Everran. Aedric line

Stirian Ven, highway. Lit. North Road

Stirsselian, Lit. North-swamp, from hasselian, swamp, from haz, earth, ilien, water

syvel, wilga tree. From syve, thick, el-ela, tree

tar, flower

tarsal, gidgee tree. Lit. sour-flower

taskgjer, Mitchell grass. From task, tussock, gjer, grass

Tasmar, Assharran province. From tassa, cloth

tathrien, red cedar. From tath, wood, rien, crimson

Taven, Lit. wood-road, from tath, wood, ven, road

Tengorial, Assharran town. Lit. cleared-land, from tengre, to clear, cut down

terrephaz, brolga. From az, blue, terre, to dance

terrepher, lyretail menura. From per, silver, terre, to dance

terrian, jacaranda. Corruption of theryx, purple, iahn, flame

Thangar, Assharran province. From thangos, hilly

Th'Iahn, aedric personal name. Lit. The Flame

thillian, diamond. Lit. light-water-fire, from thira, light, ilien, water, iahn, flame

thira, light

Thiryx, Sky-lord, worshipped in Everran. Lit. air. See Haz, Ilien and Iahn

thorgan, king

Thor'stang, aedric chess. Lit. king's-war, from thorgan, king, gastang, war

thrithan, bamboo

tingan, lyretail menura. From tingrith, all, han, tongue

tingrith, numeral. Eight, all. Quarred government, loose confederation of aedric lines

Tirien, aedric line. Lit. south water, from tirs, south, ilien, water

tirs, south. Everran region

Tirstang, Crux Australis. From tirs, south, tang, cross

tyr, narrow. Port, in Hazyk dialect

Tyr Cletho, From tyr, port, cletho, mud

Tyr Coryan, Lit. Maze-port, from tyr, port, coryan, maze, labyrinth

Tyrwash, Lit. narrow-river. Aedric line

ulfann, dingoes. From ulce, wild, fanx, fann, pl. dog

Ulven, Neolithic Gjerven tribe. From ulce, wild, Gjerven, province, q.v.

Valinhynga, Venus. Lit. horns of the morning, corruption of valin, horn, lyng, morning

Vallin Taskar, Assharran landmark. From vallin, horns, taskar, gate

Velandryxe, wisdom. Lit. high-vision, from vel, high, andeir, second or non-physical sight

velandyr, sage. Lit. high-seer

Veldisk, Phaxian plateau. From vel, high, disyk, brown

ven, highway, main road

Vendring, Assharran town. Lit. road-works, from ven, road

Ven Selloth, Milky Way. From ven, road, selloth, stars

veth, first

Vorn, aedric personal name. Lit. the tooth

Vyrenia, country. Lit. last-land, from vyrne, last

Vyrlase, Lit. Last-meeting, from vyrne, last, lase, meeting, crossing-place

vyrne, Lit. the last. Nickname of Vorn, q.v.

Vyrne Taskar, Phaxian province. Lit. last-gate, from vyrne, last, taskar, gate

wash, river

wreve, V. to master, control

wreve-lan'x, aedric art. Beast mastery, from wreve, control, lanyx, coll., beast

wreve-lethar, aedric art. Lit. to control the dream, i.e. to control or change the world. From lethar, the dream, aedric term for universe

wreviane, aedric art. Pyrokinesis

wrevurx, aedric art. To control the weather. From wreve, control, vur, sky

wrock, ridge, esp. watershed

wyre, great

wyresparyx, goanna. From wyre, great, emsparyx, lizard, from yrk, yrx, legs, and emspar, snake, from ema, poison, sparthe, to kill

Xaira, farewell, separation, aedric myth of same
xhen, aloe vera. From xhen, burnt, past. part. of xhiane, to burn

yazyk-yx, thief
yeld, blood
yeldtar, poppy. Lit. blood-flower. Juice used as soporific
yeltath, bloodwood tree. From yeld, blood, tath, wood
yst, truth
Ystanyrx, Lit. true songs. Cosmogony as preserved by Everran harpers
Ystir, Invocation. Truth it is
Ystryn, Assharran Tarot cards. Lit. truth-tellers. See also Latharyn.
yx, sing., before, pl., eyes
yxphare, aedric art. Lit. to see before. Clairvoyance

Zem-and-Zam, Assharran personal names. Lit. This-and-That
Zyphryr Coryan, Assharran capital. From zyph, city, wyre, great, coryan, maze, labyrinth

ABOUT THE AUTHOR

Sylvia Kelso lives in North Queensland, Australia, and has been writing or telling stories for as long as she remembers. *The Moving Water* is her second fantasy novel, the sequel to her well-received *Everran's Bane.* She has also published poetry in Australian literary magazines, and has a Creative Writing MA for an alternate history/SF novel set in alternate North Queenslands. She lives in a house with a lot of trees in the garden, but no cats or dogs. She makes up for this by playing Celtic music on a penny whistle and is now learning the fiddle as well.